PRAISE FOR ROCKY LEONARD'S

SECONDHAND SIGHT

"What a riveting read! This book grabbed me from the first page...Leonard creates a thrilling and chilling murder mystery, with an intriguing touch of the paranormal...The threads pull together...to a harrowing climax...and in the midst of all the mayhem, people find themselves and each other...Murder mystery and paranormal fans will love this book." — *Reader's Favorite*

"Secondhand Sight has all the elements of a good crime novel: a strong lead character, a sinister villain, bloody murder scenes plus the injection of the supernatural to add drama and mysticism to its dynamic plot." — *IP Book Reviewers*

"An unexpected mix of police procedural, thriller, supernatural and horror." — *Kirkus Reviews*

ALSO BY ROCKY LEONARD

Coastal Empire

SECONDHAND SIGHT

a novel by

ROCKY LEONARD

Each Voice Publishing

Published by Each Voice Publishing at Smashwords
www.eachvoicepub.com

ISBN: 9780615691114

Cover Design: Jason White

DEDICATION

In memory of John and Helen Remion.

ACKNOWLEDGEMENTS

The author would like to thank the following individuals:

Lisa Leonard, Betty Peltier, David W. Thornton, Bill Wassner, Jason White, Nancy L. Futral, Nigel McNaughton, Danielle Horvath and Ken Miller.

Special Thanks to:

Officer Lisa Holland, Public Relations Officer, Roswell Police Department

Inspector John Heinen and Director of Public Affairs

John Bankhead of the Georgia Bureau of Investigation

Frank F. "Chip" Tinley, RN, Clinical Analyst, ER Operations Coordinator

SECONDHAND SIGHT

PROLOGUE

"Do I need a lawyer?"

"Why do you think you need a lawyer? You got a guilty conscience?" Wassner, the cop in the rumpled suit, sneers as his eyes bore twin holes into me.

But he looks as tired as I feel.

Muffled voices passing in the hallway filter through the door. Tension grows in the silence that fills the cramped, monotone grey interview room. Wassner is sitting close enough that I can see the individual bristles in the stubble of his beard, intimidating me with his presence and invading my personal space. Even the slightest movement causes my chair to squeak, and the tiny box of a room amplifies the sound.

Wassner continues to stare me down. I rummage through the dark recesses of my memory for his partner's name, the nicer one from our earlier encounter. Maybe I can ask to speak with her, if I can only remember her name.

Forget that – it would only be a sign of weakness.

Wassner and I are adversaries, at least for the moment. His glare is relentless. I try to wait him out. Eventually, he wins our battle of silence. I break eye contact, and I can't help squirming in my chair. It's uncomfortable and my knee throbs. I think I should have ice on it. My patience reaches its limits. I give up on waiting for him to start the serious conversation.

"Do I need to remind you that I came in voluntarily?"

"You know, I've been wondering about that," Wassner says slowly, deliberately dragging out the words, making me wait for him to get to the point. "Wondering if your guilty conscience made you invent this cock-a-mamie bullshit story you've been feeding me for the last half hour. See, I think you came in here wanting to confess, but you don't know how to start. Maybe I can help. How did you know the Nelsons?"

"Is this interrogation being recorded?" I ask.

"What interrogation? I haven't asked you anything. That was my first real question."

Good point. It has taken me only a few minutes to remember why I don't like this guy. His narrowed, calculating eyes confirm the feeling is mutual.

His partner seems friendlier. And prettier. At least, she seemed the nicer of the two, before taking off with the Coke can bearing my fingerprints a few minutes ago.

Wassner leans forward to press his advantage. He snaps, "Have I read you your rights? No. That means you aren't under arrest, and this isn't an interrogation. It's simply a conversation between a police officer and a potential informant, nothing more. Of course, informants normally provide useful information, not a load of crap wrapped in sandwich bread." He sits back in his chair and glares at me contemptuously, the proverbial cat contemplating a canary dinner. "But what makes you think you can ask *me* questions, smart ass?"

Takes one to know one, asshole. I let my irritation at his rudeness get the best of me and reply sarcastically, "You just said this is a conversation. You know, like a dialogue. That usually means we're both allowed to speak freely. You have a killer running loose. You'd like to stop him. I'd like to help you, as much as humanly possible."

Perhaps not my best choice of words, considering the story I've been telling Wassner.

His face turns red. In fact, it's almost purple with rage. Wassner's jaw clenches shut, probably so that he doesn't say anything he might regret. I'm still here under a white flag, negotiating a truce, trying my best to cooperate. I can tell he's royally pissed at me, but I'm not entirely sure why. I do know that he thinks I'm jerking him around. Honestly, I can't really say that I blame him all that much. If our roles were reversed and he had just tried to tell me my story, I wouldn't have believed him either. But I'm here to help. I don't really have much choice in the matter. Somehow I have to stop this evil and I can't do it alone.

More muffled sounds filter through the door. Activity seems to be picking up outside our cramped room, a little surprising on Easter Sunday. I wonder if extra cops came in because I'm here. The thought of working in such a depressing office, with its dull, funereal gloom, is suffocating to me. The temptation to leave competes with my desire to help the police stop a murderer, but my inability to provide information they can use is frustrating to both of us.

I decide to press Wassner to clarify my status, to make sure I know where I stand. "You haven't read me my rights. You said that means I'm not under arrest. But you didn't say I'm not a suspect. Do I need to hire an attorney, or can we just continue our conversation? I came in hoping to help you stop a crazy man from killing any more people."

"What's his name?" Wassner asks.

"I don't know," I admit miserably. It's true. I don't know whether the name in my head belongs to the killer or another potential victim. But I do have a name.

"Where does he live?"

"I'm not sure," I snap, as my voice rises in frustration. "That's not the kind of help I've come here to give."

A knock at the door breaks through the growing tension in the room. The hope for a more sympathetic ear has just enough time to flit through my mind before the door swings open. An older balding man with hollow, dull brown eyes and sunken cheeks sticks his gaunt head inside. His voice is surprisingly vigorous, considering his cadaverous appearance.

"Detective Wassner, we need to talk privately."

"Sure, Captain," my adversary mutters from across the table. He scoops up his note pad as he gets up so I can't read it while he's gone. For a moment, he stares contemptuously at me, and then he tears off a blank sheet of paper and slides it in front of me. He slaps down his pen on top of the paper just a little too forcefully, to convey his annoyance at the interruption.

He thinks he's about to crack me, I decide.

Wassner smirks and says, "The paper and pen are there for your convenience, in case you have the sudden urge to make a confession. Be sure to include all the gory details."

He leaves the room, closing the door behind him. But I think I see something other than derision in his eyes. I think there's just a scintilla of doubt about me. We both know the clock is ticking, counting down to another senseless, brutal murder. We both want the same thing—to stop this madman in his tracks. Wassner may think I'm the madman, but I sense he's starting to be convinced by my story. Self-preservation wrestles against my sense of duty. Part of me really wants to go home and watch the Masters tournament on television with my wife, like most normal people in the state will be doing later today. The golf course is beautiful even when the azaleas aren't blooming.

I resist the temptation to put my ear to the door, curious to find out what they are talking about. Our conversation is headed in an ominous direction. I am here of my own free will to tell the police what I know about a serial killer operating in their back yard. The only thing that I seem to be accomplishing so far is making me into their primary suspect. I know my story sounds crazy. And time is being wasted while I try to convince the cops I'm legitimate.

I've had better days.

PART ONE
SPY WEDNESDAY

CHAPTER 1

The day my life changed forever started like any other normal workday.

The alarm clock rang. While still in bed, I listened as my wife got up, made herself some juice and crackers, dressed for work, and suffered through a few dry heaves in the bathroom. Then she was good to go. I waited for her to finish in the bathroom before starting my own routine. Two ships passing in the pre-dawn light.

I showered, shaved, and dressed before making myself breakfast. Out the door and I was off on my short commute to the office. Settled at my desk by eight a.m., I sorted through my emails, reading the important ones and deleting the spam. I checked my calendar for meetings. All clear.

My attention focused on the highest priority customer bug in my inbox. It was a problem report from a live customer site where our latest upgrade had been deployed. In spite of relentless testing by our Quality Assurance Department, the live environment exposed a serious issue. Some garbage on the line apparently caused refunds to be double posted as debits rather than properly issued as credits. For more than three hours, I played detective through my source code. I sorted through error logs, trace messages and customer updates describing the sequence of steps believed to cause the elusive problem.

Time is money in my business. To our customers, money is also money, and treating a credit as a debit really screws up the bottom line. It's not the sort of problem that customers tolerate for long. My employer, Quick Pay, is known by the two words that best describe our business: quick payment. Our software runs in cash registers, card swipe boxes, and ATMs all over the world. When a problem inconveniences our customers, the pressure to find and fix it is enormous. Time is money, but cash is especially tangible when you're losing it.

After several years with the company, working my way up the food chain to be considered a key employee, I had reached a crossroads in my career. I was comfortable with the software, liked my coworkers, had no reason to complain…but I felt like it, anyway. I needed a new challenge. Every day I fell deeper into a mind-numbed routine, simply going through the motions to earn my paycheck. I stuck around for the stability. I was about to be a father.

Don't get me wrong, I was good at my job. Maybe a little too good. On some level, work was starting to bore me. There are only so many times you can face a "crisis" scenario where the salesrep or the customer thinks the situation is life-or-death, and you realize it's not *your* life-or-death, but theirs.

My software had been deployed long enough now that I knew it did what it was supposed to do. These days, my work largely consisted of debugging what the customers or their customizations had done to screw up what otherwise worked perfectly well, and to make my software more tolerant of their screw-ups. But I was getting paid really well to keep going through the routine. And there was nothing like a baby on the way to put the importance of a steady paycheck into perspective.

Just as it started to feel like I might be getting somewhere in the trace logs, Richard derailed my train of thought. He called me into his office for a quick one-on-one meeting. No pressure, of course. It was only our best customer. I really liked my boss, but surely this charade got old for him, too. It was always the same story.

Richard was my immediate supervisor. A wiry man of medium build with a rapidly receding hairline, Richard wore wire-rimmed glasses. He kept his beard closely trimmed, giving his thin face a healthy fullness. A strong, masculine jaw line conveyed control and authority incongruous with his slightly effeminate mannerisms.

He dressed very well. Richard wore expensive tailored suits with monogrammed shirts Monday through Thursday, but on casual Friday, he opted for flannel shirts, jeans, and very expensive hiking boots. During the summer, he traded the flannel shirts for golf shirts with monogrammed logos advertising a variety of country clubs in the Atlanta area, though no one knew if he even played the game. The other members on our team joked about the "company uniform"—behind his back, of course.

I really liked Richard so I'd laugh politely and go back to minding my own business as soon as office etiquette allowed. I tried to get along with everybody. Richard spoke with the slightest trace of a lisp and his personal life was the second most popular topic for petty office gossip after who would lose their job in the next round of layoffs. Honestly, I didn't care. He was the best boss I'd ever had.

You want me to guess how long it's going to take to fix this?

A week sounded good. I grabbed a number out of thin air. I could work into the weekend if necessary, but if I could pick up my line of thought where I left it prior to his interruption, I wouldn't need that long. I had been looking at a memory dump of the request message. I suspected that a pointer had gotten whacked, stomped, or overwritten somewhere along the line.

"Give me a week to isolate, fix it, and test the patch," I half mumbled, fairly confident the job was more or less doable in that timeframe. I knew our product well enough that I assumed I could find and fix just about any bug in a week. Since I was pretty sure I'd just figured it out in my head, I felt like I was being rather generous with myself. After all, my solution *might* not work. It could happen.

"You're sure that will be enough time? I don't want to be too aggressive when I commit to a date with the customer and set their expectations."

"A week should be plenty of time. It isn't rocket science, Richard. There are only so many things that can go wrong with the devices or the code."

Pressure would not help me think harder or faster. I already knew the stakes were high because the software was released and installed in live environments. My code was responsible for processing millions of dollars in card transactions in stores, on the Internet, and anywhere else they accept debit or credit. I was absolutely sure that I now understood the cause of the problem. I could reproduce it on demand by manipulating our test host to send data that matched what we saw from the live host. That would be key to knowing when the problem was fixed. I also needed to make sure my solution wouldn't break anything else.

My stomach rumbled, calling attention to fact I'd been at this all morning. While I ate, I could think about everything that needed to be changed to make sure the fix was a solid one. Satisfied I had the bug nailed, I let myself consider running a personal errand. My plan for today's lunch hour called for eating on the run so I could squeeze in a little personal shopping. On the recommendation of my friend and coworker Tiffany, I had decided to visit a new thrift store just opened by the local Humane Society. She was an avid volunteer for the cause.

Before I could get away, Tiff stuck her head in my cubicle and asked about my plans for the weekend. "We're doing an adoption event at Petco on Saturday, but we're off Sunday because of Easter. Why don't you bring Beth and adopt a nice dog?"

I chuckled, "You are persistent, aren't you? You know we have a cat, so we can't have a dog, too." Not a week went by that she didn't try to goad me into taking in a homeless dog.

"Who made that rule? You just need to find the right dog. What about a Bassett Hound? There's one in foster care right now that might be perfect. You know, they have wonderful voices, like the beagles."

"Beagles are hunting dogs. Beth is afraid the wrong dog would terrorize the cat. But with this cat, it would more likely be the other way around," I joked. "She wants to wait until the baby is born so we can test a dog with the cat and the baby before we commit."

She didn't seem convinced.

"Hey, I brought the cat into the deal because I was a sucker. Remember when Richard posted that flyer about the cat the landlord was about to dump at the county shelter? Then you had to go and tell me that cats are more likely to get put down for lack of shelter space. I felt sorry for the miserable excuse for a feline. It's my fault we can't have a dog right now."

Tiffany laughed and teased, "You're just a big softie, aren't you?"

I shot back, "I've always liked animals better than people. But this damned cat is insane. Have I told you why her name is Abby Normal?"

She guessed, "From *Young Frankenstein*, right? I love that movie."

"Yeah, well, the cat isn't normal. The crazy damned thing will hide and pounce on my bare feet, bite the crap out of me, then lick the wound as if she's apologizing."

Tiffany scowled. "No wonder Richard was looking for someone else to take the cat. Sucker!"

To change the subject from crazy cats and perfect dogs I offered, "I'm planning to go shopping at your thrift store while I'm out for lunch. Or, should I just endorse my paycheck and give it to you?"

"The shelter could use the money," she answered with a serious expression. "You know it's for a good cause. We're hurting in this economy. Donations are way, way down. The shelter is struggling to keep the doors open and lights on. If you were a single guy, I'd take your whole check. But you do need some money to buy diapers. Just split it down the middle, and I'll sing your praises."

She was letting me off the hook. We both laughed, but mine was a little forced. I needed to get going if I was going to have time for any errands.

"Dan, you look tired. And worried. How is Beth? Is she still getting sick every morning?" she prodded. Tiffany followed Beth's progress throughout our pregnancy. More than once, she said the morning sickness was lasting too long. She sensed my concern. Beth treated throwing up every day like it was just part of being pregnant, but something didn't seem right to me. She had gone to the doctor and taken the medications intended to stave off the nausea, but nothing seemed to be working.

Tiffany was the sister I wish I had. She could read me like a book. A towering brunette with a generous personality, she was Wonder Woman with a Southern accent. Her eyes looked straight into mine while she was wearing flat heels. But Tiffany never looked down on anyone. She was the mother of two young boys, but she had been a mother hen forever. It took real effort to get on her bad side. I had only seen her lose her temper once or twice. That was enough for me. I avoided making her mad. Besides, she was one of my best friends. I knew she had my back, and vice versa.

"She's still barfing every morning. I know it's not normal, but her next appointment with the OB/GYN is next week, and she doesn't want to ruin the holiday weekend. Her last appointment was only last week."

"Oh, give me a break. If she's still sick after all that, her doctor ought to check her into the hospital until he gets this under control."

Physically, Tiffany dwarfed Beth, a petite wisp of a woman by comparison. Intellectually, or if it came to a battle of wills, the women were equals. It would be a clash of the Titans, for sure, if Tiffany were to try to tell Beth how to handle her own pregnancy. I knew she would stubbornly resist being confined to a hospital room, insisting she was fine, that she could manage better at home.

Beth and I had started a wish list for our eagerly anticipated first child. She was going a little overboard with the whole nesting instinct. She planted the idea in my head of finding good bargains on a few rarely used items. Beth's friends with children told her that the older the baby, the more wear and tear she'd find on used baby items. They loaded us down with plenty of infant clothes. She learned how to knit and started making blankets and booties for the baby. As first time parents, we didn't have anything we would need: crib, playpen, bottles, car seat...*nothing*. Saving on any items for the baby would really help stretch our budget.

Our plans called for Beth to stay home with the baby if we could afford it. I didn't want her to have to work while the kids were young, though her employer suggested she could work from home after maternity leave. We were trying to scrimp and save every penny we could, just in case the offer didn't pan out. If I could find a good crib, a car seat or even a mobile to put on a crib that would make my lunch mission successful.

I barely tasted the roast beef sandwich as I wolfed it down in the car, slurping on my iced tea to help wash down the food. I looked down and noticed a big blob of horseradish sauce on my tie. *Shit!*

The kid working the drive-through didn't put any napkins in the bag with my sandwich. I had nothing in the car to wipe up the mess. My tie was ruined. Since I was practically there already, I decided to check out the thrift store for a decent replacement. I fumed over wasting time looking for a tie instead of things for the baby. If employees of fast food restaurants worked only for tips, they would starve to death.

The Humane Society of Forsyth County's new thrift store occupied a vacant old movie theater that had once been the centerpiece of a thriving shopping center. Behind the building, a rusted out sign meant to advertise the theater to passing traffic on GA-400 had long been obscured by a thick copse of pine trees. After the theater had closed, the shopping center went through a long period of decline. Large retailers that once anchored the shopping center moved across the street to newer and nicer construction. The older complex, mostly cinder block, now housed a Chinese restaurant, a bike shop, and a frame shop in addition to the thrift store. About a third of the space available in the older shopping center remained vacant, full of dust and cobwebs.

I pressed my face against the smudged window, my hand cupped over my eyes to reduce the glare. Immediately inside the door was a large room that must have been the theater lobby. Through an open doorway, I could see someone painting a colorful mural on a bland beige interior wall. The vivid scene of dogs and cats playing in a bright green meadow would set a positive mood for the store when the artist finished her work.

Bummer. The thrift store hadn't officially opened for business. It was too late to get home for another tie. Although the sign on the door clearly indicated the store was closed, I could see movement through the windows. With most of my lunch hour wasted, I figured I might as well try to get something accomplished with my excursion.

I tugged on the handle of the locked door. I tapped on the glass and motioned for the nearest person inside, who turned the lock and cracked open the door, but stood blocking the opening.

"Hi. I'm sorry. We're not open for business yet. Our grand opening will be this coming Monday, unless I drop dead of heart failure between now and then," the ruggedly handsome man grinned and said in greeting. "Were you here to make a donation? We can take those around back, at the loading dock."

He looked too young to be the person in charge, but he spoke with authority. His alert brown eyes waited on me to respond.

I spied a display carousel of ties behind him, tucked into an alcove behind a display of dress shoes. A sign over the rack advertised the ties sold for a dollar apiece. I held up my soiled tie to show him the damage done by my lunch. "Could I just buy one of those ties to replace this one? I dribbled my lunch on it." I pulled out my wallet and offered him a five-dollar bill. "I can't wear this back to the office, and I don't have time to go home. Tell you what—I'll give you the five bucks, and you keep the change as my donation. Whaddya say? Can you help me out? I promise I'll be right in and out. Just give me a minute to find something that will pass muster for the rest of the day at work."

He frowned, but only hesitated for a second. Then he reached out and took my money, holding the door open to let me inside. As I headed for the tie rack, he walked over to the cash register and punched a few buttons. After the cash drawer popped open, he stuffed my bill under a clip. "Congratulations, you just officially became our first customer. Just let me know when you've found your tie, so I can unlock the door for you. We've gotta get this place ready for business, so nobody else gets inside, unless their bribe is more than five bucks. Sorry, but I'm it when it comes to customer service help until we officially open. You're gonna have to fend for yourself. Shop with one eye, but keep the other open so that you don't get run over, okay? And remember you're shopping in a thrift store. We don't have a refund policy. Caveat emptor—buyer beware. All sales are final."

He said it all with a pleasant smile. The man was an organic perpetual motion machine, constantly on the move. He wasn't what I expected to find working in a thrift store. His enthusiasm and energy were contagious; it was tempting to try to match his upbeat attitude, but I thought it might come off as mocking him. Besides, I wanted to get moving so I could get back to the office. I simply nodded, not seeing much opportunity to get a word in edgewise. As long as the replacement tie didn't come with a stain, there would be no complaints or regrets, even if I wore it only once.

The young man turned to get back to work, and then suddenly whirled back around on his heel to face me. He smiled as if embarrassed at being caught in a social lapse, his perfect white teeth completing the portrait of a man who should be selling Mercedes or BMWs rather than used household items in a thrift store. "Sorry, I forgot what few manners I have there for a second. I didn't even introduce myself, so you wouldn't know what to call me when you're ready to go. I'm Chuck, the store manager—well, at least I *will* be, assuming we eventually get ready to open."

I couldn't help but like the guy. I wanted to ask, *"What are you doing here?"* But I simply smiled back. "Thanks. Dan Harper. It's nice to meet you. I think the store is looking pretty good. I like the mural over there. How much more do you have to get done before Monday?"

"Don't ask," Chuck cringed. "You don't want to know." As quickly as he reversed course, he turned around again. A couple of workmen carrying a sheet of what looked like black plywood routed with grooves struggled precariously around several fragile obstacles. "Hey Michael, Julio, look where you're going with that display board. Guys—watch out for that glass showcase, damn it!"

The board they carried wobbled in their hands, threatening the display case their boss indicated. Chuck sucked in a sharp breath as if he expected the glass to shatter any minute now. Somehow, the two men regained control of the board and managed to avert disaster. Chuck breathed a sigh of relief, wiping his hand across his brow at the close call. He finally looked back at me. It took him a second to regroup his thoughts.

"Sorry about that," he said a little sheepishly. "Nice to meet you too, Dan. Good luck finding your tie over there, and thanks for helping the homeless animals. Every penny of profit benefits the no-kill animal shelter up on Kendall Bridge Road, so you are saving lives by shopping here. Your donations will be spent on food and medicine for those that can't help themselves. If you ever decide to get a pet, remember to adopt, don't shop."

His practiced marketing spiel over, Chuck hurried off to give a couple of workers loafing around in the back of the store a new set of marching orders. There obviously was plenty left to do. Soon, the idle workers were hauling out trash bags stuffed full of clothes, opening them and hanging the sorted clothing on racks. Any merchandise out of season they tossed off to the side in one pile, and the most ragged items landed in another.

Chuck's no-nonsense approach to barking orders reminded me of a drill instructor crossed with the upbeat energy of a TV evangelist. *The man sure believes in his cause.* I chuckled as I spun the tie rack, looking at my options. One caught my eye that didn't look too dated. I recognized it as good quality silk, and it didn't clash with my slacks. I pulled off my spoiled tie, and hung the new tie around my neck. I looked down to watch my hands tie the Windsor knot, a motion I'd repeated a million times before.

Not this time.

An odd dread ran down my spine the moment I draped the tie around my neck. In retrospect, I now know I should have immediately taken it off and found another. But I didn't. It was already too late. My stomach rumbled and rolled. My eyes blurred. I swayed and tried to keep my knees from buckling.

Indigestion from gulping down fast food, I chided myself. The wave of nausea slowly passed over me. I waited until I thought it was over.

I steadied myself in front of a small mirror on the wall near the tie rack. My trembling hands went through the practiced motions of tying the tie, the same moves I had made first thing in the morning, four days a week.

I looked into the mirror and gasped. Blood splatters covered the glass, obscuring my reflection in the mirror. My hands felt warm and sticky. Reluctantly, I looked down and saw them covered in wet blood. It was all over me. My mind reeled. Bile rose in my throat. I looked around frantically for the source of the spreading crimson stains.

Did I cut myself? I felt no pain. *What in the hell happened? How? Did the workers break the glass after all?* Yet when I glanced in its direction, the glass display case remained intact.

For several seconds, my mind babbled a brook of questions for which no answers came. Time crept by. I marked its passage with my breathing, the only way I could tell time hadn't stopped completely. I looked around for someone in the store to come help me. Words came to mind to cry for help, but they refused to pass my lips.

A couple of muted sounds that might pass for the bleating of a sheep rose in my throat, barely audible. No one in the store noticed me foundering in distress. I looked around helplessly, desperate to avoid looking into the mirror again. But I had to know. I forced my eyes to gaze at my own reflection once more.

My completely normal reflection looked back at me. There was no trace of blood anywhere. As quickly as it came, the sensation of tacky blood sticking to my hands faded to nothing. My hands once again felt clean and dry. I steeled my courage and looked down to confirm they were free of blood. I looked back up at the mirror, incredulous. It was as if nothing had happened. The blood splattered all over the glass and my clothes had disappeared as inexplicably as it had materialized.

Was that a hallucination? What the hell just happened to me?

Chuck reappeared, carrying a large cardboard box stuffed with household knick-knacks he began arranging on a table. He looked over and noticed that

I now wore a different tie. "Found something you like?"

I did my best to smile naturally, still speechless after the inexplicable experience. It was a relief to have Chuck close by, in case the gory visions returned. Maybe he could help me understand what had happened, if it happened again. I cleared my throat, nodded, and grunted, finding it impossible to tell him about the episode.

Just act normal. Don't let him see you sweat.

"Is something the matter? Are you okay?" Chuck asked. "You look a little pale."

I made a more serious effort to clear my throat before I dared speak again. I decided against mentioning the strange vision. I didn't want someone I had just met to think I was a complete nut. I desperately wanted to get out of the musty old building, thinking it possible the fresh paint had stirred up toxic airborne bacteria. It might be eating my brain at that very moment.

I finally found my voice. "Yeah, I'll be okay. I just feel a little funny—an upset stomach from lunch, I think. I need some fresh air, that's all. This tie will do, for work at least. I'd better go."

Chuck smiled and said, "We appreciate your business. You'll always have the honor of being our first customer. I hope you feel better. Thanks, and come back soon. Remember, we plan to be open next week."

I waved, not trusting myself to speak.

Back in the steel sanctuary of my car, I collected myself enough to suppress the images that had flashed before my eyes moments earlier. At first, I tried to deny the experience, hoping to banish the images from my mind for good.

For the first time in my life, I seriously wondered if this was what it felt like to lose my own mind.

CHAPTER 2

The uniformed guard seated at the security table gave me a small measure of comfort as I walked back into the familiar lobby of my office building, even though I knew he was only armed with a radio and pepper spray. Never again would I call the old guy Barney Fife behind his back. Well, at least it would be a while before I forgot the reassuring sight of him that day and slipped back into old habits. It was a relief to be back in the safe, sterile environment of my office.

I struggled to focus my attention back on the customer problem my boss now expected me to fix in a week, or less. Lines of code blurred before my eyes. Flashbacks of spattered blood distracted me. The vivid image of my bloody hands hovered behind my eyelids with every blink. My reaction to the sight of blood had been a lifelong issue for me, but the fact I even felt faint after a bloody hallucination was a new wrinkle in my familiar squeamishness.

I stared at my monitor, but my mind refused to stop replaying the horrific visions of phantom blood splattered all over me and the mirror in the thrift store. I shifted in my seat, considering a walk to the break room for a Coke.

Tiffany's head popped into my cubicle again. "Hey!"

I visibly started, prompting raucous laughter from her.

"Jeez, why are you so jumpy today? Are you feeling like a condemned man, the closer Beth gets to giving birth?" she asked, talking a mile a minute. "Mister, you need to learn how to relax. Personally, I recommend a glass of red wine with dinner, unless it's fish, then I'd opt for a nice white, maybe a Sauvignon Blanc. Say, did you get a chance to go by that new thrift store at lunch? Is that a different tie than you had on this morning?"

As Tiffany carried on the conversation for both of us, she was eyeing my new tie. Apparently, she was well on her way to putting two and two together and answering her own question about my new neckwear.

"Yeah, thanks for the reminder. Tiff, they're so new, they're not even open yet," I finally managed to smile back at her. "They were still setting up the store when I stopped by. The guy who's going to be the manager let me go inside anyway so I could replace the tie I ruined at lunch. I found this one to replace it. What do you think?"

I stood up, modeling my new look. Without thinking, I let my hand lift the tie for her inspection.

Gruesome images assaulted my mind immediately. This time, a nude woman who looked a little bit like Tiffany was lying down, her face turned away. Her unnaturally pale body was tinged blue with the pallor of death. The unmistakable whir of a circular saw echoed in my ears. I glanced around the cubicle, looking for the source. Something drew my gaze down. My hand felt heavy, but with a strange sense of detachment, I observed the circular saw gripped in my right hand, its blade whirling as it began to cut up the dead woman's body. My mind commanded my hand to stop, but it acted independently of my conscious control. Though I expected blood to spurt from the first cut, the body strangely produced almost none, as if she'd been drained of the life-giving fluid. Repulsed and sickened by my own actions, I seemed powerless to stop them. I could not bring myself to look away.

From another world, I heard Tiffany's voice reach through the ether.

"Dan! Dan, are you all right? You look pale. In fact, you look like you're about to pass out. I think you'd better sit down. You really don't look too good, all of a sudden—like Beth's morning sickness was contagious or something." She tried to laugh as she added, "No offense."

The concern in her tight voice was unmistakable. My body grew faint and my knees buckled. It sucked to be unable to tolerate the sight of blood. I sank down into my chair, but popped up quickly, like I'd sat on a pin. The urge to vomit became a somewhat pressing matter, superseding the dizzy feeling in my head.

"I think I need to splash some cold water on my face," I mumbled hurriedly, afraid of losing my lunch there in the cube. "Be right back."

I ran for the bathroom, sure I was about to lose it right there on the office floor before reaching my porcelain sanctuary. An ominous thought crossed my mind. The bathroom wall above the sinks was essentially one giant mirror.

What horrific reflection awaited me there?

# # #

Richard waited anxiously outside my cubicle. I knew he would be afraid the schedule to which he'd just committed could be in jeopardy. "Mother Hen Tiffany said you were feeling a bit under the weather. Why didn't you say something when we talked this morning?" Richard asked.

"I felt fine this morning. I think it's just something that bothered my stomach. Maybe something I ate at lunch. I'm not coming down with the flu or anything, I promise. You don't have to worry about me."

"Do you want me to allow for more time on the schedule for that FTR?"

FTR was company-speak for the bug I was trying to fix. The acronym stood for Field Trouble Report. By comparison, an IR was an Internal Report, meaning our own quality assurance test engineers had found the issue before the product went live in the field. Any FTR got the highest priority of queued work. Writing new code came lowest as company priority, after fixing the outstanding FTRs and IRs.

The prioritization categories weren't intended to humor our customers; they were a business necessity. Customers could tolerate a minor software inconvenience unless it added significantly to employee workload or cost them money.

My violent waking nightmare should have been a one-time episode that manifested itself for some reason in the musty old store. Instead, the visions had followed me into my turf, my office. Now I was afraid even to touch the tie. Instinct told me it was somehow responsible for my hallucinations. As desperately as I wanted to yank the cursed fabric from my neck, I resisted the temptation from fear the images would assault me again.

The beauty of being a software developer is the ability to set your own hours.

"Nah, I'm just feeling a little queasy, that's all. Would you mind if I knocked off now and got back to work on the fix tonight? I'll be fine after I've had a chance to lie down for a little while and let my stomach settle."

I had a reputation as a night owl and a hard worker who got the job done. I had a lot of good will built up with Richard. "I think if I lie down for an hour or two, I'll be good as new and ready to get back at it."

"Of course!" he quickly agreed. "Whether or not you're here in the office this afternoon won't make any difference if you can't concentrate. If you don't get to feeling better, don't worry about working later tonight. Just get it fixed this week, somehow or some way. The customer expects results. Your reputation precedes you, so I'm counting on you to deliver," he emphasized with a hand on my shoulder. "Now get out of here."

He didn't have to tell me twice.

# # #

Beth was still at work. I tried to think of a way to get the tie from around my neck without touching the damned thing. I also didn't want my wife to catch me acting so strangely, afraid of an inanimate strip of cloth. Coming up with a plausible explanation for why I was scared to touch the tie would be awkward at best.

I scrounged around the kitchen drawers for some utensil I could use to rid myself of the tie, first settling on a pair of thick yellow rubber gloves that Beth bought for cleaning the oven. I struggled in vain to get them onto my larger hands. Doubtful the thin gloves would protect me from the disturbing effects the tie anyway, I next tried a pair of salad tongs. I could grab the slippery silk, but not tightly enough that I could pull apart the firm Windsor knot. Finally, I decided that a pair of chopsticks would be ideal to loosen the knot and remove the offending tie from my neck.

I patiently worked one stick into the knot and had begun working the fat end of the tie out of the loop when our cat assumed my antics were for her amusement. She jumped on the kitchen counter and batted at the dangling fabric, catching a claw in the loosened tie. When she pulled, the tie began cinching around my neck again.

"Go on, Abby," I commanded. "I'm not in the mood to play right now!"

I moved from the kitchen to the bedroom so Beth wouldn't see me in such an embarrassing endeavor if she came home early.

Not being the most dexterous person in the world with a pair of chopsticks, it took me several painstaking attempts to work the knot loose, taking as much care as one would when handling nuclear waste. I threaded a stick through the knot but pushed it too far, jabbing myself in the neck.

Ouch! That's gonna leave a mark.

The cat watched, her tail swishing in obvious disdain for my clumsiness.

Annoyed again at my own phobia over the damned thrift store tie, I was ready to throw the chopsticks across the room and take the stupid thing off with my bare hands. But the vivid memory of bloody hands and a spinning saw blade made me determined to continue. Pulling the chopstick away loosened the knot enough that I could work the narrow end out of the loop. I finally freed myself from the cursed material.

The tie firmly clutched between the chopsticks as I held it at arm's length, I stared at the limp strip of silk in fearful fascination, half expecting the dangling material reminiscent of a dead snake to come alive and bite me. I draped the offending striped silk over the foot rail of our bed.

Evil seemed to emanate from the small article of clothing, so innocuous in appearance. Looks could be deceiving. As soon as the tie came from around my throat, I felt better.

The rumbling in the pit of my stomach calmed and the weight of dread lifted from my neck. I couldn't help wondering, *What is wrong with me? Is this some kind of self-hypnosis? Am I having a meltdown?*

I'd never tried hallucinogenic drugs of any kind. Nor had I ever been a serious drinker, certainly not one now suffering from delirium tremens. This wasn't any kind of a chemical flashback. It was some sort of a full-blown hallucination. Either a mental meltdown or...*what*?

Could some chemical substance in the fabric of the tie have caused the strange visions? Who knew what dank basement had housed the necktie before its previous owner decided to donate it to the thrift store? Mildew, mold, and fungus can be nasty stuff.

An even more ominous thought crossed my mind. *Could I have a brain tumor?*

I recalled that Charles Whitman, the Texas tower shooter, had an undetected glioblastoma before his homicidal rampage. His suicide note indicated he knew something was wrong but couldn't help himself.

Could I have killed somebody and not remember? If so, why did a tie I had found in the thrift store jar memories of a murder I had committed without any conscious recollection?

While my personal life had remained clean since my college days, I had a past. Mistakes made in the days of my more hot-tempered youth stuck with me. Once, as an undergrad at the University of Georgia, I got into a drunken brawl after I crashed a keg party at a fraternity house.

We were both drunk, but the other guy was bigger, more inebriated, and more obnoxious. He wasn't even a student at UGA, but visiting from Georgia Tech, our in-state rivals. I found out the hard way that home field advantage doesn't matter in the courtroom, especially when the opponent can afford expensive lawyers.

He was on a baseball scholarship and had an inflated opinion of himself. The hulking brute shoved his way between me and the current object of my lustful interest. The drunken ballplayer grabbed the girl I was chatting up and kissed her roughly, without as much as a hello.

I yelled, "Hey jackass!" and yanked his arm just as he was trying to stick his tongue in her mouth. She squirmed to get away from his unwelcome advances.

He let go of her and turned his angry red face to me. He put both hands in the center of my chest and shoved hard, sending me staggering off balance. In a blind fury, I charged the man three inches taller and maybe twenty pounds heavier, most of it muscle. Unbridled anger overrode my natural instincts of self-preservation.

He threw a wild and sloppy punch that made contact with my eye. He swung again. As his fist arced past my head, I stepped in and nailed him with a punch aimed for his chin. Instead, my fist smashed into his throat, injuring his larynx and costing him the second half of his junior year of baseball season. When his hands went to protect his throat, I still went after him, throwing punches until some other guys pulled me off him. My left eye swelled quickly. I'd have a hell of a shiner the next day.

The cops came. I was arrested, initially charged for underage drinking. But his family had money and wanted revenge for the damage I had done to his baseball career. When his parents found out the charges were only misdemeanors, they hired a private investigator. He found out that I once took a few martial arts classes and went as far to suggest that I be charged with aggravated assault, absurdly arguing that my hands should be considered deadly weapons. I was only an orange belt, for God's sake.

Had I been charged and convicted, the minimum sentence was a year in prison, up to twenty years. My dad had to shell out major bucks he couldn't afford to get me a decent lawyer He got the case knocked down to a plea agreement settled by pre-trial diversion and mandatory anger management classes.

I had temporarily lost control, letting my rage explode only for a minute or two. I had not thrown a punch in a decade since. It was the one and only time I let my temper turn violent. I couldn't be responsible for the murders in my visions.

Wait a minute – who said anybody's been killed?

CHAPTER 3

Candy squealed in delight. "Do you really mean it?"

Clayton smiled and said, "Baby, when *don't* I mean it? Pack whatever you need to take with you, and let's go. I've got to work this weekend."

He was tempted to smile when Candy cocked her head, reminding him of the dog he used to have when he was a kid. The bitch had also cocked her head when she didn't understand something she heard, just like Candy. She blabbered on, "We were there only a couple of weeks ago, and you had bad luck that trip. I'm just surprised we can afford to go again, so soon."

Clayton sighed with exasperation. He didn't like having to explain himself. He wasn't that good at making up answers.

"It's like I told you before, baby. You win some, you lose some. Gotta roll with the punches and besides, we're gonna change our luck. Come on girl, you need to move your ass. We've got six hours on the road before we hit Biloxi and get to the casino. For a change of pace, we're gonna stay at Beau Rivage this time and play there instead of Boomtown. I've already got us a deluxe ocean view suite, baby."

He laid it on thick, eliciting a new squeal of pleasure from Candy. During sex, he suspected she faked the squeals. The ones she made when she spent his money were real enough, he was certain of that. Good thing it wasn't really his money they were spending. It probably wouldn't matter to Candy if she knew, but it couldn't bother her if she didn't know where he got the money. Really, it was none of her business.

It occurred to Candy that she'd never seen Clayton win more than a grand or two when he gambled, but she kept her tongue. He lost more often than he won. It seemed like he only won when the house wanted him to win. Whatever he managed to score after they arrived would be gone before they left, she was sure of that. The only question was how long it would take him to blow through his stash. Clayton was one of the worst gamblers she'd ever seen. She could read his face easier than a road map as soon as he looked at his cards. She knew a real hustler when she saw one. Clayton was a lamb ready to be fleeced, not a wolf.

Of course, her last old man, Gary, hadn't really been much of a gambler either—before he got sent to prison. The word *gambler* implied risk was involved. Gary was a wolf. He ate amateurs like Clayton for breakfast.

Gary was a card sharp, a con artist, and a swindler. One who finally picked the wrong mark, and got his ass thrown in prison. Candy didn't want to upset Clayton by telling him he sucked at gambling. Not while Gary was locked up in prison for at least a couple more years. Clayton could keep her out of real trouble while she waited for her man. She didn't have to turn tricks to make ends meet until Gary got out again. Clayton sort of took care of her.

He bought her nice things and treated her okay, except when he lost his temper. Sex with him was pretty rough sometimes and he liked slap her a little. Clayton apparently liked to hurt her, but nothing too bad. She'd known worse. He pulled her hair when he took her from behind, but she didn't mind. She'd rather have a rough man in the sack than a timid mouse.

Gary hadn't been timid in the sack, either. He made Candy feel good. She thought she might love him, but that didn't mean she had to stay faithful while she waited. And it wasn't like they broke up. The State Department of Corrections, by way of the judicial system, mandated their separation. Gary was in prison for another couple of years. Out of sight, out of mind. Well, not completely. Candy had visited him at the state prison a couple of times, but not since she met Clayton. Besides, the prison in Jackson was in the middle of frigging nowhere.

Clayton tended to leave visible marks on her, like hickeys, and it would only make Gary crazy jealous. Why get him started? If she had a choice between Gary and Clayton, she'd choose Gary. But it wasn't like they had a choice, at least not for the time being. Maybe when he got out of jail, they would get back together. Candy thought about Gary often enough.

But right now, Gary could be screwing his cellmate for all she knew. When they weren't together, all bets were off. Candy remembered a time when money had run low and she turned a trick to stake Gary. The thing that bothered her was that Gary didn't seem to mind; in fact, he sort of arranged things, like he was her pimp. He even had the gall to compare their situation to that movie *Indecent Proposal* where Demi Moore sleeps with Robert Redford for a million bucks. It made her think, *O-kaay. So, I'm Demi Moore and you're Woody Harrelson? This clown you hooked me up with was no Robert Redford, and we didn't get a million bucks for it.* Maybe she needed to get rid of both Clayton and Gary and find somebody half decent.

Until Mr. Right did come along, Candy allowed Clayton to show her a good time. It only cost her a little time on her back, or her knees. No big deal. He always seemed to be able to afford to take her to nice places where she had fun. They had been to Biloxi twice this month. Spreading her legs for him a couple of times in a swank hotel was a small price to pay for the perks. It beat the hell out of trailer parks. Before Gary, she had turned tricks in a Motel 6. What a dump that place had been.

Candy realized that she needed to acquire some job skills, but she was too dumb to go back to school. The only advantage God gave her over other women was her body. She had to put it to good use, or she'd starve to death. She lacked the personality to hold down a regular job at the Waffle House.

As soon as they got to Biloxi, she knew Clayton would give her more money to gamble than she'd ever earned for a blow job. At least, that's what happened the last time they went. She could squirrel most of it away instead of burning through it on the slots or playing blackjack, like she did last time. Candy figured she needed some sort of a plan if she ever wanted to stop being like a hamster on the wheel, running until exhausted but never getting anywhere.

Although Clayton told her his job was in the medical profession, it sounded like bullshit to her. No way did she believe he was a doctor. He didn't look like any nurse she'd ever seen, either. Doctors were smart people, but soft. There wasn't anything soft about Clayton. He looked hard and his body was in great shape, Candy knew that from experience. Whatever he really did for a living, Clayton obviously made good money to afford all the stuff they did.

Candy decided that she would never ask him personal questions because she didn't care enough about him to know the answers. Their relationship was destined to be short-lived; she had a certain instinct about these things.

He could be a serial killer for all I care.

CHAPTER 4

Detective Sergeant Bill Wassner dialed the number of the Fulton County Medical Examiner's office. "Bill Wassner, Roswell PD," he began without preamble. "I'm calling about the autopsy report on Simeon Nelson. Can I speak to the ME who filed the report please? The name on it is Dr. Stuart Brannon. Yeah, I'll wait."

He never waited patiently. Wassner drummed his fingers on his desk to pass the time. He dug around in his desk drawer for another pen when he realized the one he had out didn't write, then got out a scrap of paper. He jotted down a couple of words as reminders to ask all his questions on the first phone call. Doctors don't like it when the cops call them over and over. It makes them more paranoid than normal. Who could blame them, with all the malpractice lawyers out there looking for someone to sue? But he'd never heard of an ME getting sued. Their patients never had much to say.

Wassner wrote: *multiple perps? weapons? sexual assault?*

Before Dr. Brannon picked up the receiver, he scribbled out the last reminder. The prompt to ask whether the female victim had been sexually assaulted was premature. Wassner remembered that she wasn't dead yet. Brannon didn't cut on her, just her husband. He wondered if she knew her husband was dead. When he last checked, she had not yet regained consciousness, still clinging to life somewhere in the netherworld between the living and the dead.

"This is Dr. Brannon. What can I do for you?"

"Bill Wassner with the Roswell PD, Dr. Brannon. Sorry I couldn't get there for the autopsy. Thanks for having your office fax me the report. I just have a couple of questions. You described two sets of puncture wounds on the victim, one horizontal, and one vertical. Are you describing multiple weapons? Does that mean multiple attackers, more than one perp?"

"Not unless they were the same height and had the same relative strength. Your unknown subject is right-handed, between five-ten and six-two, and very strong. I can tell by the angle of the blows. Naturally, it occurred to me the assailant was one person who used multiple weapons."

"One in each hand, or put down one and picked up another? That doesn't sound right."

"That didn't really make sense to me, either. CSI techs on the scene said they didn't find any murder weapons there, so I assumed the killer or killers took them. Then last night, it was really just a stroke of luck, but I was in Home Depot and saw something that might be what you're looking for. The weapon in this case could be double-ended, if you know what I mean. In the gardening section, I saw a tool called a mattock. It looks like a hoe on one end and an axe on the other. Nasty looking thing, especially if it's being used to hit a human being."

"What do you need from me to confirm it it's what we're looking for as a murder weapon?" Wassner asked.

"Nothing that I know of—I bought the mattock to see if the general patterns pass the eyeball test to the mold casts, but we can't do an exact match unless we find the actual murder weapon for comparison."

"That's very good, Doc. You took care of most of the questions I had in one shot. Is there anything else you can think of that would be good for me to know?"

"Nothing that wasn't already in the autopsy report that you have sitting in front of you. Cause of death, exsanguination due to blunt force trauma. Victim's time of death was approximately two thirty a.m., plus or minus thirty minutes, determined by liver temperature and lividity due to rigor mortis. Other than the fact you're looking for a total lunatic who butchered two old people in their sleep, there's not much else I can tell you. Oh, well, there is one thing I could say, but you've probably already figured it out."

"What's that?" Wassner asked, but he knew. He just needed to make sure.

Brannon said, "This guy is one sick son-of-a-bitch—I'm talking some serious overkill when I describe the degree of violence indicated by the condition of the corpse. Be careful when you catch up to this guy. He *enjoyed* hurting this man."

Yep, I could have guessed.

# # #

Wassner fidgeted at his desk while the few facts in the case he felt were solid ate at him.

It wasn't even a real desk, more like a plastic countertop attached to the fabric-lined cubicle walls than actual furniture. It didn't really bother Wassner because he hated sitting on his butt in the office. He was out on the street most of the time, relentless in his drive to break and close cases. Even when he was in the office, he rarely sat at his desk. Wassner always had to have something to do, so he would wander the maze of cubicles, looking for other detectives willing to shoot the breeze, as long as the conversation centered on somebody's open case. Wassner didn't believe in bringing his personal life into the office. It was off limits.

The other guys in his division joked, calling him Bulldog out of respect for his tenacity, and Columbo because of his perpetually rumpled look. Even if you didn't really want his help with your case, if he wasn't working something himself, Wassner would offer to listen to what you had. The wiser detectives learned from experience that those conversations often led to a break in their cases, but he never seemed to need much help himself.

Nobody remembered the last case assigned to Wassner that had stayed open for more than a week or so, but now the clock was ticking on the assault and murder in Windsor Forest, and no viable leads had surfaced. Wassner didn't like the idea of having to miss Mass during Holy Week, but this case was too important. Worse than that, Wassner's gut grumbled, but not due to hunger pangs. Something was eating at him, but he couldn't quite put his finger on it.

He walked down the corridor between cubicles and noticed Lampe, the new hire, sitting at her desk. She was probably new enough that the Captain hadn't burdened her with a very heavy caseload while she learned the ropes.

He stuck his head in her cube and said, "Hey, it's Lampe, right? I'm Bill Wassner. You got a minute?"

He pronounced her last name "lamp."

Detective Nancy Lampe looked up from her paperwork in surprise. Suspicious, her eyes shifted to his hands before she made eye contact, checking out his ring finger to see if Wassner was married. It was only her third day on the new job, and she wasn't sure how things worked in Roswell. In downtown Atlanta, every single male cop hit on her.

A very attractive, single female who got more attention than she wanted, Lampe was accustomed to her fellow officers asking for dates during her stint with the Atlanta PD. She liked knowing if they were married before they asked. As one of the more attractive members of the force, she seemed to get more than her fair share of assignments working vice on the prostitution stings. There were some women with the department that looked like they might have to pay the john to get a date, but Lampe wasn't one of them.

Her personal policy was that she didn't date coworkers, but that was beside the point. She wanted to know whether to say no with prejudice, or nicely.

Some of the idiots hinting around for a liaison didn't even have the sense to remove their wedding rings first. Lampe was already involved with someone, but that seemed not to matter to a few of the trolls in uniform.

She'd learned to look for signs of a ring and not just a gold band. She was glad to see that Wassner wore his wedding ring. It gave her a small measure of confidence that his question might even be work-related. Lampe tried not to be so suspicious, and put on her most friendly smile.

"Sorry, you startled me. Yes, what can I do for you?"

When her eyes made contact with his, she realized he'd caught her surreptitiously checking out his ring finger. Her face reddened with embarrassment. Even though she wasn't checking because of personal interest in him, she feared she'd just sent him the wrong message. Lampe kept her private life off limits and told no one of her live-in musician boyfriend because it was no one's business but hers.

Out of habit she said, "It's Lam-pee, by the way," and regretted it instantly.

In no mood for light banter, Wassner cocked his head and muttered, "Say what?"

"Sorry. I was just...you pronounced my name wrong. It's pronounced Lam-pee. It's German. It means 'light.'"

"Oh." He surprised her, becoming a little less formal. "Wassner is German, too. It means 'dweller on the water.' So, I guess we've got something in common. That's wonderful. Now, can you help me?"

Ignoring his sarcastic tone, Lampe raised an eyebrow at him. "Well?"

"Well, what?" Wassner said.

"You got a houseboat?" she asked.

It took a split second for the quip to register. In spite of himself, Wassner audibly snorted in amusement. He liked her quick wit, but there was no time for jokes. Not while the Nelson killer remained free.

"Yeah, and you look like a light bulb, a regular beacon of light in a world full of darkness," he said, refusing to smile, his words again dripping with sarcasm. "Sorry, but I don't have a lot of time for chit-chat right now. Let me cut to the chase. Normally, this sort of banter would be fun with a pretty woman like you, but at the moment, I've got one stiff in the morgue getting colder by the hour, and a second victim in the hospital with half her face ripped apart. Not a pretty sight. And the guy who did it is still running around loose out there."

His words had the intended effect. Every bit of color drained from Lampe's face. His details were more graphic than what she'd read in the papers. Lampe had also overheard some of the whispers and office gossip wafting over the maze of cubicles, but she was so new to the force that she'd been kept out of the loop. The thought sank in that Wassner was the guy working the case, and he was not there to hit on her. He asked her for help.

Wassner repeated, "So, how busy are you? I could use some help with the Nelson case."

After she recovered from her initial shock and the sting of his sarcasm, Lampe felt honored he chose to ask her for help with his case. Wassner's reputation preceded him. She could learn a lot by working on his case, and he asked *her* for help.

It never occurred to her that she happened to be the most convenient cop Wassner could find in the office at that moment.

"The murders in Windsor Forest?" her eyes widened. "Sure, what can I do for you?"

"The second victim isn't dead yet, so it's not officially a double homicide. But she's in pretty bad shape. There's a uniform assigned to her hospital room, in case the perp decides he needs to finish her off, in case he gets worried that nature won't take its course. I need you to get in touch with family, take inventory at the crime scene, make a list of identifiable stolen items, and distribute the list to the local pawn shops to see if anything turns up. The clock is ticking on this one. We need to catch a break in the worst way. I'm about to head over to Windsor Forest, poke around a little more, see if there's something we missed. I'm also going to canvass the neighborhood, looking for potential witnesses who don't realize they saw something important. You'd have to be pretty oblivious to live in the neighborhood and not realize something happened by now. It doesn't look like the kind of neighborhood where they close ranks and refuse to talk to the cops, either. Maybe nobody saw anything, which would really suck. If you could come along and get started on these lists that would really help."

"Sure. I'd love something to do besides paperwork. I'll just grab my stuff, and let's roll." As she organized her things to take with her, she thought about her newly assigned responsibilities and found herself chuckling softly as the realization slowly dawned on her.

She pinched the bridge of her nose as she shook her head in resignation. What had Wassner just asked her to do but create a new stack of paperwork?

CHAPTER 5

Lampe gasped as her mind tried to reconstruct the horror that had taken place between these four walls. The copper stench of blood greeted them at the door and permeated throughout the house.

Wassner scowled at the gore-splattered walls.

Talk to me, he implored as he wandered around, absorbing the details of the scene once more. Something about this crime scene troubled him a lot more than the ususal unsolved murder. There was a problem with the picture, but he struggled to put his finger on it. A single question refused to leave his mind…*What kind of animal could do something like this?*

As he wandered through the crime scene, several things nagged at him from his conversation with Dr. Brannon. If the ME was right in his theory about the murder weapon, it probably would have come from the garage here at the house. Wassner couldn't visualize the killer walking around the neighborhood carrying a mattock.

How did he know where to look? Did he already know it was there? Why did he go into the garage in the first place? Did he think they had something of value hidden in there?

Given the evident rage and violence of the attack on the homeowners, he wondered why the house hadn't been ransacked more thoroughly. The most troubling question kept eating at Wassner. *Does this maniac really enjoy beating old people as much as this place makes it look?*

The ME had said as much. As he investigated the interior of the garage, Wassner appreciated its tidy organization. Apparently, Mr. Nelson liked peg board. Everything hung on hooks, easy to find. A rather conspicuous gap drew his attention to an empty double hook. He closed his eyes and visualized the garden tool he'd handled earlier at Home Depot. The vacant spot appeared to be just about the perfect size to hold something shaped sort of like a pickaxe, or the mattock the ME described.

Whatever had hung there was now missing. Everything else—all the other rakes, screwdrivers, brooms, saws, and hammers, hung in their assigned places. Only the one item was missing. The empty hook on the wall stuck out like a sore thumb.

Did the killer steal the murder weapon from the victim? The question posed a real problem for Wassner. *Why not look for a knife in the kitchen, or something inside the house?*

Apparently, the killer gained access into the house by breaking through a basement window. He could have found a weapon down there, but must not have bothered looking. He must have detoured into the garage for the mattock before heading for the bedroom.

How did he know where to look, or what he was looking for? Had the killer been inside the garage before?

Wassner saw no other means of entry into the garage except through the garage door or the door leading into the house, which opened into the kitchen. *Had the garage door been left open that night?* If the assailant knew the Nelsons, he might have had an opportunity to case the house at some point before the attack.

Nothing made any sense. Wassner had plenty of questions, but no answers.

That the killer seemed to have gone into the garage intentionally continued to bother the detective as he completed his search of the garage.

Why did he come in here?

There wasn't anything in there worth stealing, except maybe Nelson's car. The mattock had been on the far wall, with the car in between. In the dark, it would have been difficult to see from that far away. It almost seemed that the killer had known exactly what he was looking for, and where to look.

He wanted the mattock.

Mr. Nelson had barely made it out of his bed, and poor Mrs. Nelson never moved until the paramedics arrived. They thought she was dead, too. She scared the shit out of the first paramedic on the scene, moaning softly when they tried to move her body. She was the killer's first target. Her neck and jaw were mangled by the mattock; she was barely breathing when they discovered she wasn't dead. It was a miracle she'd lasted as long as she did. The doctors didn't give her a very high probability of survival. There was a uniformed officer stationed outside her door at the hospital. If she learned that her husband was dead, they feared that she would lose the will to live and be gone before she could tell them who had done this to them.

"I found a few invoices and some records in a filing cabinet in the den. Jesus, Christ! What a mess! This place looks like a set from a Stephen King movie," Detective Lampe exclaimed.

Wassner turned and looked at her, but he didn't respond. His jaw tightened as he walked through the room again, this time in softer daylight. The harsh, bright lights of the crime scene techs were gone. The bodies were gone, but the faint scent of death lingered in the air. He squatted down to examine the dried blood staining the carpet at the foot of the bed, then stood and stared at the splattered wall.

"Oh man, there's blood everywhere. What the hell did that?" Lampe grimaced as she pointed to a distinct pattern on the wall near the bed.

"Arterial spray. Our killer landed a direct hit with the axe-blade end of the weapon the ME thinks was a mattock. I'm thinking the perp found it here, but probably took it with him. It wasn't found at the scene."

Anger and frustration welled up in his gut and burned in his chest. But he said nothing. Having no solid leads on the case made him antsy. They had nothing on the perp. Other than robbery, there was apparently no motive. The crime scene techs couldn't identify any fibers, hair, or prints to attribute to a suspect. The clock was ticking. Every minute that passed, the odds of apprehending a suspect grew less and less probable.

This kind of mindless brutality might happen downtown once in a blue moon, but not in his little corner of the world. Not Roswell. Sure, people got killed here, just like everywhere else. But this wasn't just a murder.

Wassner was accustomed to solving murders, catching the perps, and putting them away. Criminal activity was usually pretty straightforward, to be honest. Jilted lovers, jealous spouses, other crimes of passion, and drug deals gone bad happened in Roswell like anywhere else. But they caught those guys. And there weren't massacres like this, not like this house of horrors.

"Okay," Lampe spoke. "How can I help you catch this bastard?"

"Go through any papers you can find and organize them by date. Receipts, invoices, sales tickets, anything we can use to create a paper trail and reconstruct the movements of our victims over the previous forty-eight hours or so. Then we're gonna knock on some doors, look for witnesses. You're gonna take one side of the street, and I'll take the other. We want to know about any suspicious activity, if the neighbors noticed any strangers recently, anything out of the ordinary the night of the attack or the evenings leading up to it. Anything and everything. Got that? Leave your business card if nobody answers the door."

Lampe shrugged and got busy.

She must have some place she'd rather be. Who didn't?

Some cops were clock punchers, Wassner figured. He had never been a forty-hour-a-week kind of a guy. Whatever it took to get it done, was what he gave the job. It was why his first wife had divorced him.

Someone chopped with the hoe shaped end on Mrs. Nelson, and then planted the spike end of the mattock into Mr. Nelson's head and neck, causing the arterial spray. As Wassner visualized the attack, now that he knew the weapon involved, he shook his head at the thought of someone being so cold blooded. The killer hit the old woman while she was asleep. If the ME was right about the murder weapon, the damned thing was hardly something a stranger could lug around and remain inconspicuous.

Why bother taking the weapon with him, if he hadn't brought it and it couldn't be traced back to him?

Coldly, he wondered, *What if the killer wanted a souvenir?*

Another ugly thought struck Wassner with a rabbit punch after he looked around the bedroom a while longer. The perp surprised the Nelsons in bed. He *knew* they were home asleep. The first thing the killer did after breaking in was go for the garage. He was looking for the weapon he knew he would find there, his implement of choice to beat the hell out of these two old people for no good reason. He could have taken whatever he wanted without waking the couple if theft was his motive. And there were less brutal ways to kill them.

# # #

Wassner's feet ached, and his back was starting to hurt. So far, he had earned a big goose egg on his expedition around the neighborhood. As Wassner had instructed Lampe, he left business cards at the houses where no one answered the door, with hand-scribbled notes on the back that pled for help from any potential witnesses. The farther away Wassner wandered from ground zero, the less likely he would be to find anyone who had seen anything important.

He heard the sound of a garage door opening a few houses down. Wassner looked up from the note he was in the process of writing and admired the BMW convertible pulling into the driveway. It disappeared inside the garage, and the door closed. It was the house across the street and down one from the Nelson place.

He shortened the scribbled note on the back of his card to, *please call ASAP*, worried the bird in the hand might fly away before he made it back down the street. He hustled down to the house where he'd seen activity. Wassner paused in the driveway, catching his breath. The short jog down the street caused a little tightness in his chest. He couldn't help but wonder what the story was behind the house. He hadn't really paid attention to it before now.

He guessed that the new owners demolished the original house and started a "MacMansion" in its place...until they ran out of money. It didn't fit with the rest of the houses on the block, that was for sure. It didn't look finished. The house on the corner lot was divided into sections. What appeared to be office space or small apartment faced the street above a detached two-car garage, sort of like a carriage house. A brick walkway led to the main house, situated on the corner. The front door for the primary residence actually faced the adjoining street, leading Wassner to believe the property had a different street address than the Nelson home. The driveway that led to the garage under the carriage house entered the property on the right side of the house. An open-air patio of multi-colored paver bricks featured several symbols that Wassner could not decipher. Above the patio, there was a deck with a wrought iron railing along the edge of the wall. A potted palm tree provided a modicum of shade for a small table surrounded by a quartet of chairs. The only entrance to the apartment or office above the garage appeared to be through the garage.

Wassner followed the brick walkway to the front door and rang the doorbell. If the person he watched come home was still in the carriage house apartment, he could only hope the bell chime sounded in there as well. He trudged around to the front of the house, using the path to avoid walking on the precious little grass in the yard. *Hardly anything to make it worth owning a lawnmower*, he thought. At least the Nelsons had a little property, a back yard. He turned around to face his crime scene.

The Nelson house provided sharp contrast to this one. It was a dated-looking brick ranch on a partial basement. If the 1970s or early 1980s retro look ever came back in style, it might be a hot property. The house to its left was virtually identical but a mirror image. The majority of the houses throughout the neighborhood were similar. The Nelsons had no neighbors on their right. A thick copse of bushes obscured what looked like a small marshy area he suspected was a flood plain, but Wassner couldn't see clearly through the brush. He could only tell that no house was there, and the perp would have tracked mud into his crime scene if he'd come from that direction. If some evidence had been in there, it would have been tossed…like the murder weapon. Wassner felt pretty confident that the crime scene techs would have found something that big, if it was in there.

As for the rest of the neighborhood, some of the houses might be split level, partially bricked rather than four-sided. But nothing else on the street or adjacent blocks came close in design to the house where Wassner reached for the doorbell.

He shifted from one foot to the other as he waited for someone to answer the door.

After enough time passed to make him wonder if anyone heard anything, he pushed the doorbell again. As he gradually lost patience, he rapped several loud knocks with his knuckles, wondering to himself, *Are they deaf in there?*

Finally, he heard soft footsteps approaching. A woman obviously in the process of changing from her business attire answered the door in her bedroom slippers. She greeted Wassner coolly.

"Can I help you?" she asked.

He presented his badge, mostly to establish himself as a figure of authority. "Yes, ma'am, I'm Detective Wassner with the Roswell police department." He paused to fish a business card out of his shirt pocket to offer her. "I'm sorry to bother you, but I'm sure you're aware we had a…um…incident across the street two nights ago. We're looking for anybody who saw anything out of the ordinary either late Sunday night or early Monday morning."

Obvious concern swept over her face. "How are the Nelsons? I felt terrible when I heard what happened. I was out of town on business the night they were attacked."

"Was anyone home?" Wassner asked hopefully. "We really need to talk with anybody who saw anything out of the ordinary, either the night it happened or leading up to it."

"My partner was home that night. She said that she didn't see anything until the flashing blue lights woke her up. Rachel didn't hear anything until the sirens on the ambulance were going off right across the street. It was a total shock to her."

Wassner offered the woman his business card after jotting his cell phone number on the back. "Here's my card. If Rachel remembers anything, please don't hesitate to call. If you see anything out of the ordinary, call. Office number is on the front, and that's my cell number on the back. It's very important we find the people responsible for attacking your neighbors before they hurt somebody else. I don't think they'll come back here, but it's better safe than sorry. Keep your eyes open, and be careful."

CHAPTER 6

Beth finally made it home shortly before I left for tennis practice. I heard the garage door open as I stood in the kitchen, filling my water jug.

Almost seven months pregnant, Beth looked like a stick figure that had swallowed a bowling ball. If she had gained any weight, it was all baby. We'd been married less than a year. Beth was a petite woman with ash blond hair and blue eyes that ranged from warm to icy, depending on whether or not you angered her. Her strong Southern drawl sometimes deceived people, leading them to underestimate her. My own brother made that mistake when they first met. He hasn't repeated his mistake since.

Beth grew up in the rural South, in the southwestern part of the state, making her accent more pronounced than most native Georgians. We met at work. In addition to serving as senior UNIX system administrator for our company's main servers, she also served as our Oracle database administrator, making her a very valuable asset and a hot commodity on the open market when we agreed that we shouldn't both work for the same employer. I really liked my job, so Beth sacrificed her career for family, and looked for something with more flexibility, closer to home.

She found several jobs from which to choose practically the day she started looking, very impressive in a soft job market. In Beth's new job, she made sure everyone got paid on time by maintaining the payroll system. She knew going in that the job would be boring, but she wanted to get off the corporate ladder, and not working for the same company reduced the chance that we might both find ourselves unemployed at the same time.

Beth was technical enough to fix any problem that crashed a server or database, and was comfortable enough to teach others how to do her job. That's how we met. I took her in-house training class and found myself smitten by my teacher. I bided my time, waiting until the last day of class, before asking her to lunch. I figured if she said no, I could tuck my tail between my legs and go home to lick my wounds. The few times we spoke in class, our exchanges consisted of my asking her a question, and her giving me the answer but nothing more. She offered no hints of any personal interest in me. It took a quite a leap of faith to ask her out. She seemed almost morose, to the point of depression…until we had lunch. Maybe that's what initially attracted me to her, her aura of vulnerability. She appeared to be broken, and needed fixing.

Beth seemed a little bit sad, cool, and distant in the classroom. She was polite and friendly with all of the students, but reserved at the same time—all business, if you want to know the truth. At times, I would catch her staring out the window while the class worked on an assignment, a cloak of melancholy draped over her shoulders. Her eyes would become misty and redden. I watched her regain her composure and prepare for the next lecture segment, then glanced around the room to see if I was the only one who noticed. My heart told me that Beth was broken. I wanted to help mend her, to be her knight in shining armor.

The first couple of days in class, I thought I saw a wedding ring on her finger and hadn't allowed myself to become smitten with this sad, quiet, but very pretty woman. By Wednesday, my heart skipped a beat when I noticed that her ring finger was bare. Thursday, again there was no ring. I thought it over. What if she had just been served with divorce papers? The last thing she'd want would be a new romance. I fretted over the possibilities. How certain was I that she'd been wearing a wedding ring earlier in the week? After arguing with myself, I summoned my courage to ask her out. Friday seemed to be my ideal opportunity.

On the last day of class, we finished at noon. I waited until the last of her students left the room. I walked toward the doorway and then turned back to Beth as I asked her to lunch. If she'd said no and gunned me down in flames, I could have made my escape with only wounded pride.

I knew as soon as she lifted her eyes to meet mine that my heart was hers if she wanted me. This intelligent, beautiful woman was sleepwalking through the motions of life. Something she could not bear had drained all joy and hope from her life. Irrationally, I wanted to wrap her in my arms and protect her from whatever demons haunted her. Never the romantic type, I tried to shake off a sudden urge to kiss her.

To my satisfaction, her eyes widened and she smiled in surprise. Her eyes darted around the room, as if she expected me to be asking someone else. "Lunch? Me? Right now? Um, okay. That would be nice."

We talked in the restaurant for at least three hours. I found myself wanting to know everything about her. My burger got cold, but I didn't care. I was hooked. I had already fallen in love with her while we talked in the lull between ordering and the arrival of our meals. In Beth, I saw a goodness and purity of spirit lacking in every other woman I'd ever dated.

If she'd been ready, I would have asked her to marry me that very day, and I'm not normally an impulsive guy by any stretch of the imagination. It was a good thing I didn't. She wasn't ready. Not yet.

That day I learned why she had been wearing a wedding ring earlier in the week. Beth was a war widow. A sniper in Afghanistan had shot and killed her husband the year before. With an element of ceremony, she took off her wedding ring for good on the anniversary of his death. That Tuesday, one year later, it was finally time to move ahead. She was ready to start healing. But she wasn't ready to jump into a new relationship.

She didn't need to explain herself to me any further. I was glad she had opened up and shared such personal information on our first date. It meant she felt comfortable with me. I told myself that I needed to move slowly and give her space, respect her feelings, and not to rush her into a relationship before she was ready.

Our next few dates were magic. Beth's warm personality emerged from under her protective shell during the time we spent together. Nothing in my life had ever felt so good as being able to make her laugh. Knowing that I was the reason for the new light in her eyes made me feel complete. In spite of my best efforts to take things slowly, resistance was futile. I was hopelessly in love.

Three months after we met, I asked Beth to marry me. Two months later, she finally accepted my proposal.

Her parents drove up from Florida for the wedding, hugged us both, and drove back the next day. I had the sinking feeling they never intended to give me a chance.

They were only being protective, I told myself. They were concerned over our abbreviated courtship. I knew from our first date that she was the woman I wanted to marry and figured it took twenty-eight years for me to find her. Why couldn't they see that the light had come back into their daughter's eyes since our engagement?

We had a small wedding on a quiet stretch of beach on the Georgia coast. After the ceremony, some friends hosted a low-country boil and keg party as our reception. The next week we honeymooned in the house we had just bought together in a great location in Roswell, equidistant between our work commutes. Beth drove down GA-400 while I traversed Holcomb Bridge Road east to Norcross.

Now we were expecting a child. Her parents seemed excited at the prospect of becoming grandparents. Perhaps after the baby was born, our relationship would improve. Maybe they would even come and stay with us for a couple of days after Beth gave birth.

Not six months after our wedding day, Beth became pregnant. The positive pregnancy test sent us both into silly doe-eyed bliss and proved her gynecologist wrong. He had speculated that she would have difficulty conceiving. We were still months away from the delivery date, and my concerns worsened that her morning sickness hadn't abated. Her appetite at dinner hadn't been normal either.

She must have heard me running water in the kitchen to fill my water bottle, but Beth didn't bother to stop and say hello. She made a beeline for the bathroom off our master bedroom.

After she didn't come back out for several minutes, I followed her footsteps and found Beth curled on the floor of our bathroom, her arms wrapped around her legs. She was crying uncontrollably. I knew pregnancy hormones raged in her body, but something told me this was more than a simple crying jag. I faintly smelled vomit and my eyes followed the smell.

Poor baby. Beth had obviously hurled her stomach into the trashcan in our bathroom, not able to make it the rest of the way to the toilet.

"I'm sorry, sweetheart. I'll clean it up," she sniffed between tears.

"Don't be silly," I answered. "Are you okay? Did you fall?" I picked up the trashcan and started for the toilet. Moving the trashcan stirred its contents, sending up a stronger aroma.

"No, I felt dizzy and sat here on the floor. Please, keep going. The smell is making me nauseated again."

After dumping the contents of the otherwise empty trashcan into our toilet and flushing it, I hurried past her and out the door with the empty can. Helpless to rid her of this daily routine, I wanted to help in any way I could. I rinsed the container clean with the outside hose. I set the can upside down on the driveway to dry and returned to find her sitting cross-legged on the floor, blowing her nose.

"I'm sorry," she repeated.

"Look," I smiled. "It's my fault you're pregnant. Just aim better next time."

"You're right—it is your fault. It's those damned eyelashes of yours. And God help me when you do that eyebrow thing. I fell for a pretty face and look where it's gotten me," she teased with a weak smile that collapsed into a grimace. "I've never felt this sick in my life," Beth said. "God, I feel terrible."

I frowned at my memory of the trashcan's contents—mostly yellow bile. She'd had almost nothing on her stomach. "I'm really worried that your morning sickness lasts all day, every day. This just can't be normal, Beth. Get your purse. We're going to the emergency room."

"No, you've got tennis practice," she protested. "Get me some crackers and peanut butter to eat and I'll be fine."

I wasn't going to just head off to tennis practice and leave her in this condition. Beth really felt awful. My tennis team had a match scheduled for Saturday and tonight was our regular team practice night. Since this was a holiday weekend coming up, several team members were going out of town and the team would be shorthanded. Normally I loved practices and tolerated playing the matches, but this week I would be sorely missed from either.

The Atlanta Lawn Tennis Association (ALTA) is the largest recreational tennis league in the world. Comprised of roughly eighty thousand members including men, women and youth players of all abilities, the leagues are organized by age, gender, and skill level. For the most part, competition is evenly matched. Teams win with depth, not on the strength of a few good players. Although tennis has historically been a gentleman's game, a fact not forgotten by most of the players, team captains are another matter. The captain's approach to the league can be cutthroat and vicious, sometimes even a win-at-all-costs mentality.

ALTA is a religion to many in Atlanta. This is no friendly neighborhood league. Dedication to the game and loyalty to the team is the unwritten code of honor.

Beth and I both knew that missing practice better come with a damned good excuse.

But my baby was sick. I felt like she needed me, in spite of her protests to the contrary. Earlier, I couldn't wait to shed my work clothes, particularly the cursed tie I purchased that morning. Now dressed in a t-shirt and shorts, I forced myself to relax and took a deep breath.

"Honey, did you have anything for lunch?"

I knew the truth from the expression on her face. She hadn't been able to eat all day, but she still made me breakfast that morning. Pangs of guilt squeezed my heart. I loved this woman more than I could ever tell her, for her sacrifice for our baby, and for the way she made me feel loved. But childbirth could be dangerous, and Beth was obviously having a difficult pregnancy. The fear I might lose her choked my words.

"I'll be okay until my appointment next Tuesday. It's less than a week," Beth replied tiredly. Ever adept at changing the subject when I pestered her about her health and the baby, she asked, "You came home early. Is everything okay at work?"

Her face wore a new expression of concern. She knew how much I liked my coworkers and my job. My company had laid off about a dozen people only last year because of slow business in a stagnant economy. Our new president seemed only to know how to spend more money than the last so prospects for the short term weren't looking appreciably better. We chose to use my company's health insurance over hers. A change in jobs would put a serious crimp in our plans.

"Don't worry, there's no problem at work. My stomach was a little upset after lunch so Richard told me to knock off early and just work from home later tonight if I felt better. After I got out of my work clothes and took an antacid, I started feeling a lot better. So I changed again and dressed for tennis practice."

Beth smiled in relief. "Good. Then go on to practice. That way neither of us has to cook."

"No, I was thinking of calling that Mexican place in the Publix shopping center to order you a cup of their chicken soup to go. How does that sound for dinner?"

"As long as I don't have to cook, it sounds wonderful. I think I'll lie down until you get back with the soup. Wake me if I fall asleep."

I thought it a little odd she believed she might doze off while I went for the soup, but sure enough, when I returned, she was breathing the deep and rhythmic pattern of REM sleep, complete with twitching eyes. She must have been exhausted. But she needed to eat something. Reluctantly, I gently kissed each closed eyelid and brushed her lips lightly.

Her eyes fluttered open.

"You were right. You were sound asleep already. Why are you such a sleepy head? Did I sleep through a bad night? Why didn't you wake me?"

"You'd sleep through an earthquake, I think," she laughed. "I...had trouble sleeping."

"Nausea woke you up? Come on, I'm no expert at any of this, but even I know a woman isn't supposed to have morning sickness twenty-four hours a day. Beth, we've got to move your appointment sooner than next week."

"I'll be fine," she sighed. She opened the paper bag I had placed on the bedside table. "You didn't get anything for yourself. Why not? What are you going to do about supper?"

"Because I'm going to practice like you wanted. You know I can't run around on a tennis court with a full stomach. I have to eat something small before I get out there, like fruit. After practice is over and I've had time to cool off, I can just grab a burger or something on the way home. Since you never feed me greasy stuff like that anymore, I need my occasional fix."

"Good. Go. There is nothing you need to do here," she said, sounding relieved that I was going to give her some peace and quiet tonight. I wondered if she would even try to eat, or just fall back asleep.

"Your soup is gonna get cold. Come on, let's get you up so you can eat your dinner."

I grabbed her hands in mine and pulled her to a sitting position. She grudgingly got out of bed and followed me into the kitchen. She sat at the kitchen table in a daze. I grabbed a spoon out of the drawer and poured her customary glass of water.

"Thank you," she said. Her lack of energy was really worrying me.

"I'd better skip practice tonight."

"Why? I told you I'm fine. Just tired," she argued.

"I don't want to leave you alone so weak. As soon as I walk out that door, you're going to head right back to bed, aren't you? Maybe what bothered my stomach at lunch was a bug, not something I ate. It might hit you and the baby harder than it did me. I'm afraid to leave when you feeling this way."

"Don't be silly. You're right. After I eat my soup, I'm going back to bed. There's nothing wrong with that. Just promise me that you won't work too late, if you go to the office after practice. I hate waking up in the house by myself, especially in the middle of the night."

I smiled. "That's why I keep trying to tell you that we need a dog. A dog would bark to let you know if there was any reason for you to wake up. I went to a thrift store today that the Humane Society is opening to raise money. Tiff won't let me hear the end of it until we adopt one. What about it? Don't you want a loyal hound protecting our castle?"

"Yeah, sure," Beth said. "Abby would never let us have a dog."

"She would if we let her choose the one she could tolerate. Some dogs even *like* cats. Or, we could get a dog that is about the same size as Abby, so it would be a fair fight," I argued.

"You could bring in a giant German Shepherd and Abby would still make it a fair fight, but it's a moot point," Beth said. "We agreed to wait until the baby was born so the dog won't get jealous of the baby, remember?"

An expert negotiator, Beth diffused the tension without it escalating into an argument. I knew she wanted a dog as much or more than I did, and she was right about needing the fence to let out the dog on rainy days when we didn't want to get soaked.

Damn it, she has me off topic, as usual. I wouldn't let her win that easily. She still wanted to shoo me out the door to tennis practice.

"I should stay home…"

"If you don't feel well, then stay home. But if you're saying that because of me, I already told you that I'm going to bed as soon as I finish the soup. Don't stay here on my account. Your team expects you. And let's face it, my handsome jock of a husband, they don't stand a chance of making it to the playoffs without you." She smiled warmly, running a finger over the muscles in my serving arm.

What is it about her that makes me feel like more of a man than I know I am?

Practice was the only part of ALTA that I really enjoyed. It was only an hour and a half. The courts weren't far away. It would be a shame to miss it if Beth really didn't need me. But I felt like a heel for leaving her.

"Tell you what, keep your cell phone beside you, and I'll set my ringer on the highest volume. If you need me, call and I'll be home in ten minutes. We're playing at the park down the street where we usually practice, okay?"

"Dan, I'll be fine. I'm sleepy and have no need of your chivalry tonight. Go have fun," Beth teased.

I leaned to kiss her. My lips pressed hers for a long, possessive moment.

I love her so much it hurts. And it hurts to see her so miserable.

She put both her palms on my cheeks and scolded, "Get out of here now. Off to practice... you are keeping me from my beauty sleep."

# # #

I couldn't help but notice the cherry trees exploding in showers of pink and white as I steered my way toward our practice courts. The street underneath was littered with cherry blossom petals.

Terrific. Seasonal allergies were already killing me, with the pine trees pollinating to produce prodigious amounts of ubiquitous yellow dust, coating cars, roads, and every exposed surface outdoors. Wisps of the thick, choking pollen swirled in the breeze and coated the nose and throat of anyone outdoors in the stuff for more than a few minutes.

Most of the members of my ALTA team play to win. I play because I enjoy the game and the exercise. Not everybody has forgiven me for our loss in last season's playoffs. It boiled down to one controversial line call that I made, but I had no idea the call would be controversial when I made it. It was just the right call.

We had been in a very tight match, third set tiebreaker. My partner and I were finally challenged by players of equal caliber. Unfortunately, our test didn't come until we were playing for the city championship. When the city is the size of Atlanta, winning the title means more to some people than others. Our opponents were honest, very talented players. They pushed us to the limits, and a little beyond. In other words, we didn't hand them the match. They won...fair and square.

The guy receiving serve blistered a two-handed backhand return down the line. My partner poached, leaving the alley uncovered. The spin on the ball wanted to carry it off the court, but it barely landed in. I got there too late. The ball passed me. I rushed over to the spot where it landed, certain it had been just out, ready to make the call. Unfortunately, I could see a little bit of yellow fuzz creased the sideline. I could tell that he'd just barely clipped the line. The call was close; no one would have blamed me if I'd gotten it wrong.

But I would have blamed myself. The ball was good, so I gave them the point. It made the difference between winning and losing, but that wasn't the issue. Like golf, tennis is a gentleman's game, despite the occasional captain's shenanigans.

Our opponents never relinquished their advantage, closing out the tiebreaker by simply willing their way to win. After the match, our counterparts complimented me on my good sportsmanship. Our teammates offered slightly muted praise and condolences for the tough loss. I could tell that some of them silently blamed me for being honest. Nobody else seemed to realize the exhilaration I felt from getting pushed to the limits and finding the integrity within myself to do the right thing, to make the right call.

It does matter how you play the game.

Mike Wu spotted me approaching the practice courts and raised his racket in greeting, with his usual muted enthusiasm. It didn't bother him any more than losing the final bothered me. He was my partner at number one doubles for our tennis team out of Roswell Park, a twelve pack of courts crammed into an impressively organized nook of the expansive wooded refuge. Even though we had lost the final, our team got promoted to the next level, A-1. Our next stop would be double A, where the college players and former touring pros waited for us. When we rose to a level above our abilities, we would no longer need worry about winning at all costs.

A walking trail meandered beside the courts we had reserved for tonight's practice. The foot traffic was brisk with walkers and joggers out enjoying the glorious spring evening in spite of the heavy pollen. The day had been warm, but at night the air began to cool down quite a bit. As I approached, I watched Mike scurry around the court, warming up our number two doubles team, Holger Weisskopf and John Rothstein. All three players were solid and rock steady on both wings. John had a couple of weapons, while Holger played an aggressive serve-and-volley game with consistency, but no real put-away shots. The ball crisscrossed the net with mechanical precision, crisp groundstrokes and solid volleys exchanged, but they almost looked bored. Unlike points played under match conditions, during practice each player deliberately hit a return shot designed for the opponent on the other side of the net to have a play on the ball. Nobody aimed for lines or corners.

Mike floated around the court, a jitterbug of a player who formed a human backboard on his side of the court. His movements appeared effortless. Mike's day job was litigation; he was a corporate attorney for the local media conglomerate that owned radio, television, and newspapers in Atlanta. Our games complemented each other perfectly; he was lightning quick, while I brought thunder in my groundstrokes and service game.

During ALTA matches, most opponents played away from me because I went for big shots, falling for the mistake of trying to play to Mike. He won matches by rarely making unforced errors, setting the table for me by forcing them away from the net, where I would close to pounce on any overhead or easy volley in the empty space Mike created for me.

The down side to Mike as partner was that he never hit many clean winners. He worried our opponents to death. He lacked any sort of killer instinct, which is where I fit into the picture. I had no qualms about going for broke, anywhere, or any time. I hated to lob, or hit defensive shots, unless as a last resort.

Our practices were on Wednesday nights. We played league matches on Saturday mornings. Both the one and two seed teams played at nine o'clock, so it didn't really matter who played at one and who played at two except to Holger and John…but mostly to Holger. There was a very intense, mostly good-natured rivalry between those guys, Mike, and me. It was starting to bug Holger that I knew how to beat them and that we won most of the time when we squared off against each other. Claiming the top spot on the team was clearly eating at him.

Holger grew up in Germany, immigrating after college and his youthful Olympic competition. He was some kind of international investment banker—young, athletic, naturally aggressive, and agile. He settled in California, married a Georgia girl, and migrated back to the east coast with her. He now suffered in the stifling summer heat of Atlanta like the rest of us. There's nothing like baking on a hard court in the middle of the day when it's over a hundred degrees in the shade.

The pollen really seemed to bother my allergies tonight. My eyes itched and watered constantly, making it difficult to see the ball clearly. My sinuses kept draining and made me feel a little sick after I worked up a pretty good lather running around the court. But I held it together, and we finished off Holger and John in two tight sets. I gathered my gear and said a quick goodbye.

I was glad I decided to come out to practice after all. The brisk exercise and routine of tennis practice had cleared my head of any lingering uneasiness about the strange images that filled my head earlier in the day. Something about the familiar sights and sounds of the tennis courts allowed me to dismiss those distant memories as mere aberrations. The only thing on my mind now was getting back home to Beth.

CHAPTER 7

My gut told me to go straight home and check on my wife. I felt guilty for leaving her, even though she had insisted. My sweatshirt clung to my body, drenched with sweat from my exertion in the muggy night. My body felt sticky. I ached for a long, hot shower as soon as I got home. I put my towel over the car seat so that sweat from my saturated clothing wouldn't absorb into the leather.

Fog began to settle in as I drove home, a gray curtain of gloom. A misting drizzle hung in the air like a wet blanket, forcing me to slow my speed and actually obey the residential limits. It was a little after eight o'clock, and I was hungry, tired, and more than a little slimy. My garage door wouldn't open fast enough.

I dropped off my tennis gear in the appointed spot and called out to Beth, announcing my return home, the conquering hero. She didn't respond. I peeled off my wet shirt and left it in the laundry room before I wandered through the house, expecting to find her in the kitchen on the phone, or on the living room sofa watching television.

After calling her name several times but getting no answer, I got nervous. An involuntary shudder gave me the chills. As goose bumps popped up on my bare arms and chest, I headed for our closet to get a dry t-shirt. The light was on in the master bathroom. My heart froze when my eyes fell on her small bare foot lying on the white ceramic tile.

I jumped over the cat and bolted to the bathroom. My knees buckled on me when I reached Beth lying on the bathroom floor, unconscious. Panic forced blinding tears to my eyes.

"Beth, answer me. Come on baby, answer me. Answer me, Beth," I urged her insistently, trying to focus my adrenalin toward action instead of panic. Years of living the precise analytical life of an engineer kicked in, and I reached for the pocket where I normally carried my cell phone.

Shit! It was still in my tennis bag.

I took the steps down to where I'd left it, three at a time. My pants were also soaked with sweat, making them cling uncomfortably to my legs, and my tired legs balked at the exertion I demanded of them. I slipped on the steps as I stumbled back up to Beth, righted myself with one arm and kept going, my eyes on the buttons as I punched in 9-1-1.

I could see that her chest moved rhythmically. Her eyelids fluttered as if she was trying to open them when she heard her name, but she remained unconscious, her eyes closed.

"Beth, what happened? Wake up! Beth!" I didn't want to shake her, afraid she might have broken a bone when she fell. I stroked her pale arm briskly, trying to warm her and bring some color back to her skin. I was still pleading with her to wake up when the operator answered.

"9-1-1 operator. What is the nature of your emergency, please?"

An ugly red welt darkened Beth's forehead. Tissue holder lay on the floor behind the toilet, torn off the wall. She'd been kneeling to throw up when she passed out and hit her head.

"My wife fell and hit her head. She's unconscious and she's pregnant," I said in a staccato burst of words.

"Is she breathing normally?"

"Yes, she seems to be." I tried to keep from hyperventilating, forcing myself to slow down. A vague old adage about a real man being able to keep his head when those around him were losing theirs offered me an unexpected anchor.

Get a grip. Take control. Handle this. She needs you.

I took one quick, settling breath and described her injury. "There's a dark bruise on her head. I think she passed out and hit her head on something as she fell. I'm afraid to move her in case her neck is hurt."

"Just stay with her until emergency personnel arrive to take care of her. An ambulance is being dispatched to your location. Please confirm the street address for the phone number from which you are calling."

She rattled off our street address, which I confirmed. I asked them to hurry.

"Don't panic, sir. Emergency personnel will be there any minute. Stay with your wife, and tell me how she's doing. Don't try to move her as long as she's breathing normally. If she shows any difficulty in breathing, only then you should turn her head to the side so she can keep her airways clear."

"She seems to be breathing okay," I said.

The operator asked, "Has she ever had a seizure before? Are her extremities twitching or showing any signs of involuntary movement?"

"No, she's just lying there. When I said her name, her eyelids moved like she was trying to open them. Now she's not reacting at all."

The voice remained calm, but her words were not soothing. "Check her pulse."

I began to wonder if the operator was simply trying to keep me preoccupied with trying to minister to Beth in order to help calm *me* down until the paramedics arrived. If that was her plan, it was working. Beth's pulse felt weak and slower than normal. New pangs of terror fought to take away my control, but I forced myself to stay calm and conveyed the information back to the operator.

"I can feel her pulse, but it's weak."

"Just hang on with me for a few more seconds. The ambulance should be almost there by now. The crew en route is one of our best teams. They'll take great care of your wife and baby. Don't worry, okay?"

The more she talked, the more I doubted her sincerity. How could she know who was driving the ambulance approaching my house?

She's only telling me what she thinks I want to hear.

At the same time, I took comfort in her reassurances. She was right there with me, every step of the way, and a steadying voice on the other end of the phone.

In the distance, I heard sirens wail. Flashing red lights lit the windows from outside our house. I again took three steps at a time, jumping down the short flight separating the living room from our foyer. As the doorbell rang, I snatched open the door, vaguely aware I was still bare chested and smelled of sweat.

No time for niceties. I'm sure they've seen worse.

A paramedic and an EMT waited on my front stoop. I looked at the male EMT, who towered over me even standing on the lower step. His imposing height at that moment sent a wave of relief over me, as if I had seen a row of cavalry cresting the horizon in an old movie.

"Hello," I said awkwardly, not knowing what else to say.

"Where is our emergency?" the paramedic asked. Her nametag identified her as "Wright," but neither of them offered a name. She was comically shorter than her partner, but seemed to be the one in charge. I led them to the master bathroom, where Beth remained unconscious on the floor. I moved out of their way to let them work.

Wright checked Beth's vital signs. She spoke into the handset clipped to her collar, communicating with the doctors back at the hospital. She brusquely directed her partner to bring equipment in from the ambulance. In my dazed state, I only heard her say "spine board" and "C collar" before a new wave of panic swept over me. The tall cavalry officer disappeared to get them.

I heard Wright speak into her lapel mic, "Victim is approximately thirty year old white female with a fall from a probable standing position, with a visible hematoma on the right temple area. Patient is presently unconscious. Blood pressure is ninety over fifty. Heart rate one twenty, mild sinus tachycardia. Skin color pink and warm, but slightly diaphoretic. Patient is estimated to be at least six months pregnant, but appears slightly underweight."

A couple of seconds passed like an eternity before Wright's radio squawked, "Got it. Let's check for hypoglycemia. Please test the blood sugar, stat."

With a series of smooth, practiced moves that were quick but not hurried, Wright had her answer in seconds. She radioed, "Finger stick blood sugar is low."

I nodded along as if they cared about my opinion, understanding only about half the medical speak. I volunteered, "Beth didn't stop having morning sickness after her first trimester. It's like all day, every day. She keeps her regular appointments with our obstetrician and eats as much as she can, but she has trouble keeping things down. Her doctor's name, the obstetrician is Dr. Grover. Beth…"

Wright didn't have to tell me to shut up because her radio squawked again, "Start her on 500cc bolus of normal saline with fifty cc's of fifty percent dextrose to bring her around. Then get her in here. Just to be safe, use the spine board and C collar during transport, please."

As if on cue, the giant reappeared with the medical devices the doctor had just now ordered, but Wright had anticipated.

"Roger that." Wright never stopped moving, quick but unhurried. With an economy of motion, she introduced an IV needle into Beth's arm and secured it with tape. She looked at her partner and said, "Load a syringe with an ampoule of D-fifty and get it ready for me, okay?"

When he handed it to her, she pressed lightly on the plunger until liquid squirted, and then injected the remaining contents into the IV tubing. Beth's eyes popped wide open almost instantaneously, though she appeared somewhat disoriented.

"What happened? Dan?" she asked for me, her voice still groggy.

From behind Wright, I said to her, "You fell and hit your head pretty hard. You were knocked out when I found you, so I called for the ambulance."

Wright spoke into her radio, "She's awake. Going to evaluate neurological responses."

She asked Beth, "What is your name?"

"Beth Harper. What's yours?"

Wright suppressed a half-smile at Beth's sarcastic response. Next, she asked Beth to confirm her age, the city where we lived and our current street address. The answers were all the right ones, so she signaled to her partner Beth was ready for transport to the hospital.

"Wait a minute," Beth protested. "If I got all the answers right, why do I still have to go to the hospital?" She tried to resist the super-sized EMT as he immobilized her head with the cervical collar and strapped her down to the spine board.

Wright smiled apologetically. "We have to figure out why you fell." She turned to her partner and said, "You heard. Let's get her to the hospital ASAP."

"But I don't want to go to the hospital," Beth protested.

"Sweetie, you don't get a vote," I said sympathetically. "Even if you did, it would be three against one. I'm with the paramedics on this one. Besides, once they've got you strapped down like that, we have to pay them to release you. The insurance won't cover their visit if you don't go to the hospital," I fibbed, not knowing if it was true. "I'm going to ride in the ambulance with you."

Her eyes cleared and her voice got stronger. She insisted, "Dan, you need to follow the ambulance with our car. Otherwise, we'll have to get a cab back home."

I looked at the driver, the burly EMT. "Where are we going, North Fulton?"

Both paramedic and EMT nodded yes.

"I'll be right behind you."

Half an hour later in the emergency room, they finally let me see her again. The attending physician announced that he decided to admit her to the hospital.

"She has zero body fat. Her body is digesting muscle to feed nutrition to the baby," he said. "Unless her OB says differently tomorrow, she probably needs to stay a few days. We'll keep her on intravenous fluids and monitor her condition."

After moving Beth to a room, the nurses swarmed like ants around her, attaching tubes, sensors, and every conceivable type of monitor that beeped and hissed. Her pulse, heart rate, and other vital signs drew glowing lines on a monochrome screen mounted to a rolling stand that the technicians and doctors danced around.

My vocal concern about Beth's lack of body fat caught the attention of one of her doctors.

"Don't worry; she's going to be ok," he reassured me. Your wife is a real trooper. The baby's fine — he or she hasn't missed a meal. Your wife told us she kept taking the prenatal vitamins her obstetrician prescribed even though she wasn't able to keep them down for long. We're going to start her on anti-nausea medication so she can take solid foods as soon as she feels like it. Jello is already on the way, and we'll go slowly. Once her condition has stabilized, I can send her home with a prescription for Phenergan in pill form. It's the same anti-nausea medication we've introduced into her IV."

I breathed a sigh of relief. "Thank you for taking care of her," I said. Emotions welled again, now that I could allow myself to crack. I brusquely brushed my eyes with the back of my hand. "I couldn't handle losing her."

"She'll be fine. I need to continue my rounds. Give her some time to rest. You can stay in the room with her a little longer if you'd like, but you really need to let her get some sleep. Go home, get some rest yourself, and come back in the morning. She'll be fine. The nurses on this floor are the best."

"Will do. Thanks again," I said as I turned to look at Beth.

She looked so pale and fragile lying there in bed. My finger twirled a tendril of her hair at her shoulder. I never thought I could feel this way about anyone, but this woman held my heart in her hands. Guilt twisted my gut again, reminding me that she'd become so sick with our baby.

A suppressed voice from my subconsciousness reminded me I was a poor comparison to her first husband, the strong soldier hero. Recalling my crazy hallucinations and hysteria over a stupid thrift store tie only added to my sense of weakness. Old insecurities taunted me again. I didn't deserve her.

I leaned over to kiss her cool forehead and promised, "Beth, I will never let anything hurt you again. I am so sorry I left you tonight." I buried my head in the blankets on her bed for a long while. Eventually some semblance of control came back to me and I left, closing the door softly behind me.

I went outside the hospital where the reception was better to use my cell phone. I called her parents down in Florida to let them know what had happened. Their doubt in my ability to take care of their daughter came through in her father's relentless questions over every detail of her collapse, treatment, and prognosis. Grudgingly, he accepted that I had done all he thought to suggest. He would have to trust me to care for her. They were both sick with the flu and would have to wait to travel up to see their daughter. The last thing on earth Beth needed was a new reason to get sick to her stomach.

CHAPTER 8

Roswell had a small but efficient police force to serve its population of about ninety thousand people. The city was located far enough north of the Perimeter that most of the street crime was confined to the large apartment complexes off Holcomb Bridge Road, clustered near the GA-400 corridor that connected the northern suburbs to downtown Atlanta. Unlike their big-city counterparts, the Roswell police department simply grouped plainclothes detectives into one of two categories, one for crimes against persons, and the other for crimes against property. Lampe was a property detective.

Only about twenty miles north of downtown Atlanta, Roswell was close enough to the big city that major crimes could invade the quiet suburban community. Sometimes the offender managed to escape and disappear into the sprawling metropolis of greater Atlanta. As far as the rest of the world was concerned, Roswell was part of Atlanta. But it was really a small city with a rich history of its own, tucked under a bigger city's coat tails.

Wassner was assigned to crimes against persons. The other detectives sometimes joked it was because he was such a people sort of guy. He was as tenacious as a bulldog, appropriate given his alma mater, the University of Georgia.

An hour passed with Wassner's head buried in the medical examiner's report. Lieutenant Anestos, the day shift supervisor, stuck his head in the cubicle door to say hello. "Hey, how's it going on the Windsor Forest case?"

"Just freaking fabulous. I asked Lampe to help me out a little. She's running down any pawned items with the roster of pawn shops. No suspects, no forensic evidence worth mentioning. Motive was apparently robbery. Reason for murder unclear—the victims were attacked while still asleep in bed. No witnesses. My gut is telling me that this wasn't our boy's first time out. I'm pretty sure that our perp has done this sort of thing before."

"What makes you say that?"

"Mostly my gut," Wassner admitted. "Something about the crime scene, I guess. The fact he seemed so...*methodical*. The place wasn't completely ransacked. The rage behind the attack doesn't fit the brutality of the scene. It doesn't look like he got frustrated when he couldn't find what he wanted. He got inside, found his weapon, attacked the people with a bloody vengeance, and then robbed the place at his leisure. It feels like this guy really *enjoyed* the killing. He likes hurting people."

"Jesus Christ!" Anestos swore under his breath.

"No, I think we can rule him out as a suspect," Wassner quipped dryly.

"You keep saying *he*."

"I can't see a woman doing this one. Too bloody, much too violent. Some strong muscles swung that mattock."

Anestos shifted uncomfortably on his feet. "The quarterly cross-metro PD conference was just last week. There wasn't anything out of the other PDs with scenes remotely approaching this MO," he said. "Unless this guy's new in town, there's nothing to back your hunch he's a repeat offender." He thought for a moment and added, "There was a bludgeoning homicide in Sugar Hill, but it was looking like a crime of passion, and I think they had a suspect, maybe already solved the case. Guy was beaten to death with his own golf club while his wife was out of town on business. I can check with Forsyth County, but I don't think robbery was the motive. I think they were looking at a jealous lover angle."

"Was the golf club found at the crime scene?"

Anestos frowned, deepening the permanent worry lines etched into his forehead by years on the force. Wassner had his full attention now. "I think they said that the golf club used on the guy was his pitching wedge, and it was missing, if memory serves me correctly. So, what are you trying to tell me? You really think our guy is a serial killer? Can you tie this guy to Sugar Hill?"

"Let me keep digging and see if I can find any other cases with a similar MO," Wassner said. "Pretty soon I'm going to call my guy in the GBI to see if I can get him to create a profile and run it through VICAP."

"You're starting to make a good argument. Maybe you should've been a lawyer. Why are you still waiting to call the GBI? I'm thinking that you're about to pick up the phone any minute, right?"

"Yeah. I wanted to look at the Sugar Hill incident first, develop any leads we could before I made the call, but I'm about there," Wassner said. "I've pieced some things together. The crime scene techs found no extra DNA at the Nelson house. We need some forensic evidence. We've got to find a common denominator between victims, if there *is* any connection between them. How does the perp pick his target?"

"What about the victims?" Anestos suggested. "Have you built a profile on them yet? Maybe the GBI can help with that. Anything suspicious that might connect the Nelsons to Sugar Hill? Any recent trips or unfamiliar visitors? Is our survivor able to answer any questions yet?"

"Not really," Wassner muttered. "She did regain consciousness. She can write, but that's about it. She's on so many pain meds, it's hard to get anything out of her that we can use. That's the problem…these were a couple of old retired people. She belonged to a book club, and he was a member of the VFW. They were just a pair of old geezers who didn't get out much. I don't get the anger. Shit, they were half dead as it was. Not knowing anything about her mental state before the attack, I have no way to know how reliable a witness she'll turn out to be. She could've been senile or well on the way there before the attack."

"I don't need to tell you that the press will be crawling up the chief's ass if we don't make some quick progress on this one, or, God forbid, there's another one in our jurisdiction."

"If I'm right, Roswell is far from being this guy's only hunting ground. He thinks he owns the whole city of Atlanta."

"And he doesn't?"

That brought a scowl to Wassner's face. It looked natural, like it belonged there. "Was there a reason you dropped by, other than to annoy me?"

"Yes, to ask if you need more help. The mayor is worried about this one."

Oh, no. The "we're a team" speech is coming next, Wassner thought to himself. "Let me think about it. Lampe already agreed to give me a hand with the pawn shops. There is such a thing as having too many cooks in the kitchen, you know?"

"We're all part of the same team," Anestos said, right on cue. "Any resource you need, say the word, and it will be put at your disposal. We need a break on this one, and pretty quick, Detective Wassner."

# # #

After Anestos stopped bothering him, Wassner flipped through his Rolodex until he found the right card. He dialed his contact with the Georgia Bureau of Investigation, a guy he knew from all the way back to his high school days, ancient history. Because their personalities were so much alike, Wassner slipped into old habits when he heard his friend's voice on the line.

"Gradick, investigations," the GBI agent answered the phone.

"Aren't you supposed to say 'GBI' or something like that? What if I dialed the wrong number? You didn't say what you investigate or who you do it for," Wassner cracked.

"You called to waste my time, Wassner? What do you want?"

"Help, *Special Investigator* Gradick. I'm touched you recognized my voice. And yeah, I've been doing fine. Thanks for asking."

"Let's try this one more time. What do you want, *asshole*. It hasn't been that long since the last time you called me to ask a favor. Nobody else has the balls to call my private line unless it's a matter of life or death. Who else in the Roswell police department knows the number for the direct line to my desk? I've got this thing called Caller ID. Ever heard of it? Don't answer that question; it'll just waste more of my time. Get to the point. I'm busy."

"Damn, Craig, who licked the molasses off of your bread? All right, I'll get right down to business. I need you to open up a parallel investigation to a case I'm working. I'm looking for murders that match a sick profile. The victims are attacked in their own homes while they sleep, with something the assailant finds in the house. Nothing as clean as a knife or gun. This guy likes to wale on people with the meanest weapon he can find. He takes the weapon with him. Burglary is almost an afterthought. There was one murder here in Roswell. The ME thinks a gardening mattock was the weapon used in the attack."

"Jesus! That's nasty. I know what a mattock is," Gradick said. "I've got one at home. Before you ask, no, it wasn't used recently to kill somebody. Why don't you think this case is a crime of passion? What makes you think there are more? Where? Before I decide if I'm going to open a new investigation, you're gonna have to give me everything you've got." A more serious tone entered his voice. "Give me a second. Let me get a pen. Okay, from the top. Victim's name, date of the attack, mode of entry, weapon used, any notable items on the pawn list. I'm ready whenever you are. Go."

Wassner laid out the details of everything he knew about the Roswell and Sugar Hill attacks. "If this is the same guy, he's moving haphazardly from one jurisdiction to another, and he's putting some distance in between one victim and the next. There aren't many common denominators I've been able to identify yet. Cause of death in both cases was blunt force from whatever the killer decided to pick up there in the house. Both times, he took the weapon with him. He apparently got into to the houses by means he seemed to know about beforehand. In other words, I think our guy cased his targets before hitting them. B and E through the basement window, and the perp had to know there wasn't an alarm."

"Not necessarily," Gradick countered. "You know as well as I do, if it turns out we're looking for a meth head, all bets are off. Those people are idiots. But looking over what you've put together, it's interesting. You might be on to something. Okay. I've got it. If I decide you're not chasing your tail, we'll open our own investigation. I'll keep you in the loop since you brought it to me. You'll get everything we get. Scout's honor."

"You were never a Scout, were you?"

"What difference does that make? It's just an expression," Gradick deflected. "Those crime scenes are spread out, pretty far apart," he added doubtfully. "It sounded like you thought the perp had prior knowledge of the place in Roswell before the attack. How did you say he got inside? The Sugar Hill detective—what was his name? Did he have any idea how the perp got inside at his crime scene? Have y'all compared notes on papers and receipts to see if any names show up in both places?"

"Slow down, my friend accustomed to working for the big government bureaucracy. The lowly detectives here in Roswell don't get other cops to ask, 'how high?' when we say jump. My boss doesn't think the crimes are related. Thinks they're too far apart. So he says talk to the guys in Sugar Hill, but don't waste too much time spinning your wheels. You, on the other hand, can cast a bigger net and see if our boy's MO turns up in any other jurisdictions. You game?"

"Of course," Gradick said. "I've got nothing better to do, right? I sit here, waiting for your call. 'Cause you'd never send me flowers."

"Did I tell you my wife left me? I still wear my wedding ring, because now I'm married to my job," Wassner deadpanned.

"I'm shocked. And stunned," Gradick cracked. "You about to ask me out on a date?"

"Her loss could be your gain. She makes more money than I do, so I inherited the season tickets. You could be my date to the Auburn game this year. It's a home game."

"Go Dawgs. My wife looks forward to the peace and quiet when I'm not around on my days off. Of course I'll be your date, as long as you don't expect me to put out for you, big guy."

CHAPTER 9

It happened on the way home from the hospital. I must have blacked out behind the wheel. I remembered turning right onto Alpharetta Highway heading home, and then I snapped out of a trance and found myself parked with the engine shut off in front of a strange, dark house on an unfamiliar street, nowhere near my neighborhood.

How in the hell did I get here?

On a moonless night, the cul-de-sac where I found myself parked was almost pitch black, as dark as it ever gets considering all the ambient light created by the sprawling metropolis of Atlanta. Wherever I was, I could tell it was close enough to share the night sky glow of the big city.

As my eyes adjusted to the dark, I saw that I was near the dead end of a cul-de-sac. The dark house loomed forebodingly. A brief flash of light teased me with a quick glimpse of something draped across the front entrance. I couldn't tell what it was.

Several houses down the street, in the yard of a corner lot, a streetlight flickered and struggled to come on. It cast a dull, pale glow that pulsed rhythmically like a bug zapper, illuminating the eerie shadows surrounding the house where I parked. Something was definitely wrong with this picture.

My heart began to race. My palms grew clammy. I started to reach for my cell phone but stopped myself. *Who could I call? What would I tell them?*

I had no memory of driving here. After several disoriented seconds, I reached for the keys to start my car. As common sense screamed at me to leave, I found myself still staring at the house, watching for the lights to come on or other signs of activity.

Dread battled with a growing concern about drawing unwanted attention. If a stranger parked on the curb directly in front of my house late at night, I knew Beth would be shaking me awake to call the cops. It was only a little after eleven, but it would be tough explaining to a police officer why I was loitering in front of a strange house since I didn't even know myself. I still smelled of dried sweat from tennis practice, sat parked in front of the house of a complete stranger, while my wife slept in a hospital bed.

Mr. Harper, can you say…stalker?

Yet I remained frozen in place, my hand resting on the gearshift.

Something else didn't feel right. It wasn't simply a case of me being in the wrong place at the wrong time. I was already here, so I might as well try to figure out why.

I cut off the engine and opened the car door, taking the flashlight from the glove compartment with me. In my mind, I pieced together a cover story to explain being here. It was off the main road with minimal street traffic where I could check my tire pressure on the way home from the hospital. Around Atlanta, enough Good Samaritans and stranded motorists get struck by passing vehicles that my story might hold water.

Was this subdivision on my way home from the hospital? Where was home in relation to this place? Was this really on the way?"

I asked myself one question too many and knew a cop would easily catch me in a lie. I was not good enough at it.

Better move quick.

I circled my vehicle, directed the beam at each of the tires just in case any neighbors had spotted me parked there and wondered what I was doing. When I was on the side of the car nearest the curb, I dared to look away from the car and directly at the house, my glance timed with the flickering streetlight for an optimal chance of actually seeing anything.

The shadowy house was set back a fair distance from the street, so I still had to strain my eyes in the dark to focus on its silhouette. The roofline frowned menacingly against the night sky. I fought the urge to panic like a child. An odd fluttering sound whispered in the trees, raising the hair on the back of my neck. It didn't belong there; I could tell that much for sure.

Furtively, I glanced up and down the street at the nearest neighbors, looking for snoopers behind moving curtains. No one seemed interested in what I was doing, in fact there were no signs of life anywhere along the deserted street. I took a chance of pointing my flashlight beam at the soft fluttering sound coming from the trees.

Yellow crime scene tape blocked the sidewalk leading to the front door. Something stirred from deep inside me, telling me that this house had a connection to the cursed tie I bought from the thrift store. The suppressed visions flooded back with a vengeance.

I jumped back into my car, my hands literally shaking in fear. I was ready to make my escape. The car keys slipped through my fingers and fell into the ink black of the floorboard. My fingers scrambled like hungry spiders over the carpet. Finally, flesh touched metal, but too hard—the keys slid away from my hand, further under my feet. I cursed as the fear tightened in my chest.

My fingers firmly grasped the keys once more. My pulse still raced. Blood pounded in my temples, forced to my brain by my contorted position cramped under the steering wheel. It gradually eased when I sat upright. I took several deep breaths and cranked the car engine.

Get a grip on yourself, I admonished. But at that moment, I wanted nothing more than to get away from this place, far away.

Suppressing the urge to speed away—mostly afraid of drawing attention to screeching tires—I navigated my way out of the neighborhood to the front of the subdivision and to the main cross street, which I was relieved to recognize. I looked over my shoulder at the subdivision sign inviting those coming from the opposite direction into the neighborhood: *Windsor Forest.*

The homes appeared older, but the neighborhood was well maintained. The house was far enough away from the streetlight that I hadn't been able to see it clearly. In my haste to leave, I failed to make note of the street address, but I remembered the name of the street from the corner sign I had passed on my way out: *Maid Marian Lane.*

I stifled an incongruous urge to laugh. *Shouldn't Maid Marian Lane be in Sherwood Forest rather than Windsor Forest?* It took a few more turns before I found myself back on a main thoroughfare and headed in the right direction, for home. The experience spooked me.

As I neared home, I tried to rationalize a logical explanation for the episode. The practical me needed to compartmentalize this quickly.

Sure…I was distracted and tired, my mind on Beth. That let me drive aimlessly for a while. Stress could do that to a person. It may not be normal to zone out like that, but at least I kept the presence of mind to pull off onto a quiet street instead of going *zombie* in the middle of a busy intersection. And I managed to snap out of it…no harm done. There was no reason for me to make a connection between the house and the visions I associated with the old necktie I bought from that thrift shop. In fact, the nightmarish connection actually supported my rationalization that tonight was just a random episode of stress-induced sleep walking…er…driving.

# # #

"Detective Wassner? This is Judy Zenor calling. I'm sorry to bother you so late. I had no idea this was your cell phone number. I expected to leave a voice message. Anyway, you gave me your business card this afternoon when you stopped by my house and asked if I had seen anything out of the ordinary the night the Nelsons were attacked. Do you remember me?"

She paused long enough to hear his confirmation that indeed he remembered her. "My house is almost right across the street from theirs. I was out of town, and you asked if my partner would call you if she saw anything. Well, I asked and she didn't. But I thought you might like to know, I was on our deck a little while ago, and I saw a car parked on the curb by their house. No, I'm sorry. I couldn't see the tag number. Um, it was a dark color, and I think it was one of those hybrid cars, maybe a Prius. You know, Toyota. The motor was really quiet; I can tell you that much. Yes, if I see the car in the neighborhood again, you can be sure that I'll call right away."

To Wassner's expression of gratitude she responded, "Yes, sir. Glad to be able to help. I hope you catch the people who were responsible, and soon."

# # #

Of course, that made sense. There was no reason to believe anything other than stress and lack of sleep was to blame for this nonsense. Fatigue must be making me delirious. As structure and reason set my world upright again, fear gave way to a calm exhaustion by the time I pulled into my own familiar driveway.

Famished from skipping dinner, I thumbed a speed dial entry in my cell phone as I pulled into the garage. I thought I remembered the Thai place nearby ran deliveries until midnight. Yep, my order would be here in thirty minutes.

Safely within the walls of my own house, I powered up my laptop so I could get some work done after my shower. I took my time, letting the warm water relax my tense muscles, soothing my raw nerves.

As I had after tennis practice, I set aside brooding thoughts of strange visions and inexplicable detours. The phantoms faded away, replaced by the need to solve the problem I left behind at work earlier in the day. As I toweled dry and pulled on clean shorts and a shirt, my mind was already sorting through the clues I had uncovered in the customer's trace files that morning.

I walked barefoot back to my laptop and started poring over the detailed logs while comparing the trace output to the source code. By the time my dinner arrived, I thought I'd identified the section of code where the problem had occurred.

The host defined these fixed length messages. Each message contained a header and a message body. The host for this customer had apparently increased the size of its message header, which messed up the module that parsed the data. The code that formatted the message depending on host type must have incorrectly calculated the size of the data buffer for reading the host response. So, I needed to address the issue of reading fewer bytes than the host sent in reply.

If I didn't take pride in my work, I could have simply assigned values for the message length of a given host by switching into a case statement that set the length into a variable based on host type, but that would not be the most elegant solution. Besides, another programmer might one day see that I had cheated and taken a short cut to force the message length. We called such clumsy solutions kludges.

Why didn't I just associate the expected message length with a new tag I could read out of the host-specific configuration file? Full recompiles of the code wouldn't be necessary in the event of future changes if the message length were stored externally in a file and read in at runtime. But it took more work to make the message lengths configurable. The solution continued to develop in my mind as I considered what it would take to implement it.

While I ate, I ruminated about how to code the solution, and test the results. Confident I could recreate the problem and that the patch I devised and coded would solve it, I decided to reward myself with a stiff drink. I triggered the process that compiled all the source modules of our product and bundled it into a new install.

A cabinet hiding an eighteen-year-old bottle of scotch surrendered its cache without resistance. I poured a drink for myself with a heavy hand, over ice with a light splash of water. After a sip to sample the water to scotch ratio, I decided to let the ice melt a bit.

I had sweated profusely during tennis, robbing me of fluids that I hadn't replaced, so I opened and downed a bottled water while I waited for the compiler to finish. Then another sip of the smooth golden whiskey. *Perfect.*

I sat again at my laptop and unit tested my new build. Everything seemed in order, ready for integration and then regression testing. The burn of alcohol down my throat relaxed me as I celebrated a successful end to the evening. I finished my drink and generously poured another, more certain than ever I was home for the night.

Beth needs her rest, and I need to get too drunk to drive.

I thought about shutting down my computer for the night, the warmth of the whiskey smoothing my ruffled feathers, but on a whim, I decided to search for information that might explain the yellow tape fluttering at the house on Maid Marian Lane. I tried entering "crime scene" into the search engine, but the results were vague and unrelated.

I shortened the search criteria, just looking for "Maid Marian Lane," and I found a small item in the local paper. In it, the reporter described a brutal home invasion that left one person dead and a survivor clinging to life.

That sobered me up a bit.

CHAPTER 10

Around two a.m., I sent Richard an email explaining what had happened with Beth, about her being in the hospital and asking if he would have QA conduct a full regression test for me on the completed code fix. I explained that I planned to take some time off until things settled down a bit at home. I uploaded the new build into the test environment. Normally I performed a full complement of tests before turning over the code, but this way we could adhere to the schedule and get the code to the customer next week without requiring my physical presence in the office.

They could always reach me in an emergency. Besides, QA wasn't swamped with work so it was a win/win situation. It gave idle people something to do during a time of year when management reconsidered staffing levels and adjusted their budgets for mid-year. Having something productive to do always gives one a little extra job security. At least I was helping them look busy.

In my email, I offered to come in to the office once we knew Beth was improving. I told Richard that I planned to work the next night to make up for time lost at work during the day. He's never had a problem with me doing something like this before, and these were extenuating circumstances. I asked him to phone me if QA found something. I felt uncomfortable with the idea of being completely out of pocket during normal business hours.

I wished I had thought to send the email before I'd had anything to drink and hoped it read coherently. I had felt a little more lucid and alert before the second scotch. Finally, I shut down my laptop, packed it away, and wandered into our bedroom.

It felt empty and too quiet with Beth gone. Abby slept curled up at the foot of our bed. The memory of finding Beth's crumpled form on the bathroom floor just a few feet away came rushing back to me. I dealt with pangs of regret as I remembered how pale she had looked, how worthless I had felt to find her there, unconscious and alone. Her first husband would have been there for her. Was she thinking that, too? I was a selfish bastard, out hitting tennis balls while she was…

Stop it. You're just torturing yourself. She loves you. She told you to go to practice tonight. Insisted, even.

Needing something to distract me from pointless self-recrimination, I turned on the boob tube. Television offered nothing of real interest. I considered watching the news, but decided the reality of the news might further addle my state of mind. I'd successfully convinced myself that the events of the day—except for Beth's trip to the hospital—were the product of an overworked mind. I must have seen something in the paper that morning which triggered the bizarre waking nightmares and the erratic driving episode.

I flipped the channel to a science fiction program and left it there.

A few hours later, I awoke with the television on and a crick in my neck. At first, I thought the channel had stopped broadcasting and the sound coming from the set was white noise, but then voices registered in my ears, and I realized the hissing sound was Abby Normal. She was upset that we had an uninvited guest standing at the foot of my bed.

I started at the sight of a short, stooping old man who grinned mischievously at me. He held out his right hand. It clutched a playing card. His closely cropped white hair was wet and beads of water hung in his short beard, as if he'd been sweating profusely or been caught in a torrential rainstorm. Water dripped from the card. He turned over his dark-skinned hand, palm up, to show me the card. It was a Joker, but the harlequin was a sinister-looking skeleton. Alarmed, I bolted upright in bed and threw off the covers. For whatever reason, I didn't feel threatened by the stranger. Perhaps it was his age, his smile, or a combination of both. I jumped out of bed and demanded, "Who the hell are you? What are you doing in my house?"

Without a word, he shrugged, turned, and fled down the hall. Or maybe I should say he *flew* down the hall. Literally, he moved so fast it shocked me. He took two steps and was gone, off to the races. An old guy like that shouldn't be quite so agile. He hadn't seemed threatening and didn't appear to be a burglar, just some old kook who had wandered into my house in the middle of the night. Except that it seemed he awakened me deliberately. A faint sense of foreboding told me to slow down. The old man who didn't act as old as he looked could be leading me right into a trap.

The cold ceramic tile on my kitchen floor reminded me that I was barefoot, increasing my doubts about the wisdom of what I was doing. I should be calling the police instead of following him around. The old man didn't feel threatening, but still...I sensed danger as I crept stealthily toward the last place I had seen him before he vanished around a corner.

Then things really got weird.

An old, gray woman with sunken eyes but no mouth materialized from the darkness of my living room and grabbed at my arms. Just below her nose, her face seemed to dissolve into an amorphous mist. Both fascinated and horrified, I recoiled from the grotesque apparition as it neared, forgetting all about the old man I'd been chasing. She reached toward me, but I realized that she wasn't really...*there*. Her hands made motions in thin air, a series of strange hand signals.

She looked very sad, but in a scary sort of way. Her eyes looked off in the darkened gloom, apparently oblivious to my presence. My eyes followed hers, just in time to see a vague shape wielding what looked like a pickaxe as it swung through the air, hacking down on a human form writhing on the floor in agony. My eyes adjusted to the light and saw blood as it spurted and sprayed all over my living room walls. Crimson pools spread from underneath the body that no longer moved.

What the hell! Who are these people and what in the world are they doing in my living room? If the old woman isn't real, what about the guy with the pickaxe?

I found myself staring again at the old woman again. Her mouth wasn't missing. It was covered, wrapped in cloth like a mummy. Suddenly she didn't look so scary, more like the old guy who started this nightmare. In her hands, she now held a notepad and pen, and she gestured to get my attention. I watched as her withered hand scrawled in a laborious effort to communicate with me. Finally, she turned the pad to show me what she had written.

SNAKE SK

She stopped to rest, and leaned backward. She had been reaching toward me earlier, but now she lay in a hospital bed like a frail bird.

*Wait a damned minute. How did I get into **her** room? Where am I?*

I was sure I had been asleep in my bed, inside my own home, when the nightmare started. I could tell that this old woman with the bandaged face wasn't afraid of me. For some strange reason, I sensed that she looked to me for help. The grinning little leprechaun of a man who had awakened me reappeared suddenly. He cleared his throat, distracting me from what I had wanted to do. I wanted to ask the old woman what the words on the notepad meant. I wanted to ask her where the man with the pickaxe had gone, and what had happened to his victim on the floor.

Shouldn't we be calling the police?

Both killer and victim had vanished without a trace.

This has gotten way too weird.

I clearly remembered waking up from a deep sleep, but the surreal events since being roused from sleep made me wonder if someone had drugged me. My diminutive, uninvited guest impishly waved to catch my attention, then darted out the front door, with me in hot pursuit.

This can't be happening. It feels wrong. I must not be in my own house anymore. These people are complete strangers. I'm going to end up being the one who gets into trouble.

My pursuit of the old man certainly seemed real enough. The tile floor had felt ice cold. Now I could feel the grainy looseness of sand between my bare toes.

Wait a minute…sand?

By reflex, I looked down at my feet.

Where did this sand come from? There's not any sand anywhere close to my house.

As that thought registered, a pale white hand reached up from beneath the surface of the sand. With serpentine swiftness, the fingers curled an incredibly powerful grip around my ankle and started to pull me under. With a panicked yelp, I struggled to break free. The sand sucked at my legs like quicksand. The fingers of the cold hand still held my ankle with a vise-like grip. With an effort borne of sheer panic, I fell on my butt and began kicking and flailing with my other foot until the ghostly hand released me.

My eyes blinked in amazement. I saw the arm flopping around on top of the sand like a fish out of water. There was no body attached. The severed appendage wriggled like a snake and burrowed itself in the sand once more, lying in wait for its next victim.

Did my Thai dinner come laced with LSD or something? What in the hell was going on here? How did I get here?

I felt hopelessly lost and disoriented. Desperately, I wanted to snap out of this dream. I wanted my life to go back to normal. I wanted to be back in the comfort of my own home, in the safety of my own bed, not wandering around in the middle of the night, running after a nut job who apparently wanted me to chase him. I wanted to click the heels on Dorothy's red slippers three times and wake up in my own bed. This wasn't or Kansas *or* Oz. It was a hellish nightmare.

And then just as quickly as it started, it was over. I was back home, safely in my own bed. I blinked, and there I was in my own bedroom. I looked down, and to my great surprise, *I saw myself* lying in bed. In fact, I was still asleep. My dream self reentered my prostrate body. I awoke from the nightmare and sat up in bed, the clear memory of my impish visitor's face still etched into my mind. Strangely, I still remembered every last detail from my nightmare.

Of course, he hadn't been real. None of it had been real. But it had all been so vivid, so bizarre, that I couldn't help remembering his smiling face, withered and dark like a raisin from the sun. I brooded about the old woman and the severed arm long after my nightmare had finally ended.

I was fully awake and I was exhausted. I felt like I needed another shower, but I hesitated. It would have been my third shower of the day. My t-shirt was soaked with sweat, so I changed shirts yet again before getting back in bed.

I hadn't had nightmares that intense in years. And it was just a nightmare...but why had that stranger's face looked hauntingly familiar? I wondered how my hallucinations, the strange events of earlier in the day, and now this nightmare were related. *Damn that thrift store tie.*

Damn that spicy Thai dinner. I'd had enough culinary adventures for a while. Rich or spicy food seems to have a weird effect on me occasionally. Tonight was apparently one of those nights, especially after my strange experience of snapping out of a stupor, parked on Maid Marian Lane.

Was it the scotch that fueled my dreams tonight? How many drinks did I end up having before bed? I wasn't ready to say, damn the scotch.

Except the episode at Maid Marian Lane came before the Thai food. Or the scotch.

If these had been bad dreams about something happening to Beth, me, or the baby, it might make some level of sense. Bizarre nightmares of ghoulish acts involving total strangers seemed an annoying intrusion into my well-deserved and badly needed sleep.

The more I thought about it, the more it bothered me that the perspective in the visions came through my own eyes as the work of a vicious killer. I felt sickened by what my hands were doing, but also strangely detached. A killer would have to be emotionless to kill that methodically, that brutally.

Could I really be a murderer?

How would that be possible? Was my subconscious mind searching for a scapegoat onto which I could transfer all these violent fixations, or was my mind suppressing a dark and secret desire from my own psyche? Was I trying to hide something from myself? Since that brawl in the frat house years ago, I hadn't lost control of my temper so completely, not even once. At least, not that I remembered...

Another pang of doubt ripped through my gut, followed by a paralyzing question: Could a brain tumor trigger psychotic episodes allowing me to lead a double life?

Am I responsible for these attacks?

Now fully awake, I threw off the bed covers to cool off. I turned on the lamp on the bedside table and stared at the ceiling, thinking about my strange, violent nightmare. It would have been hard for me to go back to sleep after that ordeal anyway.

I was afraid that the specters haunting my dreams would return if I tried to go back to sleep. Shaken, I reached into the past for some vague memory of protection and comfort.

My religious faith had always been sort of ambiguous. I wanted to believe in God, but had difficulty reconciling religious faith with science. The problem stemmed from the fact that I accepted the Big Bang theory and that the Earth was billions of years old, but that didn't seem to agree with the biblical account of creation. In my neatly ordered world, things had to make sense.

During my childhood in the Bible Belt, I regularly attended Sunday school. It was the social norm and I never thought about it as being optional. The Church taught that the Earth was only a few thousand years old and that God had created everything. That was all well and good until Charles Darwin's theory challenged that in biology class in high school and then again in college. His theory made sense to me, especially after we studied the geological record and fossils.

On the other hand, I struggled with the idea of man descending from ape-like ancestors without at least the guiding influence of some sort of superior intellect, like maybe an alien intelligence. All the intricate puzzle pieces that comprised life on Earth seemed too complex to have randomly fit into place without a cosmic designer of some sort. But to really believe that also required belief in the supernatural.

There was the rub. I'd outgrown myths and fairy tales.

As kids, we found it easy to mix imagination with reality. Well-intentioned Christian parents pretended to be Santa Claus and the Easter Bunny, inadvertently associating religion with invisible, imaginary characters. It's no wonder the number of atheists and agnostics grew each year. I became one while in college.

Nobody knew how I really felt about God or that I didn't really believe, not even Beth. We got married in a church. I knew she still believed in an invisible man in the sky, but not me.

We lived in the Bible Belt, but it wasn't like everybody went to church every Sunday anymore. Times had changed since we were kids, but I wouldn't dream of suggesting we stop going as a couple. Beth didn't object too strenuously when I sometimes made excuses not to go with her. I also had to admit that I'd made a few business contacts through church.

But let's face facts. It's easier to get a tee time on Sunday morning than it is on Sunday afternoon.

The Bible says somewhere that the father heads the household and holds responsibility for the family's faith. Beth expected me to fulfill that role, so I went through the motions. In truth, I enjoyed my conversations with Pastor Tom and had yet to doze off in one of his sermons. It seemed harmless enough to keep going.

I loved Beth and would never hurt her. I remember the one occasion I nearly summoned the courage to reveal my agnosticism to her. When I began the conversation and dropped a couple of hints in the direction it was leading, a troubled expression crept over her face. I realized that the fate of our relationship could depend on what I said next. If I professed not to believe in God, it might irrevocably damage our marriage. My inner voice warned me that she would interpret that to mean I thought her first husband had died in vain. That his ultimate sacrifice only cut short a vibrant life too young, and nothing remained for his rotting corpse but to be eaten by worms, his life extinguished like flipping a light switch.

So I lied.

Something gnawed at me for the lie to my wife about something so important to her. Was it my guilty conscience or a black mark on my soul? I hadn't believed in a soul for a while now.

But I still knew right from wrong. I did not believe I could be a killer.

PART TWO
MAUNDY THURSDAY

CHAPTER 11

Clayton and Candy reached the hotel, checked in, had sex, then Clayton dropped a wad of cash on the bed and told Candy it was hers to spend. He strutted out of the room and headed to the casino, confident this would be his night. For the length of time it took Candy to shower and dress, he had a brief run of luck. He ordered a Jack and Coke to celebrate, up maybe two grand when she walked up to the table. She stood there for a moment, and then retreated to a safe spot where she could watch him in action.

He didn't even know that Candy was standing there. She watched him play, flirting with a woman standing next to him. She didn't care; she had no real feelings for Clayton, unless contempt counted for anything. He was a man who needed to have an attentive woman doting on him; she was willing to play the part, up to a point.

Sex was part of his benefits package, but the affection she pretended to have for him was an act.

Tonight, underneath that clean-cut look, she sensed a hidden danger. She saw something different in him tonight than she'd ever seen before. Clayton's new persona scared Candy, just a little bit. Something cold lurked behind his eyes.

He was a chameleon, Candy realized. Clayton blended into the woodwork in whatever environment he found himself, fooling others into thinking he was something he wasn't. He wore long sleeves in the casino, she guessed to hide the tattoo on his arm. The personality cloak Clayton wore tonight was some sort of a hotshot doctor. Candy decided that the woman standing next to him looked like a working girl. Apparently, the hotel security hadn't been tipped to her presence there.

Having been rousted a time or two for soliciting herself, it occurred to Candy that security might think she was there working, too, if she was hanging out there by herself, not gambling away any money. She moved further away from the poker table, jockeying for a spot at the nearest slot machine. From there she could more or less see what Clayton was doing, but he wouldn't see her immediately if he happened to turn and look in her direction. She fed the machine, pulled the lever, but didn't even watch the wheels spin. She knew it was a sucker's game, but she kept playing periodically, just enough to justify keeping the spot. When a waitress passed, she ordered a glass of wine, having decided to make herself comfortable. She staked out her turf with a little more authority by ordering the drink. If Clayton noticed her now, she could claim she didn't even realize he was there. He told her to have fun, right?

Candy didn't worry about casino security hassling her at this point; her secret weapon was the room key. She had every right to be there, but she suspected the hooker trying to work on Clayton did not. She wondered if Clayton would find somewhere to sneak off and have sex with the whore, thinking about whether or not she had the right to get indignant about it if he did. The only thing that concerned her was whether Clayton had a condom with him because she worried about sexually transmitted diseases coming from another working girl.

It turned out she had nothing to worry about, though. As the size of the stack of chips in front of Clayton reversed course and began to shrink, the prostitute looked like she was ready to move on to greener pastures. He kept drinking. He lost even faster.

The waitress arrived with her glass of wine. By the time Candy turned her attention back to Clayton, a scene was in the making. Hotel security had arrived at the table; a couple of burly men wearing matching blazers bracketed Clayton on either side. They weren't there to hassle the hooker. Candy thought she overheard Clayton slur either the word "thief" or "cheat," neither being good words to use in a gambling establishment. *Uh oh.*

If he got thrown out of the hotel, she would be going with him. Candy pulled the room key out of her purse, grabbed her glass of wine, and hurried over to Clayton's side. Holding her purse in one hand, she displayed the plastic key card in her fingers clutching her wine glass as she took a sip so the security people could see they were hotel guests. "Sweetie, I'm sorry I took so long and kept you waiting. We're going to be late for our reservations at Jia."

"Huh?" Clayton asked drunkenly.

"Our dinner reservations, remember? We're going to be late. Come on, collect your chips and let's go," Candy bluffed. The blazers each took a step away, letting Candy pass between them to reach Clayton's side. As long as the drunk wasn't making a scene or accusing the dealer of cheating him, they could let it slide. But the eye-in-the-sky would be watching him from now on. High-class places like the casino couldn't tolerate frivolous accusations about their integrity.

Clayton stared at Candy for a long minute as his eyes cleared a little. He seemed to realize what had happened. "Okay. I need to eat something. I'm going to run up to the room for a minute before we eat. Are you coming with me?"

Candy thought, *what the hell.* "Sure."

As soon as the door closed behind them, Candy regretted her decision. Clayton slapped her hard across the face, knocking her to the floor. He didn't seem the least bit drunk. He pounced on her before she had a chance to get to her feet, straddling her body and pinning her down as she lay on the floor, each heavy knee crushing down on her arms with searing pain.

The wiry son-of-a-bitch felt like he weighed a ton with all of his weight shifted onto those two pressure points. "Don't you ever, *ever*, embarrass me in public like that again, do you hear me?" he screamed, spittle flying into her face as he raged.

"I'm sorry," Candy whimpered, struggling for relief from the excruciating pain of Clayton's weight. Her arms felt like they were nailed to the floor. She writhed helplessly as his fingers slowly wrapped around her throat. She was sure he would choke her.

"I could snap your neck like a twig right now if I wanted," Clayton said. "You know that, don't you?"

She nodded vigorously, terrified out of her wits.

Clayton sneered at her before taking a deep breath, which seemed to calm him down a little. He slipped his knees from her arms onto the floor next to them, not letting her up. Instead, he unzipped his pants.

"While you're down there, make yourself useful," he ordered.

CHAPTER 12

I finally managed to get in a couple of hours of recuperative sleep before dawn after tossing and turning for a couple more. I was surprised how much comfort I took in the early rays of light illuminating the vague but familiar shapes in my bedroom after the black and disturbing night.

A long, hot shower helped clear my groggy head. Today would be a better day, I assured myself as I shaved. While splashing cold water on my face, I chided myself for letting my imagination run wild the day before.

Witches, goblins, ghosts, Santa Claus and the Easter Bunny simply did not exist. Disembodied limbs did not attack casual passersby. *I'm just overly worried about Beth*, I told myself. *My mind is inventing some wacky shit for a distraction*. The necktie might have been coated with some strange hallucinogen. Mildew and mold can be nasty stuff.

It had worn off now, so today I'd be fine. All I needed to worry about was making sure to never touch that damned tie again. The dreams were just bad dreams, nothing more. The house with the yellow crime scene tape in Windsor Forest—well, that was pretty weird. It had to be a coincidence.

But I didn't really believe in coincidences.

I remembered finding the short article last night when I searched online for any news about Maid Marian Lane. It had to be the same street where I found myself parked after blacking out the night before...while I drove home.

Blacking out was one thing. Zoning out behind the wheel of my car while it was moving added an element of danger to the equation. I worried about the potential for having a serious or even fatal accident if it happened again.

Enough with the psychoanalysis and melodrama. It was one bad day, that's all. You aren't dying or losing your mind. Shake it off.

# # #

Knowing that I ought to leave this business alone, I fought against a compulsion to find answers to questions that I didn't understand or know how to ask, or where I should direct them. As if I were tracing a bug through a software program, the engineer in me just couldn't let go of this until I had found the root cause.

The Humane Society thrift store was not my only connection with whatever ignited the fuse that turned my sanity into dry kindling yesterday. There was also the house on Maid Marian Lane.

What if I had imagined the whole thing? The weird dream-within-a-dream sensation came back to me. Could all the strangeness of yesterday have been confined to my dreams last night? The paperwork from Beth's admission to the hospital last night lay on the chest of drawers. I hadn't dreamed all of it.

Beth. What will she think about my crazy dreams?

I decided then that I'd keep my temporary insanity to myself. The last thing Beth needed right now was to find out that her husband was chasing after ghosts and lurking around crime scenes. No, I would not be sharing any of this with my wife. But I needed to see her, needed that calming effect of meeting her gaze. The love and trust I always saw in her eyes would ground me again I was sure.

But rather than heading north up Alpharetta Highway to visit my wife in the hospital, I turned south and returned to the mysterious house where I found myself after blacking out last night. Against my better judgment, I was back there instead of going to Beth. I needed to understand what had happened, how, and why.

In bright daylight, the Windsor Forest subdivision proved more comical than scary. My bearings were a little off, so I turned the wrong direction coming off Houze Way. The developer must have been either bored or severely hung over when he named the roads, I decided. At least half the street names brought golf courses to mind. I made my way along Bent Grass Drive and crossed Putting Green Lane, passing Chipping Court and Par Circle. The only problem with his theme was that the neighborhood had no golf course.

The homes were older, most with dated exteriors, but appeared well built. Homeowners seemed to be slowly updating the look of their homes as some of the houses changed hands. New homeowners moved in and upgraded, replacing windows and garage doors with stylish new designs, replacing roofs with architectural shingles, and making other cosmetic upgrades to the exterior and landscaping. The desire to renovate was proving to be contagious as neighbors recognized the spruced up house next door now made their own look shabby.

When the developer apparently changed his mind and decided to nix the golf course, his street naming convention changed dramatically. As I worked my way along Windsor Trail toward Maid Marian Lane, I saw Robin Court and Friar Tuck Way. I turned onto Falstaff Drive, and there was the cul-de-sac. I recognized the house from last night.

I parked at the curb and left the engine running. For several long moments, I stared in disbelief at the yellow tape. It was real, all right. It seemed that I hadn't been there but a few seconds when a marked Roswell patrol car suddenly whipped in front of my car, blocking my way. A natural instinct to run flitted through my mind, but I quickly dismissed the notion. It had been my experience that the best way to avoid trouble with the police was to avoid them altogether, but it was too late for that. I hadn't done anything wrong. Attempting to run away now would be interpreted as an admission of guilt. Of what, I had no idea. So, I got my driver's license and proof of insurance out of my wallet and waited as the officer approached.

"License and registration, please," the police officer said, ignoring the fact I was offering them to him. I kept my hand extended until he finally took them. He took his sweet time in doing so. His eyes, hidden behind dark sunglasses, told me nothing.

"Is there a problem? Have I done something wrong?" I asked.

He ignored my question, glanced at my license and insurance card, and curtly said, "Wait here, please." But it obviously wasn't a request.

He stalked back to his patrol car, presumably to call his dispatcher and see if there were any outstanding warrants for me or if the vehicle was stolen. After what seemed an eternity, he rapped on my car window. When I rolled the window down he asked, "Is this still your current address, Mr. Harper?"

"Yes, sir," I answered respectfully, intent on not giving him any cause to take offense.

Finally, he asked me what he really wanted to know. "Mr. Harper, you're parked near the scene of a recent crime. Only last night, a witness reported a car matching this description involved in suspicious activity in this same spot. That makes me think you might've been here more than once in the last twenty-four hours. So, I'm gonna ask you nicely, but I want you to think about the answer carefully because you don't want to lie to me. Exactly what *are* you doing here?"

Shit! I was totally unprepared to answer a rather obvious question. Why *was* I there? I wished I knew. I needed to come up with something that sounded convincing, and fast…he'd never believe the truth.

I should have kept thinking just a little bit longer before opening my mouth. "I'm not actually parked. The engine's still running; you just can't hear it. It's a hybrid."

"Are you getting smart with me?" The officer's tone warned that he was losing patience with me quickly. He took a deep breath and said, "Mr. Harper, you're parked in front of a house where very serious crime occurred only a few days ago, and I'm asking for your cooperation. The perpetrator hasn't been apprehended. What's your business here? You can decline to answer, or you can ask for a lawyer. But all of that'll happen at the station, not in a pleasant exchange here on the street. Would you like try again?"

My flippant answer bought me a few seconds, but I failed to use them wisely. I tried, "Um…I play tennis in ALTA. We've got an away match somewhere near this neighborhood on Saturday. I was just trying to make sure I know how to find the courts. My wife's in the hospital, and I might be cutting it close Saturday morning. There's a default rule if you're more than fifteen minutes late. The whole team has to forfeit if I don't make it on time."

That's the best I could do?

The cop seemed to read my mind. "Mr. Harper, that sounds an awful lot like bullshit to me. Today's only Thursday. If your wife is in the hospital, it seems like you'd worry more about her than a tennis match. I'm trying to think of the nearest subdivision with tennis courts. What was the name of the subdivision where you're gonna play?"

The best defense is a good offense, right? Since I couldn't think of a subdivision name quickly enough, I went on the offensive. "Officer, I'm really sorry, but my wife is expecting me at the hospital. Have I done something wrong? Is it a crime to park your car on the street for a minute or two while you try to get your bearings, figure out where you are? I didn't even get out of my car. I'm not trespassing on private property. Streets have a public right of way, don't they?"

"Okay, what's your wife's name? What hospital?"

I told him. "Wait here," he ordered, all business. He walked out of earshot and called out on his radio, waiting another eternity before he rejoined me.

"Okay, that checks out."

"Can I go now?"

"Mr. Harper, I still want to know why you're parked here, hanging around this crime scene. We've had a little problem with people who follow the news looking to prey on people who already are victims. We've had houses and vehicles burglarized while the family was at the cemetery. Did you know the family in this house? Do you have any business being here? You never answered my question. Have you ever been here before?"

I still didn't answer. "I had no idea this was someplace special," I lied. "I didn't even notice the yellow tape over there until you mentioned it. What happened? Did someone die?"

"None of your business. You don't want to get involved in this if you aren't already. I certainly wouldn't want to catch you interfering with a police investigation." Suddenly he changed gears, catching me off-guard again. "Where did you say your tennis match was on Saturday?"

Blindsided by the question, I said the name of the team we were playing this weekend, even though it was a home match on the schedule: River Ridge.

"Try again. That subdivision is nowhere near here. It's more than five miles away, at least."

The best defense is a good offense, I reminded myself once more.

"Why are you harassing me? I got lost looking for some tennis courts. I only stopped here to get my bearings. I hadn't even been here a minute, and I was about to leave. You may have woken up on the wrong side of the bed, but I've done nothing wrong. I'm sorry. I parked in front of the wrong house. I got lost."

He ignored me and asked, "Where do you work, Mr. Harper?"

I told him but added a question of my own. "What's that got to do with anything?"

"What's the address and phone number there?"

My wallet was still in my hand. I fished out a business card and gave it to him. "Satisfied?" I was annoyed and not bothering to hide it now. "Listen, if I'm not under arrest, I need to be going."

"To see your wife in the hospital, right? You're telling me that your wife's in the hospital while you're driving around looking for some tennis courts for a match that you aren't playing for another two days? And I'm supposed to believe that?" he asked sarcastically.

"Believe whatever you want. Unless I'm under arrest, I'd like my license and insurance card back so I can get out of here. Otherwise, I'll need to call my attorney."

"You can wait to call your attorney when you really need one. I'm letting you go. We've got your name and address on record." He offered back my identification cards, but when I reached for them, he twisted his fingers, pulling them away again while he warned, "One more thing, Mr. Harper…you get 'lost' in this subdivision again, I predict you'll get lost in the shuffle somewhere in between the Fulton County jail and Roswell city lockup. You might go missing for a couple of weeks before you find your way to a phone where you can make that call. Do you understand what I'm telling you?"

He handed over my cards. When I firmly grasped my identification once more, I said, "Yes sir. I received your warning, loud and clear."

"It wasn't a warning. That was a promise."

CHAPTER 13

On my way to the hospital, I berated myself for taking that unnecessary detour directly into trouble. What had possessed me to retrace my steps from last night? I was certain that I'd never seen the house before, never even been in this neighborhood. Yet last night I had ventured quite a bit out of my way to get there and, most troubling, had no memory of the drive.

The crime scene was real. I hadn't imagined it or the cop who just harassed me. Of course, that didn't mean there was any sort of connection between it and my nightmares. The last thing I needed to do was get into trouble with the law, with my pregnant wife hospitalized.

I don't need to get involved. I didn't know anything about what happened in that house or why. I took small comfort in the thought that my car was still headed in the right direction, back to Beth.

Enough of this nonsense.

After finding a parking place and stopping by the gift shop for a couple of magazines in case Beth ever stopped knitting for the baby, I went in to see my wife. The color had returned to her face a good bit. I was surprised to see she was awake when I tiptoed into her hospital room, trying not to disturb her in case she'd been resting. A breakfast tray sat in front of her, the remnants of grits and a piece of toast left on her plate. It looked like she'd eaten some fruit as well. I was elated. She didn't look the least bit concerned about an upset stomach after her limited meal.

I kissed her good morning and complimented her on her improved color as the machines surrounding her hummed and buzzed, masking a few of my words until I matched their pattern.

"Good morning, sweetheart. How did you sleep last night?"

"Like a baby," I lied. I was getting more adept with practice. "How about you? You look so much better than you did last night. Have you seen the doctor yet?"

"Not yet. Dan…" she hesitated. "I'm sorry I let things get so bad. I was stubborn. Let me say it before you do. You told me so." Her chin quivered. "I didn't mean to put the baby in danger. I honestly didn't know how serious it was. I'm sorry..." Her voice trailed off and she looked at me, her eyes full of apology.

I breathed a heavy sigh. She had been expecting the lecture I was about to give her, the one about not taking care of herself and not listening to me. I didn't have the heart to scold her, to make her feel even worse than she did already.

129

"Beth, when I saw you lying there, it almost killed me. If you hadn't been all right, I would have never been able to forgive myself." She flinched, and I softened, "But what matters is that you're going to be okay now. I love you, even if you are the most stubborn woman in all of Georgia."

She smiled and reached her arms out to me. I pulled her head to my chest and stroked her hair. She fit snugly against my shoulder, as if that was where she was always meant to be. I asked gently, "So tell me the truth now. How are you? Really?"

"I'm feeling better. Actually, even though I ate most of my breakfast, I'm still hungry. I was kind of hoping you'd get some fruit in the cafeteria. You know…something the doctor can't find objectionable. Could I please have some peaches or grapes if they have some that look good? I hate asking you to run an errand for me when you just got here, but they won't let me leave the room yet."

"I would love to get you something else to eat. Just make sure you don't overdo it, okay? Take your time. Eat a little, wait a little while, then have some more. But honey, if you want something, all you have to do is say the word. If the cafeteria doesn't have it, I'll run over to Harry's Farmers Market. They always have some good fruit no matter what time of year it is because they import from all over the world."

Beth laughed. "What, are you going to film a commercial for them, or something? You sound like Harry. I'm sure the cafeteria will have something I like. You just got here. I don't want you running off again so soon, okay?"

"Okay. It's great that your appetite is coming back. You're right; I can probably get you something here that's perfectly good. I certainly don't want to get you anything exotic that might upset your stomach again. How about strawberries?"

"That might be okay. Or maybe some peaches would be good, something like that. Please, no papaya, though. Remember, I'm allergic." As she spoke, I felt her eyes inspecting me. As she saw something that didn't meet with her approval, her sparkling blue eyes clouded with concern. She frowned and said, "Why won't you tell me the truth? You look tired. There are dark circles under your eyes. I might be sick, but I'm not blind."

"You're right. I did not sleep very well," I confessed. "I really missed you. I tossed and turned all night long." It surprised me that she kept after me about my apparently haggard appearance. *I must really look like shit*, I thought.

I chose not to alarm her by adding that I might also be losing my mind.

No way do I tell her about the blackout or the hallucinations. Recounting nighttime chases, ghostly visitors in our own bedroom, severed limbs, and nightmares that included copious amounts of blood to someone hospitalized for problems with nausea seemed like a really bad idea.

"My brilliant husband, did you get your new problem at work solved? I don't want you to get in trouble with your boss on my account. I'm perfectly fine here in the hospital," Beth said, her voice upbeat. But she wasn't smiling. She was unhappy with me. She knew I was holding out on her. She was always able to see right through me. What could I possibly tell her—the truth? Part of me wanted to tell her everything and ask for advice from my partner and best friend.

No, that is just selfish. Now is not the time.

"No, it's fine. There's no way they're going to get mad at me for extenuating circumstances like these. Besides, I'm pretty sure I've already delivered the fix for it. Instead of the usual routine, QA will do the full unit testing along with their normal integration and regression testing. It's not that much extra work for them, and it's not like they're busting it to get a new release out. Tiff promised she could pick up the slack while I am out. I asked Richard to shepherd it through the QA process for me and just keep me posted if something comes up that needs my attention. Otherwise, I wanted some time off to be here for you. Work is important, but nothing is more important to me than you."

It was a sappy thing to say, but it brought a big smile to Beth's face. She still looked exhausted, so tired it appeared she might doze off at any moment. I could tell she was really glad to have me there. Maybe I could pull up a chair and nap beside her after I got back with her fruit. I squeezed her hand as I thought about how close I'd come to losing both her and the baby. Way too close for comfort.

Is it too risky for her to continue carrying our child? Should we have the pregnancy terminated? I didn't dare voice those questions aloud. Beth would never put her own life above the baby. But how could I raise a child alone, if the unthinkable were to happen to her?

I thought about asking the doctor, but if Beth ever found out, there would be hell to pay. Soon her eyes closed. I thought she might be asleep, but they popped back open every time my grip relaxed on her hand.

I started when the doctor tapped on the door. He went to the sink and scrubbed his hands, glancing at her chart before putting on a fresh pair of latex gloves. "You aren't allergic to latex, correct?" he asked Beth to confirm.

"No. How long will I need to stay here?" Beth asked him.

"Why are we meeting here instead of my office?" Dr. Grover clucked disapprovingly. "You should've called to let us know the severity of your nausea. I remember that you have an aversion to taking unnecessary medication, but I assure you that I would prescribe nothing that would put your baby at risk. I think you realize what a close call you had. I think you'll need to stay here through the weekend. I want to make absolutely sure your condition has stabilized before sending you home."

"But it's Easter this weekend," Beth protested with a frown. "I'll miss church."

"I'm sure God will forgive you," the doctor said with something approaching a smirk. "I'm sure Jesus loves the little children enough to want them to be born."

Uh oh.

"I don't think that's very funny," Beth stiffened.

I'd better change the subject before this gets any worse.

"Before you got here, Beth told me that she was feeling better and still hungry after breakfast. I

133

thought as long as she didn't overdo it, you might say she could have more to eat. Hopefully, she's going to start making up for lost time and gain back some weight. She said she wanted some peaches. Is it okay for me to go get her some more fruit?"

Silently his eyes thanked me. Dr. Grover said, "No acidic fruits and no sweets until she's gone at least twenty-four hours without becoming nauseous. Nothing that might make her queasy, but the idea is to get as much weight back on her as we can, as soon as possible. Don't let her eat herself sick now that she feels like eating again. Bland foods—have at it—but don't overdo it."

"Good deal. Beth, I'm going to check in the cafeteria. If they don't have something that looks good, I promise I won't run off to Harry's without letting you know. How about some cheese and peanut butter crackers? Those are always safe."

"Crackers are okay, and cheese," Dr. Grover agreed. "Remember, everything in moderation, especially until we see how your stomach tolerates the food over a longer period of time. Your digestive tract is still working on breakfast. You probably shouldn't eat anything else for at least another half hour. More frequent, smaller meals are actually better for the digestion. We don't want to undo the good we've done so far and extend your stay here."

"You've got that right," she laughed. "I'm ready to get out of here. Dan, please can you run get me something more to eat?"

I smiled patiently. "Yes, my dear," I bowed with a flourish as I left to hunt and gather for my expectant wife.

CHAPTER 14

I *know* I punched the elevator button for the main lobby of the hospital. No other buttons were lit. But for some reason, I got off on the wrong floor when the elevator door opened. If someone had called the elevator, they must have caught another before mine stopped on that floor.

Lost in my thoughts about Beth, I paid no attention to where I was going, heading in the direction I knew the cafeteria should be. I failed to notice immediately that I was not walking through the lobby that should have been between the cafeteria and me.

I felt a vibration in my pocket. In retrospect, I'm now surer of it than ever.

Thinking it was my cell phone, I reached to retrieve it. I stopped in my tracks while I fished around in my pocket for my phone. To my surprise, when I looked at the display the phone was turned off. Suddenly aware that I wasn't headed in the right direction, dread ran up my spine. That was becoming a familiar sensation, unfortunately.

Sensing movement at the door of the nearest hospital room, I noticed it was slightly ajar. The next thing I knew, my hand was on the doorknob. I found myself about to walk into a total stranger's room.

From inside, I heard a voice whisper, "Wait until he comes inside," but the guy closest to me decided not to wait. A linebacker-sized policeman in uniform threw open the door, latched a steel grip onto my arm and whipped me around. He slammed me to the door, flattening me against the wood with one giant hand while roughly frisking me with the other.

A second cop in a rumpled business suit followed in his wake. He took control of the situation and said, "Check him for weapons and let's get him out of the doorway. We don't need to cause a commotion here in the hospital. Cuff him in case he tries something stupid. I think we can handle him between the two of us, don't you? Actually, three of us counting Lampe. She's probably a lot tougher than she looks. "

I found myself cuffed as ordered, with rough hands rudely probing every square inch of my body.

"He's clean, Detective Wassner," the ape in the uniform said.

"What in the hell do you think you're doing?" I protested when I managed to find my voice again.

"Shut up," growled the uniformed cop rough handling me. He deftly fished my wallet from my pocket with one hand while the other kept me pinned against the door. He tossed it to Wassner. I heard murmurs between two of the nurses watching from their station, but they had no interest intervening in my behalf.

"Bring him inside where we can speak a little more privately," Wassner said.

"What's this all about," I croaked, more alarmed by the minute. "Why does walking around a hospital land me in trouble?"

I heard the handcuffs click around my wrists behind my back. This was no joke. Why was I a magnet for trouble all of a sudden?

Wassner smiled mirthlessly and said, "You aren't in trouble for being in the hospital, but for where you were headed once you got here. Why were you loitering around outside this room, Mr. Harper? What's your business here?"

I didn't speak. He threw a sharp glance at the block of granite wearing blue and said, "Ease up. Not so rough. We don't want to leave any bruises on him, especially if he tells us a good story in a minute. He's not going anywhere. Let's let him talk. See what kind of story he's got for us. If he even blinks twice at our witness here, take him down, and don't be gentle. If he's our guy, he's used to rough stuff."

Confused, I looked from one cop to the other. Wassner, the detective holding my wallet, was about my height, around six feet tall. He outweighed me by at least twenty pounds. But he was thick and muscled, not fat, with a long, broad nose and sharp, quick eyes under mousy brown hair. Streaks of grey blended in at the sideburns, giving him a distinguished look. Or that's how I imagine he would look if his eyes were not shooting bullets into me.

I started getting mad, trying to work myself into a righteous indignation. "My lawyer might consider this false arrest," I bluffed. "I was on my way to the cafeteria to get my wife something to eat. She's pregnant. Her room is on the third floor. Apparently, I got lost. I must have gotten off the elevator at the wrong floor. You guys pop out of nowhere, throw me up against the door, and cuff me like a criminal. You've got the wrong guy. This is a big mistake."

A very attractive woman moved to stand between the foot of the bed and me. "What's his story?" she directed to Wassner, a quick tilt of her chin aimed at me.

He shrugged and said, "Ask him. Spivey grabbed him as soon as he touched the doorknob. He's saying that his wife is here in the hospital, and he was coming in this room by accident. Isn't that right?" he looked at me.

I might be happily married, but I am human. And sometimes charming. I smiled at the woman and said, "Yes, that's right. My name is Dan Harper. My wife Beth is in Room 302. She's here for complications from her pregnancy. I'm sorry I bothered you…"

I finally looked past her, at the patient lying in bed. My heart stopped. Someone had savagely attacked the poor woman. Her wounds looked horrific, even though gauze and bandages obscured the most gruesome of her injuries. The dressings covering her facial injuries literally took my breath away, paralyzing me with revulsion at whatever could have done this to her.

Apparently, Detective Lampe didn't notice. She dialed a number and spoke softly into her phone. A few seconds later, she nodded at Wassner.

He sighed, took a deep breath, and said with no trace of apology in his voice, "Criminals are who we usually deal with, Mr. Harper. It's our job to serve and protect. Tonight, the person most in need of our services is this poor lady in the bed behind us. Sorry we inconvenienced you. Cut him loose, Spivey."

I kept staring at the woman in bed while Spivey moved slowly, digging for his cuff keys. The old woman looked like she was wearing a fright wig, her grey hair sticking up as if she'd stuck a finger into an electric socket. Thick white bandages wrapped around her neck, beginning below the neckline of her hospital gown and ending just under her nose. She looked like half a mummy. The bandages immobilized her jaws.

Somehow, I knew. I'd seen this woman in my nightmare. The woman with no mouth.

The next thought flitted through my mind involuntarily, the engineer in me still doing a root cause analysis. *Could she have been involved with whatever happened at Maid Marian Lane?*

The pretty detective got my attention by asking, "So how did you get off the elevator on this floor? There aren't any signs for the cafeteria. Why did you start roaming around when you noticed you were on the wrong floor?"

"I thought I explained that I wasn't paying attention. The elevator door opened and I got out. I didn't notice I was on the wrong floor until I was in here."

"But you didn't notice that there weren't any signs pointing toward the cafeteria? It's not like this floor looks like the main lobby. I don't understand how you could have made the mistake," Lampe said. But she smiled, like she wanted to help me give a better answer.

"I told you. My wife almost *died* yesterday. They admitted her last night, through the emergency room. I'm still a little shook up, okay? I'm sorry. My mind isn't clicking on all cylinders today, but I think that's understandable. Period, or exclamation point if you prefer. I've never seen this woman before in my life."

My voice trailed off a little at the ugly albeit irrational thought that they might ask me to take a polygraph test. I wondered if seeing the woman in my nightmare would show up as a lie in my subconscious mind.

The old woman's mouth was completely hidden, the lower part of her face completely wrapped in gauze. Unable to look away, I met her eyes. I knew instantly that she was the old woman that haunted my dreams. She was one who wrote the cryptic note in my nightmare. I'd never laid eyes on her, but I had met her in a vision.

The old woman abruptly sat upright, suddenly alert, and motioning wildly. She pantomimed writing, so Wassner produced a pen and a notepad, offering them to her. I got a sinking feeling in the pit of my stomach, remembering my dream and knowing what she was about to write.

Wassner turned to me and smiled triumphantly, as if he expected her to identify me as her assailant. He said, "You know, I was just about to ask if she could recognize the man who beat her husband to death and put her in the hospital. It seems the sight of you inspired her to want to write me a note without even any prompting. We caught you just outside her door, headed this way. If she points the finger in your direction, I'm thinking your ass is grass, and I'm a lawnmower."

"That cliché is older than I am," I muttered, but then wondered why I was bent on making things worse.

Fortunately, Wassner paid me no attention. His eyes remained fixed on the old woman in bed.

She held notepad and pen in shaking hands, laboring to write, just as I had watched her do in my dream. The same smell of blood from my visions suddenly filled the room. It was overwhelming, but no one else seemed to notice. A heavy blanket of dread hung over me and grew more suffocating as each moment passed. The old woman looked up from her efforts to stare at me with blackened and bloodshot eyes, giving me the uncomfortable certainty that she recognized me. I shifted on my feet, withering under her steady gaze.

Lampe walked over and looked at what she'd written on the page. She frowned, looking a bit confused. She made eye contact with Wassner, giving him an almost imperceptible shake of her head.

But I saw it as an opening, a chance to escape. "Why did you bring me into this woman's room?" I asked defensively. "Who is she?"

My knees were weak. I helplessly looked at the injured woman, struggling to maintain my composure as the world reeled around me. If she wrote what I expected, there would be nothing for the cops to tie to me. But it would confirm my dream. It would force me to admit that was real, no matter how much I wanted to deny it. I felt my grasp on reality slip. The idea that very real brutality caused my nightmares was almost too much for me to comprehend. I would have to question my own role in the nightmare. I had seen many of the images through the eyes of a murderer.

Get a grip! You've already made these cops suspicious!

Wassner watched me curiously, his eyes flitting between the woman lying in the bed and me. My face must have betrayed me, confessing I knew more than I claimed. He looked at her and apologized, saying, "We're sorry...we caught this man entering your room. You're in no danger. He can't hurt you. Detective Lampe is right there, next to you. Neither I nor Officer Spivey will let anything happen," he assured her.

"I've never seen her before in my life," I lied again. I didn't like the shrill, unnatural notes or the desperation in my voice. "I'm at the hospital because my wife is here and I'm in this room because she asked for some fruit. Like I told you, I was going to the cafeteria. I've got nothing to do with whatever happened to this poor woman."

The old woman's dazed, drug-addled expression became more alert. Maybe the chemical cocktail wore off just enough that she could focus her attention on writing. She had appeared oblivious when I first noticed her, but now her eyes sharpened, awareness creeping in, and she suddenly became quite lucid.

She scrawled again on the notepad with a determined, laboring pen. The effort even to write a couple of simple words proved taxing for her. Her eyes blazed with intensity as I watched each character formed painstakingly. Her intense concentration made the effort seem almost heroic, as if she were summoning her last breath to communicate some secret about her attacker.

I wanted to scream at the top of my lungs, *I didn't do anything wrong!* But I remained silent, and watched her pen write in a slow, measured effort. She wasn't writing about me. Though I could not see the actual letters as she formed them on the paper, I could watch the movement of the pen. My mind deciphered the movements, reversing them in mirror image and backward order. I recognized what she was writing.

She stopped, leaned back in her bed, and closed her eyes. The effort must have drained her. The pad relaxed in her grip, and she appeared to doze off. Lampe gently extracted the tablet from between the old woman's fingers and tossed it over to Wassner. He frowned when he read the words. I craned my neck to look around him and saw,

SNAKE SKULL

I thought back to my nightmare from last night. My best guess to complete the second word had been *snake skin*. Snake and skull didn't normally go together.

An almost hysterical impulse to giggle tickled in my throat, but I suppressed it quickly. This was no laughing matter. My dreams and reality were converging. There was no denying that I was involved in a very real, very dangerous situation. I slipped instinctively into the software developer's familiar, comfortable problem-solving mode.

Snake skull? It was obviously meant as a clue. *But to what?*

I stopped myself from asking the old woman any questions. The cops intimidated me. I was completely vulnerable and they controlled the situation. As much as I needed information from her, I kept quiet. I already knew more about the killer than the cops did. I was sure of that much. I hadn't asked to come into this mess, but my life was tangled with hers now. An overpowering need to get out of the room engulfed me.

As if on cue, Spivey jingled the cuff keys in his fingers. He nodded at me and asked Wassner, "Do you still want to let him go?"

Wassner nodded, "Show him the door, and cut him loose."

Spivey released me from the handcuffs and pushed me toward the door, not too rough but enough to get me moving. Over my shoulder, Wassner made it clear that they knew where to find me. I hurried off to find the cafeteria, anxious to put this encounter behind me.

A nagging fear followed me. Sooner or later, Wassner would compare notes with the uniformed officer who checked my ID a few hours earlier on Maid Marian Lane and he would show up on my doorstep.

# # #

The three of them stepped into the hallway after Harper was gone. Wassner didn't want the old woman to hear them. "What do you think?" Wassner asked Lampe.

She shrugged. "He tells a good story," she said.

"What's eating you?" Spivey asked nervously after waiting his turn, anticipating the answer.

"I'm pissed you didn't wait to see if that asshole was actually going to enter the room," Wassner hissed angrily. "You could have waited at least until his foot crossed the frigging threshold. We should've given him time to make a more overt move. Now we'll never know for sure what he was about to do. We can only speculate. And now, if he was our guy, we've tipped our hand. He knows we're in her room, watching in case he comes back to finish her off. We blew it."

"You meant to say *I* blew it. But I thought Detective Lampe said his story checked out. His wife is here in the hospital, two floors up."

"His wife gave him an excuse to be in the hospital. It didn't give him an excuse to be on this floor, damn it!" Wassner thundered.

Spivey got progressively more uncomfortable the longer the conversation lasted. He looked to Lampe, who shrugged in apology. He said defensively, "Look, he made an honest mistake. A guy with a pregnant wife in the hospital—does that sound like your guy?"

"If our case depends on throwing out anything that doesn't make sense on the surface, it will never get solved. We have no idea what we're looking at—a crime of passion disguised as a robbery. Or a robbery disguised as a crime of passion. Take your pick."

His voice rose as he became more frustrated at a missed opportunity. "If this was a robbery, why beat the shit out of the old people? Go back in there and take a really good look at her. I don't know if it's the dope the doctors have given her for the pain or her brain got scrambled from the beating she took, but she's no help, or at least I can't make heads or tails out of what she's trying to tell us. What in the hell does 'snake skull' mean? Is it a reference to a place, an event, or even a stupid belt buckle? Who the hell knows? Either way, unless this guy Harper has a tattoo of a snake or a skull on his ass, the clue she just gave us doesn't have anything to do with him. She didn't recognize him, so either he's not the guy, or she didn't see anything. She doesn't have much in the way of a motive for lying to us, does she? So why would a total stranger butcher her husband and do this to her? What did they ever do to deserve it? Why would anyone do something like this?"

Spivey thought hard about the question and then shrugged his shoulders in frustration. "I don't know…because the maniac enjoyed it?"

Wassner cocked an eyebrow at the uniformed lug in surprise and replied, "You just might be right about that one."

CHAPTER 15

Beth enjoyed the peaches, poking her fork around in the empty fruit cup as if she could eat more. I didn't want her to eat too much, too fast. I still worried about making her sick, in spite of the intravenous anti-nausea medicine pumping into her arm. She pouted, resentful that the doctor had implied that she would remain bedridden here for several more days.

She needed to add weight, her doctors insisted. I agreed, but keeping her here once she started feeling better would be tough. Her impatience and stubbornness would soon win her release over my objections.

But I now found myself dreading her release. I needed to decipher the visions and nightmares while she was still safe here. I wouldn't be able to keep it from her once she came home. She couldn't get caught up in this. The best way to protect her was to keep her here until I could figure out what was going on.

I forced myself to talk about baby names for about an hour before I excused myself to run by the office and check on how things were going with QA's testing. I felt like a juggler, grabbing each ball and quickly tossing it back in the air.

According to Tiffany, the testing was going well so far. She promised she'd call my cell phone if anything changed. I touched base with Richard long enough to stick my head in his office before I skipped out again, promising to keep him posted on Beth's condition and thanking him for the flowers he had the office send. Richard assumed that I was on my way to the hospital to visit Beth, not on my way back. I didn't bother to correct him. The company got their hours and a pound of flesh out of me, so I didn't feel guilty about the time.

I had plenty to worry about now, besides Beth. The police were developing an unfavorable opinion of me. My hallucinations were not pure fantasy. A killer was on the prowl, and I was watching his brutality escalate. I'd begun the new day in denial, but as the old woman wrote out the words, I slowly began to accept the truth.

And what is my connection to this "truth," if that's what it is? Am I the cat or the mouse? Am I the killer or am I his nemesis?

Bad dreams in the dark of night were one thing. Chance encounters with police conducting a criminal investigation during the harsh light of day were another matter entirely. I needed to get to the bottom of my own erratic behavior. Before one can develop a solution, one must first identify the cause of the problem.

My surreal ordeal started with my visit to the thrift store and the purchase of that damned necktie. Perhaps more information awaited me there. On impulse, I altered my course home to grab lunch and instead headed to the thrift store. As I drove, I tried to plan what to say or do upon arriving. I couldn't keep manufacturing excuses to shop before the store opened. Yet I found myself grimly determined to follow the clues in these strange, invasive dreams and visions. I wanted to know, *why me?*

Several odd scenarios played out in my mind.

Hi, remember me? I'm your first customer, back to shop for another tie. The first one must have been dipped in LSD. I've had some interesting hallucinations since I shopped in here yesterday.

Hey Chuck, would you mind if I hang around a while to see if any murderers drop by to donate items to the thrift store?

If I were Chuck, I wouldn't let me back into the store. It was important for me to get back inside. Maybe I could think of a way to make myself useful.

The front door to the thrift store was unlocked. Chuck stood near the top rung on a tall, orange ladder. He was removing a florescent light bulb from an overhead fixture. I reached over, handed him the new light bulb, and then offered to take the burned out bulb off his hands.

Chuck greeted me with a smile of recognition and climbed down from the ladder. I said, "Hi, Chuck. Dan Harper. I bought a tie from you yesterday. I meant to ask you then if you needed any volunteers to help get the store up and running. I confess that I have an ulterior motive. My wife is expecting and we're pinching pennies. I'll be able to keep an eye out for baby equipment if I volunteer in the store."

I left out the part about Beth in the hospital. I knew it wouldn't sound believable that I would be looking for volunteer opportunities at a time like this. In fact, it would sound downright insensitive. But the tie that started these horrible visions came from this store. I needed to find out more about its origin.

He slapped a friendly arm across my shoulder and laughed. "Are you kidding? Free labor? I'll take it. When can you start?"

"Do you need any help right now? I've got some time today, in fact. How soon can you put me to use?"

Chuck jumped at the offer. "I've got a delivery of some furniture I'm expecting shortly, and I need to clear the loading dock area so we can bring it inside. It would be a big help if you could clear that out of the way for me. Somebody left a pile of trash bags full of good clothes out there. The intake area is so full that the bags are blocking the roll door on the loading dock and we need to get them inside and up the stairs. There're a million things to finish on my to-do list before we have our grand opening Monday."

"Wow, that's only four days away." I looked around the thrift store and took in the disarray. There was a good deal of work to complete in the short time left.

Chuck correctly interpreted my doubts from my facial expression. I couldn't see them getting everything done on time.

"There were some delays in getting the lease finalized. Now every day we aren't open is money lost. We have to get the doors open some way, somehow."

"It looks like you're gonna be busy the next few days. I'm off work for the rest of today and all of tomorrow, so I can lend a hand here and there. Where did you say I can find the stairs?"

Chuck motioned toward the front door. "To the left of the cash register, next to the men's bathroom there's another door on the left marked OFFICE. You can't miss it. The light switch for the stairwell is on the left hand wall at the base of the stairs, and there's another switch for the projection room at the top of the stairs as soon as you turn the corner to the left. If you get those bags of clothes to the top of the stairs, that would be great. I've got a guy who says he can build a clothing rack for me that runs the length of the projection room wall. That will give me about ninety more feet of clothes racks, so we'll be able to hang everything when it comes in, which will make things easier to sort. We have to be able to organize clothing according to season. With summer coming soon, nobody is looking for winter clothes. We can store all the heavy winter stuff upstairs and leave the summer stuff down here until the seasons change, know what I mean?"

His infectious enthusiasm had me laughing easily. I mused again at the great fortune the small charitable organization had found in their engaging new thrift store manager. *Sure would like to know more about his story someday. Maybe he's trust fund baby who doesn't have to work for a living, out to change the world.*

Following Chuck's directions, I went to the back and found the pile of plastic garbage bags. They bulged with clothing stuffed inside, forming misshapen lumps. The plastic stretched under the weight of the clothes as I picked up the first bag. Even though they weren't completely full, the bags were heavy. I grabbed a bag in each hand and headed for the stairway. It would take several trips up and down the stairs. I was in no hurry. Each trip through the store provided a chance to look for clues.

The projection room upstairs was a long, narrow corridor with several framed window-like openings on the right wall where movie projectors once sat. I saw where the clothes rack should go and visualized how easy it would be to put together. Volunteering to build the racks Chuck needed would give me unfettered access to the store. The left wall was solid cinderblock, easy enough to use as a solid anchor in my developing design.

Pulled by curiosity, I looked out the nearest projector hole down on the showroom floor, envisioning the old theater filled with seats. How many noisy kids and young couples in heat had filled those seats in years past? The clicking whir of celluloid through an old movie projector and crackling speakers trumpeting the production company fanfare sounded again from youthful memories. I wondered idly how many county locals could trace their conception to the back row of seats and the intoxicating aroma of buttered popcorn. Shaking off the daydream, I dropped the heavy bags in my hand and returned downstairs to bring up another load.

Passing Chuck on the way down, I paused long enough to volunteer my services to build the clothes rack. "Hey, Chuck…you said somebody else would build that rack, but it looks like you needed it yesterday. Tell you what, since I have the day off from work, and I'd be glad to knock it out for you. I'll just run home and grab a few tools after I finish moving these bags of clothes upstairs. How does that sound?"

Chuck grinned widely and said, "Twist my arm! Throw me in that briar patch!" His face contorted as if he suddenly felt great pain. "Oh, damn it! I had another cliché on the tip of my tongue, and it ran off before it could come out of my mouth."

I laughed along with him. I was really starting to like Chuck.

Several boxes stacked at the far end of the projection room held what appeared to be shoes. I carried the next load of bags to the far end of the gloomy, poorly lit room and dropped them. The ceiling was rather low. Only about eight feet separated the floor from drop ceiling. Can lights were spaced about every eight feet, but several were missing bulbs.

My back was to the exit. I felt a hand touch my shoulder. Someone had been exceptionally quiet sneaking up on me. I whirled around expecting to see Chuck, but no one was there. There was no place for anyone to hide in the sparse room, either.

On my way back to the loading dock, I passed Chuck again as he got off the ladder. "Was anybody just upstairs?" I asked lightly.

"No. It's just you and me. Pedro and Andrew left in the box truck to pick up that furniture I was telling you about. There's a whole basement full an old lady decided to donate. She said some of them were antiques, so I volunteered my guys to do a pick up from her. We're the only two people in the store."

"That's really weird. I could've sworn there was somebody else upstairs in the projection room when I dropped off the first load of clothes up there."

Chuck laughed and said, "Did the landlord put you up to this?"

"What are you talking about?"

"He told me a cock-and-bull story about this place being haunted when he leased the theater to me— pretended it was part of the "full disclosure" on the lease. I could tell he was pulling my leg, but I've got to hand it to him. He never stepped out of character once he brought it up. It was kind of hokey the way he worked it. The lease agreement specifies our hours of operation. We can be in the store at all hours, but we're not supposed to be open between five a.m. and eight a.m. because of deliveries to the Chinese restaurant next door. They get fresh seafood shipped in and the parking lot here is small. The delivery truck needs the space to maneuver. That's why the owner of the building doesn't want us here all hours of the day and night, so he made up that story about ghosts and had the landlord spook us into daylight hours."

Don't let him start thinking you're a nutcase. Move on.

I forced a half-laugh to diffuse the moment and said, "I didn't say that I thought I saw a ghost. And I promise I'm not trying to pull your leg. I really thought somebody else might have been up there because a shadow blocked the light coming from the other end of the room for a second. It must just have been something else. No big deal."

"You're telling me. I don't believe in ghosts or any of that crap."

I snorted derisively in agreement, "Me either."

But I was less confident than I sounded. I was sure somebody just touched my shoulder, but nobody was there. Against all reason, I had begun to believe that someone, or *something*, was trying to reach out from another world and get my attention.

And it was working.

CHAPTER 16

What was I thinking? I had a patch in QA, a wife in the hospital, an ALTA match on Saturday, and I had just committed to knocking out a construction project on the side. *Brilliant.* I didn't need ghosts and homicide detectives to complicate my life. I seemed hell bent on doing a fine job of that on my own.

I shook my head and looked over the pile of building materials Chuck said would be at the back of the store. After sorting through what he had on hand, I finished my plan for constructing the clothes rack. I announced that I would get right to work after a quick run home for a few tools.

"Were you serious about coming back again today to get started?" Chuck said.

"Yeah, I am. This shouldn't take all that long, if I have all the tools with me. I just made a list of what else I'm going to need. If I don't finish it today, I'll knock the rest of it out in the morning. It'll be a lot easier to organize all this if you can get all the clothing out of these bags and hung so that you can see what you have. While I'm here, I can keep one eye open for things to help my wife with her nesting."

"That all sounds great as far as I'm concerned. Okay, the president of our board laid out a policy for me for accepting volunteers, especially before letting them work on anything that could be dangerous. We have insurance but don't want volunteers doing anything that puts them in harm's way unless they sign a liability waiver. I already set her mind at ease by telling her you aren't asking for credit toward community service hours. Was I lying?"

I chuckled, "No, I'm not working off any sort of community service for the courts. I can sign a waiver that lets me to use my own power tools to build a clothes rack for you. It's not that big of a deal."

"Good enough for me. Before you get started, can I borrow your driver's license and make a quick copy? The powers-that-be asked that I keep one for everyone who works at the store so we can do a criminal background check. It's just to protect the Humane Society, honestly."

"No problem." I pulled my license from my wallet, thinking it was getting a lot more use than usual these past couple of days. I suppressed a twinge of concern as I couldn't help but wonder if the ugly blemish on my record from my ancient past would surface. Too late to worry about that now. "I'll hang out for a couple of minutes. If it's okay with you, I want to browse around to see if there's anything Beth might like for the baby."

While he went off to copy my license, I found a decent car seat designed for newborns in the children's section of the store. *No stains. Clasps all work. Neutral colors. Manufacturer I've heard of before. Bingo.*

I carried it, left it on the counter by the cash register, and went back for more bargain hunting.

Unable to resist, I wandered through the electronics section. The selection and quality of donated goods impressed me. There were a few older computer monitors and dot matrix printers, but there were also some flat screen monitors and one or two recent model laser printers.

I spied an old HP flatbed Laser Jet like one I had at home on a shelf about knee level. My fingers blindly probed the right side of the printer and found the release button, and I lifted out the print cartridge.

Heavy. It feels almost full, I thought.

I put the cartridge back inside and closed the door, then checked for a price tag. At twenty dollars, the printer was only a fraction of what a new print cartridge cost. I decided to buy it, but I didn't want to carry it around while I shopped. The power and serial cords were wadded up in a tangled mess atop the printer. I looped the cords and secured them with a twist tie I found lying nearby, then carried the printer to the checkout counter.

I distinctly remember placing the cord bundle on top of the printer so that I wouldn't lose the power cord. The printer wouldn't work without it. There was absolutely nothing under the cord bundle when I left the printer on the counter. I am quite certain of that fact. Nothing.

I wandered back through the store again, but I didn't find any baby equipment in the same near-mint condition as the car seat, so I returned to the counter to wait for Chuck. In my head, I summed up the cost of the car seat and the printer, added tax, and dug out my wallet to get the right combination of bills.

I looked at the printer and did a double take. A single piece of paper lay *under* the cords I had secured only a few minutes earlier. The printed page lay face down in the output tray. I touched the paper with my fingertips.

It still feels warm.

I picked up the paper and turned it over. There were only a couple of lines on the page.

Hidden Hills

Peter Driscoll

I didn't bother arguing with myself about improbability. I recognized this as the new clue I sought by coming here.

The obvious questions ran through my mind. *Who is Peter Driscoll? Does "Hidden Hills" point to a location?* But in one sense, it didn't really matter. I knew it meant *something*.

My heart pounded in my chest. I thought over the plausible explanations. Chuck could not have slipped downstairs to plant the note on the printer in the short time I walked through the store. Besides, I would have heard him coming downstairs. I could now hear his footsteps coming down the steps. Chuck sounded like a herd of buffalo coming from his office. Those old steps were simply too noisy for traversing in stealth.

This was no accident. No coincidence. *Something* was definitely trying to get my attention.

All right, you got me. I'm the one who came here for clues. Now what am I supposed to do with this?

I folded up the sheet of paper and stuffed it into my back pocket. No sense making Chuck think he let a nut case volunteer in his new thrift store. I pulled out enough cash to cover my purchases, ready to pay. Chuck burst through the door leading from upstairs. The man never moved slowly. I didn't think his engine ran at any speed other than full throttle.

He noticed me waiting by the cash register, offering back my license when he came within arm's length. "Sorry. It took a few minutes for the copier to warm up."

"No problem. I found a couple of things I decided to buy, if you don't mind. I made sure what I picked out already had a price tag on it."

Chuck laughed. "You're gonna spend your whole paycheck here if you're not careful."

"No danger I'll blow through my check at these prices."

"Then, by all means, keep spending money. We keep getting donations dropped off and we haven't even solicited them from the community yet. The word spread through the Humane Society network and people just started showing up and dropping things off. The store is about to overflow. I can't get everything ready the way that I want and we still have a steady stream of people dropping by to donate clothes, toys, furniture...you name it. It's a happy problem to be sure, but it would be nice to be ready to open when we said we would be. Let's face it—we have zero acquisition costs, unless you count the gas to drive to somebody's house and empty the basement of furniture. The name of the game in a thrift store is turnover. You need to turn the store's inventory at least once a month. We want to price things to sell, period. Your money is just as good as anybody's. If items stay on the shelf for any length of time, they're priced too high."

"You've done this before."

"Not a thrift store, but I've worked retail," Chuck said. "It isn't rocket science."

He calculated the tax. "You've got about two bucks in change coming to you. I still don't have any money in the drawer. Do you mind donating the change to the Humane Society, or would you rather grab another tie or two from the rack?"

I feigned nonchalance as I told him to keep the change.

"I'd much rather make a donation than choke myself with another tie," I joked lamely. "Honestly, the damned things feel like a hangman's noose around my neck."

CHAPTER 17

As I drove down Alpharetta Highway toward home, a gaudy crimson and gold sign with bold lettering caught my eye. It seemed odd to me that I noticed it only now. I drove this stretch of road almost every day. The sign was weathered enough that I could easily tell, even from a distance, that it had been there a while. In large letters, the sign read:

SISTER ANITA
PSYCHIC – MEDIUM - ASTROLOGIST
INTUITIVE AND SPIRITUAL CONSULTANT

I thought about stopping. *I must really be losing my mind. Psychics. Really?*

I thought about what my brother Kevin might say. The voice in my head even sounded like Kevin. But I turned the car around at the next side street. I drove past the place once more, debating whether to give in to my urge to stop.

Why don't you just pull the money out of your wallet and set it on fire? We're trying to save money so Beth can stay home with the baby.

Rather than passing the place a third time, I turned into the parking lot. I continued arguing with myself about whether or not I should waste even a nickel on this sort of nonsense. *What is she going to do, look into her crystal ball and explain all my nightmares and the ghostly clues?*

What the hell. After the events of yesterday and last night, what harm could come from just checking the place out?

Well, for one thing, you know perfectly well it's a con game. Sister Anita had to be some sort of a con artist. To accept that psychic communication could be real required me to accept that our minds or souls could exist independently of our physical bodies. To consider a supernatural realm would challenge my orderly agnostic view of the universe.

Are you seriously going to fall for some hocus pocus, mumbo jumbo crap about talking to dead people?

My rational mind was doing its best to win the argument. Then my primordial *id* spoke up. *This is real. You are in over your head. You need help.*

The thrift store business with the tie was one thing. Then the vision at the office…the blackout…finding the woman with no mouth as a real woman in a hospital…the tapestry of gruesome clues in my dream last night. What was logical about any of that?

Having already accepted that some frighteningly real crimes bound me and that *something* seemed to be relying on my problem-solving skills, I needed to learn how to get more from the visions. I couldn't ignore an opportunity to find out more about the supernatural from a potential expert in the field. There was a reason I noticed the sign after so many times driving by and not seeing it. I realized that I was fighting a losing battle. I was going inside to meet Sister Anita. I told myself at least to set a budget to limit how much money I was willing to spend. No more than twenty-five bucks at the most.

I can't believe I'm even considering this...if she charges more than twenty-five bucks for an appointment, let that be the decision point. Make an excuse and leave. If she will see you, pay in cash. Don't volunteer any information. Only answer questions with yes or no. Don't elaborate. Tell the truth, but don't fall for any bullshit.

I pulled the bills out of my wallet, embarrassed at the thought of Beth seeing charges for a psychic on our bill, just in case she looked.

Braced for a new experience, I walked through the psychic's parking lot. My cheeks burned as I couldn't help but feel some embarrassment at the thought of doing something like this—something I would normally think preposterous.

The business had obviously once been a private residence. As the city grew and expanded, the rural artery on which the home sat became a main thoroughfare. It was now valuable frontage on a well-traveled highway, zoned commercial. Now even handicapped-accessible.

The small parking lot claimed most of the front yard. My older model car joined a BMW SUV and a Land Rover. As I walked toward the entrance, I caught a glimpse of another vehicle parked in behind the house—a late model Jaguar. Apparently, the psychic act paid pretty well.

The receptionist, a big black woman with her hair braided into cornrows decorated with colorful beads, looked up as I walked through the front door. She smiled brightly. At first, I assumed she was merely happy to see another sucker with money walk through the door. I was wrong. Her bright white teeth lit her face, with a genuine happiness to see me.

"How are you, darlin'? I'm Teresa, the office manager. You here for an appointment with Sister Anita?" she asked in a rich, tropical voice. When I didn't answer immediately, she added flirtatiously, "You sure are a pretty white boy."

I couldn't get offended, not with the gentle, teasing way she said it, like we were part of the same conspiracy. Her islands accent sounded a little contrived to me, setting off a warning alarm in my head. I could feel my face flush with mild embarrassment, but I couldn't help but laugh with her.

"Thank you, my dear. And you are a lovely sight, I must say." Grinning, I bent to kiss her hand and looked up with the blue eyes that usually got me either forgiveness or permission.

Lay on the charm. You came this far, so may as well go with the flow.

Teresa beamed. Apparently, I had won a new friend.

Now that I was inside, little daggers of doubts poked at me. Forty-eight hours ago, wild horses couldn't have dragged me inside this place. If Kevin ever found out, I'd never hear the end of it.

I pressed on with a false bravado, "No, I don't have an appointment. I guess you could say I stopped on impulse." Thinking I might have given myself an excuse to exit gracefully, I added, "If I need to make an appointment and come back later…"

"No, darlin'. She'll make time for you. If you can wait ten minutes, Sister Anita will see you."

She showed me to the waiting room while Sister Anita finished her reading in progress. I really didn't want to wait, but ten minutes didn't seem like too long to ask. I looked at my watch. Besides, I'd be sitting in traffic at this time of day otherwise, so I might as well stick this out and see what she had to say. But the longer I waited, the antsier I became.

Although no one came or went from the back room, Teresa reappeared ten minutes later and led me down the hall. In a small, dimly lit room, I met Sister Anita. I introduced myself as Daniel, offering her my given name for some inexplicable reason.

After meeting Teresa, I half-expected Whoopi Goldberg's character from the movie *Ghost* to play my spirit guide. Instead, I got Fran Drescher's character from *The Nanny*, or at least the accent.

Sister Anita had a heavy nasal Jersey accent. She was a little on the chubby side, shorter and younger than I expected. She was a bleached blonde who would have fit right in with *The Real Housewives of Atlanta,* if they taped it on the *Jersey Shore*. Incorrectly, I had assumed that because Teresa was black, that Anita would be, too. Honestly, before going there I had no idea what to expect. She looked more like a suburban socialite than a professional medium. Rather than a table with a crystal ball, she pointed me toward a leather recliner and asked me to get comfortable.

She smiled demurely and said, "Have a seat, please. Tell me, what brought you here?"

I thought to myself, *I wish I knew. What in the hell am I doing here?* "I don't know, honestly."

"Are you interested in having your palm read, or your fortune told?"

Neither will work, I told myself. "No, that's not why I came."

She closed her eyes for a moment and cocked her head, as if listening to a voice only she could hear. Sister Anita frowned, and then she said something that set me reeling. Her eyes fluttered open, and she exclaimed, "You have the gift!" Her voice changed, getting deeper, more masculine. She eyed me curiously. "Daniel, why do you doubt the gift?"

I protested weakly, "What are you talking about?"

"Your gift of sight through touch. Are you familiar with psychometry?" she asked.

"I've heard the word before," I shrugged.

Sister Anita continued, "We are energy. Psychometry is the art of touching an object and accepting images or impressions about that object, essentially taking the residual energy as input into your senses. You aren't quite ready to believe in yourself and your abilities. Not yet. I sense that you are not here because a loved one has passed. You are here because you are haunted by the spirit of one you do not know...Peter? Peter...Bristol? The last name might not be quite right. But did Peter lead you here?"

Icicles froze in my heart. That was a hell of a lucky guess. She hadn't nailed the name perfectly, but it was close enough for me. "Nobody brought me here, exactly. There's just been some weird stuff happening over the last couple of days. Where did that name come from?"

She ignored my question, further surprising me by saying, "I'm sorry, but I can't help you. I won't take your money. Please see Teresa for your refund."

She was refusing to help? She lost her desire to fleece me? My money wasn't good enough? What kind of con game was this woman running? How could she possibly guess and even come close to getting that name right?

As if reading my mind, Sister Anita explained, "You don't need to pay for my help. What little help I can give, I give to you as my brother, freely. One day you may see fit to repay the favor. One day I might need your help. What I have for you today is advice. Trust your instincts. When you touch something and receive a vision, you can believe what you see is real, whether past, present, or in rare cases, the future. But you have the gift to see something that has happened or will happen. Do not be afraid of the visions. Do not fear...*involvement*. Do you believe in God, Daniel Harper?"

"What does that have to do with anything?" I asked defensively, thrown off by the abrupt change of subject.

"Everything...and nothing," Sister Anita said. "Being open to the possibility of God makes you open to the possibilities of the world around you. How do you think you got here on Earth, anyway? Why are you here? Do you think the only reason you breathe with each sunrise is to earn your paycheck, make babies with your wife, and mow the lawn once a week? Play golf…no, you look more like a tennis player to me."

"Are you reading me, or profiling me?"

"Maybe a little bit of both. I do not deny that sometimes I receive false impressions. Feedback is actually quite important to me, letting me know how close to the mark I am with my reading. It's not like reading a book or watching a movie where everything unfolds in pretty much a straightforward fashion."

Forgetting that I argued with myself before coming here, I suddenly did not want to leave. After working through my reservations about being here, Sister Anita's comprehension and explanation of my visions was like a rope thrown to a drowning man. I needed to know more. A twinge of anxiety, or perhaps even anger, struggled to surface.

"Now wait a minute. I waited my turn and paid my money. I just got here for help, and you're turning me away…"

She held out her hand palm up to stop me. It silenced me. Even though we couldn't be more than a few years difference in age, she addressed me, "Child, you came with a mind more than clouded by doubt. You don't yet believe. Until you are more receptive and open to the truth, you should not seek it. All the help that you need will be here for you…when the time comes."

Incredulous, I said, "You are refusing to take my money. This can't be real."

She shrugged and smiled apologetically. "That's exactly my point, why I can't take your money. I can't help you at this time. You'd be wasting it. Your mind is not yet...*receptive*. You will be welcome back when the time is right."

"What a crock!" I shouted.

"Daniel, you don't even know why you're here. You don't know what you believe. You need to search your soul. Your gift has found you. The question you must ask yourself is...what are you going to do with it?"

"What gift? You don't even know me."

She frowned at me. "Now sugar, don't play dumb with me. I didn't say that I wouldn't *like* to help you. As I just said, I can't at this time. Today, it would only be a waste of my time and your money because your gift has revealed itself to you, but you have not embraced it. Open the inner eyes of your mind. Free yourself from your religion of logic. For me to be able to help you, first you must be receptive to help. The universe seeks balance. You will know when the time has come."

Anger simmered as I stood to leave. If there's one thing I can't stand, it's being jerked around.

"Go along now," Sister Anita said. "Teresa will refund your money. You have to give yourself permission to believe before coming back here. You must open your eyes, especially when you've got them screwed shut. You're a software man. What is this software? You make systems with rules and constraints imposed by your mind. Open the systems within your mind. Become receptive to the world around you...not just the one you see, feel, and touch."

How could she possibly know that? About my playing tennis? She guessed Peter Bristol—which was close enough to Driscoll. How did she guess his name? Nobody made me come here. It was my idea. *This can't be a setup, can it?*

I walked to Teresa's desk in stunned silence, my mind reeling from what I would normally consider gibberish. But Sister Anita's demeanor bothered me. How had she known what I did for a living? I wanted to believe she'd been feeding me a load of crap, but how did she know these things?

Worse yet, I knew she was right about me. I had no idea how to open my mind enough to stop the murders. What's more, I was afraid. I had to wrestle with my doubts and overcome my fears if I had any hope of finding the answers in time. My courage to unravel the visions could come too late for his next victims.

CHAPTER 18

For most of my drive home, I berated myself for my foolishness of having visited Sister Anita. Tempting me into believing I had some kind of psychic ability only made matters worse. As much as I hated to admit it, I should get some psychological counseling instead.

I dialed the number for Beth's hospital room. She answered sleepily.

"Hi baby. I didn't mean to wake you."

"It's okay. I had just dozed off. This nausea medicine makes me drowsy. Where are you?"

"I was headed home and thought I'd check to see if you needed anything. I could bring it back tonight when I come."

"No, you don't need to do that. Dan, you looked so tired when you were here earlier today. I want you to stay put, get some sleep tonight, okay? They already brought my dinner and I'm full and content. I'll be sound asleep again before you could get back here."

"What, you don't want me to come tuck you in?" I teased.

"Tempting as that sounds, I think I'd rather have you well rested for when they decide to let me out of here," she hinted suggestively.

I laughed. She *was* feeling better.

"Okay, if you're sure."

"I'm sure. I'll see you tomorrow. Love you."

"Love you, too. Good night, baby."

I turned on the radio and found it tuned to a golden oldie station. Mike Oldfield's classic *Tubular Bells*, the theme song to the move *The Exorcist,* raked against my ears like a knife against my throat. Creeped out, I turned the radio off and finished my drive home in silence. I parked in the driveway, but left the car running as I jumped out to check the mail, waiting as the garage door opened.

Our neighborhood is Providence Oaks. It is small subdivision off Upper Hembree Road, a small development of higher-end starter homes built in the late 1990s, with a scattering of cul-de-sacs distributed evenly around the main drive that circles in and back out of the single entranceway. Most of the houses followed one of the basic layouts of three bedrooms, two full baths, living room, dining room, and kitchen on the same level. A few houses near the entrance to the subdivision had different floor plans designed by an earlier developer. Three different construction companies built houses in Providence Oaks, but the entire second phase of the subdivision, including our house, was built by the last and largest one.

The builder varied the exterior of each house so they weren't literally carbon copies of each other by flip-flopping the location of the garage and putting brick facing on some houses, stacked stone on others, but, by and large, we all had the same basic floor plans. Our house sat on a hill, making it possible to include an unfinished basement that would give us future room to expand.

Everyone in the small community was friendly enough. The homeowner's association hosted block parties several times a year. We showed up with buns, salad, or whatever they asked us to bring. We enjoyed the sense of community, of belonging. It was a quiet corner of suburbia that seemed a safe place to start our family.

We were close friends with the Martins, who lived across the street until Scott got a promotion a couple of months ago that required he and Leslie relocate to Arizona. Beth and I were sorry to see them go, but things change and people have to move. It sucks when the people are your favorite neighbors. Scott had a great sense of humor, and the four of us all liked the same music. We have nothing against our new neighbors who bought their house, of course. We just hadn't had time to get to know them.

My new neighbor in the former Martin residence was working in his yard when I got home. He gave me a friendly wave and yelled something that I couldn't quite understand. It sounded an awful lot like "Wait!" but then he hustled inside before I had a chance to respond.

Beth and I hadn't been very good neighbors when we noticed the moving truck last month. She had been struggling with morning sickness so I bought a coffee cake from the grocery store, said "hello" as I thrust it in their hand when they opened the door, then apologized for my inability to stay over my shoulder as I dashed back home.

My attention focused on retrieving the mail out of my mailbox so by the time it registered that he was speaking to me, he had already disappeared. I couldn't imagine what he might want, but didn't want to be rude. So I waited there at the mailbox for a little while before giving up and pulling the car into the garage. I figured I must have misunderstood him.

Pleased with my purchases from the thrift store, I thought Beth would appreciate the great bargain I found on a newborn car seat. Once she had our baby, it would be the first piece of equipment we would need as we left the hospital.

Daylight was beginning to fade when I got home. I thought about food, having decided to call for takeout. Maybe some pizza. I could eat most of it tonight and still have a few cold slices for breakfast in the morning…a breakfast of champions.

After thinking about the best place to hide the car seat in order to surprise Beth when she got home from the hospital, I ran upstairs and stored it in the guest bedroom closet. I stopped by the home office Beth and I shared long enough to power on my laptop.

Pizza delivery for sure tonight. I was preoccupied with getting to the bottom of my weird experiences and didn't want to waste time either preparing dinner or going out to get it.

Unload the car, load up my tools, and get to work figuring out the link between Driscoll and Maid Marian Lane. There had to be some sort of a connection between the name "Peter Driscoll" and house at the center of so much recent misery for me.

Moving quickly, I finished unloading my purchases, and then I loaded the tools necessary to finish building the clothing rack I had promised Chuck at the thrift store. I had a good start on the design, prepped the installation area, and collected building materials this afternoon. All that remained tomorrow was the assembly.

While I checked off my mental list of circular saw, drill and drill bits plus other assorted hand tools, my mind drifted back to the strange events of the day and the mysterious piece of paper I now carried in my pocket. I looked across the street but didn't see my neighbor. He must have been waving to say hello and I had misunderstood or something. On my way inside the house for the final time, I closed the garage door.

The printer cable was still lying on top of the printer so I plugged it into my laptop and went to the kitchen to pour myself a scotch while the equipment warmed up. My stomach growled to remind me that I hadn't eaten since breakfast. I wandered around the kitchen, looking for the coupon bearing the phone number of the pizza joint that should have been stuck to the refrigerator door with a magnet. The doorbell rang.

It was my new neighbor. He carried a heaping plate covered with tin foil in one hand. He held his other hand out and said, "Hi, I'm Sam Leman, your neighbor across the street. Barbara, my wife, saw the ambulance over here last night. She knew someone went to the hospital and if one of you rolled in tonight, you wouldn't have your mind on cooking. She asked me to bring over some dinner for you."

The heavenly aromas made my choice easy. "Twist my arm. I was just about to call out for a pizza. That plate smells a heck of a lot better than hot dough covered in tomato sauce and cheese. Would you like to come inside?"

Sam shook his head and said, "I don't want to intrude. I hope that it's nothing serious and your wife is able to come home soon." With that, he began turning away, as if to leave. Apparently, I had set some sort of precedent by dumping off food at his house and running away.

He stopped when I held out my hand. "I know we met briefly once before. My name's Dan Harper. Look, I'm really sorry I ran off last time before we could even do proper introductions. Are you sure you won't come inside? Beth has been having some complications with her pregnancy. She's especially having trouble with morning sickness that doesn't ever stop. The doctors are keeping her in the hospital for a day or two while she puts back on a little weight. I can't tell you enough how much I appreciate your kindness and the food. It smells delicious. Are you sure you won't come inside for a minute?"

We shook hands. He shrugged and said, "Nice to meet you, Dan. I can't stay, but for a minute. Barbara is waiting on me to eat and I want you to enjoy your dinner while it's still warm."

"I can always stick it in the microwave to heat it up," I said.

Sam curled his lip in disapproval. Apparently, dinner was meant to be eaten hot off the stove in the Leman household.

We continued talking in my foyer. Sam surveyed the split-foyer layout, his eyes taking in the short flight of stairs leading up to the main living area, then the second set of stairs heading down toward the garage, unfinished basement, and laundry room. He smirked and said sarcastically, "What a unique floor plan! You've got to tell me the name of your architect."

We both laughed, but I was trying to be polite.

Sam said, "It scared Barbara when she saw the flashing lights over here. She was afraid something bad had happened to your wife."

The way he said it made me wonder whether she had a habit of watching her neighbors or if the flashing lights had attracted her attention. I wasn't about to think the worst of a woman who had just cooked me dinner, though.

I shook my head. "Beth fell. She's still in the hospital. She hit her head, and they worried about a concussion, but she was also underweight from being sick so often. The doctors believe both she and the baby will be fine. She's anxious to get back home as soon as they let her. She gave us all a bit of a scare, but she'll be home soon."

"Thank God!" Sam said.

"Absolutely," I said, but reflexively shrugged my shoulders.

Sam seemed to be unusually perceptive. "Is anything else the matter?"

Uh Oh, I thought. Sounds like I started something.

"Um…no. I'm worried about Beth and didn't sleep well last night. It's been a tough day. This smells delicious," I said, changing the subject and hoping Sam would not pursue it further.

To my relief, he didn't. "Well, I do hope you enjoy dinner. Let us know if there's anything we can do to help." He reached into his shirt pocket, and pulled out a card. "I wrote our home number on the back of my business card. Please don't hesitate to call if you need something. My wife will want to help."

That seemed like a little bit of an odd way to phrase it, as if she called all the shots and Sam only did what he was told, but I didn't know enough about them to pass judgment on their relationship. Besides, the smell of dinner was making me hungry.

"I'll return your plate sometime tomorrow if that's okay," I said.

"No hurry," Sam said. As he reached for the door, the chain around his neck swung out so that I could identify the symbol on his necklace as a small gold Star of David.

So imagine my surprise when I uncovered my dinner and found fried pork chops, corn, green beans, and mashed potatoes and gravy. No wonder it smelled so delicious. It was Southern cooking at its best.

# # #

After I hand-washed the one dish from my delicious dinner, I fed Abby Normal before going into our home office where my computer waited.

Trolling the Internet for information that might help me understand my bizarre dreams and daytime encounters with the cops, I hit pay dirt quickly. When

I searched for "Peter Driscoll" and "Hidden Hills" together, the search returned so few hits that I didn't have to read much.

Hidden Hills was the name of a neighborhood in the city of Stone Mountain. Someone named Peter Driscoll was the former president of their homeowner's association, according to an article I found published in an online edition of the Atlanta newspaper.

The article featured an interview with Driscoll about the closing of the country club and golf course that used to be part of the amenities of the subdivision. The club had been sold to a private enterprise that subsequently went out of business and closed both the golf course and tennis complex, deeming them unprofitable in the declining economy. Driscoll was described in the article as a retired school superintendent, disappointed to lose his home course advantage over his golfing buddies.

The limited description of him sounded nothing like that of a psychotic killer.

But how does one describe a murderer?

CHAPTER 19

I spent my remaining waking hours that evening trying to make sense out of the tidbits of information, like disconnected puzzle pieces scattered on my desktop. My eyes grew bleary from staring at the computer screen, looking for any connection between Hidden Hills, Peter Driscoll, and the house on Maid Marian Lane. I repeated my searches using "Peter Driscoll" and "Hidden Hills" with combinations of "Maid Marian Lane" and "Windsor Forest" but found no new clues.

Then it occurred to me that I still didn't know the name of the people who owned the house on Maid Marian Lane. I had assumed until now the woman with no mouth was connected to that house. What if instead she had some relationship to Hidden Hills? Could she know Driscoll?

Perhaps the only common denominator in all of this was *me*.

As difficult as it would be to consider that I could be the killer, the visions a product of my own tortured conscience, it would be the easy answer to the puzzle. If I were a detective, I would be my own prime suspect. But it didn't *feel* true. These names, places, and clues were completely unfamiliar. There was no sense of "that vaguely rings a bell."

Zero, zip, nothing. Nada. Nothing in my own life tied any of this together.

I was working off assumptions. The facts were few. I happened to drive and park in front of the murder scene while in some sort of weird mental fog the night after I first touched the tie from the thrift store. And I almost went into the wrong room at the hospital. That much was real and true, but the rest was conjecture.

Windsor Forest and Hidden Hills were at least forty miles apart. It bothered me that I still didn't know who owned the crime-scene house on Maid Marian Lane. So I asked the Internet.

I typed in the street address along with the words "property owner" and clicked the search button. Not surprisingly, the county posted helpful property valuation, ownership history and tax records to a website called city-data.com that displayed in a matter of seconds. There were even street maps and satellite photos of the house.

Nobody has any privacy anymore.

That search produced the name of the property owner: Simeon Nelson. The listing included nothing about a wife. Apparently, they didn't have joint ownership of the house.

Undeterred, I subscribed to an online service that provided access to all types of ancestral documents such as birth, death, and marriage records, and again hit pay dirt. I located the marriage certificate of Simeon Nelson and Miss Grace Stokes about thirty-five years ago.

After brooding over the impulse for a couple of minutes, I dialed the hospital and asked the switchboard operator for Grace Nelson's room. When she said, "Please hold while I transfer your call," I hung up. Even though I was sure the call to the room couldn't be traced back to me, I didn't want the phone to ring in her room and disturb the poor woman if she had managed to get some rest.

Two puzzle pieces locked into place. Grace Nelson, resident of Maid Marian Lane, was the woman with no mouth.

# # #

Grace and Simeon Nelson were married, but I couldn't find any connection between them and Peter Driscoll. After considerable internet trolling, I ascertained that Grace had been a homemaker. That little tidbit of information virtually eliminated the possibility she met Driscoll professionally. The probability that they knew each other was limited to their possible connections through social encounters. What was the likelihood that they knew each other, living that far apart?

Could Grace and Peter have been lovers? She was white and Driscoll was black. The difference in their races might have made that taboo in years past, but not anymore. No one would have raised an eyebrow to see the two of them dining together in Atlanta today. No, the distance between Stone Mountain and Roswell made their relationship unlikely.

Grace Nelson originally hailed from a small town up north called Newark, Ohio. For a nominal fee, a subscription database revealed she married Simeon in Lexington, Kentucky. They moved to their house in Roswell in the early 1980s.

Driscoll grew up in the Stone Mountain area, graduated from Redland High School, and lived in the Hidden Hills subdivision since the early 1970s. He had been left a widower by Renee Allen Driscoll, with no children.

Nelson sold insurance as an independent broker. Driscoll was an educator. Maybe he bought insurance from Nelson somewhere along the line. If there was some sort of relationship between them, I wasn't seeing it. If it turned out that Driscoll had also been attacked, maybe the only real connection between him and Nelson was the identity of their assailant.

The old article that quoted Peter Driscoll did not list his street address. I figured that out by searching phone directory listings in the Stone Mountain zip codes. The article was a few years old, but I had a hunch Peter still lived in a house in the Hidden Hills subdivision. The zip code was easy enough to figure out from the current MLS listings. That was enough for another search engine to produce a street address. MapQuest provided directions to an address on Brasswood Court, and I soon stared at an aerial view of the house that I felt confident was his.

It may be well past Nineteen Eighty-Four, but Big Brother is alive and well. Pity nobody seems to notice or care.

I knew I had to pay Peter Driscoll a visit in the morning, but my gut told me that he would not be the vicious killer who attacked the Nelsons. He would be an old man himself. Maybe he could point me in the right direction. Driscoll had something to tell me. Otherwise, why would the ethereal presence shadowing my every step for the last forty-eight hours lead me to his doorstep?

Now appropriately named, the country club life once offered in Hidden Hills had vanished. At one time, the epitome of luxury living in Stone Mountain, the country club and golf course were now closed. Like so many developments across the country, Hidden Hills had been hit hard when the real estate bubble collapsed.

Many homes were in foreclosure or for sale, dirt-cheap. The real estate listings for homes in the neighborhood reflected the housing bust. If the pictures that went with the MLS listings I pulled up were the best that could be taken, Peter Driscoll had to be depressed. His property value had gone down the toilet.

Even the name Hidden Hills resonated with me, provoking an odd certainty that answers awaited me there. The nagging voice of insecurity muttered in my ear, telling me there was nothing a software developer like me could do to stop a deranged killer on a murder spree. It was a job best left to the professionals. Kevin would say I was being irrational.

Screw Kevin. I can't fight this anymore. I don't even want to fight it. I want to understand what is happening to me, and make it stop.

I wanted to solve the puzzle, believing peace of mind would come with it. No, *something* was directing me to find Peter Driscoll. *Hopefully, he knows of a man with a snake skull tattoo.*

I set my alarm for five a.m., planning to drive to Stone Mountain and look for Driscoll's house. I had no idea what I would do when I got there or what I would say if someone answered his door.

One more scotch before bed.

I feared new nightmares, but desperately needed to sleep. The scotch acted like a sedative. By a little after nine o'clock my eyes burned with fatigue and aching shoulders barked in anger. My body felt completely drained of energy after a sleepless night and a long, troubling day. One last shot in my glass ought to finish the job.

After I poured that last measure of whiskey to soothe my frazzled nerves, the thought that I was drinking a lot more than usual crossed my mind. For tonight, a little extra liquid courage might be the perfect lubricant to loosen the wheels in my brain frozen by fear and dissolve my natural reluctance to get involved in somebody else's business.

I decided the need for sleep justified that extra shot of scotch. Besides, I had already poured it into my glass. It was too hard to put it back in the bottle without making an even bigger mess.

CHAPTER 20

My dreams of the previous evening paled in comparison to the orgy of blood that ruined my sleep this night. My eyes popped open as I sensed movement. My first thought was of the cat, but I recognized the danger much too late.

A golf club smashed down on my head before I could move. Curiously, I felt no pain, only the sickening crunch of the club as it struck my temple. I thought I must be dead, now floating above the still form lying in bed.

My throat constricted with a feeling of impotent rage as my attacker struck my helpless body once more. My eyes followed the arc of the golf club from back swing to impact with bitter frustration. Blood splattered against the wall. I had to be dead.

As the initial shock wore off, it dawned on me that this was not my bedroom. The layout was all wrong. The closet was on the wrong side of the room. Abby hadn't been curled up in the crook of my knee, as was her habit. When I looked toward the foot of the bed, I recognized my soggy friend from last night standing in the doorway. In the dim light, once again I noticed water dripping from his clothes. He must have been for another swim before coming to see me. And where had he brought me tonight?

Finally, I forced my attention on the bastard wielding the golf club. His back was turned to me, paying me no attention as he ransacked the bedroom, stealing the dead man's valuables. The killer pocketed jewelry and cash as he casually rummaged through the drawers before dumping the remaining contents on the floor, scattering them around to make sure he didn't miss anything.

Anger coursed through my veins as I watched, helpless to prevent this travesty. The man in bed never stood a chance. From the looks of the corpse, he would have been no match for the animal who attacked him even if he had been awake. A younger, faster, stronger man attacked him in his sleep. He was totally defenseless.

As I floated above the bed, I reached for the bedpost on the foot rail, ready to launch myself through the air at this monster. As I moved into position, an icy hand grabbed a firm hold on my foot. It was my wet friend. His flaccid expression seemed grotesquely inappropriate, given the circumstances. Then he smiled at me. I struggled in his grasp, recoiling from his touch as his lifeless eyes locked onto mine.

My ankle was caught in his iron-fisted grip, which seemed unnaturally strong considering his age and slight physique. For a brief moment, the opaque film of death cleared from his eyes and I saw compassion and warmth from the real person underneath, the life that had been there before death took him. Curiosity replaced my indignant anger. His kind brown eyes bore deep into mine, communicating an understanding of what had just happened, if not why.

Reason crept back as I absorbed the brutality acted out for my benefit. The only motive driving the killer that I could fathom was robbery, but that didn't justify the violence of the murder.

My waterlogged friend looked at a blank wall. I followed his gaze and then road signs began passing by in front of my eyes. I recognized the drive down GA-400. The old man looked at me, and his eyes communicated, *You can't change the past. That is not why we are here.*

I had to ask, *Am I dead?*

For a brief moment, his smile was warm and genuine. His bloated and ruined face reanimated, appearing to me as it had in life.

If you were dead, what good would you be to me? You bought the tie. It connected me to you through my killer.

His lips never moved. Startled by his unspoken words that clearly registered in my brain, I had answered him in thought. My mystery visitor still heard me, loud and clear.

I still had not had a good look at the killer's face. I'd been too caught up in freeing myself from the grasp of a dead man. I implored him to let me go, furrowing my brow with effort as I concentrated my thoughts on him. *Let me go! I need to get a good look at him in case I get the chance to identify him somewhere down the line. I haven't even seen his face clearly.*

My strange new friend shook his head. *You think you could identify him in court? What would you tell the police? They won't believe you. In fact, they'll think you are a suspect. You're going to have to think of a way of a more subtle way to get the police on his trail. Look, he's leaving now.*

He released his grip on my ankle. He was right. The killer was leaving. Apparently, I was now free to follow him and see where he went. As he walked out of the bedroom, I went after him. As I crossed the threshold, we not only entered a different room, we were now in a different house. Vertigo hit me as I fought a wave of nausea, struggling to acclimate to a new time and space.

The bedroom I had just left behind, complete with its grisly murder scene, seemed warm and friendly compared with this new place. This house really gave me the creeps. As I opened the door and stepped through, I found myself tracking a now-familiar evil down his rickety steps, apparently into a basement with only one way out. Despite my current lack of physical form, a faint musty smell assaulted my senses.

I had followed a voracious lion into his den. Even though I knew I lacked physical form, the thought of being here made me apprehensive. The murderer didn't seem to sense that I was there, but the thought that he even might sent my heart racing. I'd seen how savagely he attacked his victims. I was following the footsteps of a lunatic.

A noise like a scream filled the cramped space, but it was a higher pitched, metallic whine. After the hallucination I had in front of Tiffany yesterday, I recognized the sound immediately.

It's a circular saw.

The poor woman on the table did not move a muscle. The predator hovered over her. Though he faced me, he didn't react to my presence. The glare off the splashguard shield protecting his face from his gruesome work prevented me from making out his features. From the corner of my eye, I recognized the shape of a long handled flashlight that might make a useful weapon, but as I reached for it, my hand passed through the shaft.

I instinctively dived to stop him, at the same time knowing there wasn't much I could do to stop him without my physical body. I didn't relish the idea of confronting a mad man wielding a power tool, but I just couldn't stand there and watch as he hacked up that poor woman's body, either.

The rotating saw ripped through the bone and took off her arm in seconds. I recognized the pallor of death in her skin color. It was a small measure of comfort to know that she was already dead. He was coldly mutilating the corpse of someone he had murdered earlier, not cutting up a live woman. Her stiff limbs resisted movement. I wondered if he had frozen her body first, so her dismemberment wouldn't create too much of a mess. *What kind of a monster plans in advance how best to dissect his victims?*

Rage quickly grew to match my helplessness. This *animal* was literally getting away with murder while I stood by and watched, powerless to intervene as he bludgeoned a man to death and now hacked up a woman's body. Mindless of my lack of substance, I lowered my shoulder and plowed into his stomach with every ounce of my strength, but passed right through him. The only effect my effort had was to cause both of us an involuntary shudder. I resigned myself to the fact I was no more than the invisible fly-on-the-wall, watching the sinister scene unfold.

His face shield, now covered with gore, still hid the features of this ruthless killer. His build was engrained into my memory, but his face continued to elude me. The illusion mocked and teased me. The killer always seemed at the wrong angle for me to get a good look at his face or something obstructed my view. His size and build were not uncommon, though. I needed some way to identify this man.

Or his house. I knew we were in his basement, but I began to look around to see if anything in the room would stand out, letting me be sure I would recognize the place if I saw it again.

Too late. His grisly work over, my killer headed for the stairs.

Where was the little old man? As soon as the question popped into my head, I glanced around the room for him. He wasn't there. Apparently, I'd come by myself. I nonchalantly followed the killer up the stairs...and froze when he hesitated and turned to look down in my direction. I looked up at him, but the backlit glare from the light on the wall behind him obscured my sight. There was no place for me to hide. If he could see me after all, I was a dead man...but he shrugged, turned, and continued up the stairs.

Why can't I see his face?

Crossing the threshold, I expected to be in a room on the main level. Instead, I found myself outside, walking on an unkempt concrete path a little larger than a normal sidewalk. It was overgrown with grass and weeds.

Unease crept into my bones. *Beware of sand*, I reminded myself.

I'd seen this place last night. *What had brought me back here?* The question lingered in my mind when I saw my wet little companion once more.

Not again. But sure enough, he had something else to show me. We stood there together and watched a man digging in the distance. He lifted his head and cocked it, apparently warned by some sound we couldn't hear. He slithered into the woods, out of our sight.

An oddly familiar form approached in the distance, an old man walking his dog on the untended golf cart path. In sudden recognition, I looked to my companion with surprise. His lips pursed with grim tension. He directed my attention back to his doppelganger as the killer reemerged from hiding and viciously struck him. One savage blow of the killer's fist in the side of the head felled him easily. He pounced on top of the old man and bashed his head against the paved path several times, making sure he was unconscious or dead. The old man's dog ran off, dragging its leash behind. It all happened so fast, the old man didn't have time to yell in protest. It was over in seconds.

The killer moved in haste, anxious to destroy any evidence of what he'd done. I wondered why. He didn't act as worried in the houses where he murdered people. What was special about this place?

The killer tied off my companion's lifeless body with cinder blocks, while a spectral form of the dead man dispassionately watched the scene from my side. With some effort, the killer dragged the body away from my field of vision.

I started to follow, but the spirit of the man I'd just seen murdered caught my arm and shook his head. *Don't bother*, he said.

For some reason, that woke me up.

PART THREE
GOOD FRIDAY

CHAPTER 21

GBI Agent Craig Gradick dialed Wassner's cell phone number bright and early, but it sounded like he had interrupted his grouchy friend in the middle of something. Wassner recognized the phone number of the incoming call and answered, "Yeah. What have you got?"

"And Good Friday morning to you, too. Do you want to know why I called, or are you going to waste all morning exchanging pleasantries with me?" Gradick asked sarcastically.

"Oh, wow. It's Good Friday, already?" He'd actually been to early Mass, knowing full well the significance of the day, but he humored Gradick. "Man, where is the time going?" He paused for effect. "Okay, so there's some chitchat for you. Now, tell me why you called. Spill it. The suspense is killing me."

"You could actually be a first class government agent, Detective Wassner, if you didn't have issues with authority. But don't we all? You just have a penchant for expressing yourself a little too clearly sometimes. Diplomacy wouldn't kill you, you know? You have the tenacity of a bulldog, which is good for a detective, but you have the personality to match, which is not so good for the career. Do you ever think about what you could accomplish, if you ever learned to kiss a little ass?"

"The appeal is limited, I'd have to say."

"It's your career."

Wassner quickly tired of the banter. "Gradick? I'm still waiting for you to tell me why you called. I'm busy here. Can you cut to the chase, please?"

"Sorry, Bill. Okay, okay, so I'll get to the point. I do believe you've stumbled onto something. In addition to your murder investigation in Roswell, and the one you mentioned in Sugar Hill, I found a third one in Smyrna with some similarities: unknown assailant, burglary and assault, victim was brutally murdered, murder weapon was missing. ME believes the missing murder weapon was a meat cleaver."

"Brutal!" Wassner exclaimed. "That had to hurt. Was that the only other case?"

"That's with limiting the search within the last three months. We might find more if we go farther back. But then again, these three are all bunched together in the last couple of months. Maybe our perp is just getting started, which sort of makes sense, if you think about it. He's only going to get better with time. Not sloppier. The longer the serial killer goes without getting caught, the better he gets at avoiding detection and capture. But you knew that already. My hunch is that we're looking for the same guy on all three, but he's probably a newbie, relatively speaking," Gradick replied.

"So, we are looking for a serial, apparently. What's bugging this guy? What's made him so mad at these people? How does he know people in Smyrna, Roswell, and Sugar Hill? Do you think these are just random targets?"

Gradick thought about the questions for a while. "Hmm. The only problem with the random target idea is the mode of entry. Each case suggests prior knowledge of the residence. Well, that and the demographic profiles of the victims are all over the map. It looked like our boy might be targeting the geriatric crowd for easy pickings, but the guy in Smyrna wasn't all that old—mid to late forties. You were the one who suggested he knew where he was going, weren't you? If we don't catch this guy soon, the papers will have a field day with the story. They'll probably call this guy 'The Souvenir Killer' or some crap like that. Reporters eat this shit on a cracker. Nobody likes a happy ending. It isn't interesting enough. Nobody cares, unless there's a body count."

"The problem is, if this really is all the work of the same guy, the body count is starting to add up pretty quick. We need to find this maniac, and soon." Wassner thought for a moment, then dug around for his notepad. "Hey, hang on a minute, will you?"

"Sure. It's not like I've got something better to do." But he waited, because Wassner never asked for an extra second of his time on the job. It was all business, until they were off the clock. And it looked like Wassner had already taken one shot in the dark and scored a bull's eye. He felt inclined to give his gruff friend the benefit of the doubt.

"This is a little bit of a long shot, but I know you're working with the profilers. I ran the name of this guy already. He doesn't have any priors, but we caught him outside the hospital room of the surviving victim in my case. He had an excuse for being in the hospital, but not that floor, and certainly not the room of our witness. Name is Daniel Harper. He's about six foot, dark brown hair, blue eyes. He's one who'd be used to having women fall for his good looks, and like I said, no criminal record. Have the profilers given you anything on whether or not our guy might be married? Could he act normal most of the time, be a chameleon that nobody sees?"

Gradick snorted in disbelief. "What are you, a profiling expert too? So far, the profiler building the case hasn't constructed an extensive outline, but she has said that he's someone who blends into the crowd. The victims don't notice when he cases their house. Might be a cable guy, handyman, carpet cleaner...but the profiler agrees with one thing you said. He's getting inside the house and nobody cares or notices. So how does some freak waltz inside, case the place, and leave without anyone getting nervous? What electrician, service tech, or termite guy has a territory this big?"

Wassner had a thought. "I've got another detective here contacting the pawn shops to see if anything from the list of items missing from my crime scene turns up. She's going through the household papers and documents that were scattered all over the place, to try to construct a timeline of who came to the house, when and why they were there. We can cross-check our timeline with the Forsyth County Sheriff's department to see if we hit on anything that matches up with the Sugar Hill case."

"I'll be in touch with them shortly. If they've come up with any promising leads, I'll run them back by you to see if your detective can find a match. I'm impressed that you're willing to admit you can use help once in a while. I thought you were too stubborn to think so."

"This guy needs to be stopped. Whatever it takes," Wassner said. "A bullet to the head ought to work."

CHAPTER 22

I didn't sleep after awaking from my nightmare. Since I had first touched the fateful tie from the thrift store, the forces haunting my dreams and waking visions were constantly driving me toward Hidden Hills, to find Peter Driscoll.

My departure for Stone Mountain avoided the early morning traffic. So few cars were on the road that I decided to avoid the I-285 bypass. I opted for the straight shot across the eastern suburbs to the circuitous route of the expressway. Traffic was so light I was able to read some of the road signs as I passed, a distracted luxury I normally did not afford myself. My route began on Holcomb Bridge Road. It turned into Jimmy Carter Boulevard as I passed through Norcross, changing names again to Mountain Industrial Boulevard as I passed through Tucker.

Usually I kept my eyes glued to the road because of the inherent dangers presented by typical Atlanta traffic, but this early morning I found myself amused by some of the signs I passed. Best Friend Park advised drivers it was time to register for dance workshops, presumably with your best friend as dance partner. Dr. Creflo Dollar's World Changers Church offered salvation on Cash Court. The Tile House sold flooring products on Granite Way. The street names all seemed amusingly appropriate.

Did these businesses pay a premium for the privilege of naming the streets, or were these assigned by a county employee with a decent sense of humor?

I also planned what might I say to Peter Driscoll when he answered his door this morning. *Excuse me, sir, but do you have any tattoos, particularly with snakes or skulls? Have you murdered anyone recently? Do you have any idea why a ghost printed your name on a piece of paper in a thrift store in Cumming?*

Okay, so that last question was likely to get the door slammed in my face. Actually, all of those questions were likely to get the door slammed in my face. How about a simple, *Do you know a man named Simeon Nelson?* That sounded harmless enough. It might even work.

However, what was the likelihood the answer would be yes? These men lived almost forty miles apart. The only reason I believed they were connected was the link of the thrift store. The tie came from the thrift store, and the printer printed its mysterious message there. How could any items belonging to Peter Driscoll get all the way from Stone Mountain to Cumming? It made more sense to believe something from Nelson found its way there. Roswell was only a few exits down GA-400.

What in the hell am I doing? What seemed to make perfect sense in the dark of night seemed foolhardy in dawn's early light. If Peter Driscoll were connected or somehow involved with the attack on Simeon and Grace Nelson, approaching him directly and raising his suspicions could prove the worst possible idea.

But I didn't know what else to do.

I found my way down South Hairston and turned left into the Hidden Hills subdivision. A festive banner announced a birthday party, either about to happen or recently celebrated. The street names reflected the neighborhood's former status as a golf course community: Clubgreen Summit, Fieldgreen Drive, and Wedgewood Way. The main road was divided by wide medians, most populated by dense woods or a virtually impenetrable mass of brush.

The hairs stood up on the back of my neck as the thought popped into my head...*a body could be hidden there*. I shook off the thought. *Your mind is playing tricks on you, my boy.*

Intuition took over. An odd feeling enveloped me, a sense of déjà vu.

I've been here before.

# # #

I didn't recognize any house or landmark in particular. Some of the homes in the neighborhood still looked to be in decent shape, but many mirrored the condition of the links. The golf course appeared to have been in steady and rapid decline since the club closed.

The neighborhood seemed to be in various stages of decay in an eerie sequence reminiscent of the progression of death. A fairly well maintained house just beginning to show its age stood beside one with an overgrown yard and a thick mat of pine needles piled high on its roof. Next door to them was a house with rotted eaves, the gutters barely hanging by a single nail.

Going...going...gone.

Gloom hung over the neighborhood like a thick fog. As I turned onto South Hidden Hills Parkway, I realized I was not really following my directions to Driscoll's house any longer. Instinct had completely taken over. I glanced at my watch. Making this trip well before the morning rush hour had me here earlier than I expected. I had time to burn. Well before seven a.m., it was way too early to call on Mr. Driscoll.

I didn't want to park in front of the Driscoll house and sit in the car waiting for an hour or more to pass. It made me antsy to sit still, and it would make me really nervous to sit still in this neighborhood. Hidden Hills had once been a very nice, exclusive neighborhood, but it had been in decline for a number of years.

People would naturally be more suspicious and more likely to call police and report unusual activity. Having little experience interacting with the police and not having enjoyed my recent encounter with the two detectives at the hospital or the officer at Maid Marian Lane, I stayed on the move. *It's harder to hit a moving target.*

Admittedly, I found myself curious to see what an abandoned golf course looked like. I wondered if the neighborhood residents still maintained the clubhouse to use for parties and special events. I figured it was expensive to maintain a golf course, but the clubhouse was only a building, so there might be a chance it was still in use. Besides, exploring gave me something to do for an hour, to kill time.

Remembering from my internet search that the club had an address on Biffle Road, I meandered through the subdivision until I recognized the name on a street sign. I followed Biffle along the golf course until I found the driveway leading to the clubhouse. The main entrance to the clubhouse had been permanently blocked off from vehicle traffic by steel poles embedded in the asphalt. All signage had been removed. It would have been easy to miss if I had not been looking for it.

I drove past, and then did a U-turn after I noticed a back entrance remained unblocked.

Apparently, a homeowner near the clubhouse kept the rear access to the clubhouse open to use as his personal driveway. A truck was parked facing the road, leaving me only inches to spare as I squeezed between it and a pile of logs.

Logs were piled everywhere. Fallen trees had been chopped into logs and stacked where they fell, forcing me to weave around them. I navigated around more fallen limbs to reach the parking lot, where I stopped between the clubhouse and the old cart shack.

Debris, apparently damaged sheetrock removed from the clubhouse, was stacked outside. I wondered if the cops would hassle me if they found me here. I also wondered if they ever made it this far. The entrance to the old clubhouse complex had been hard to find, and the road didn't exactly look well-traveled. Plus, it was still really early.

I got out and wandered around, curious to observe the decay up close and personal. I was far enough away from any houses not to disturb the early morning quiet by opening and closing my car door.

If somebody showed me pictures of the clubhouse interior and told me a bomb had done the damage, I could have believed it. The roof had an exposed hole. As I gingerly walked around the scattered debris, the stench of mildew and mold began to overpower me. Feeling no magnetic pull to this old building other than morbid curiosity, I decided that continued exposure to the fungi I saw growing on the rubble was a bad idea.

Leaving the ramshackle clubhouse behind, I turned my attention to the old cart shack next door, which was in much the same condition. There just wasn't much there inside the building to see.

On the other side of the cart shack was a really depressing sight—the old tennis complex for the club. There were four traditional hard courts on the right with lights, four on the left without, and two lighted clay courts in the middle. Birds nested among the broken, long dim light fixtures. All ten courts were without nets and not just cracked, but missing huge chunks of court surface.

What a waste.

The folks who make the documentary series *Life after People* would have a field day in this neighborhood. We often chide ourselves about humanity's impact on the environment, but this very real example of how quickly nature erases human impact and reclaims its territory stunned me.

My foray as an explorer put me in a somber mood. I checked my watch again. It was a little after six thirty. My self-imposed moratorium of an earliest arrival time for Mr. Driscoll's was seven a.m., but I was ready to leave this depressing place. I got back in my car and turned on the console light.

CHAPTER 23

As I sat there killing time, I remembered that my mother would kill me if she found out that Beth was in the hospital without my calling to tell her. Mom answered on the fourth ring, just before the voice mail answered. I knew her dogs would have awakened her by now.

"Hey, Mom. It's Dan."

Mom somehow detected distress in my voice, even in those four short words. "Son, what's the matter?"

I saw no reason to beat around the bush. "Beth and the baby are both going to be okay, but she fell Wednesday night and hit her head. Her doctor decided to keep her in the hospital until she's a little stronger. She's been sick and she just got too weak."

"Oh, my God! Is Beth going to be okay? And the baby?"

"Yes, Mom, they're both going to be fine. I told you she'd been having problems with morning sickness. Apparently, Beth blacked out and her head hit as she was falling. It might end up being a blessing in disguise. The doctor said that she'd lost too much weight because of throwing up all the time. She had almost zero body fat. Her body was digesting muscle to feed the baby. Things were rapidly approaching the danger zone from what the doctor was saying. I could have lost them both." My voice cracked with emotion, choking over those last words.

"I'll call and book the next available flight. Don't worry about picking me up from the airport. I'll get a taxi. What's the name of the hospital? I'll come straight there."

"No, Mom, that's not necessary. Beth is going to be in the hospital until she puts on enough weight to make her doctor happy. At least wait until she comes home from the hospital. But it won't be that much longer before the baby is due, just a couple more months. We're going to really need your help once she comes home with the baby, if you can come then and stay for a while."

"Are you sure?"

"Yes, ma'am. If you want to give Beth a call in a little while, she's in North Fulton Hospital. Ask the operator for her room. I've got the number for the switchboard written down somewhere."

Somewhere was back home, but I didn't tell Mom that, nor did I let on where I was. Or why.

"Daniel?"

"Yes, ma'am?"

"Is anything else the matter? Don't take this the wrong way, but you really don't sound good. You sound like you are absolutely exhausted."

"I'll be okay. I'm just tired."

Mom waited me out.

"I knew Beth was sick more than she should have been, but how could I know that it was lasting all day? We work in different offices. I don't see her all day. She didn't tell me how bad it was. I could see when she picked at dinner. Now I know it was because she was feeling queasy all the time. I kept telling her that she needed to go see the doctor, and she kept telling me that her next appointment was only a couple of days away and it could wait. You know how stubborn Beth can be." I took in a deep breath, realizing how guilty I sounded. "I should have insisted, though."

"Your wife is a proud woman. She has a strong constitution and a strong will. I'm not suggesting it's your fault. Are you sure that's all that's bothering you?"

If my mother was anything, she was persistent. Was it mother's intuition?

When I didn't answer, she pressed the issue. "What aren't you telling me, Daniel? There's something else bothering you. I know you're upset about Beth, but that's not the only thing that's bothering you. Is everything okay at work? You aren't having problems with your job, are you?"

Mom had definitely caught on to the fact something was bothering me, and I realized I had to tell her something. Because she always saw right through my attempts to lie, I didn't bother to try. I skirted the truth as closely as I dared. "It's nothing, really. Work is fine. After the adventure with Beth, going to the hospital and all that business, when I finally got home, I couldn't get a good night's sleep.

Actually, before I even got home, something weird happened. I sort of blacked out behind the wheel and found myself parked in front of a strange house in a strange neighborhood. I have no idea how I got there."

She was silent for a moment. "That doesn't sound like nothing to me."

"What made it even weirder was that something bad had happened at that particular house. I don't know exactly what it was, but that yellow tape the police use to cordon off a crime scene was all over the place."

"You said you blacked out while you were driving?"

The sound that came from my throat was nothing like my normal laugh. "The detour to the house wasn't the only thing. I had this...nightmare afterward. That dream was so weird, I don't know even how to begin to describe it. Look, all of this weird behavior has probably got more to do with stress or a reaction to spicy food than anything. You don't need to worry...I'm not losing my mind. I'm just a little stressed out, mostly about Beth and the baby. That's all."

My protest sounded like I wanted to convince myself as much as my mother. "Why don't you call your brother and tell him about this? Maybe he's got a friend in the area who can help you. Maybe he can just prescribe something for you and fax it to your local pharmacy."

"Better living through chemistry," I muttered under my breath. I didn't bother to argue with her, but I was pretty sure that a Georgia pharmacy would question an Illinois psychiatrist prescribing medications across state lines. But Kevin would know, and he probably had a friend here in town who could handle it for him. The thing was I didn't want to dope myself into oblivion.

"Don't be smart with me, young man. Your brother might be kind enough to give you a mild sedative, if you need it."

It's funny how she can selectively hear anything I say when she wants. "Mom, I only had one, okay, two bad nights. I don't want to bother Kevin with my personal problems or tell him all about the gory details of a bad dream. I'm not his patient. He won't get paid for…consulting with me. I'm sure he hears plenty of this crap all day at work as it is."

"He won't care about getting paid. He's your brother. Son, it's not normal for you to operate a motor vehicle and have no memory of it, or to find yourself in a strange neighborhood with no recollection of how you got there. Call your brother."

"Okay, I promise."

Fat chance.

I said goodbye to my mother. Anxious to be on my way, I found my printed directions and refreshed my memory about how to get from the now decrepit clubhouse to Driscoll's address on Brasswood Court.

CHAPTER 24

Again, I found myself questioning my own judgment. What possessed me to get my mother all riled up, the first thing this morning? Yeah, I needed to let her know that Beth went into the hospital, but that stuff about blacking out while driving the car was getting her upset unnecessarily. I really needed to become a better liar.

As I neared the Driscoll address, a street sign caught my attention as powerfully as if the sign pole had grown legs and leapt into my path. The sign read *Clearlake Court*. In my head, it resonated as if spoken aloud. The name hit me like a ton a bricks. The feeling I'd been here grew stronger than ever. And I knew when. This place hosted my dreams.

I pulled in and parked on Clearlake Court, even though Driscoll lived a few blocks away, on Brasswood Court. My instinct had proved too reliable in the last couple of days not to trust it now. So I followed my gut.

I had no good reason to get out of my car and begin to wander the neighborhood. But that's exactly what I did. A sense of *knowing* that the answers to my questions lurked nearby compelled me. My eye had been drawn to a large retention pond as I passed on the road. So there I headed. My dream friend always looked wet. There had to be a reason. Water seemed the obvious answer. This wasn't a lake and the water didn't look clear, but it was near where the little voice inside my head told me to stop.

My eyes swept over the landscape and back, searching in vain for the vantage point from which my ghostly associate and I witnessed the reenactment of his murder. It all looked so familiar, but it wasn't quite right. I could feel that I was close. The pond was right there in front of me. I worked my way toward the water's edge.

The large, black pond looked to be about an acre in diameter. Sort of big for a pond, but it would be a stretch to give it the label of "lake." It followed a rough "J" shape, a dog-leg left, in golf parlance.

A formidable barrier of small trees and bamboo obscured my view of the water's edge, forcing me to weave through the dense brush. Even though it was still early morning, the air was dense and muggy. I began to perspire from the effort of making my way through the brush and trees to the pond bank.

What if I found an honest-to-God dead body? Not a corpse in a casket some mortician at a funeral home had spent hours making presentable but an ugly bloated vision worth a lifetime of nightmares?

Is this something I really want to do? Do I have a choice?

The answer was obviously no. The idea of finding a submerged corpse in those murky depths really horrified me, but the dreams wouldn't stop if I chickened out. My heart raced at the idea of making such a discovery. I won't deny an element of titillation spurred me on, but I also believed these visions came to me for a reason—more than simply touching a stupid piece of cloth in a store full of used goods. I pressed forward, looking for resolution. And a dead body.

Though I took my time and circled the pond slowly, nothing hideous floated beneath the surface, at least not where I could see. My nightmares did include a boat transporting the body out into the middle of the pond, so I walked along the bank, peering as far out into the murky recesses and amid the clumps of marsh grass as I could see. Thick groves of pines and river birch limited access to the very edge of the water in a few areas, but I managed. And I was fairly certain that no body was in the pond, submerged and hidden from my sight.

A wave of disappointment hit me. I felt let down. Or that I had let my nighttime visitor down by not finding his body. The mosquitoes began to swarm, and I began to itch as the blood-sucking insects found their mark. On cue as I felt the heat rise, the cicadas started serenading me, letting me know the morning sun was doing its job. The brambles scratched and clawed at my trousers, leaving me to pick out broken pieces of thorn that embedded in the khaki fabric and pricked my skin with every step.

I was completely miserable, beyond ready to give up my search and go home. The whole notion that bad dreams could lead me to find real murder victims now seemed patently absurd as the bright light of day illuminated the world around me.

There had to be more to my dreams and the events of the past several days that I just wasn't seeing. The delusion that a supernatural entity was guiding me to solve a mystery began to evaporate as my internal debate gained steam. I took several deep breaths, allowing the knots in my stomach muscles finally to relax. Maybe taking a couple of pills to help me sleep wasn't such a bad idea. I made my way back to the road, ready to walk back to my car and return home.

This has all been for nothing.

I tried to convince myself that it was worthwhile to stop by Driscoll's house before leaving Hidden Hills for good, but I'd lost my enthusiasm for adventure. And I did not intend to come back here after this monumental waste of time.

I really had myself going there for a while, but it had to be a coincidence, my imagination running wild, stress causing some sort of mild mental breakdown. *Starting to believe in ghosts, boogey men, and psychics. What will be next? What's wrong with you?*

I just needed a couple of days of pure rest and relaxation. If it hadn't been a holiday weekend coming up, this would have been a good week to skip ALTA. If we weren't short-handed, I would back out of playing this week's match. I frowned when I started down the first cul-de-sac I came across. The street sign was missing. Clearlake Court, where my car was parked, turned out to be the *second* cul-de-sac after the pond. On my initial drive by, I didn't even notice the first.

I retraced my steps. As I walked toward my parked car, lost deep in thought, a loud chattering noise captured my attention. A boisterous squirrel approached me from a patch of nearby brush. My initial thought was rabies and I scoured the vicinity for anything to use as a weapon; but the creature detoured, passing me by as it raced deep into the unmarked cul-de-sac, drawing my attention back in that direction as it disappeared in the distance.

Just before it vanished, unless my eyes played tricks on me, the squirrel did the impossible—it stopped in its tracks and nodded its head in the direction it was going, as if to say *follow me*, before scampering headlong to disappear into a bed of liriope.

As my eyes tracked the squirrel, I noticed something I hadn't seen before, coming from the opposite direction. Earlier I had seen only an overgrown abundance of foliage amid a few houses on a dead end street. The squirrel attracted my attention to the end of the block as I stood at the perfect angle to catch a glimmer of sunlight reflecting off a second body of black water.

There's another pond back there?

This second body of water, whatever it was, could not be the same pond I'd just searched. I forgot about Peter Driscoll, my wife, and everything I'd just told myself about this search being a waste of time. I suddenly knew that I'd been searching in the wrong place all along.

So of course, I followed the squirrel.

A now-familiar voice told me this was the water I saw in my dream. I followed the trail blazed by my animal guide until I reached the edge of dark water, looking for confirmation of the murder I had witnessed in my nightmare.

CHAPTER 25

Okay, so taking navigation directions from a squirrel undermined my disbelief yet again. I vacillated back to believing in ghosts and fairy tales. Well, at least ghosts. Now I was okay having a conversation with woodland creatures. The only thing missing from this morning so far was Rod Serling coming out of the bushes to tell me that I had just entered *The Twilight Zone*.

Just as I had almost convinced myself that my spirit guide was a product of my overactive imagination, the damned squirrel absconded with the bulk of my doubt as it deliberately drew my attention to this larger pond.

This second body of water was huge, more like a small lake compared to the first retention pond. It was much too large to have been a water hazard on the former golf course. I moved quickly through the trees, trying to get off private property as fast as I could because I never stopped expecting cops to appear at any moment to arrest me for trespassing. The later the morning wore on, the more concerned I was about being caught in someone's backyard. I couldn't exactly plead ignorance, having walked through their front yard to get here.

To my left was a small utility shed near the water's edge. The woods obscured it enough that I couldn't see it clearly, yet a detailed image of peeling red paint and rusty hinges flashed through my mind. I felt drawn in that direction, no longer by curiosity but intuition.

Doing my best not to sound like a herd of buffalo crashing through the dry pine branches that had fallen during winter, I made my way for the little shack on the west bank. Stealth was simply not working out for me. It seemed that I could not take a step without finding a dry, brittle tree branch to snap underfoot.

It would have been nice for the possessed squirrel to scout a better route through the dense brush than I was managing. But the farther I staggered, the more I recognized I probably could fire several gunshots before anyone would notice me. As long as I didn't explode or spontaneously combust, it didn't appear that anyone would pay me any mind.

My natural paranoia eased as I told myself it was late enough that people should have heard or questioned me by now if anyone cared that I was a stranger wandering around the neighborhood. It was as if I were invisible.

The brush suddenly cleared, thanks to a small pier of poured concrete. A narrow channel cut through the concrete, connecting a small stream to this new pond.

It was a big body of water, for sure. I had no idea how deep it was, but it appeared to be about three hundred yards long and maybe one hundred fifty to one hundred seventy five yards across at the widest point. There were houses behind me on the south end of the lake and houses to the east. Only the lone shed stood to the west and nothing but woods were visible from the far side of the shed to the northern tip of the pond. It was a little difficult to see much that far away, but a house is kind of hard to miss.

A swarm of mosquitoes followed me to the shed, which I gave a cursory look. It appeared to have once housed a device akin to a bilge pump. There were giant tubes leading to dark recesses underground. I envisioned something creepy jumping out in surprise if I flashed my keychain flashlight in there. I exercised discretion and chose to move on. The clearing beyond the shed intrigued me more.

A larger building almost completely obscured by the woods stood only about fifty yards off to the left. Based on its relative distance from the clubhouse and the apparent proximity of several holes on the golf course, I deduced it must be an old greens keeper's building where the lawnmowers were once kept and maintained. Sure enough, as I approached I could see the shell of a rusted out mower, the engine stripped long ago. The door to the building had signs posted that warned against trespassing, the first such warning I'd seen since beginning my trek. I had broken that law routinely all morning, so I ignored the sign. I entered the large steel building cautiously given the decay of everything else I'd seen.

The interior was dark. I switched on the small flashlight on my keychain and shone the beam around, not really knowing what I was looking for but searching the building nonetheless. I crossed what looked like an old maintenance bay to a set of doors. They were both locked. Tentatively I rapped on each door, knowing it had been months, if not years since anyone had opened them. I heard the rustle of a creature scurrying for cover as something moved behind me.

"Okay folks, next up we have another special guest on our psycho show. Please let's give a warm welcome for Willie the talking rat," I attempted to joke.

That very moment I heard a voice—not with my ears, but inside my head. It clearly said, *not here.*

I looked around quickly as if I expected someone to be there. I knew the words had not been spoken aloud. My heart raced. After a moment to reflect on this feat of communication outside my dreams by my normally silent companion, I vented my frustration.

Aloud, I answered the unknown.

"Very funny. Okay, *mystery man*! Who are you, Driscoll? Speak to me! I've driven 30 miles without a clue about what I'm doing. Why don't we skip the part where you leave me in suspense? Why don't you just tell me why I'm here? Am I looking for something in particular? Am I looking for Peter Driscoll? Is this place connected to the attack on the Nelsons?"

Only the chirp of crickets replied.

"Look, I don't have all day. Let's cut to the chase so I can get on with my life. The mother of my unborn child is in the hospital, and I'm sweating my balls off in a decrepit old building. I've got better things to do. I have a job, a wife, and a whole life that I'm currently ignoring. If I'm not at the hospital, I should be at work—not running around an overgrown old golf course, getting torn up by briars, eaten alive by mosquitoes, and led around by a *frigging squirrel*."

I shined my flashlight on my watch. I said sharply to the empty room, "I need to get back home. It's time I should drop by to see if Peter Driscoll is home. Maybe he can tell me something that will explain why I'm here since you've apparently clammed up again."

My shirt stuck to my skin, damp with sweat. I hoped I wouldn't smell too bad when I introduced myself to Mr. Driscoll. If I still planned to go, it was time to visit him. And that had been the whole reason for my trip.

I retraced my steps toward the entrance to the building. I froze in my tracks as I got near the doorway. In the daylight, I could clearly see my footsteps in the dust. I also saw a second set of footprints leading out of the building toward the water. It was easy to tell them from mine. They were wet.

At that moment, I was sure there really was a body in the pond. That's what had brought me here. All that remained was for me to find it. I left the building and walked to the far side of the shack, drawn as if by a magnet. I looked to the left, and a new feeling of déjà vu overwhelmed me. The submerged body from my nightmare waited nearby.

Very close. I can feel it.

I spotted a clearing. It looked exactly like the place I'd been standing in my dream last night when I saw the murder. In the trees, off in the distance I thought I caught a glimpse of the little old man persistently haunting my dreams, just before he blended into the black brush.

On cue, a small swarm of mosquitoes found me and buzzed around my head, miniature forces of evil trying to drive me in the opposite direction, away from the water. I was truly miserable, but I knew the body was very near. I wasn't completely sure, but it looked like a hand hidden underneath a thick mass of algae.

The rakes for the nearest sand trap were long gone, but I found a long, sturdy pine tree branch with which I managed to stir the algae. The dead hand in my imagination was nothing more than a knot of small branches clustered at the end of a stick.

I sighed aloud in frustration. All I saw was muddy water, swirling in the wake of my stick. I almost threw it away. Then, only a few feet further out, I saw the old man's body floating about a foot under the surface, exactly as I'd seen in my dreams.

I could see him clearly now. The reason the arms seemed to beckon to me was the bloating of gases that tried to force his body to the surface, but apparently his legs were weighted down to prevent that from happening. He stared at me sightlessly through the murky water, the ripples from the wake of my stick making his arms wave wider at me. His dead eyes met mine through the dirty water.

An involuntary scream of terror tried to escape my throat. Fortunately, I couldn't muster more than a squeak. My vocal cords refused to cooperate. Then common sense made me hesitate. The last thing I needed to do was attract attention to myself. What excuse could I possibly give for snooping around so far away from home?

There was no way on earth I intended to go into the pond to retrieve a corpse.

I had spent more than an hour wandering around a golf course, looking for a dead body that I'd only seen in a dream. Someone might have noticed as I drove around exploring. After my experience yesterday, the last thing I wanted to do was to have to explain myself to the cops. They would be most skeptical of my story.

On the other hand, reporting the body was the right thing to do. Anonymously reporting my discovery seemed the most sensible way to handle it.

I found what I came looking for...now what?

How could I report finding his body? I really didn't want to get directly involved. I couldn't just call from a pay phone. Those had become scarce since the advent of the cell phone. I hadn't seen a phone booth in Atlanta for a number of years.

How might I call 9-1-1 and report the body anonymously? Maybe I could find a courtesy phone at the hospital. Maybe write an anonymous letter and mail it?

That would take forever.

It's time for me to get the hell out of here and go visit my wife.

Before I left, it occurred to me that I ought to make it as easy as possible for the cops to find the body. I backtracked to the shed, where I remembered seeing something I suspected might be a long abandoned flagstick. Sure enough, it even sported an old dirty flag. I hurried back to the bank nearest the body and drove the stick into the ground, making sure it stayed upright.

Feeling inexplicably guilty for leaving the drowned man, I avoided looking at his face again and whispered in his direction, "I will send someone for you. I found you. You can leave me alone now."

The cops would find the body rather easily with that marker left for them. I was ready to get out of there and go home, or at least to the hospital to see Beth.

But I'm only a couple of blocks from Driscoll's house. I was too close not to drive by and see if I could confirm the identity of the man in the water.

I was pretty sure it was Driscoll. His house appeared to have been well kept, but his grass was beginning to look overgrown. Several newspapers lay untouched in the driveway. I pulled a blank envelope from my glove compartment and held it out prominently while I snatched open his mailbox to take a quick look inside. I pretended to wedge my blank envelope in with his mail, but truthfully, the box was crammed full. I accepted what I already knew. The body in the lake was Peter Driscoll.

Now I just needed to figure out who killed him, and why.

CHAPTER 26

As I sat in my car, parked in Driscoll's driveway, my cell phone rang.

I looked at the caller ID. I didn't recognize the number, but could tell the call originated from Illinois. It had to be my brother, Kevin. He must be calling from home. It was too early for him to be at the office. I don't call him at home. Only his cell phone number is programmed into mine. Kevin's wife and I don't get along very well. It was awfully early in the morning for Kevin, an hour behind me, in a different time zone.

While my phone continued to ring, I shifted into reverse and backed out of the driveway. I just wanted to keep on the move in case I decided to answer the phone. I didn't want to answer the call, thinking about what to say. Mom probably thought I sounded crazy, so she had called Kevin to get his opinion. She must have woken him up, got him irritated, and motivated him to call me. Between talking to Mom and taking Kevin's call, I had discovered a dead body.

So I felt vindicated, up to a point.

But I had already made the decision not to get involved. I wanted to call the cops and give them an anonymous tip, not jump into the middle of a murder investigation with both feet. It was a pretty safe bet that detectives would be swarming all over Hidden Hills once I provided the cops with specific directions on where to find Driscoll's body. Still, the cops would want to talk to me for hours, and all I would be able to say is the location of his body came to me in a dream. Hell, I wouldn't believe me, either.

Telling Kevin about my discovery was out of the question, especially if I had no intention of getting involved. Why should I? I didn't really know anything except where to find the body, and I certainly couldn't explain how I came about that knowledge. Nobody in his right, or highly analytical mind, would believe me, and that especially meant Kevin.

My older brother Kevin is the primary reason that I don't believe in God. He has always intimidated me. When he stopped believing, I stopped believing in short order. It only took his ridiculing me a couple of times when I was still young and vulnerable. After college, it was easy enough to become comfortable with my non-belief.

Right before the call transferred to voice mail, I broke down and answered my phone. "Kevin! How's it going? Give me three guesses why you're calling. I won't need the first two."

"Hey, Dan. Yeah, I just got off the phone with Mom."

"Terrific. I'm sorry, Kevin. She shouldn't have bothered you."

"From what little she told me, maybe she should have. She said that you blacked out behind the wheel while you were driving. Mom has been known to exaggerate a bit, but not that much. If true, that is not good, my younger sibling. So why don't you give me your version of events? I know your wife is expecting and you are probably under a great deal of stress. Is work okay? Did you have anything to drink before the blackout? Did you feel faint right before it happened? Were you in an accident?"

"That was at least five of your allotted twenty questions, Dr. Freud. I'm already feeling better, simply because you called."

Sarcasm aside, I sighed as I thought about telling him at least part of the truth. Mom had put him up to calling me, and he was on the phone. I was going to have to tell him something to get him off my back now so I might as well tell him everything except about finding a real, honest-to-God dead body.

Who knows? Maybe he will decipher something in the dreams that I missed. I could use some fresh clues. No need to tell him his little brother has turned into a damned psychic.

Kevin was a psychiatrist, a well-respected doctor. He was also a bit of a pretentious know-it-all. After meeting a couple of his professional friends when we visited Chicago to watch Kevin receive a prestigious award, I figured that he was more the rule than the exception.

Like most doctors, Kevin believed his opinion mattered most, his judgment the last to come under scrutiny. It had always been tough being his little brother, even before he became the big city doctor of world renown, his career on the rise after several well-received publications of books and articles lauded by his peers.

He became the doctor in the family. By comparison, I was a lowly software developer with a bachelor's degree. I didn't even bother to get my master's degree. Our parents had already put both of us through college, Kevin all the way to his doctorate. Sure, he won scholarships and received grants that paid for most of his advanced education, but they didn't cover his room and board. The year Kevin spent in England on scholarship to Oxford might have encouraged my father to work himself into an early grave, if my shenanigans had not.

I wasn't about to have my mother spend the money she had inherited upon his death on education beyond my undergraduate degree. I could always foot my own way if I wanted a Master's degree or decided I needed it to advance at work. I worried about a lot of things, but my ability to do my job wasn't one of them.

"No, I didn't have an accident or anything like that," I finally said into Kevin's waiting silence. "Beth was taken to the hospital by ambulance. After she was admitted, I went home. Or at least, I went on my way home, but for some reason, I took a detour. I remember driving down the road, and it was like I blinked and the next thing I knew, the car was parked in a strange neighborhood in front of a house where it looked like something bad might have happened. You know, there was crime scene tape all over the place, but I didn't recognize the house. I didn't remember driving there or stopping. It's like somebody snapped his fingers and I came out of my trance. There wasn't anything wrong with the car. It started right back up. I checked the tires, nothing."

"Very strange," Kevin murmured. He didn't bother to couch or sugar coat his professional opinion when speaking to me. "Have you taken any prescriptions or over-the-counter medicines that you aren't accustomed to using?"

"No, nothing. Not even an aspirin. Allergy season hasn't even started yet. I've been getting exercise regularly, and I'm not drinking much. More accurately, I've had almost no alcohol at all since Beth got pregnant. I don't think it's fair for me to drink in front of her when she won't even take a sip of wine while she's carrying the baby. I think she's even switched to grape juice at communion instead of that thimble-full of wine they offer."

"Are you going to church with her?" Kevin asked. Neither of us was too big on religion. We'd had enough obligatory attendance when we were kids.

"I've been a few times. It makes Beth happy when I go through the motions." I felt that defensive edge creeping into my mind, sure the ridicule was about to come.

"It won't hurt you." Kevin surprised me by saying. He sounded sincere. But I remained suspicious, anticipating the trap.

"A vivid imagination has never hurt anybody."

"Cute. Dan, I'm serious. Maybe you should offer to buy lunch for the pastor of the church where she goes. He can probably give you some pretty good counseling for less than twenty bucks, depending on where you take him to eat."

"Look, I don't need some pastor I barely know digging into my life over a sandwich while I'm trying to enjoy my meal. All of this crap started…" I stopped myself.

"Started when? What aren't you telling me?" Kevin demanded.

"The past couple of days have been an anomaly. It started Wednesday at lunch. I got a spot on my tie. I stopped by a thrift store and bought a cheap replacement. When I put that tie around my neck, I had this weird vision, or hallucination. It was…very *violent*. Sickening, really. It was like I'd watched some terrible, brutal horror movie and forgotten it, but then it replayed in my mind for some reason—when I put on this tie. Every time I touched the damned thing, I had another vision. I had to use a pair of chopsticks to get it off my neck."

Kevin didn't say a word. It was the worst thing he could have said. Nothing.

I described the vivid dream sequences of Wednesday and Thursday night. Kevin's silence made me wonder if he'd dropped off the line.

"Beyond that, it's just been some flashbacks and odd coincidences," I finished lamely. I knew I had better stop before I blabbered on about my conversations with the police, Sister Anita, or the voice in my head.

I heard him sigh.

No matter how hard I tried to modulate my voice, the next words from my mouth sounded shrill and defensive. "Look, I'm not suffering from some sort of nervous breakdown, okay? It was an aberration. Today I've been fine, back to normal," I lied.

Kevin finally spoke. His voice was tight and measured. Now he was stressed. I could tell my outburst really worried him. "I'm going to check my calendar. I haven't taken any time off recently, nor have I been down to Atlanta in a while. Could you look into hotels that are near you? I don't want to impose, but I'd like to come and see both you and your lovely bride. She should know your whole family is concerned for her well-being and wishes her a speedy recovery."

"Cut the crap, Kevin. You don't want to come to Atlanta all of a sudden. You don't have a spontaneous bone in your body. You're trying to diagnose me over the phone, and since you can't, you've decided to come shrink my head in person. Thanks, but no thanks. I've got enough going on as it is without entertaining company. If I'm still having issues in another day or two, then we'll talk about it."

Kevin said, "I'm just worried about you, little brother. I'm coming down to talk some sense into you. You're worried about your family, but maybe you should worry about yourself."

"What are you talking about?"

"About getting these procedures done. You need to have a CAT and probably a PET scan run as soon as possible in order to rule out blastomas as a potential explanation for these sudden hallucinations. What you're describing is not normal, Dan."

"Damn it, I had a waking nightmare; it's not a brain tumor. I'm hanging up the phone now. By the way, Freud wasn't worthy of shining Carl Jung's shoes," I taunted.

"Look, if you think it was just some sort of bad dream or a nightmare, why don't you talk with a friend of mine who might be able to interpret it for you?"

Suddenly, I found myself sorely tempted to spill the beans and tell Kevin about the body I had found. An idea popped into my head. "Let me ask you a hypothetical question. What if I find out that these dreams are based on some psychic connection? What if I find out that something really bad happened — should I pretend it's just a figment of my imagination, or call the police?"

My older brother wasn't joking in the least when he said, "If you find out that your dreams reveal details of actual murders and those details turn out to be true, don't bother calling the cops. Call and get yourself the best lawyer money can buy."

That settled that question in my mind. "Kevin, I don't want to get my head shrunk by one of your buddies, okay? I don't have a freaking brain tumor, for God's sake. I'm not crazy, and there's no subliminal message or symbolism to translate. My wife is pregnant and in the hospital. I had a couple of bad dreams. That's about all there is to it. So just give it a rest. Don't call any of your buddies to do a number on my head, and everything will get back to normal. Let's not overreact just because Mom said jump, okay? We're both grown men, perfectly capable of thinking for ourselves."

Kevin didn't respond right away. I realized my voice had become increasingly shrill the longer the argument continued. My older brother still intimidated me to some degree, even after all these years. His intimidating older-brother presence only increased my irritation with the intrusion into my personal affairs. I should never have said anything to my mother. Even though she meant well, her concerns were unfounded.

I softened my tone a bit. "Hey, I'm sorry for getting a little worked up about it, but between work and now Beth...you know, it's been a tough couple of days. Let's not jump the gun on diagnosing my visions. I just don't think it's that important in the big scheme of things. If I have another episode, you'll be the first to know. I promise I'll call you. But right now I've gotta go or I'll be late for work. Bye."

Angrily, I thumbed the button to disconnect the call. I didn't give him a chance to get another word in edgewise. That had been a childish way to end the conversation, and not one to set my brother's mind at ease.

I don't have a frigging tumor, I fumed. I don't even have a headache.

At least, I hadn't had one *before* speaking with Kevin.

CHAPTER 27

Peter Driscoll's bloated face floating underwater haunted me all the way home.

I nearly rear-ended the vehicle in front of me more than once as my mind reconstructed the image of his floating arms beckoning to me.

I am way too squeamish for detective work.

I wondered about Driscoll's family, and if he had any. They would want closure. It appeared he lived alone, but he could have children living elsewhere. It might take another couple of days for the postman to deliver the letter if that's how I chose to notify the police. I couldn't leave him alone there for days.

How can I explain finding the body without becoming the primary suspect?

I remembered reading stories about detectives using psychics to help them solve difficult cases, but I was not a willing psychic. I was a reluctant, coerced witness following a not-so-anonymous tip from an invisible friend. A sense of duty compelled me to keep following the clues to stop his killer. I didn't ask for any of this. He had dragged me into some serious shit, but he couldn't have made the connection with me unless Sister Anita was right. I was a psychic satellite dish, tuned in to the gruesome story Driscoll needed to tell.

The next step in wrapping this up was phoning in the body. An idea popped into my head. The police didn't perform traces or track numbers for non-emergency calls to the main switchboard. How about if I just looked up the main number for the local Stone Mountain police precinct and called them directly? If I waited and called from the hospital, going through their switchboard to make an outbound local call, even with caller ID, the cops would have hundreds of potential individuals at the hospital that could have provided the tip.

I probed my idea for weaknesses. It felt like a plan that might work. To execute it, I only had to survive another ten miles of bumper-to-bumper traffic across suburban Atlanta to get home, grab a quick shower, then find a way to call the Stone Mountain police from the hospital without getting caught. I focused my attention on driving.

The only way to get off the roller coaster was to wait to the end of the ride.

# # #

I stopped by my office before heading to the hospital, just long enough to make a cameo appearance that would satisfy my boss. Keeping my job was still important to me. Richard offered to let me use more flextime, but I asked permission to claim Monday as one of my floating holidays, and he acquiesced. The patch would be released on Monday, but I anticipated Beth would be coming home by then, and I wanted to be with her when she first got back.

My efficient production of the new patch pleased Richard, especially since Tiffany's minions had not been able to break it. He remained happy with my work, so I would remain employed for the foreseeable future. Richard reminded me that it was almost time for my annual performance review. He asked me to compile a list of major accomplishments over the past year to help remind him of all my good work, essentially asking me to sing my own praises. I promised to work on it first thing Tuesday morning.

Next, I made my obligatory stop by Tiffany's desk to say hello, and goodbye until Tuesday. I gave her an update on Beth's condition because she'd never forgive me for not telling her at the first opportunity. The fact I'd only told my own mother an hour or so earlier would not have bought me the least bit of leniency. When she wasn't busy playing the part of mother hen, Tiffany filled the role of the fiercely protective sister I never had. She cajoled Beth's room number out of me, expecting to be treated no differently than my intimate family.

"Dan, I'm not kidding around. I'm sorry to be so blunt, but you look terrible. Is there anything I can do to help? I'm really worried about you."

"Just think happy thoughts and send them my way. Things will get better soon. They have to, I think. I just need a good night's sleep. When Beth comes home from the hospital, I'm sure I'll sleep better," I placated her so she would let me leave.

"Why don't you see if they'll let you sleep on a cot in the hospital?"

"I'll ask." Actually, I wouldn't. Once I called the police and reported finding the body, I suspected my nightmares would end.

"Well, I don't know if I can get by the hospital after work today. If not, I'll come see Beth tomorrow. You have my cell phone number, don't you? Call me if anything changes."

# # #

Beth looked a lot better after a second decent night of rest and rehydration. She greeted me with a big smile. It quickly turned into a frown. "What happened to you?" she asked.

Confused, I shrugged. "Nothing. What do you mean?"

"How did you get those scratches on your face and neck?"

A mirror hung above a small sink outside the bathroom. I glanced at my reflection and inspected the damage. "Oh, that. I went for a walk around the neighborhood last night and some kids were playing ball. They lost it in some briars. I heard them arguing about how to get it back, so I gave them a hand and fetched it for them."

The lie seemed okay when it formed in my mind a split second before it passed so easily through my lips. My jaws clenched shut to prevent further words.

What if she asked which house? She knew I didn't normally go for walks around the neighborhood by myself like that.

But Beth didn't challenge me. "You're such a good man! What a nice thing to do."

238

Then why do I feel like dirt for lying to you?

I sat beside her on the bed, avoiding the web of tubes and equipment. She buried her face on my shoulder. I kissed the top of her head, my lips lingering on her soft blonde hair. I breathed in the familiar smell of lavender. It was Beth's scent. The ache in my shoulders eased. We sat holding each other for a while, not talking, just enjoying the closeness of each other. Eventually she lifted her head and touched her lips to mine gently.

A fierce need to protect her welled in me, a determination she would never experience any of the violence I had witnessed these past few days. I could never let that kind of evil touch her or our child. I returned her kiss firmly, possessively. When a buzzer on one of the machines interrupted us seconds later, we were both breathing heavily.

"If that is what I have to look forward to when I come home, Daniel, they will be hard pressed to keep me here much longer," she teased, a smile spreading across her beautiful face. "The doctor says I need to gain three more pounds, and we can return to the privacy of our own home."

"Well, you're not going to do that by eating hospital food."

"It's funny you would say that. I have a craving…"

"Great!" I answered.

She looked at me expectantly. "Well…feed me!"

"Of course, dear. What would you like?"

Ah, pregnancy food cravings. It had been so long since Beth had any real sort of appetite, I'd forgotten what I had been missing. I'd heard the "pickles and ice cream" jokes, but Beth had stuck to her bland food diet since she'd been struggling with the sickness. Apparently, the medicine added to her IV fluids was doing the trick.

The next stop in my future — or stops I should say — would be grocery stores. I agreed to undertake a quest for raisin bars, whatever the hell those were. Beth tried to describe them to me before I went looking for them.

"Oh, like Fig Newtons! No problem," I said.

"They're raisin, not fig. They're longer than Fig Newtons, and thinner. My best guess is that you'll find them on the cookie aisle."

The grocery store closest to the hospital had raisin cookies that sort of fit her description. *Piece of cake*, I thought.

However, when I returned to Beth's room, disappointment was written all over her face. "But they're raisin cookies," I protested. "That's what you said you wanted."

"Yes, they are raisin cookies. But see? These have icing on them. The crackers I'm trying to describe have a soft cracker exterior that's light brown, sort of like a Fig Newton. But they are long and thin, not short and fat like Fig Newtons."

"All right," I said, matching her disappointment. "I'll keep looking until I find whatever it is that you are describing."

"Thanks, sweetheart," Beth stopped me as I headed toward the door. "Dan? One more thing."

"Yes, dear?" I asked, suppressing any trace of frustration in my voice. If anyone deserved a little special treatment right now, it was Beth.

"Since you are going to the grocery store for me, will you bring back a bag of pork rinds?"

Cringing at the thought, I promised I would. *What in the hell are pork rinds?*

Ah, the things you do for love.

CHAPTER 28

Kevin Harper rapped on the open door several times as he stuck his head inside Dr. Allison Reese's office and asked, "Got a minute? Can I buy you a cup of coffee while I pick your brain about something?"

She looked at him skeptically, and then thought, *what the hell. I wouldn't mind getting my daily Starbucks fix for free.* The amenities downstairs weren't bad at all. It was one of the perks of working at the teaching hospital for a major university.

"Sure," she said. "Let me grab my purse."

As they walked toward the cafeteria she asked, "What can I do for you?" She smiled nervously. Kevin Harper's stature in the department now surpassed her own. Whether he intended it, asking for her opinion was flattering, but not without pressure. "I'm assuming we are having a hypothetical discussion, or is this about specific symptoms of an actual patient who shall remain anonymous? Would you rather wait to get started until we're both sitting down?"

"Oh, no, it's not that big of a deal. I'm not taking notes. I have a few questions about one of your specialties: dream interpretation. Actually, I'd like to pick your brain about a patient of mine presenting some interesting, um, symptoms." He paused, then lied, "We've done a CAT scan and found no tumors or abnormalities in the brain to explain the strange behavior he has been exhibiting. He reports having a recurring dream where he wakes up to find he's been sleeping in a strange house, with an intruder lurking at the foot of his bed. There's a chase, dead bodies, vivid nightmares of mutilated bodies and faceless women…"

"Recurrent nightmares?" Dr. Reese sounded a little surprised.

Kevin sighed and then added, "There is no history of substance abuse, no illegal drug use, so no easy explanation involving psychotropic drug ingestion. The patient is hallucinating freely without any physiological or pharmaceutical justification. If it were a tumor, I'd prescribe steroids to shrink it and have the surgeons try to cut it all out. If the cause were determined to be illicit drug use, I'd suggest to the family they pack him off to rehab. The tox screen was negative, but I suppose it could always be a rare form of hallucinogen. Maybe even one the patient didn't realize he ingested. But what if it is none of the above? What other options are plausible?"

She slipped habitually into lecture mode. "Dreams are the vehicles by which our subconscious minds communicate with our conscious minds. They contain messages that reveal the inner secrets we keep from ourselves. Repetitive dreams force you to pay attention, to confront the underlying issues serving as catalyst. The fact the recurring dreams are frightening or nightmarish in nature simply reinforces the idea that the unresolved problem inspiring the dream continues to be an issue. It is nothing more than the mechanism by which the subconscious mind demands we pay attention and confront the problem."

"Any suggestions?"

"Recommend that your patient record the details of each dream. Look for variations, and especially the introduction of new symbols, as keys or triggers to unravel the mystery of the message involved. Also, look for patterns by comparing events that occur during waking hours relative to the timing of new nightmares. Does the patient experience a nightmare every night?"

Kevin could tell; the hook was set.

"Tell me more. What are these other symptoms to which you are referring?" Reese asked. Harper's description of the problem patient intrigued her. "Are these waking hallucinations, or nightmares occurring within a dream state? You said the dream is recurring and that it involves waking up inside the dream?"

"Both. My patient is upset because the dream, which repeats frequently, started suddenly without warning or explanation and it is really interfering with his ability to sleep. He's struggling to maintain his productivity at work," he said, embellishing the tale a little as he went along.

"Recurring dreams are quite common. Is your patient going through any sort of a transitional phase in his life?"

"I believe he said his wife is expecting their first child."

Reese smiled. "That would certainly qualify as a stress inducing life event. What are some of the details in this dream, pray tell?"

"Brutal violence, for one thing," Kevin said.

"Sadism suggests repressed anger, often stemming from childhood incidents. Where does this violence take place? In a familiar setting?"

"My patient mentioned being on sand or sandy ground."

"Was it a beach? Were there sand dunes, or a sand castle? Beaches are near salt water, which represents tears and suffering, or a form of emotional outburst."

"Interesting," Kevin observed. "I didn't realize sand was so significant."

"Sand dunes signify a desire for the dreamer to be sheltered from reality. Sand castles are psychological constructions within the mind reflecting delusions of grandeur."

That made Kevin chuckle. Reese got a little defensive, adding, "Sand usually represents changes in latitudes or attitudes. Sorry for the lame attempt at a Jimmy Buffett line. Seriously, sand suggests the dreamer is spinning wheels, wasting time. Think of the expression, the sands of time. It relates to wasting time, or letting time pass you by. Perhaps your patient is frustrated with lack of advancement in job opportunities. Was the sand wet?"

"He didn't say. He mentioned sand, but not water. Why do you ask?"

"Wet sand indicates a lack of balance in the life of the dreamer. If it turns out the sand was in a sand box, that's a completely different story. It usually means the dreamer is taking some situation too seriously."

"Fascinating," Kevin smiled to himself. She now cared about his problem, and she didn't even know it related to his own brother. He had successfully shielded himself from Dan's craziness. He looked around the cafeteria. "There aren't many tables available. Why don't you grab that one in the corner, to give us a little privacy while I bore you with the details? How do you like your mocha?"

"Make mine a skinny mocha. Peppermint, please."

A few minutes later, Kevin joined her at the table, placing her cup in front of her as he sat across the table. "So, here's the deal," he began. "The patient does not display any obvious symptoms or neuroses during waking hours. Except over time, sleep deprivation is beginning to cause some physical distress. The patient is reporting persistent nightmares that, ah, he insists have some psychological connection to an unknown reality."

"Well, you know, I've dabbled more than a bit in dream analysis," Reese said. "But without speaking with your patient and being able to put the symbols into proper context, this will only serve as a guideline, not an interpretation meant to be taken literally."

Of course, Kevin knew. That's why he had bought her a Starbucks skinny mocha, a cheap price to pick the brain of the best expert on the subject in the city of Chicago.

"Tell me about your patient's nightmare, what you can remember," Reese prompted.

Kevin had to refrain from snorting indignantly. After all, his memory was virtually eidetic. "Well, let's see. The patient claims that part of the dream is recurring, but new details seem to be added with each iteration. I'll try to differentiate between the repeated and new detail. Agreed?"

He didn't wait for her answer. It was Kevin's turn to slip into lecture mode as he regurgitated every minute detail of Dan's dreams. "My patient consistently claims to dream he awakens in a strange house to find a stranger standing at the foot of his bed. He follows or chases the stranger, depending on your perspective. My patient reports seeing a faceless woman in this strange house who writes a strange note to him that says 'Snake Skull.' I said faceless, but the patient only said she had no mouth. The dream continues. As he chases the mysterious intruder, the landscape changes from the grassy field to a beach scene. As he runs across the sands, suddenly, a woman's arms appear and grab at him, trying to drag him underground. He panics and runs, forgetting the man he's chasing. He finds a man's body floating beneath the surface of a pond or a still body of water. The corpse is staring at him from beneath the surface of the water. Then he wakes up."

"Oh, my," Reese said. "That sounds very stressful. No wonder your patient is losing sleep. Perhaps you could prescribe him a mild sedative. Or maybe something a little stronger. Since we psychologists don't prescribe any medications, your opinion would be the expert one. How much sleep per night does your patient report getting?"

"Four to five hours per night on average," Kevin said a little impatiently. He didn't buy her a cup of coffee to answer a bunch of questions. He wanted to get answers, not give them. "What do you think?"

"Well, the good news is, if we correctly decode the symbols of the dream, the nightmares may come to an end. First, the house represents your patient. The house always represents self. The fact that the house is unfamiliar to him is very interesting, especially if you combine that with the symbol of the faceless woman. If the dream is symbolic in nature, it might mean that your patient is uncomfortable in his own body. Do you know if he has ever expressed any homosexual tendencies?"

Kevin bit his lip to keep from laughing. He could imagine the response that question would elicit from his little brother, especially when he was married and expecting a kid. "He hasn't said anything about it, no. On his patient questionnaire, he listed a spouse with a female name, if that helps."

"Could be latent. He could be suppressing primitive, subconscious urges," Reese offered.

"I'll keep that in mind," Kevin said. "Anything else on decoding the rest of the dream?"

"Oh, goodness, yes. I was just getting started. The fact that aspects of the dream are recurring indicates unresolved issues remain in the patient's personal life. If we can get the patient to understand his dream, it should not recur," she repeated.

I get it. Solve the mystery and the nightmare disappears. Get to the point! Kevin thought to himself. Instead, he smiled and murmured, "Makes sense. Please, continue."

"A house the patient doesn't recognize suggests there is some aspect of his personality with which he can't identify, or something about himself he seeks to learn. The chase aspect of the dream is another interesting symbol. It suggests the patient seeks to assert control over his life. He's following his own past. It would be interesting to know how the patient felt about waking up in a strange house."

"I actually thought to ask," Kevin said. "The patient said he didn't feel safe in the house."

"So, he's uncomfortable in his own skin," Reese reviewed. "He's chasing this stranger and the faceless woman…"

"No, he only chased the man. He saw the woman and she gestured to him, but he wasn't chasing her, too. Do you think it was the same symbol in the woman who grabbed him from underneath the sand?"

"Let's slow down and identify each dream symbol individually, in the order they come in the dream. We begin in the house. A strange house, but it represents the patient himself. Next, we have a laughing trespasser, standing at the foot of his bed. He's a short, older man, perhaps representing the future. Our patient gets out of bed and begins to chase the stranger. He runs through green fields, which symbolize prosperity, and then bogs down in sand, a classic symbol of work stagnation. At this point a woman grabs at our patient from under the sand, correct?" Reese waited for Kevin to nod in agreement. "Does the patient have a female superior or dominant female coworker perhaps impeding his advancement in the workplace? These images do seem to point in one direction, but without the patient here to confirm or deny the analysis, we have no idea if my conjecture as to the meaning of these symbols is correct."

"I am sorry that I don't have detailed notes about the patient with me," Kevin said. "But I do recall the patient and his wife are expecting their first child. Would that affect your analysis?"

"Yes, it would, to some degree. On the other hand, if the patient is suffering from latent homosexual tendencies and suppressing his primal urges, the sexual tension could manifest itself into nightmares, and they might be triggered by traumatic experiences such as the death of a parent or spouse, marriage, divorce, or the birth of a child."

Kevin's mind had begun to wander, dismissing Reese's diagnosis as nothing more than claptrap. He knew his brother far better than she did. Well, technically she didn't even know she was helping him unravel the mystery of his own brother's weird sojourn into the nocturnal realm of fictitious monsters and "the boogeyman." Dan was much too old for this sort of nonsense. The last words Reese muttered resonated around his brain, though. "...or the birth of a child."

Dan's wife was expecting. Of course, he felt tremendous stress! This is simply a psychosomatic trauma Dan induced to justify his irrational fear of fatherhood, or failing to be a good father. If he'd only followed big brother's example and had the vasectomy, this would not have been an issue.

Reese asked, "Do you know if the wife was pregnant when they got married? Perhaps the woman's arms snaring him in the sand relates to how he became married, if he felt trapped into the relationship. It would make some degree of sense."

"No. That's not it. I'm sure of that much. Look, you've been very helpful. Thanks, Allison. I really appreciate your taking time to answer my questions."

She smiled. "No problem, Kevin. I got a free cup of coffee out of the deal."

CHAPTER 29

Under normal circumstances, I would have been tempted to buy a box of Graham crackers, a box of raisins and simply smash the crackers together. If Beth wasn't pregnant and sick, I might even try it. I still needed to report a serious crime to the proper authorities. However, that would be failing my duties as hunter and gatherer, ignoring the eons of primeval instinct bred into my genetic makeup. I should be willing to crawl over broken glass to get her anything she wanted to eat.

Take care of your baby's mama. Preserve your progeny.

Confidence in my ability to carry on my own gene pool dimmed as my second foray to forage for those damned raisin bars failed to produce the desired results. Not only was I unable to find any cookies that matched her description, the stock clerks in every grocery store I scoured couldn't find them either. Not only that, but they weren't sure if they were familiar with any cookies that met my description.

Apparently, I sucked pretty badly at this whole hunter/gatherer thing. Wasn't much of a purchaser, either.

With grim determination, I set out again. This time, I was on a mission to procure raisin bars *and* pork rinds.

Having no luck with the stores closest to my house or the hospital, I drove aimlessly north past Windward Parkway. The windows rolled down and Bob Dylan on the CD player, it was relaxing drive that I was in no hurry to end. Noticing one of the rare independent grocery stores still in business on McGinnis Ferry Road just over the Forsyth County line, I decided it was worth a shot. The IGA symbol on the front door reminded me of the grocery stores that used to dot small towns across the state.

I found the sparse cookie and snack aisle. I startled the young kid stocking the shelves when I raised both my arms over my head in victory and shouted, "Eureka! Victory is mine!" After trying all the big chain grocery stores in John's Creek, Alpharetta, Roswell, and Cumming, I was pretty sure I had found both of my objectives.

The package actually called them raisin biscuits, but they were long, thin, cookies with raisins in between two flat brown wafers. They had to be the right thing, or I would have to give it up. *Yum. Don't those look delicious? She hasn't eaten in months, and this is what she craves?*

Pork rinds looked even less appealing than they had sounded, and apparently they came in a variety of flavors, just like potato chips. I settled on the plain variety and headed to the counter with my bounty.

On the way up to the register, much to my surprise, I noticed a pay phone on the wall by the entrance to the restrooms.

This would be better than calling from the hospital, I thought.

Being a cheapskate, I called information from my cell phone and got the non-emergency listing for the DeKalb police department. I didn't have anything on which to write, so I jotted the number on the inside of my wrist.

I fed the appropriate coins into the phone and dialed the number.

"DeKalb Police Department. How may I route your call?"

I spoke softly, in case the stock boy wandered within earshot. "Um...I'd like to report a dead body."

"Could you repeat that, sir?"

When I didn't answer, the dispatcher prodded, "Who's calling, please?"

"Look, I'd rather not get involved. I was wandering around an old golf course in a subdivision called Hidden Hills. Behind Clearlake Court, there is a big pond. About twenty yards past the old greens keeper's building, about eight feet off shore or so, there's a dead guy in the water. It looks like he might have been weighted down or something. It doesn't look like he fell in by accident, that's for sure. Hidden Hills subdivision, the body is in the pond behind Clearlake Court. There's a flagstick marking the spot nearest the edge of the pond where you can see his body. I'm afraid the people who killed him will come after me if they find out I called the police, so please, catch them soon. This is all I can really tell you. It's all I know."

Well, that isn't exactly true, but let's not split hairs, shall we?

The dispatcher was a professional. He didn't get excited or raise his voice in speaking with me. "Sir, if I could just get a little more information…"

I slammed down the receiver before the voice on the phone could ask any more questions and wiped the sweat from my palm on my pants leg. The phone began to ring as I retrieved my items for purchase and hurried to the checkout line.

"Did you find everything you needed, Mr. Harper?" the cashier asked.

"*What*? What did you just ask me? How did you know my name?" I demanded.

The young girl snapped her gum as she gave me her best bored stare. "What are you talking about, mister? How would I know your name?" she asked. "I've never even laid eyes on you before in my life."

Nice trick, I thought silently. "I'm really sorry. I thought I heard you say my name."

The cashier just shook her head in bewilderment and tried to blow a bubble, but a hole popped in her gum and she ended up sticking out her tongue at me. She wasn't the only one worried about me. I was worried about me. By now, I should know better than ignore any supernatural sign.

My receipt read, *Have a nice day. You're not done yet.*

I was sure my receipt was the only one the cash register had printed that day with the taunting postscript.

How can I have a nice day if you are going to keep bugging me unless I help you catch a serial killer?

I returned to the hospital with my spoils, hoping to win my love's approval.

# # #

Beth was ecstatic. Two-for-two. The pork rinds were a bases-clearing double, and the raisin bars a grand slam home run. All hail the conquering hero, master of raisin and pork delights. Before I left the hospital, I remembered my ALTA match was tomorrow morning and reminded Beth that I was still scheduled to play.

"Shouldn't I ask Steve to get a substitute for me?" I asked.

I think Beth wanted to say yes but didn't want me to miss playing since it does help me keep in shape. Sitting in front a computer all day at work, we both knew the exercise was important. So she encouraged, "Go ahead and play your match. You already told me that the team is shorthanded this week because of Easter. I'll be here when you're done."

"I'll go shower right after my match and come straight here afterward," I said. "I don't want to be all sweaty when I visit and gross out the rest of the hospital. But I'll tell the guys that I can't hang around and watch the later matches. As long as I bring the beer, they won't care. Actually, their attitude will be...more for us. By the way, Tiff said she wants to stop by after work today or tomorrow."

"Let me say thanks for showering before you come, on behalf of me and the entire hospital staff," she laughed. "I'll be glad to see Tiffany, of course. But why do you have to leave so early today?"

"I offered to help at the thrift store so I can get first crack at the best infant merchandise as it comes in the store. I'm building a clothes rack for them in the old projection area upstairs. They have a lot of floor space but need to use the storage areas better. It's just a couple of hours of sweat equity, so we get first dibs on the good stuff at the store."

"That's why I keep you around," Beth laughed. "You're so good with a hammer and nail. And clever, to boot."

It was sort of an inside joke. When we first met, I never hesitated to call in the apartment handyman to do many things it turned out I was perfectly capable of doing myself, once Beth goaded me into making an effort. Over the past year, I'd gotten rather handy with my growing collection of hand tools and power equipment. I now actually enjoyed receiving a Home Depot gift card.

But it had not always been this way. Remembering a favorite line from a movie we both liked, I gave her my best Jack Nicholson impression, "I love you. You make me want to be a better man."

"I love you, too. Don't forget to wear your goggles," Beth pragmatically reminded me.

# # #

I set the guide on my table saw and ran several two by fours through, making a sizeable stack of material. I cut an equal number of pressure treated boards and nailed them to the floor, then cut a second batch to shoot into the wall. My old-fashioned nail gun used gunpowder to literally shoot a single nail at a time into the concrete with terrific force. For this kind of job, it worked better than the newer models.

After each shot, the spent shell cartridge would automatically eject when I opened the breech, flying out to litter the floor of the dimly lit room. I hated leaving litter behind, but I had to be able to see the litter before I could pick it up. It was still dim and musty up there.

Every three feet along the floor, I set a pressure-treated stud base. After the first few shots, I heard footsteps running up the stairs. Chuck burst into the room, an alarmed look on his face. "Is everything okay?" he asked. "I thought I heard gunshots."

Already in the process of reloading, I laughed and held up the unused powder pellet. "You did hear gunshots. But my gun fires nails, not bullets."

While Chuck watched, I jammed the head of the nail into the barrel, pressed the apparatus against the piece of wood on the floor and pulled the trigger. The nail drove through the wood into the poured concrete floor, holding fast. "Try to wiggle it now," I challenged.

Chuck squatted down beside me and tried to move the wood. "Not bad," he said. "But how does this become part of my new clothes rack? Why are you nailing wood to the floor?"

"I'll show you," I answered. "Hand me that long level, please."

I stood the level upright and made sure the bubble indicated it was square. I took a foot long piece of wood and shot two more nails through it into the cinder block wall. Then I screwed in a second piece to form an "L". For extra stability, I screwed a prefabricated steel bracket designed to strengthen the joint. Using my compressor nail gun, I attached a two-by-four to the side of the base plate and the piece of wood protruding from the wall. I bored a one-inch hole about a foot down from where it attached at the top. When I repeated the design three feet down the wall, I could run a length of my galvanized pipe through. I grabbed the pole with both hands and lifted my feet off the floor. The pipe didn't even flex.

"Hey, that's pretty good," Chuck said. "How much weight will the rack hold?"

"If you're just hanging clothes, I think it will hold as much as you can squeeze on the rod. There's no real danger of the rack pulling away from the wall because the weight is really distributed on these upright two-by-fours here." I tapped the boards with my knuckles, quite satisfied with my engineering. "Knock on wood."

"I really like what you're doing, Dan. How soon can you be finished? I'm hoping we can use this soon. Like later today."

I couldn't help but laugh. "You hate being pushy, but it doesn't stop you, huh?"

Chuck laughed, too. "I can't help myself." Exaggerating his voice for dramatic effect, he continued, "Somebody, please help me!"

The words were barely out of his mouth when an open box of donated items fell from its perch with a loud clatter. A tennis ball bounced out of the box and slowly rolled to a stop between his feet. Chuck looked down and laughed again, but this time there was no mirth in the sound.

"Creepy," he said after a long look my way. "Glad it's you working up here by yourself and not me."

As I listened to the sound of his footsteps retreating downstairs, I thought to myself, *keep busy. The sooner you're done, the sooner you can get out of here.*

CHAPTER 30

Sam Leman was planting flowers by his mailbox when I pulled into my driveway and stopped to check the mail. I waved with the hand holding the day's quota of bills and junk mail. One of the envelopes slipped through my fingers. I bent to pick it up, and on the way back up, saw him approaching.

"Hi, Sam," I said. "That salvia will look great in full bloom. Hey, I've got your dish in the dishwasher. If you hang around for a second, I'll grab it and bring it right out to you."

"No worries, no hurry," he said. "Actually, I was coming over to invite you for dinner."

"I wouldn't think of imposing on you two nights in a row. Thank you so much for the offer. When Beth comes home and is feeling better, we'll have to reciprocate and have you over for a cookout or something."

Sam began to protest, but I cut him off.

"Okay, if you insist, but my wife won't believe that I tried very hard. Why don't you at least come over so that I can introduce you?"

"Sure. Let me pull the car in the garage, and I'll follow you over." Socializing was the last thing I wanted to do tonight, but I was stuck. After he'd been so considerate I was obligated by the southern code of conduct.

Besides, I liked Sam. The truth was that I wanted to stay home in peace and quiet to do some serious thinking about everything that had happened today. I had a clear indication from the message on the sales receipt that the recent but constant turmoil in my life was not over yet.

You're not done yet. What did that mean? I reported the body. What else could there be?

Apparently, I had errands yet to run for Mr. Driscoll. I knew I would never have another decent night's sleep if I didn't keep trying to put the puzzle pieces together.

As we entered Sam's house, my eye was drawn to the grand piano taking up half their living room. He called out, "Barbara, we're back! I brought Dan."

His wife appeared from the direction of their kitchen as she dried her hands on a dishtowel. The enticing smell of dinner followed her through the open door, assaulting my senses and making my mouth water. I started to regret declining Sam's offer.

"Hi, I'm Dan Harper," I said, as we shook hands. Sam's lovely wife, Barbara, smiled shyly.

"Thank you for the wonderful dinner plate you send me last night," I said. "It was very thoughtful."

"I'm so glad you enjoyed it."

Sam ratted me out, frowning as he said, "I invited Daniel to have dinner with us, but he says he can't stay. I guess I should have mentioned that tonight we're having your world-famous chicken and dumplings, with cinnamon apples and broccoli with cheese. How he could turn down such a meal, I'll never know."

Barbara extended her arms toward me and said, "I set the table for three. Please, won't you stay and eat with us, Dan?"

Sam could have warned me. I shot him a withering look. I was roped in to staying for dinner and he knew it as soon as he insisted I come over. The aroma of dinner would weaken even the stiffest resolve. He grinned and winked at me, clearly amused at my predicament.

Barbara's hospitality eroded my determination to get home. Seeing no polite way to excuse myself now, I said, "Barbara, I'd be honored to join you. It smells delicious."

Delighted, she grabbed my hands and assured me, "We're happy to have you. But your wife, tell me, is she better?"

"Yes. She's got to stay in the hospital until she gains a bit more weight. They'll probably keep her at least through the weekend." Wondering if I was repeating myself, I finished the story I'd told so many times in recent days, "She had no measurable body fat when they admitted her, not good for a woman as far into her pregnancy as she is. Her body was digesting muscle to feed the baby."

Serious concern darkened Barbara's face. "Oh, no! That's terrible! The poor thing! And the baby will be all right?"

"Yes, she's eating again and starting to gain weight. She sent me out today to find a few things she is craving. That's a good sign. We were hoping she could come home this weekend, but it looks like she'll be there until Monday or Tuesday. As long as she gains weight, keeps eating, and doesn't get sick anymore, the doctors say both she and the baby will be fine."

"Thank God for such good news! Now, I always cook enough for leftovers. I work from home about half of the time, and it gives me an easy option for lunch. Shall we eat?"

"You never have to ask me twice," Sam said.

# # #

Dinner tasted even better than it smelled. Barbara replenished the food on my plate as soon as I ate it. I would be waddling around the tennis court in the morning if I weren't careful. She waited politely while I dug into my meal, but after a few minutes she restarted our conversation. "So, are you and your wife originally from Atlanta?"

I laughed. "Is anybody who lives here a native? I don't think I've met more than one or two people born in the Atlanta area. We're both from South Georgia. I grew up in Savannah and she was raised in Albany. How about you two?"

Sam interjected, "I'm originally from Nevada. Barbara's a California girl." He reached out to hold her hand resting on the table.

They seemed happy. I wonder how many other couples ever managed to find what Beth and I share.

Barbara smiled and asked, "How did the two of you meet? College sweethearts?"

"No, we went to different schools. I graduated from the University of Georgia and she got her degree from Georgia State. We met here in Atlanta, after we were both working with the same company. She changed jobs after we married, so all our eggs weren't in the same basket, so to speak."

"Love at first sight?"

"More like infatuation at first sight. Of course, Beth hadn't noticed me and at first she wouldn't give me the time of day. She was still getting over her first husband."

"First husband? Oh, she was married before. He left her?" Her blunt question took me aback, but she didn't seem to realize she had danced over the line of propriety. Mildly amused, I imagined how Beth's Southern gentility would flinch at Barbara's direct west coast style.

I saw no harm in answering her, "Not voluntarily. He was killed in combat in Afghanistan about a year before we met. She really wasn't interested in starting a relationship, but my persistence paid off. Actually, I think her former sister-in-law had something to do with her deciding to date again."

"I'm sorry. It was really none of my business. I didn't mean to pry."

"Yes, she did," Sam teased playfully. "But she can't help herself."

I laughed as Barbara blushed. Trying to change the subject, I said, "So, how long have the two of you been married?"

Sam said, "Our seventh anniversary will be this May. Memorial Day."

"How easy to remember can that be? Good thinking, Sam," I looked from one to the other and added, "Given how strong Barbara's maternal instincts seem to be, I'm a little surprised that you two don't have any children. When are you two going to have a baby? Y'all would make great parents."

Barbara made a choking sound. I looked over and saw tears welling in her eyes. *Oh, shit. I said something wrong.* Yep, it was a bad idea to assume lack of children means lack of trying. It was my turn to err on the wrong side of propriety.

Barbara jumped out of her chair, mumbled "Excuse me," and hurried from the table.

"I'm sorry. I didn't mean…"

Sam held up his hand to stop me and said quietly, "We lost a child, our daughter, last year. She was born with a congenital heart defect and would have been five next January. There were other…genetic issues. She wasn't a viable candidate for a transplant. Barbara took the loss exceptionally hard. She stayed home and cared for her. Her boss was great, let her move to fulltime telecommuting. Since Ruthie's death, she's started going into the office part time, just to get out of the house once in a while. Barbara hasn't been willing to have another child yet. Don't worry. Barbara will be all right. She understands. You didn't know."

I shifted uncomfortably in my chair. I still felt like crawling under the table. "I'm so sorry. I had no idea. I didn't mean…"

"How could you know?"

"Well, the evening was perfectly wonderful until I put my foot in my mouth," I said.

"Don't be ridiculous. In fact, I'm glad you brought it up. You are absolutely right. We should have another child. Barbara was a wonderful mother. The doctors said they can do an amniocentesis test and tell us if something is wrong with the baby. There's only one problem with that. I don't think Barbara would be willing to terminate the pregnancy, regardless of the results. She would insist that God's will be done."

"If she wouldn't be willing to take action on the information, why go to the trouble of finding out whether or not the baby has a birth defect? Why bother doing the amniocentesis?"

Sam smiled cryptically. "That's an excellent question."

But he didn't answer it.

"Ssssh. I hear Barbara coming," Sam said.

Barbara emerged from the powder room. She settled back into her seat at the table and said brightly, "Sorry to rush out like that. I had something in my eye. These new contact lenses are giving me fits."

Sam shot me a look that begged me to drop the subject. He said, "Dan, I noticed you unloading a fine looking saw from your trunk. That's a professional grade piece of equipment. Are you into woodworking?"

Thankful for the change of subject, I told Sam about my project at the thrift store. It turned out Sam was good with his hands, even building furniture as a hobby. Our dinner conversation shifted to animated debate over jigsaw brands and trying to outdo each other's story of the time a Dremel bit averted disaster.

After helping Barbara with the dishes, we went down to Sam's workshop area in the partially finished basement. Sam's chest puffed proudly when I let out a long, appreciative whistle.

Impressed and envious of the array of tools Sam had collected, I asked him about some of the specialty woodworking equipment I'd never used before. His current project, a reproduction Victorian hall table, showed the fine skill of a craftsman, an artisan.

Sam could teach me a thing or two, that's for sure. I would love to build a simple piece of furniture, maybe something for the nursery.

But the unsolved puzzle entangling me in a netherworld web would not leave me alone, even here. Leaning casually against a worktable in Sam's shop, my hand rested accidentally on a metal tool behind me. I turned to see what I touched. It was a simple circular handsaw.

The sound of comfortable laughter with my nice, normal, new neighbors faded, replaced by the shrill whir of the saw blade from my vision. Doubting whether I would ever have a normal life again, I shook off the intrusive memory and sighed.

"Sam, you win, hands down. You definitely have better toys." Pointing at the clock hanging on the wall of the workshop, I added, "It's time I headed home. Barbara, thank you again for another wonderful meal.

I look forward to Beth feeling better so I can introduce her to you both. You're been great these past couple of days."

# # #

I opened a can of tuna and fed the cat, who enthusiastically reminded me of that contractual responsibility by attacking my feet.

I poured myself a heavy scotch to sip as I reflected on the day.

I had solved the riddle of why my spirit guide had led me to Hidden Hills—to discover Peter Driscoll's body. At least, that's what I thought for most of the evening. But then an ugly, nagging question began bouncing around my brain and refused to leave.

The corpse in the pond was Driscoll. How was he connected to Nelson?

For the life of me, I couldn't think how they might know each other. Both were old men. Maybe they had known each other years before. Whatever relationship might connect the two men—other than the fact they both seemed to be dead—must either be from the ancient past, or tangential in nature.

Could they have been members of the same organization—Shriners, Freemasons, a group like that? Old army buddies? It wouldn't be a church or something regular where you met every week, I didn't think. Their houses were too far apart. Were they in the military together? Maybe both went to the same high school, decades ago. How could I figure out their connection? What if there wasn't a connection? But if that was the case, how did Nelson and Driscoll both appear in the same nightmare?

I had plenty of questions, but no answers. I also couldn't think of where to start looking for them.

Except the thrift store.

CHAPTER 31

Clayton drove straight through from Biloxi, anxious to get out of Mississippi and back on his home turf. He stopped only for gas, worried the cops would be looking for his car. With the way his luck had gone on this trip, if that bitch Candy managed to survive the housing projects, she would surely have the police looking for him by now.

She must have read his mind and known he was ready to get rid of her ass, once and for all. They weren't out of the Biloxi city limits when she jumped out of the car once Clayton stopped at a traffic light. She ran like hell into a nearby housing project. After the stupid bitch found the debit card he'd kept from one of his adventures, as he liked to call them, she immediately went from being a convenient asset to a major liability. She knew something she shouldn't know.

Clayton was annoyed that she had just enough sense to make her break for it while she had a chance.

She was hurting pretty bad and chose running blindly into a war zone they called a neighborhood to get away from him. He'd been tempted to chase her down, but Candy didn't even know his real name. Unless he let himself get caught on the scene, he could burn his bridge to her without killing her.

He would leave her stupid ass behind and get rid of the card. But first, he'd try using it at that ATM machine outside the bank, now that the housing project was far enough away. Then he needed to get the hell out of Dodge.

When he caught her with the stolen card in her hand, the look in her eyes told him she had put two and two together. She must have recognized the name from newspaper reports. Then again, all she needed to see was that the name Clayton didn't appear anywhere on the card. So she knew something was wrong. Or at least, she suspected something, and that was enough for him.

Clayton had brought the card along in case his cash reserves ran too low. He knew to be careful, not to use the card any place other than an ATM, where he could test the PIN without getting caught. Most people used their birthday for the PIN number of their debit card because it was easiest to remember. If his educated guesses didn't pan out, the worst that could happen was the ATM would eat the card.

It had been the first time he beat the ever-living shit out of Candy and really lost control of his temper. She dared to embarrass him in public. He regained just enough control of his emotions to get her up to the room before he went to work on her. She was lucky that he didn't pummel her face beyond recognition. The hotel staff would recognize the signs of domestic violence and call the cops on him, no question. He grabbed a washcloth and forcibly gagged Candy with it just before smashing his fist into her ribcage.

Clayton worked her ribs over pretty good, stopping after he was sure he'd broken a couple of them. He was satisfied to see tears of pain and terror flooding her eyes. *Serves her right. Women get more docile and submissive after you beat the shit out of them*, Clayton mused.

Candy acted cowed, like a scared little lamb, ready to be slaughtered. She refused to make eye contact, answered him in a meek, submissive voice, and convinced Clayton that she had become putty in his hands.

He grabbed her by the throat and almost choked her to death before he realized he'd have trouble dumping her body if he killed her inside the hotel, so he decided not to strangle her. Not yet. Instead, he planned to dump her somewhere nobody would find her body for a while, out in the middle of nowhere between Biloxi and Atlanta.

He had even gone so far as to entertain the idea of keeping her around for a little while longer, right before the bitch jumped out of the car and ran away. Apparently, she wasn't as dumb as she looked, and made her escape at the first opportunity. *Good riddance. She can't touch me.*

But she anticipated his intent, and escaped while she had a chance.

Oh, well.

# # #

Once he crossed the state line from Alabama into Georgia, Clayton began to relax a little. He'd worried about bruising and the imprint of his fingers around her throat adding credibility to Candy's complaint if she called the police and filed charges. But now she was two states away. If the cops were looking for him, they would have caught up to him on the road. He was home free...except for the cops he saw crawling over his subdivision in full force.

Clayton's pulse quickened as he approached the home stretch. He could see a swarm of cops ahead, and the activity was heavy enough it slowed down traffic ahead, making him wonder if the bitch somehow knew enough about him that she managed to call out the cops after all. He relaxed after he could see it wasn't a roadblock, but rubberneckers slowing down, fascinated by the police activity.

He was certain that Candy didn't know where he lived, and he knew that he had never told her his real last name. He borrowed one from a guy at work. How many men in Atlanta had the first name of Clayton? More than the cops would care about checking, that was for sure. She'd never been to his house in Stone Mountain. Stupid bitch didn't care about him. Even though she was probably still alive—she had been moving pretty good the last time he saw her—if she had called the cops, what could she have told them, once he got out of eyesight?

Nothing. She wasn't smart enough to memorize his tag number. So, the question was what were the cops doing in his neighborhood, fucking up traffic from here halfway to South Hairston?

He struggled to suppress the temptation to break loose to avoid the police activity and keep on the move. He forced himself to concentrate on taking deep breaths, forcing himself to calm down in the face of danger. He didn't feel the normal thrill and rush of adrenaline when he was out on the hunt. Now, he experienced the fear of the hunted. Something felt awfully wrong about the police being there, so close to home. Fortunately, traffic was so bottled up that he had time to recover his composure. He asked himself, *why are the cops here?*

Panic gnawed at him as he remembered the two bodies he hid well enough. He expected them never to be found, unless the golf course reopened one day. The old man in the lake. The woman he strangled, mostly by accident, now chopped up and buried in the fairway sand traps on hole sixteen. All three sand traps, to be specific. He felt a slight twinge of regret, remembering the almost fond feelings he had for her as they made love. It was a pity it got out of hand. The funny thing now was Clayton couldn't even remember her name. But he remembered strangling and dismembering her well enough. If the police found parts of her, they would be crawling all over the neighborhood before you knew it.

Sure enough, the cops cordoned off the cul-de-sac near the pond where the old man slept with the minnows. As Clayton watched from his spot in the traffic jam, paramedics wheeled a cart bearing a body bag toward the back of an ambulance, waiting with the engine running and rear door already open, probably to keep the air conditioning running. He guessed the body had decomposed enough to stink like hell by now, visualizing the bloated stomach puffed out with gases eager to escape the confines of dead intestines.

The mental image of rotted flesh repulsed him. *Why can't they just stay dead?*

CHAPTER 32

My dreams on Good Friday night began pleasantly enough. Hazy dreams of making love enticed me with warm embraces and promises of sexual gratification. In the midst of a fiercely passionate kiss, something about the situation felt very wrong. I abruptly pulled up and looked down in shock to see that I was not making love to Beth, but my good friend and confidante, Tiffany.

As I grappled with the question of how I could let myself cheat on my pregnant wife with a woman who was like a sister to me, my dream went from bad to worse.

I realized the woman wasn't Tiffany, but looked very much like her. She had a small mole on her jaw and was a few years younger than Tiffany, but the resemblance was close enough they could almost pass for twins.

My nameless lover was very pretty, in spite of glistening sweat pasting her hair to her head, apparently from the vigor of our passions. Her face was red and flushed with the passion of physical exertion. We must have been going at it pretty good when I came to my senses.

Things went bad. As her face began to turn beet red and then scarlet, I slowly realized that it was because my hands were locked around her neck with a vise grip. Terror filled her helpless eyes, pleading into mine to stop. I slowly choked the life out of her. Every scrap of free will within my soul rebelled. My hands simply refused to obey, as if they had a mind of their own. She slapped feebly at my arms as her body slowly surrendered to death. Eventually she stopped trying to resist. Her body went limp.

Abruptly I sat up in bed, the horrible dream over. Abby Normal growled, then hunched her back and hissed at the darkness lurking at the foot of my bed, just as she did two nights ago. I wondered what she saw down by where the tie still hung. My eyes adjusted to the darkness, eventually making out a human form hovering at the foot of my bed. The last person on earth or maybe the last person from hell that I expected to see at this point was Driscoll, but there he was, sopping wet, a crooked, apologetic smile on his face.

Seriously? You are here again?

No more chasing after him this time, I decided. The media reports hadn't named Driscoll in the press releases due to pending notification of next of kin, but I knew they had found his body. The evening news led with a flurry of police activity in DeKalb County. I watched long enough to recognize the subdivision, confirming that they had found my marker in Hidden Hills and pulled Driscoll from his watery grave.

I owed him nothing more. I would stay in bed, get some desperately needed rest, and my life would get back to normal.

Driscoll needed to go to the light, rest in peace, or do whatever the hell ghosts are supposed to do once their bodies had been found.

It was time for him to leave me alone.

I closed my eyes, hoping he would go away.

My persistent, diminutive, most unwanted guest persisted, waking me into another nightmare like the ghost of Christmas Past. This time he gently brushed against my foot to wake me up.

I sat up in bed and looked at the clock. Three in the morning? Irritated, I said, "Why can't I get a good night's sleep just this once?"

He smiled apologetically and shook his head. He went to the open doorway of my bedroom and turned to wait for me there. It dawned on me that he had *touched* me, and I had felt it. I reached for the bed covers and sure enough, my hand passed through them as I tried to turn them back and get out of bed. I was in his ethereal realm already. *His world.*

But I wasn't dead. I could clearly see my physical form still lying in bed and hoped the subtle, rhythmic movements meant I was getting some sleep in spite of this.

Oh yeah, you're still alive.

I whipped my head around to stare at my spectral companion. *He could read my mind?* "How can you talk to me without speaking?" I demanded aloud.

Our physical brains and our minds are separable. Some people call it spirit. Others may call it the conscious mind or the soul. Your essence has been temporarily released from your physical flesh. My mortal body and essence have been permanently separated because of my murder. Justice has not been served. In this state, I cannot set things right. Not without your help. Your gift spoke to me when you touched the tie once worn by my murderer. We...connected. It was shown to me that your gift could be used for good. You can help me. If it is your choice.

"I'd like to help, but I have a wife, a job, and a kid on the way. I'm not a cop or detective. I don't even own a gun. I'm a computer programmer, for God's sake! *Why me?*"

Why not you? You have a special gift. When I was alive, I would have never recognized it in you in a million years. But now I haven't got a worry in the world about my job. My life is over. A new journey is about to begin.

Almost comically, his shoulders flexed in a familiar movement. Although he no longer breathed or spoke, my ghost companion still knew how to sigh.

I can see things in a whole new light, you might say. It takes some adjustment to get used to being dead. I'm still kind of new at this myself.

I found myself feeling a bit sorry for my spectral friend. In spite of my frustration at another interrupted night of sleep and reluctance to get directly involved, an odd feeling of pride rose in me. "What specifically is this gift that makes me special?"

I didn't say you were special. I said you'd been given a special gift that you are close to realizing and perhaps utilizing to your full potential. Every human is special. Every human has value. Whether they choose to appreciate their individual gifts and use them to their full potential is a product of free will. A time of new enlightenment or of deeper darkness will soon come. It is your choice to help or not. You can wake up right now, and I will not return to bother you again. But you know what will continue to happen if you do nothing.

"All that is necessary for the triumph of evil is that good men do nothing."

Ah, you know Edmund Burke.

"Actually, there is some dispute about whether Burke actually wrote or said those specific words. A lot of people think…"

In a surprisingly stern and authoritative tone for a voice without sound, my friend interrupted, *We are wasting time, young man. You forget yourself. After visiting the world of the dead, I now know Edmund Burke. You could say I've met what was once the man. Those were his words. Burke also said, "There is nothing that God has judged good for us that He has not given us the means to accomplish, both in the natural and the moral world."*

"Are you saying there is a God?"

We're wasting time we don't have. If we don't hurry, we'll be late.

# # #

I found myself outside my house standing next to him. The waterlogged ghost nodded his head toward the west. I felt sure that some unspeakable horror awaited me there, but I had no choice. I followed, drawn toward my destiny.

I should have guessed that we would be in pursuit of the killer.

"Why can't I see his face?"

You must learn.

"Learn what? Just show me."

Learn patience. Learn to listen to the world around you. Pay attention to the silence. What do you hear?

"I don't hear anything. That's why it's called *silence*. Every morning I wake up more and more tired. Interrupting my sleep every night is beginning to have an adverse effect on my ability to think clearly. I can't believe…"

I stopped talking because my companion was ignoring me. His eyes were closed. He cocked his head, straining to hear something I could not. I followed his example. Closing my eyes, I listened to the silence. And in the quiet, I heard something.

In the distance, a faint *skrrrip* sound drew my attention. A few seconds passed, and then I heard it again. Something was happening off to the west. I turned to my left and started moving toward the sound. A different muffled noise caught my ears next, and my speed increased as I felt drawn toward the source. I flew northwest, several hundred feet above Holcomb Bridge Road in the opposite direction of Stone Mountain. I recognized I-575 as I passed through Woodstock along Highway 92.

While I didn't have to worry about traffic lights or speed limits, I was trying to keep track of where I was going. I knew I would most likely want to find my way back.

# # #

Little River Marina loomed high on the bluff above Lake Allatoona, a scattering of buildings stretching from the waterfront docks up to the summit of a small hill protected from the elements by a thick band of pine trees. A dry dock at least three stories high looked like an ordinary steel building had been sliced in half along the peak of the roof, and then each half shoved about seventy five to a hundred yards apart so the heavy equipment could get in and out, moving boats to and from the water.

Between the massive steel support beams reaching from floor to ceiling, the honeycomb inside looked like a giant shoe rack, but one full of boats instead.

Illuminated by the silver moonlight filtering through the black clouds overhead, the marina was closed for the night. Across Bell's Ferry Road, the Little River Bar and Grill was still alive with drunken patrons. It was a squat building of cinder block construction brightened with colorful pennants flaunting support for the various college football teams of the Southeastern Conference.

I floated over the roof, enthralled by the splendor of the moonlight reflected on the water, illuminating the dark beauty of the little bay behind the canteen. I drifted over the parking lot and looked down. Several cars remained in the lot, but it was late. Activity in the bar was winding down. They were about to close for the night. A slightly drunk patron dropped his car keys and cursed when he accidentally kicked them under his car.

I'm glad I won't be on the road with this idiot, I thought.

I was only vaguely familiar with the area, so the compound behind the grill surprised me. A short dirt road led to a small array of lake cottages that looked like rental properties. At the shoreline, a stationary dock sported a green aluminum roof that gleamed bright in the moonlight. Two covered jet skis were moored to a floating dock attached to the larger stationary dock. Adjacent to the nearest cottage, a pontoon boat sat on a trailer. It was also covered to protect it from the elements.

A spur of the short dirt road led up the hill to a larger house. Instinct told me the rental cottages and all the bells and whistles below belonged to the homeowner of the larger house.

That's where he'll be headed.

I still had no idea who "he" was. How could I stop him? I wasn't even there, really.

The faint tinkle of breaking glass drifted across the inky darkness. I followed the sound. A dark, stout figure slithered across the window frame and dropped inside. I knew the killer was about to make his move, but how could I stop him from within the dream?

I was too late.

Like a spectator to a traffic accident who couldn't bring himself to look away from the gore, I approached the manor house. Suddenly, it burst into flames. In spite of my apparent invincibility in the spirit state in which I traveled, I hesitated to get closer to the fire.

Smoke billowed out the broken window. I floated above the ground and looked through the bedroom window. Two mutilated bodies lay on the floor. Almost as soon as I saw them, both bodies were completely immolated, charred beyond recognition. Obviously, accelerant hastened the inferno. Acrid smoke filled my nostrils. I hadn't expected to be able to experience sensory input like smell. Knowing the odor emanated from the burning bodies of human beings that had been alive only seconds earlier turned my stomach.

The only consolation for me was the knowledge neither body made the least effort to save itself. They were both stone dead before their murderer burned them beyond recognition.

PART FOUR
HOLY SATURDAY

CHAPTER 33

I bolted upright in bed before dawn and immediately snapped out of my nightmare, right into a new one called reality. It was my most vivid dream yet. I should have expected no less. Witness to yet another of the killer's senseless slayings, I recalled enough of the details to know where to find the bodies.

Four a.m. — barely time to confirm the deaths and make it back to pack a cooler and grab my tennis bag before heading to the match. Bitterly, I regretted not asking for a sub today. Tennis had become just another weight around my neck, no longer a pleasure, but an obligation.

I thought again about calling to withdraw from match, but it didn't give Steve much time to find a substitute. It also wasn't fair to Mike, my partner. God, but tennis seemed so trivial now.

But how often does one find dead bodies to report to the police?

My drive out to Lake Allatoona was filled with anticipatory dread. Finding Driscoll's body in the pond was bad enough. The murder scene in last night's vision held gruesome images of charred bodies. I would lay eyes on the ruins, then find another pay phone and call the cops to tell them the killer had struck again.

I hated the idea of "discovering" the burnt house. Perhaps a neighbor had seen the fire and called emergency services. I just wanted to fulfill my obligation and return home, nothing more. I did not intend to poke around the ruins of the house to look for clues as to why the killer picked these two poor people.

Well, based on what I remembered of the house from my dream, maybe *poor* wasn't the right adjective. They lived quite well.

But nobody deserved to die this way. I had driven several miles toward Woodstock and Lake Allatoona in Cherokee County, when it occurred to me that I'd neglected to print a map. I thought about turning around, but the images of familiar landmarks were seared into my memory. I felt sure I could find the house without a map.

The route remained emblazoned in my brain. There weren't that many turns, and I knew the road names. I drove straight to the house.

It showed no signs of fire. *He hasn't killed them yet!*

I pulled my car into their circular driveway, my headlights illuminating windows across the entire side of the house as I approached.

Movement of someone escaping from the house caught my eye. My joy in their survival was short lived; from his familiar form and the speed and animal prowess with which he moved, I thought I recognized the killer. His victims must still be inside.

Puzzled, I tentatively approached the front door. About halfway between my car and the door, the porch light turned on. For a brief second that felt like an eternity, I froze like a deer in headlights before quickly scurrying back to my car. How could I explain my presence there before five a.m.?

Then a sinking feeling stabbed me in the stomach. *Where did the killer go? I'd let him get away.*

I'd had more than my fair share of unpleasant interviews with the police within the last few days to last a lifetime. The last thing on earth I wanted to do was explain trespassing in a stranger's yard, when I should be asleep in my bed.

Then it hit me: *the lights came on.*

The people inside were not dead. They were alive, awake, and alert. The house was not on fire. Their death had not yet happened. A wave of relief swept over me. On my drive home, I allowed myself to feel a sense of accomplishment.

I stopped this one.

# # #

Daniel Harper was being followed, but not by the police. Clayton had watched in amazement when Dan's car pulled up in front of the house, the beams of his headlights narrowly missing him in the pre-dawn light. Clayton retreated immediately to the adjacent boat ramp where his car was hidden in the dark, only intending to make good his escape.

He drove slowly down the road from the lake, headed toward his home in Stone Mountain, but then he recognized the black car as Dan passed him. Realizing a probable stranger, not the police, had foiled his plans, Clayton decided to follow the car to see where it led.

It surprised Clayton to see how far the stranger had driven, just in time to scare him off from his plans to rob and kill the inhabitants. *Was he a relative?*

That didn't really make sense. Whoever was in the car had run away as fast as Clayton had, even passing him on the road. Clayton had to increase his speed to keep the man's vehicle within sight. *Who is this guy? What brought him to the lake? How did he know I was there?*

Clayton believed Daniel's appearance was a sign of bad luck. But now he followed to make sure he knew where bad luck lived.

CHAPTER 34

Grumbles and complaints rumbled around the squad room in a collective murmur. Nobody liked being called in for an all-hands-on-deck meeting over a holiday weekend.

DeKalb County Police Captain Ben Hodges, the highest ranking officer at the meeting, called the detectives to order with a curt, "All right. Shut up, and take your seats. Let's get this show on the road. Let's get one thing straight—I'm no more thrilled to be working a double homicide case this weekend than any of you people are. But that's why we get paid the big bucks."

A couple of guys snickered at the joke, but it wasn't really that funny. The room got quiet. "Okay, what have we got on IDs for the victims? Anything?"

Warren cleared his throat and said, "The ME identified the floater as a resident of the neighborhood, name of Peter Driscoll."

Somebody in back said, "Wasn't doing much floating with those blocks tied to him, was he, Warren? Looked like more of a sinker to me."

Hodges cut off the scattered giggles with an icy glare. "Enough horseshit. Don't interrupt again, unless you've got something *really* important to say." The laughter abruptly stopped.

Warren continued, "Cause of death on the old man, blunt force trauma. ME says the backside of his head was a mess, and there was no water in the lungs, so he was dead before his murderer put him in the pond. No ID on the woman yet. Her fingerprints weren't on file, so she wasn't a pro or at least not one with a record. She wasn't a hooker. We're going through missing persons reports trying to match our Jane Doe, but the ME said our approximate time of death was screwed up because her body was frozen before she was cut up and buried."

"We've got to get an ID on the woman to see why she and Driscoll are both dead, and buried pretty close to each other," Hodges snorted in frustration.

Somebody said, "Technically, Driscoll wasn't buried. Just submerged."

Nobody laughed that time. They could tell Hodges was pissed and trying to place the voice. If he figured out who made that last wisecrack, that guy would be cleaning toilets in the jail for the next month.

Hodges called on Rey Sanchez. "Anything on our tipster?"

Sanchez shook his head sadly. "Nope. Well, at least not much. Anonymous call came from a pay phone in a small grocery store on McGinnis Ferry in south Forsyth County. As a courtesy, of course, I touched base with the locals to let them know I was in their jurisdiction on official business, and dusted the phone for prints. Even though a fingerprint on a pay phone probably wouldn't stand up in court, I figured it was worth a shot to see if I could run any prints through IAFIS and potentially ID our caller, but it was drilling a dry well. The phone had been wiped clean. Nothing but smudges."

"Nice idea, anyway. It was worth a shot."

"It would be really nice to talk to this guy and find out how he knew what he knew. If he's not the guy, he knows the guy who did our two victims. Well, it might have been worth the trip, anyway. One of the Forsyth County Sheriff's deputies dropped in while I dusted the phone, to shoot the breeze and let the store owner see a local badge.

While we were talking, he dropped that the scuttlebutt around their department is that a hotshot in Roswell thinks a murder in his jurisdiction has a lot in common with something that happened on their turf. It's a heck of a long shot, but what do you think of the possibility that a serial is working over there, and we've got a double murder over here?"

Hodges's eyebrows knitted together as he calculated the odds the crimes were all connected. He shook his head, "Not likely."

Sanchez protested, "But our tip originated from their jurisdiction. That means it's possible, even if it's not likely."

"Good point," Hodges smiled...for about a second. "Okay, people, listen up. We're going to canvas Hidden Hills today, and we're going to keep at it until we find somebody who knows something about these two dead people, right here under our noses. Now, get your asses in gear."

# # #

Clayton glanced at the bony, shriveled woman in the bed. She was just like the majority of his customers who required medical equipment to prolong their miserable lives. Old and withered, she reeked of coming death, the smell that he associated with his childhood. As he counted out the catheters he was supposed to leave behind on this delivery, his mind drifted back the old woman who came to die at his house.

He hadn't been abused as a child so much as neglected. His father died in a traffic accident when Clayton was six years old. With the loss of his father and the onset of financial problems, Clayton's mother had to take her mother out of the assisted living facility. He remembered when his mother brought the old bag of bones into their house and set her up in the guest room.

He hadn't hated his grandmother before she moved into their home. He hadn't really known her. His parents never took him to visit her in the nursing home. Her mind was too far gone to know them, so they saw no reason to upset their young son.

Time blurred in his memories. Practically overnight, he had lost his father, replaced by an old hag who did nothing but lay in bed, a black hole for energy that required virtually all of his mother's attention. It turned into a non-stop vigil that sucked the light out of his mother's eyes. He spent years watching the grandmother he'd never met before she invaded his comfortable life, watching and waiting for her to die.

He waited. And waited.

He was too young to remember the old woman except as a breathing corpse, kept alive by machines and his mother, the bedridden shell of a person he'd never really known. But over time, he developed a deep resentment for this inanimate lump of flesh that had once been a human being.

When he came home from school, the house smelled like her. He was too ashamed to bring his friends over any more. He grew more introverted and brooded frequently, remembering the Cub Scout camping trips, amusement parks and fun activities from his past life. He wanted his childhood back the way it had been, before his father died. Their neighborhood changed. Clayton's friends moved away, but his mom couldn't afford to follow the trend. He was stuck in their hellish day-to-day existence, biding time until the angel of death remembered his grandmother.

Clayton learned to vent his frustrations by killing small animals he caught near the house. Each time, he fantasized he was killing his grandmother, putting her out of his, and her, misery. He thought he could find the courage to suffocate her with the pillow, the next time his mother ran an errand. But he realized that if his mother ever found out, she would never forgive him.

Eventually, his grandmother succumbed to her disease, before Clayton worked up the courage to turn his fantasy into reality. But his childish dream of reconnecting with his mother died with the old woman—the years of round-the-clock caregiving had worn his mother down. She suffered a stroke and died shortly after the funeral of her own mother, leaving young Clayton alone and bitter in the world.

How he hated the weak ones. It went against nature, keeping them alive just because society felt obligated to use its artificial, life-extending technology. A few generations ago, the weak simply died, leaving the strong to move on with their lives. Survival of the fittest. That was how things were meant to be.

It felt good to Clayton to set things right.

CHAPTER 35

Our ALTA opponents, or at least one of them, pissed me off on first sight in the parking lot. While trying to relax my frazzled nerves with my eyes closed, listening to some Mozart, the jerk pulled in and parked right next to me, even though the lot was almost empty. With the top down on his BMW, music blaring full blast, he effectively destroyed the tranquil moment of peace that I so desperately sought as I tried my best to get into the mood to play tennis. The truth was that I felt more like hitting a person than a tennis ball. My eyes snapped open to glare at him, but his bright pink shirt bothered my eyes, so I closed them once more.

Stay cool. Get this over with.

Soon enough, I recognized the engine sound of Mike's car and opened my eyes. I had been waiting for him to arrive before going to the court to stretch and warm up. Feeling the pressure building once more, the disappointment of having last night's nightmare in spite of finding and reporting Driscoll's body, it was all getting to be a little too much for me to take.

I felt a little fatigued, but I came to the court with a keen sense of purpose, determined to win the match quickly and get to the hospital. I needed the comfort of my partner, my confidant. I needed Beth.

Mike asked, "You okay?"

He always asks me if I'm ready, but I don't remember Mike asking if I was okay before. I must really look haggard. "Beth was admitted to the hospital Wednesday night. I found her, unconscious, when I got home from practice."

"Oh, shit. She's gonna be okay, right?"

I nodded but said nothing. We walked in silence toward the tennis hut to get our court assignments. There were eleven available courts in total, but we weren't the only team that played out of the park.

"I'm really sorry, Dan. I knew things weren't right on Wednesday. Steve should have subbed out for you this week."

"I could have insisted, but I knew we didn't have enough guys. We would have moved everybody up a spot, and had to forfeit the fives. Even if you and I lose in straight sets, it would be better than screwing up the whole lineup and forfeiting the last point. This way, we put out the best lineup possible."

Mike stared at me in disbelief. "Dan, I know you're a team player, but there comes a time when you have to put your family first. Your wife and kid are more important than any job, any game, *anything*. You know what? This team could lose every point this week, and the world would not end. It's just a game."

His words were English, but sounded foreign to me. Gradually, his point sank in and made sense. I wanted to believe it was fatigue and not my normal pig-headedness that had me on the court today.

# # #

All the way to the tennis hut, Pink Shirt's bag clinked with every step. For reasons entirely irrational to me, I began to detest the man intensely. So naturally, he was one of the number one seeds from the other team. Mike and I would play him and his partner.

The clinking sound came from his bag tags. He had a real collection of them. Mine were home in a drawer, where they belonged. Bag tags for winning the division meant nothing to me. Maybe they intimidated some opponents and got in their heads, but the ornaments did nothing on the court for *my* game. If psyching out my opponent was the only way to win, I'd rather lose.

They were decent enough players, Pink Shirt and his partner. Under normal circumstances, the match could have even been fun. But I wasn't in the mood for a long, athletic, match. I was ready to go for a winner on every shot, win or lose. I'd come to play, but Mike's speech made sense. Just before we started the match, I explained to Mike my strategy for the day. I was proposing my normal style of play, on steroids. No second serves, only first serves. Go for the returns. Live or die at the net.

He smiled. "Sounds like fun. Let's see what happens."

What happened was that we split the first two sets in the time it normally took Mike and me to play a first set tiebreaker. We won the first easily, mostly because the reckless nature of our strategy caught them by surprise. They made adjustments and won the second set with equal ease. During the break at the split, just before the third set, Steve came up on the bleacher side of the fence and said to me, "These aren't grass courts, you know. Points can last more than two or three shots. Slow down, and play your normal game. What's with you guys today, anyway?"

I looked at Steve and snapped, "Worry about your own match, why don't you?" With a wounded look, he retreated to join other team members as they watched our match, surely to report what an asshole I'd just been. I felt bad.

In the first game of the third set, Pink Shirt started with the bad calls. First, he called me for a foot fault when I aced his partner.

"Excuse me?" I asked.

"You stepped across the baseline before your serve landed in the court. That's a foot fault. Second serve."

"You're making a *foot-fault* call from the other side of the net? Would you like to come check the mark?"

"What mark? There isn't a mark for a foot fault."

"There's a clear mark where you can see I drag the toe of my left foot with my service motion, and I'll give you a buck if you can find one that crosses the base line. I bring my feet together and get my legs under me to push my body into the serve. If you come check the court here, you'll see little white streaks grouped right here where I normally stand in both the deuce and the ad courts. You can see where every one of these marks is behind the baseline by several inches. I'm sorry. You're clearly mistaken."

"But it's my call. Second serve," he smirked.

Normally, I would have shrugged it off. It was just a fault call. But today, I was in no mood to take any shit off anyone. So, rather than directing my second serve into the box, I pulled the old John McEnroe stunt of trying to hit the net man with the second serve, winning a cheap point the easy way. My second serve was blasted right into his body, but he danced out of the way, narrowly evading it.

Mike turned around, and cocked his head at me. Pink Shirt's eyes widened with mild alarm, but then he smiled. He realized I'd thrown away the point because of him. "Deuce," he called out triumphantly.

When he deliberately made a bad call to claim the next point, I was just about ready to strangle Pink Shirt. Mike had lobbed over his head. Pink Shirt swung and nearly whiffed, but the *tick* of his racquet as it grazed the ball was clearly audible to both of us, so Mike and I stopped play. Pink Shirt's partner apparently didn't hear, because he tracked down the lob and fired a groundstroke that passed easily between Mike and me uncontested, since neither of us made a move because the point ended when Pink Shirt's racquet touched the ball.

Our opponents slapped hands in celebration. "Ad-out."

I watched in stunned disbelief as Pink Shirt went over and slapped hands with his partner.

My short fuse ran out, and I smacked the net cord violently with my racquet. "What the hell are you doing? You're cheating to claim that point, too? Are you trying to say your racquet didn't make contact with that lob? That's funny because my partner and I both heard it and stopped play because the point was over."

"I *didn't* make contact. It was a clean miss."

Mike, who never complained, walked up and calmly said, "I'm pretty sure that I heard contact, too."

"Are you calling me a liar?" Pink Shirt bristled. "Pretty sure and damned sure aren't the same thing. It's my call. Our point."

"You're a damned liar and a cheat!" I yelled, angrily waving my racquet.

Both our partners intervened before things got more out of hand. Mike stepped in between to create a buffer between Pink Shirt and me.

"Let it go, Dan." Mike said to me quietly. "It's just a tennis match. You've got a wife in the hospital. You don't need to get into a fistfight with this jerk over an ALTA match. He's trying to goad you because he can't win unless he gets inside your head. Let's just concentrate on closing them out and finishing this match."

Steve came back to the fence near our end of the court and motioned for Mike and me to come near. Apparently, our voices carried. "If there's consistent disagreement on line calls and awarding points, you can request members from each team to serve as linesmen. I saw you guys get jobbed on at least one of those calls. We can put an end to it, right here and now."

"If this asshole cheats on another line call, I'm going to break every string in this frame when I smash my racquet over his head. Mike, you're right.

I've got no time for this shit. So, Steve, did you just volunteer to be a line judge?" I fumed.

Steve grinned and motioned to some guys who'd been watching us from the stands near another of our assigned courts. The group moved in our direction. They were a mixture of guys from each team. He lowered his voice and said, "Apparently this dork has a bit of a reputation as a sore loser. They say he's not really such a bad guy off the court, when you get to know him. His teammates are more than a little embarrassed by him today. You don't have to worry about honest calls from this point forward."

I turned to my partner and said, "I'm sorry if I've embarrassed you. Mike, I'm sorry. I shouldn't have blown my stack like that."

"No worries, Dan. We've been friends for too long to let something little like this guy's antics cause problems between us."

"Thanks."

The purloined point wasn't the last one our adversaries won, but it might as well have been. We came back to win my serve, and then closed out the set without losing a game, giving them the bagel in that final set.

My anger and frustration with the last few days channeled into my shots. I stung clean winners off both wings, and my serve was not seriously challenged after the ad-out point. On several occasions, I blasted shots right at his midsection, causing Pink Shirt to scramble out of the way.

He hurriedly threw his gear in his bag after the match and scurried off, as if he were afraid of me, even though I had calmed down after the bad calls stopped. Apparently, the newfound fury in my game was palpable. Before leaving, Pink Shirt's partner apologized profusely on his behalf, and I uttered a half-hearted acknowledgment of my own bad behavior as my temper still simmered.

Mike asked me, "So, where in the hell did this new killer instinct in you come from?"

I just shrugged my shoulders. "Beats me," I said. But I thought about Pink Shirt.

He shouldn't have pissed me off.

CHAPTER 36

To my surprise, when I arrived to visit Beth in the hospital she informed me that her doctor was sending her home. Now she was supposed to check out as soon as possible. He had just informed her an hour earlier.

"But you're still on an IV!" I said, my voice rising in frustration. "I thought you were supposed to stay here until you added more weight and were eating normally. I mean, honey, I want you to come home, but I expected to stay with you here tonight. How is this going to work at home? Are you ready to come off the IV? Where is your doctor? I mean the obstetrician. I want to talk to him *now*."

"Shhh, honey. The nurses will hear you. Apparently, the insurance company said they wouldn't pay for hospitalization any longer. In-home nursing care is covered, but not extended hospitalization for pregnancy. Dr. Grover seems very upset. He's not to blame. The insurance representatives said their PPO policy calls for in-home nursing care. They said it should be sufficient given my condition. We'd have to fight with the insurance company."

"There's going to be a nurse staying at our house?" I asked, feeling a little better in spite of the intrusion that would mean. Beth was my only real concern, at the moment.

"Well, not exactly…a nurse will come by the house, set up the machine, and train us on how to use it when she can't be there. They will keep checking on me every day, even over the weekend, they said. According to the doctor, he's going to keep me on fluids until my weight gets back into an acceptable range."

"What? Who's supposed to change your IV bags, me?"

Beth squirmed, anticipating the worst. "Don't frown so much, honey. It's not that big of a deal, really. The bag only has to be changed three or four times a day. I'm supposed to eat a normal diet. Mostly I'm prescribed bed rest. As far as the duties at home are concerned, it's just going to be a matter of changing out the bag of electrolytes whenever the pump alarm goes off. The nurse will check on the needle in my arm every day and bring supplies. If I have any more problems with nausea, there will be some Phenergan you can add to the fluids. But really, the insurance company is right. There's no reason for me to stay in the hospital any longer. And I want to go home."

"I want you to come home, baby. But your health and the baby are the most important things right now.

As long as there's no danger you'll get sick again, I'll shut up. But you said I'm going to be responsible for changing your IV bags?"

Not convincing even herself, Beth managed, "It's okay. We'll both pay attention and know how it's supposed to be done, so if you forget something, I can help talk you through it. You're smarter than any nurse I've seen lately, and I trust you with my life. We can do this. Don't let the insurance company get you upset. As long as I keep eating and use the nausea medicine, everything will be fine. I'll be off this IV pump in no time. You know how stubborn I can be. Before I got so sick, I didn't want to take anything because I was afraid of hurting the baby. Now the doctor has convinced me the Phenergan is safe, and it's a lot better for me to stay healthy than refuse to take my prescriptions and put the baby in danger that way. Now you'll be able to monitor how well I'm eating, and you'll be responsible for giving me the Phenergan, so I can't refuse."

I didn't share her confidence. "That machine looks complicated."

"Oh, come on, Dan! You program computers for a living. Are you telling me you're afraid of operating a little electric pump?"

"It's a little electric pump that could kill you if I do something wrong, pump air into your veins, cause an overdose… I've got no medical training, no experience with what to do if something goes wrong."

"If something goes wrong, you call 9-1-1 again. Between the two of us, we can handle just about anything—maybe not nuclear physics or rocket science, but this is just pulling off an empty bag and putting on a full one. I trust you, Dan, more than I trust any nurse in a hospital. Once you know what you're supposed to do, you'll be able to handle it. And I want to come home," she finished in a soft, pleading voice.

Her words jarred me and I knew why the last few days had been so difficult to weather. It was because she wasn't there beside me. I drew in a deep breath. "I want you home too, baby. You're right. I need you. We can do just about anything when we're together."

"What do you mean, just about anything? What can't we accomplish?"

Wearing my best goofy smile, I said, "Hmmm…walk on water? Teleport?"

Beth hugged me and said, "That's the spirit!"

"I know what you're saying. We have yet to meet our match—although that parquet floor we put down in the guest bedroom came pretty close."

Beth smiled broadly at the memory. "We kicked parquet butt!"

"Yeah, but nobody was going to die if the floor didn't get installed properly," I couldn't help but say. "That's my only concern about this pump."

Footsteps in the hall got louder, and then a knock came at the door. It was Tiffany. She carried a stack of magazines and a few skeins of yarn for my wife, suddenly the knitting fool as she remained confined to bed.

After last night's dream of steamy sex with her twin, my greeting was awkward and stilted. She didn't seem to notice. "Just wanted to check on your better half," she said to me. "Hi, Beth. Everybody's been worried about you. Are you feeling better?"

Beth laughed, "I'd better be. They're sending me home today. The insurance company mandated in-home nursing care as the preferred treatment plan."

Tiffany's expression of disbelief spoke volumes. "You're kidding me. Cheapskate bastards! That's absolutely absurd." She whipped around to face me. "Have you called HR?"

"No. Why?"

"An individual complaint from one person probably gets ignored. An *official* complaint from a human resources representative of a company with over a thousand employees probably gets taken a lot more seriously. This just isn't right," Tiffany glowered. I recognized the look. She was off on a righteous mission to right all wrongs against me. I warmed at her protective concern. I was lucky to have her as a friend, and I shuddered anew at what befell her twin.

# # #

Clayton wondered if he was heading into a trap. When the dispatcher made the call and gave him the delivery address, of course he recognized it immediately. He had been there only this morning. But nobody else knew that, did they? Clayton was certain that the man had not been aware he had tailed him home.

So why was he here? The order looked legitimate enough. Could it be a coincidence? It might, but Clayton didn't really believe in coincidences.

If the cops thought they knew something but weren't sure, they might have arranged a fake invoice to flush him out, concoct something to bring him here and see what he'd do. Clayton drove slowly on his approach, scanning the streets for unmarked vehicles. An instinct for self-preservation percolated in the reptilian part of his brain, tempering his compulsion to seek thrills.

He parked the van and went through the motions of collecting the components of the order, half expecting the police to swarm around him at any second. What were the odds that the stranger who had interrupted his latest adventure would have medical needs that required his services? While Clayton might not be the greatest gambler in the world, he knew enough about probability to understand that the odds were against him. He would not go down without a fight. He slipped a scalpel into the pocket of his lab coat, determined to take as many cops with him as possible.

On high alert, he approached the front door and rang the bell. As he waited, his left hand fingered the scalpel in his coat pocket. He heard footsteps approach, and then the door swung open. With his right hand, out of habit, he adjusted the knot in the tie he wore to legitimize his professional image as a supplier of medical equipment. His hand then reached out for the IV stand beside him.

The woman who answered the door looked hauntingly familiar. Then it hit him. Clayton stared at her for several seconds, dumbfounded to the point of being unable to speak. His mind shouted silently, *what the hell? I killed you already*.

She was a dead ringer for the woman he had strangled a few months ago, his first kill. Hers was the body he had dismembered and scattered around the dead golf course, like macabre clues in a scavenger hunt. His first taste, an accidental crime of passion, caused him no end of consternation. *What is the best way to dispose of a dead body you didn't plan to have?*

Fortunately, the woman answering the door paid more attention to the equipment he had beside him than to Clayton. Had she seen the expression on his face when he first laid eyes on her, she would never have let him into the house. But she looked at the equipment he brought and paid virtually no attention to Clayton whatsoever.

Finally, he found his voice. "I have a delivery of an infusion pump intravenous delivery system. Is this the Harper residence?"

"Yes, you've got the right house. Sorry, I'm just a visitor," she offered. "The lady of the house is upstairs in bed, but your timing is impeccable. The nurse just got here a few minutes ago to set up the IV and get her situated. Please, come inside."

He knew he wasn't looking at a ghost, because ghosts don't exist. It might have been her come back to life though, the resemblance was so striking. He felt himself getting hard at the thought of having her again, reliving the thrill of squeezing the life out of her hot, and sweaty body. He drank in the moment she surrendered her life to him.

"Beth, the deliveryman with the IV equipment is here," she called out.

A voice answered, "Please bring him up, Tiff."

Tiffany said to Clayton, "If you could bring everything up to the master bedroom, to your left at the top of the stairs that would be great. Just follow me. Watch out that the cat doesn't try to get outside."

She led him upstairs. Clayton's mind reeled as he watched her walk up the steps — *who is this woman?* He willed away his erection. Dutifully, he followed his guide to the master bedroom, where a plump, middle-aged woman wearing a stethoscope around her neck fussed around her patient, who sat propped up into a reclined sitting position with the help of several pillows. Clayton's eyes darted about, looking for the man he followed here last night. This was the same house, he was sure of it. So, where was he?

He slipped on a mask of normalcy and asked, "Where do you want this set up?" gesturing toward the equipment in tow.

The nurse said, "Here's good," and pointed to a location on the far side of the bed. Clayton lugged his gear, but then stopped dead in his tracks at the foot of the bed and stared at the tie draped over the footboard. He recognized it immediately as his old tie. He tossed it into a donation bin somewhere. He couldn't remember where. Near the Sugar Hill adventure maybe? He remembered it was a damned uncomfortable tie. He couldn't keep it loose enough. Seemed like the thing always tightened around his neck.

So, these bitches are trying to mess with my head, he fumed silently.

"What are you doing?" the nurse asked. "I said to put the stand over here."

Clayton stared at her, tempted to pull out his scalpel and go to work on these three cows right then and there. They were toying with him, he was sure. The room had to be wired. His heart raced. He came expecting the cops and they were probably waiting for him to strike. He wondered if he could kill all three of them before the cops killed him. In the back of his mind, Clayton realized that he'd always expected to go out in a blaze of glory. Live fast, die hard. He had no intention of being captured and left to rot in prison.

"Sorry," he managed. "The tie there on the foot of your bed caught my eye. I used to have one just like it."

The woman in bed followed his pointed finger. "Oh, that," she said. "My husband bought it at a thrift store, and then decided he didn't like it for some strange reason. He only wore it one time, and it's been there ever since."

The woman he had already killed once asked, "Does she need to sign anything?"

"No, everything has been handled. Here's a copy of your paperwork."

CHAPTER 37

With Beth home from the hospital, I spent time puttering around the house.

Sam had dutifully showed up on our doorstep in the late afternoon, bearing a covered dish of chicken and dumplings left over our dinner together last night. He said Barbara hoped it would be mild enough for Beth to eat. He refused to come inside this time, citing a pressing errand. But I wondered if his experience with his daughter's illness made him uncomfortable around beeping medical equipment and tubes.

After enjoying a small plate of the chicken and dumplings, Beth napped quietly. As much as I objected to the in-home care arrangement, it felt good to have her home. Her presence brought a normalcy…a goodness…back to the house.

I turned on the downstairs television and flipped over to a Braves game. The drone of sportscaster voices created soothing, familiar background noise for me to muddle through the backlog of household chores I neglected for the past few days.

It caught my attention when the sportscaster announced the next Braves hitter would be...Dan Harper!

My head whipped around. I stared in wonder at the screen. My ears alerted to hear my own name; I knew full well that nobody on the Braves lineup shared my name. The voice was no longer that of the announcer I recognized, but one that sounded like it might have belonged to my waterlogged friend. The sounds of baseball filtered out, and I only heard two phrases, a name, and an address.

The name was Clayton Farmer. The street address sounded familiar. It was one I remembered from Hidden Hills.

# # #

The alarm on Beth's IV pump went off in the middle of the night. For the first time in days, I had fallen into a deep, restful sleep untroubled by nightmarish visitors. The alarm sounded several times before I managed to wake up enough to identify the sound and its importance.

I jumped up and staggered over to that side of the bed, fumbling with the replacement bag of saline solution as I unhooked the old bag and connected the new one. I shook off sleep and tried to go through the motions the nurse had taught me earlier in the day.

The realization of my mistake suddenly struck me like a hammer. I hadn't shut off the pump and clamped the line while I changed the bag. That meant a large bubble of air captured by the machine and now snaked its way through the tube that fed Beth's arm. I knew air bubbles in the blood stream could kill a person. Panicking, I turned on the bedside light, no longer worried about waking Beth.

She was groggy, but my desperation brought her fully alert. That strong center of gravity I felt any time we worked together grounded me. She would always be right there with me, every step of the way. Just having her awake, aware of the danger we shared, somehow began to calm me down.

"Dan, it's going to be okay. Remember, the nurse explained how we can bleed air from the line through the port she showed us. Wasn't there a button that shut off the pump? Yes, that's the one. Take a deep breath, honey. It's going to be okay. Find one of those hypodermic needles she left. Just use the syringe to tap the port. Stick it in the port with the plunger all the way in. Then draw it down until you pull liquid again. That will suck all the air out of the line."

Even with the pump paused, I tried to hurry and moved too quickly. "Ow! Shit!"

I had stabbed my thumb with the needle. More accurately, I had buried the needle into the meat of the thumb on my right hand in my haste, all the way to the base of the syringe. The pain was excruciating. I felt compelled to get a fresh needle, not wanting to contaminate the fluid going into my wife's body with my body fluids.

Ironically, it occurred to me that was how this all got started anyway, right?

Following her coaching, I extracted the air bubble and turned the pump back on. It resumed the rhythmic pulse and beep pattern that earlier had lulled me to sleep.

"You did great, honey," Beth stroked me. "It was just a slip because you are so tired. You shouldn't have to deal with all this alone. When it goes off, shake me awake too, okay? Turn on the light and let's get through it together. You're taking good care of me."

Except I could have killed her with my careless mistake. I knew the lapse had been caused by a lack of sleep. The specters that persistently invaded my dreams were now putting the life of my wife into jeopardy.

This stops here. Now.

# # #

Clayton giggled to himself. It was crazy to come back here, he knew. The police could have been warned. They could be watching the place right now. A team of detectives could be inside the house, staking it out. This could be his worst mistake ever.

No guts, no glory.

That was sort of the whole point. Clayton didn't care anymore.

The first murder was an accident. The problem was that he *enjoyed* it. His second murder was instinctive, self-preservation. He enjoyed that one even more. The spontaneity of the kill provided most of the thrill. The burglary murders seemed tainted in comparison.

The fact that he cased the houses for an easy mode of entry, alarm systems, and potential caches for hiding money and valuables that would be easy to pawn detracted from Clayton's ability to enjoy his memory of those murders. Those almost seemed like work. After the first one, he would have quit, finding it too easy. But the sweet release he found in every blow he landed on their pitiful, weak bodies stuck with him. *It felt good. Like an orgasm. It made him hungry for more.*

The one thing every one of his victims had in common was the feeling of power they gave him as he watched them surrender their last moments of life to him. He reveled at their futile struggles to regain control over what he now held in his hands—the power of life and death over the weak ones.

He chose death. It gave him pleasure.

Clayton was curious about his own death. He wondered what happened after he snuffed the life from his victims as easily as a priest extinguished a candle at the end of the service.

Did they go somewhere?

His delusional sense of power evolved to the point where Clayton didn't simply reject God; he believed he *was* a god. He had the power to smite the chosen, or anointed ones, on the most capricious of whims.

Somewhere deep in the recesses of his brain, Clayton knew his behavior had spiraled way out of control, but he couldn't stop. He had no interest in trying. The cops had found the body in the pond at Hidden Hills. Maybe they knew about the woman. To be precise, she was a lot of little pieces of a woman scattered around a string of sand traps.

Clayton found himself wanting to giggle again. He slapped himself in the face. *You've still got to be able to fool people, dummy. Be serious. Nobody will let you close enough to kill them if you let on that you've gone completely insane.*

PART FIVE
EASTER SUNDAY

CHAPTER 38

Trying to recover from a rough night of struggling with the IV bags, I started a pot of coffee and fetched the newspaper. *At least the dream ghouls left me alone. Maybe they're finally done with me.*

Back inside with the paper, I turned my attention to making breakfast. Since I couldn't read while I worked, I tuned the television to the local news.

I realized it was important for me to monitor Beth's intake of food as well as make sure she didn't get sick after eating. She had passed out last week because she stopped eating, convinced she would only throw up anything she ate. She had admitted she thought by keeping her stomach empty for a while, she could get control over the nausea. She tried drinking fruit drinks and smoothies to maintain her caloric intake, but it had been a losing battle.

Hot buttered toast with a sliced orange and banana ought to be safe enough. Some oatmeal might be good, too. Healthy and easy to digest.

Thankfully, I wasn't cooking anything that required close monitoring when I heard the anchor announce an overnight tragedy. His words grabbed me by the shoulders and shook hard. As I scrambled to see the television screen, I banged my knee, hard, on the solid oak buffet. Bolts of pain shot up my leg, but my brain overrode any urge to linger and nurse my injury. I limped ahead to confirm my worst fears.

He reported a house fire at Lake Allatoona involving multiple deaths. No sooner had my brain processed his words than bile began to form in my throat. I could not help feeling responsible. It had to be the same house I had visited in the wee hours of Saturday morning, once in my dreams, and a second time in desperation to stop something that I fooled myself into believing had been thwarted. I assumed when everyone was okay after I got to Lake Allatoona, nothing would happen. Now these needless deaths were on my hands. I had done nothing to stop the killer. I only delayed the inevitable.

The breakfast plate wobbled in my unsteady hands as Beth took it from me. Alarmed, she grabbed my hands in hers, "Dan, you are shaking. Here, climb back into bed beside me. You had a rough night. Let's rest together,"

I looked my wife in the eyes, reading her concern. "I have to tell you something," I said. "Actually, I have to tell you a lot of stuff. I know this is gonna sound crazy, but I swear it's the truth."

"I know you won't lie to me," Beth said cautiously. She smiled and quipped, "Except when you tell me how beautiful I am when my feet are swollen, my belly is huge, and I'm starting to break out for the first time since high school."

"All those things are unimportant and temporary. What I'm about to tell you is neither."

So, I started with buying the tie in the thrift store and went on to my first night of horrors. My words came freely, my voice often cracking with fear or anger, but it felt good to finally share the truth with someone. My story culminated with the murders at Lake Allatoona on the news only minutes ago. Beth listened without interruption. As I admitted my feelings of guilt and regret for not saving those people, her eyes brimmed with tears.

"Oh, Dan. I love you so much," she said. "This is awful. Why didn't you tell me earlier?"

"I didn't want to upset you," I said lamely. "And I didn't think you would believe me. I had trouble believing it myself. It all seems so crazy. But there *was* a body in the pond in Stone Mountain. I reported it to the police, but anonymously. I had no explanation for how I knew it was there. Ever since I touched that damned thrift store tie, I haven't been able to break the connection to me. I haven't wanted to get directly involved, but this maniac has to be stopped. Now there have been more murders, out at Lake Allatoona. I drove out there early Saturday morning, before the tennis match. I thought it stopped him, but the murders happened anyway, a day later. Look, I know this sounds crazy…"

"I do believe you," Beth assured me. "But what are you going to do? What can you do?"

"I need to go see the police and tell them everything I know. Granted, it isn't all that much, certainly nothing they can use to arrest and prosecute anybody, but I feel like have to do something. I have to help by offering them what little I know. This is really going to sound crazy, but last night, during the Braves game, a message came to me…a name and an address. Clayton Farmer was the name, and the street is one I remember seeing in Hidden Hills, the same subdivision where I discovered Peter Driscoll's body. I think it may be the guy, but I don't know how the police could do anything but watch him. What's that phrase they always use in the cop shows…? Probable cause, that's it. Well, they don't have probable cause for a search warrant or anything like that. It would just be my tip based on psychic visions. Maybe it will help the cops to know all these cases are connected. Maybe they can keep Farmer under surveillance until he tries doing something else. Hell, I don't really even know for sure that Farmer isn't going to end up being another victim, but that gut feeling I'm learning to trust more and more tells me he's the one and he needs to be stopped right away, before he hurts anybody else."

"Have you spoken with your mother about this?"

I peered at my wife, my friend, my partner. She fidgeted, looking at my forehead instead of meeting my eyes.

"Yes, a little bit. I talked with her yesterday. But I left out the crazier parts of the story, and it was before I found Driscoll's body. She called Kevin right away and put a bug in his ear. For the record, I love being psychoanalyzed by my brother, over the phone, by ambush interview," I said sarcastically.

"You spoke with Kevin? What did he say about this?" Beth asked cautiously.

Dear God. She thinks I might be going off the deep end, too. Beth no, please no. I need you now more than ever.

"I didn't tell him about finding Driscoll's body. I thought this would all be over when I called the DeKalb police and reported the location of the body. Kevin said that he thinks I might have a brain tumor. How's that for a pleasant thought?"

"Oh, that's ridiculous," Beth laughed. But a hint of worry lurked in her voice. Funny I could read the mind of a dead man, but the thoughts of my own wife remained a mystery to me.

"It ought to sound ridiculous because it is ridiculous. I don't even have a headache. There's nothing wrong with me, except that my normal reality hasn't been so normal lately."

She quietly replied, "I think it's pretty safe to say that's the understatement of the year."

CHAPTER 39

I knew roughly where to find the Roswell police headquarters. It was near the public library. I circled a few blocks in old town Roswell until I found Hill Street.

The police department building sat on the left hand side of the road. I parked near the entrance of the administration building and took a moment to admire the monstrosity across the street known as City Hall.

During my time playing tennis out of Roswell Park, I knew the police station was only about a block away from a Krispy Kreme doughnut shop, within easy walking distance on the way to the square. The neon red "Hot Doughnuts Now" sign had always proved to be an irresistible beacon. Hot Krispy Kreme glazed doughnuts just out of the oven really are *that* good. They melt in your mouth.

The Roswell Police Department building reminded me of an office where I once worked. A solid but somewhat nondescript red brick two story building, it didn't look like a police department would be housed there, except for the boldly lettered sign identifying the DETENTION facility in a large annex from the main building.

An armed officer in uniform greeted me just inside the glass foyer. He sat at a table with a clipboard. Apparently, one needed an appointment before being asked to step through the metal detectors. The uniformed officer, a thin man with a receding hairline, met my frown with one of his own. He adjusted his wire-rimmed glasses on the peak of his nose as he stared at me.

"Is there a problem?" he asked.

"I need to speak with somebody about a crime. A murder. It happened on a street called Maid Marian Lane."

His eyes widened in surprise, and then he reached for the phone.

# # #

Detective Wassner's eyes narrowed in suspicion the moment he recognized me. "What a pleasant surprise," he said disingenuously. "I was planning on paying you a visit today and you just saved me a trip. Your name has popped up one too many times in the course of my investigation. I'm sure you remember our meeting at the hospital. A patrolman recently let me know he chatted with you after he found you parked outside my crime scene. Since I don't believe in coincidences, you've got a hell of a lot of explaining to do."

"Oh, I'll tell you everything I know," I promised. "But I seriously doubt you'll believe me."

"If you're coming here voluntarily to tell me the truth, you won't have any problem. Tell you what, how about some privacy for this little heart-to-heart conversation? We've got a small conference room I can borrow for a few minutes, and you can tell me all about what brought you here today. You've got my undivided attention." The longer he spoke, the nicer his demeanor became. I sensed he thought I'd come in to confess, and in a way I had. But it was not the type of confession he would be expecting. He continued, "Can I get you anything? Cup of coffee? Coke? We've got diet too, if you prefer."

He directed me through the metal detectors while the uniformed officer watched me carefully. I placed my keys and wallet in the small dish he offered, and then passed through the arch without issue. I stopped at the front desk with Detective Wassner long enough to sign the visitor's book. The guy with the clipboard handed me a guest badge that I clipped to my shirt.

"No thanks, I'm fine. I'd really like to tell you what I know as soon as possible. I don't know how you are going to stop this guy or even figure out who he is, but you're the detective. You're supposed to know how to catch a killer."

Wassner stiffened, obviously keen to keep me talking.

He led me through a door, past a hive of cubicles almost identical to the ones in my office. *Strange, I expected an open area crowded with a bunch of old metal desks and overstuffed filing cabinets.* That brief lapse into assumptions and stereotypes only reinforced my decision to come here. I was an amateur, a rookie drafted into a role way out of my league.

I followed him to the conference room. Wassner pointed at a chair. "Have a seat."

He sat across the table from me. Over his shoulder, I looked into the video camera attached to the wall. Conference room my ass. This was an interrogation room. I squirmed in discomfort at the thought. The metal folding chair didn't help matters.

I looked across the table at the stone-faced Wassner. "I assume you're the detective in charge of the investigation of the attack on the woman in whose hospital room we met. I swear that was the only time in my life that I ever laid eyes on her. But I assume she lives in the Windsor Forest subdivision off Houze Way."

His expression didn't change, but it hadn't been a surprise to him that I knew where she lived. He already told me he knew about my conversation with the cop in front of her house. After hesitating a moment to give Wassner a chance to interject a comment, I continued, "I already told you the truth at the hospital. Like I just said, until I met you, I'd never laid eyes on that woman in my entire life. But the whole truth is…it wasn't the first time I'd ever seen her."

Wassner's eyebrows furrowed. He couldn't mask his surprise, but he quickly regained his composure. In a calm, measured tone he asked, "Excuse me, but how can you see somebody without ever laying eyes on them?"

"Look, I'm not a nut. I know this is gonna sound crazy. You can't know how hard I argued with myself that it's not real. But this is the God's honest truth—I was led to her house and the hospital room in a dream. Or maybe it was a vision, I don't know. I bought a tie from a thrift store. When I put it around my neck, I saw something terrible. I had a vision of…murder. Blood, people dying in awful ways. I can't really explain what happened, but I can tell you something did happen. Now, it won't stop."

I leaned forward in my desperation to convince him. He leaned forward too, encouraging me to keep talking. "What happened? What are we talking about here? Did you see something, or didn't you?"

"It's not that simple. Oh, believe me, I *saw* something. But I wasn't there when it happened. I didn't do it. I don't know who did it. I just know he's done it before, in Stone Mountain. Two other places. One place he used a meat cleaver…"

Not realizing until the word passed my lips that I could name the place, I finished, "…Smyrna. Somewhere in Forsyth County he used a golf club. Last night, he killed somebody out at Lake Allatoona."

Wassner said, "Whoa, whoa, wait a minute. You came in here this morning to tell me that my perp from Windsor Forest has killed multiple people spread all over metropolitan Atlanta? You saw this in a *dream*? Get out of here. You're wasting my time," Wassner bluffed. I knew better. He was hooked.

"I don't know who he is, but I've been getting hints on where he's going to go or what he might do next. I think I know what the Joker playing card meant. The killer is a gambler. He steals from people after he's killed them…but he likes killing them. The murders all seem so *violent*. He doesn't just shoot or stab people, he beats or hacks them to death with something he steals from the house and takes with him."

Wassner's eyebrows shot up. "Would you excuse me for a second? I need to take a leak. Are you sure I can't get you something to drink?" He grinned mischievously. "I promise I'll wash my hands."

"Sure. I'll take a Coke, if you don't mind," I said.

# # #

When he returned, Wassner brought the Coke he promised, along with a large plastic cup full of ice that I found thoughtful. His female partner from the hospital accompanied him. I looked at her with mild surprise. *Odd that both of them are here on a Sunday.*

Wassner said, "You remember my partner, Detective Lampe, don't you? You met her at the hospital. Detective Lampe, Daniel Harper. He was kind enough to come in voluntarily to offer us information to help our investigation." She nodded at me, folded her arms, and leaned against the wall.

He poured a little of the Coke over the ice and set the cup and can in front of me, but after the fizz died, the liquid hadn't even covered the ice. Out of habit, I poured the rest of the can into the cup and squeezed the can hard enough to bend the metal a little as a sign the can was now empty. Wassner gave Lampe a barely perceptible nod. With a gloved hand, she snatched the empty can off the table and scurried out the room, holding it like a trophy. I stared after her in stunned silence, and then looked across the table at Wassner.

He gave me a wicked smile and said, "You mentioned a murder in Smyrna. It just so happens that I'd heard about the same case from a buddy of mine in the GBI. The murder weapon was available in the house, but it was not the most obvious weapon the killer could have picked up in either place. He seemed to know it was there in advance, and he took it with him when he left. My friend caught a little bit of a lucky break because the killer left a bloody partial fingerprint at the scene."

His smile softened into a more sympathetic expression.

"The boys in the lab can run your print against his and tell me if you're my guy pretty quick, before the end of this conversation if I'm lucky. But since I already know who you are and where you live, I don't need print results to tell me you know more than you should about some nasty business. Based on what you seem to know, I'm guessing that you're really here to confess and just need a little time to figure out the best way to word it. I'm sorry for the Coke can stunt, I really am. I probably should have told you that I don't believe in psychics. I don't believe you got your information from any damned dreams. I admit the bit with Detective Lampe was shock treatment, my attempt to get you to recognize why you came here and do the right thing."

He paused, offering me to opportunity speak. I met his gaze but kept quiet.

Well, this is going well. A couple more minutes and he'll have me in cuffs again.

"The fact you came in of your own accord tells me that you want to do the right thing, but you don't know how. Your fingerprint will tell us soon enough whether or not you did it. Then you can tell me *why* you did it. You aren't a bad person. The fact that you came here tells me that much. We can get you the help you need. All you've got to do is tell the truth," he coached.

I was shell-shocked, and disappointed in myself for my own gullibility. Of course, the cop suspected me. My story sounded ridiculous, even to the most sympathetic ear. My own wife thought I was losing my mind. And as recently as a week ago, I would never have believed me, either.

My frustration boiled over. "Do I need a lawyer?"

# # #

Lampe smiled when she stuck her head into the room, but there was nothing friendly about her face. She said to Wassner, "Guess what? Our guest has a violent history. A decade ago, some agg-assault charges got knocked down. He took a pre-trial diversion into anger management classes. Our friend here has a bit of a temper. Maybe he needs a refresher course in self-control."

I blinked at her in surprise. "I thought that bullshit was supposed to be expunged from my record after I finished the classes. I haven't been in any trouble in a long time. I was a stupid kid, drinking underage at a fraternity house keg party. It was the on-campus equivalent of a bar fight."

Wassner smirked, "Nothing ever really goes away."

They took turns, trying to wear me down or break my story. Wassner grilled me for over an hour, and then Lampe came back in to spell him for a thirty-minute break. She used a much kinder and gentler approach to bludgeon me over the head with the same questions, over and over. She asked them in

330

different patterns and phrased them a hundred different ways, trying to see if I'd ever answer them differently.

Finally, I had enough. I stood up from the uncomfortable chair and leaned my back against the wall. "Am I under arrest?" I demanded. "Because if I'm not, I'd like to go home now. My wife has been left alone for several hours, and it's my responsibility to change her IV bag. The cheapskate bastards with the insurance company won't allow her to stay in the hospital, where she ought to be. If you are going to keep me here much longer, you need to send somebody to my house to take care of her."

Footsteps echoed down the hall. "Sounds like the rhino is heading back this way," she said.

"Pardon me?"

"Sorry, I wasn't really talking to you," she deflected. "I'm still sort of new to this department, learning my way around. Wassner apparently has a nickname. The guys call him Columbo because he's a little rumpled-looking most of the time, and he always gets his man. But I've decided to call him the rhino."

"Why is that?"

"Because he'll trample all over you and crush you like a bug, if you make him angry enough," she smiled sweetly. "My suggestion would be that you cooperate fully, and start telling us the truth. I really do think he's had about enough of your bullshit."

CHAPTER 40

Wassner scowled as he reentered the interrogation room. "The fingerprints didn't match," he grumbled. "I had them double check and confirm it."

"I told you that I didn't do it," I protested. "Why would I come in here and tell you a story about psychic visions if I was guilty?"

Wassner could not suppress a sarcastic smile. "Because you're crazy, an attention seeker, or just a regular pain in the ass," he offered helpfully.

He moved to where I stood against the wall. I squirmed involuntarily, cornered by his invasion of my personal space. He leveled his eyes at mine and slapped his palm to the wall beside my ear, leaning only inches from my face. His low, steady voice scoffed, "Let's face it...you tell me you're a psychic. That gives me three choices. You're either a total nut job, the perp himself, or an accomplice. The fourth option would be that you really are a psychic, but the problem is that I don't believe in psychics, therefore making you a nutcase or an accomplice. The only reason I give you that much credit is because you lucked out with a couple of wild guesses about the souvenirs and the one in Sugar Hill."

Sugar Hill. That would be the Forsyth County murder. The location name hit a chord of truth in my brain as another puzzle piece snapped into place.

"Plus two in Stone Mountain," I said, ducking away from him and going back to the chair. It was only slightly less uncomfortable than having Wassner in my face. "And now there are the dead people by the Little River Marina at Lake Allatoona as well."

Wassner spun around and stared at me. He appraised me with a suspicious glare, debating his next tactic. I sensed he wanted the answers he knew I held. He seemed to decide humoring me about the visions was the quickest way to get to what he wanted.

"How does our killer know all these people?" Wassner asked. "I assume he isn't just randomly selecting names out of the phonebook. How's he choosing his victims?"

I shook my head in frustration. "I wish I knew."

"The key to catching this guy, assuming all this bullshit you're telling me is on the up-and-up, is gonna be finding the patterns that tell him which houses to hit. Let's start with him taking the murder weapon. How did he know the murder weapon would be available and where to look for it? If he went into the kitchen for a knife every time and made do with a meat cleaver, that's one thing. But if he's going into the storage closet and getting a golf club in one house and rummaging through the garage for a mattock in the other, it no longer sounds like the same guy. Unless, of course, he's been in each of the houses before and knows where to find his weapon of choice. But how is he doing that, when Smyrna and Sugar Hill are at least forty miles apart? If what you just said is true and the same guy did people in Stone Mountain and Allatoona, that's about a fifty-mile radius. How are all of these people connected?" Wassner demanded.

"How should I know?" I protested.

"How do you know any of this shit you've been telling me?" Wassner shot back. "You explain it all by telling me you're psychic."

"That's not what I said," I replied. "I touched a tie and had visions, bad dreams, whatever you want to call it. I didn't claim to be a psychic, at least not one who knows what he's doing. I said I had some visions, that's all. I can't help what happened. Look, I'm not any happier about it than you are."

I paused to collect my thoughts, but the next words that came from my mouth didn't seem to be mine.

"Something is using me to communicate with you. This evil man needs to be stopped. You're very good at your job, and you were on the right track before Daniel came in to see you. I'm just trying to prod you a little further in the right direction. We are here to assist, not interfere. If our help is no longer required, we shall get out of your way and let you go about your business."

Wassner stared at me strangely.

He spoke in measured tones. "What happened to your voice just now? What's this "we" business, and talking in the third person? How did you know I was thinking my perp could be a repeat offender before you came here? Who *are* you?"

I shook my head helplessly. I had no explanation for what had just happened.

"Okay, there is one thing I've been holding back, because I don't want you to think I'm giving you the killer on a platter and it turns out to be the wrong guy. I don't know for sure that this name that came to me isn't another future victim, and not the killer…but last night I got a name and address. Clayton Farmer and the address are out in Hidden Hills, where I found Peter Driscoll's body and reported it to the police. I don't know what it means for sure, but I am sure it means *something*. It's either the guy, or somebody he plans to kill. Maybe you could work with the DeKalb police to keep Farmer under surveillance until he does something, or somebody tries to kill him."

Lampe made eye contact with Wassner and nodded toward the door, some silent communication taking place between them. "Would you excuse us for a minute?" Wassner asked me. "We'll be back in a flash," he promised.

"Sure," I said. "But I really do need to get home to my wife."

Like I really had a whole lot of choice in the matter.

# # #

"What do you think?" Lampe asked.

"What do you mean, that he's really psychic?" Wassner laughed derisively. "If he's legit, that would be a first. Besides, what good is any help from this guy? Any testimony from him would get ripped to shreds by a half decent defense attorney. Psychics are useless witnesses in the courtroom, from everything I know about the judicial system."

Lampe's eyes narrowed. "Let me rephrase the question. What do *you* think?"

"I think he knows too much for an innocent bystander. I'm pissed the thumbprint didn't match. Maybe that just means he's got an accomplice."

"But his alibi checked out at the hospital. Can you see a guy with a wife in the hospital about to spit out a kid running around murdering strangers for a couple of bucks? His credit check came back golden. He doesn't need the kind of money our perp has apparently been getting, unless he's got a well-hidden drug habit or a mistress."

Wassner started laughing. "Spit out a kid? You've got a way with words, Nancy."

"You're being evasive," she replied. "You still haven't said whether or not you think he's our perp."

"You think he's telling the truth?" Wassner asked incredulously.

"Honestly, I don't know. Maybe he's trying to protect somebody, the real witness. He doesn't fit the profile of the guy who did the Nelsons, but he could be a total sociopath. You want my gut reaction? He's telling the truth. I know it sounds crazy. You don't have to say anything, so don't. That's what I think, though. Wait a minute…didn't he say the name he had was Clayton Farmer? That name sounds familiar. Hang on a second."

She ducked into her cubicle while Wassner waited. He thought about everything Dan Harper had told him that morning, and asked himself why Harper would come in and tell the story he just recounted, unless he was completely insane or telling the truth. Wassner frowned.

Lampe's face was flushed with excitement when she returned, waving an invoice in her hand. "I thought the name was familiar. Clayton Farmer home-delivered some special medical supplies to the Nelson house two weeks prior to their attack."

CHAPTER 41

Finally, I broke down and confessed to Wassner. I admitted that I had lied to him about one thing, that I hadn't been worried about checking on Beth. The nurse who set up the IV yesterday said she would come by after church, and I'd changed the bag right before I left. It should be several more hours before the new bag of fluid emptied, and I expected to be home by then.

At that moment, I found myself back at the last place on earth that I wanted to be—Hidden Hills, parked in front of the address for Clayton Farmer given to me by my supernatural friend. But it made sense, or at least as much as anything else had since last Wednesday when all this craziness started. I dreaded the thought of going inside, but how else would I know for sure if this was really the guy? How could I tell the cops to arrest Clayton Farmer unless I knew more about him than simply his name and address?

Wassner sat in the car with me, watching the house. To my surprise, he had followed me out of the station after he and Lampe told me I was free to go. He said, not really asking, "You aren't really going home, are you? You drove all the way out to Allatoona on a hunch. I think you're going out to his place to see Farmer, aren't you?"

"What's it to you?" I shot back. "It's not in your jurisdiction."

Wassner shrugged, "You live in Roswell and pay taxes. Therefore, you help pay my salary. If I let you go out of my jurisdiction and you get yourself killed trying to play detective, I might have to take a pay cut."

When he saw the suspicion written all over my face, he got serious and added, "Okay, it was a bad joke. Look, I just punched out. I'm officially off duty. You've told me enough that I believe you're probably about to go do something stupid, like break into this guy's house to confirm he's our killer. The problem is, if he catches you in the act, you're gonna become his next victim. Since you'd be trespassing, he might be able to even claim justifiable homicide and turn this around on you. Like I said, I'm off the clock, just another concerned citizen. I was thinking about taking a ride with my new friend Dan to see this golf course in Stone Mountain that's free to play, as long as you don't mind weeds in the fairway."

He nailed me. I knew that was where I had to go next, but I protested, "You can't be along for the ride and watch me break the law, can you? How about this…I ring the doorbell. If he answers the door, I ask him if he knows Peter Driscoll. We see how he reacts.

It's broad daylight in his front yard, so I don't expect he'll jump outside and snuff me right there on the spot. Maybe I can get a read on the guy, tune in on him somehow."

Wassner didn't look convinced, but he kept listening. I sensed that he wanted this guy as much as I did and would go along with just about anything at this point.

"If he's not home, I'm going inside the guy's house to see if I can find anything to confirm he's the right guy, any tangible evidence. If so, I can become your informant and give you the information. You can turn around and convince a judge to establish probable cause and get a search warrant." Knowing it sounded too easy, I trailed off.

We stood there in silence, both weighing the odds.

"Only problem with your plan is DeKalb County isn't in my jurisdiction," Wassner growled. "So I'm not interested in search warrants or protecting my job. I'm not going to the GBI for help because I'd have to tell Gradick I'm listening to a psychic. No, the more official routes I go with this, the longer it takes to get anything done." His voice turned icy, "This guy has got to be stopped, whatever it takes. I think you underestimate just how crazy this guy is, Dan. If this is his house and he's home, he'll kill you. His crime scenes have given us the profile of a man whose rage is completely out of control."

The words hit home. Knowing that I was in way over my head was what brought me to the station today.

"But you're sworn to uphold the law. You can't just break into someone's house. That has to be against some code of conduct, at least. You need a legitimate excuse for coming in the house without a warrant, or it causes you problems on the job."

Wassner snapped, "If push comes to shove, screw the job. I want this guy's head on a platter. Everybody has an excuse for the evil they are willing to ignore in themselves, but this guy is different than most people. He's not making any bones about the fact he enjoys butchering people for no reason, except that he *likes* to hurt people. Evil triumphs when good men are afraid to take action."

I gnawed at my lip—his words were close enough to Edmund Burke's to resonate with me. The thought of an experienced cop with a gun and a badge sounded a lot better to me than playing the Lone Ranger. Wassner was right. If Clayton Farmer was the murderer and he caught me in his home, I would end up just as dead as his other victims.

The detective obviously felt as strongly as I did about ending this madman's spree of terror.

"Okay, Wassner, let's go lion hunting."

# # #

The place looked deserted, nobody home. After glancing around the cul-de-sac at the neighbors' windows, I was satisfied no one was paying the least bit of attention to us. Following yesterday's heavy police activity, you would think somebody would be on alert, or at least keep an eye open. Not here.

My gut told me this was *his* house. The name on the mailbox wasn't his, but there was a letter inside addressed to him.

As Wassner checked his Glock, the danger of the situation only strengthened my determination to see this through. "Stay behind me," he warned me. "Inside the house, my weapon will be out and ready. I don't want to shoot you by accident."

We waited impatiently, ringing the doorbell several times.

The idea of being found snooping around the killer's lair made me as nervous as a cat caught in the dog pound. However, the same instinct that told me this house belonged to a killer also told me that he wasn't home. It *felt* empty.

"He's not here," I said with certainty. I gave up wondering how the intuitive bits of information formed in my mind. "We can get in through the patio door."

Wassner shot me a look, but kept his mouth shut. He led the way to the back deck, grabbed the handle on the old sliding glass door, and pulled. It was locked. Wassner scowled and shot me a look.

"Well, that did us a lot of good," I muttered half-aloud.

Lift the door and push it open. The lock is old. It will give.

"Here, let me take a look," I said. When Wassner stepped aside, I grabbed the door handle, pinched my fingers on the far edge of the door to hold it in both hands. I lifted with all my strength and then pushed the door against the latch with all my weight. The brittle, worn metal latch hook inside the door snapped off, and the door slid open with a little extra effort.

"Oops," I said.

Wassner grinned and shook his head. He entered the house and headed toward the shadowy bedrooms, his gun leading the way.

I willed my body forward, following him deeper into the dark and foreboding house. Farmer kept all the windows covered and shades drawn in the back, where the bedrooms were located. Until we stopped him, the killing would continue. My dreams would continue to be invaded, and ultimately my conscience would snap under the shame of being too paralyzed by fear to take action. I had no choice. I had to be here. I needed to confirm his identity and find something that tied him to at least one of the murders.

I let down the people at Lake Allatoona. Now they were dead. I couldn't live with the thought of failing someone else. If evidence existed in Farmer's house, I felt confident we would find it.

Once again, my gut told me that I would recognize the evidence when I found it.

Wassner whispered, "Stay close. You may be sure that Farmer isn't here now, but you don't know when he might return. Let's make this quick."

Trust your gut, I had come to learn. It told me we should look in the empty bedroom. "The one on the right," I said confidently.

Sure enough, hidden in the guest bedroom closet, we found a bloody collection of souvenirs from the various crime scenes. Wassner's admonition not to touch them was unnecessary. If a necktie could spark hallucinations, touching the actual implements of death would send me over the edge.

Meat cleaver, bloody golf club, a wicked-looking garden tool...this sadistic bastard liked to strike hard, allowing his rage to work out through his muscles as he beat and hacked his victims to death. After finding his trophy case, I had seen enough. I wanted to get out of there as fast as I could.

"We should leave," I managed.

Wassner nodded in agreement. "I don't know how you did it, but you found him. He's the one. Now let's get him."

When I turned for the door, I happened to notice several white coats mixed in with other hanging clothes. The coats *pulled* me back to the closet.

Wassner and I made eye contact. I shrugged and lifted my hand toward a white sleeve. He cocked his head, watching me with curiosity as I clenched the fabric and closed my eyes.

Immediately I was staring at the outside of a startlingly familiar house. My heart skipped a beat as I recognized my own home.

A desperate, "NO..." struggled through my constricted throat. I didn't need to worry about this homicidal madman catching me in his house. I knew exactly where he was—the insane predator stalked my house.

My eyes popped open. I looked at Wassner desperately. "He's watching my house, right now, this very second!"

Wassner said, "Are you sure?" But he was already reaching for his cell phone.

The bastard is stalking me and my wife at the very moment I'm sneaking around his house. My phone was already in my hand, and I fumbled in my panic to reach Beth. I flipped it open and pressed the buttons to speed-dial my home number. Busy signal. *Get off the damned phone!*

One more try, with the same result. I couldn't reach Beth to warn her of the imminent danger lurking outside.

Helpless to reach her, I listened to the detective bark out instructions.

"Lampe, it's Wassner. We found confirmation that we're looking for the right guy, but more importantly, I just got a tip where our killer is, right this second. Listen...the guy we talked to, Harper. Providence Oaks. Have the dispatcher put out a code on the radio and get all available units over there, ASAP. We were right about Harper. He's not the guy. The suspect's name is Clayton Farmer. He's going after Harper and his family. Get people there, and get them there quick. *Move it*, or we're gonna have another crime scene to process on our home turf."

Wassner snapped his cell phone shut and looked at me. Reading the anxiety in my face, he nodded toward the door and said, "Don't worry about me. Go see about your family."

# # #

Watching the stunned man finally snap out of it and run for the door, Wassner dialed another number. "Gradick? Call the DeKalb police and tell them to get to Hidden Hills subdivision. I found our boy. Get over here as soon as you can and come get me. I'm going to sit on his house until a judge signs off on a warrant, or just in case he decides to come back home."

Gradick said, "What? You found him? Are you sure?"

In measured tones, Wassner gave him Farmer's name and address. He said grimly, "A tip led me to the residence of our perp. I noticed signs of a break in and took steps to secure the residence. While I checked to make sure the intruders were no longer on the premises, evidence that a crime had been committed was discovered in plain view."

Bullshit. Gradick recognized the careful wording. *He's way out on a limb on this one.* But if Wassner had managed to nail the creep, he wasn't going to quibble over protocol. He made up his mind to go along with whatever cover story Wassner was feeding him.

"I got another tip from that same reliable source that he's about to make another move, in my neck of the woods again. If he makes it out of Roswell, I want to be here waiting for him—at least until there's another welcoming committee to take my place. So yeah, I'm going to be sitting on his place until you get here. By the way, let DeKalb know that anybody in plain clothes who might get here first should use my name so I know they're okay. I've never seen what this guy looks like, and I don't want to shoot any good guys."

# # #

On the way to the car, I tried my home number once more, but still got a busy signal. A sinking feeling in my stomach led me to suspect Farmer had tampered with the phone line. I tried Beth's cell phone, but got no answer, making my anxiety worsen.

As I put my key in the ignition, I remembered my neighbor Sam and dug his phone number out of my wallet after cranking the engine.

He answered his cell phone right away. "Sam, thank God! This is Dan, from across the street. Are you home? Listen, I don't have time to explain, but I need to ask, do you own a gun? Good. Would you take it with you and go make sure my wife is okay? Be very careful. I believe there's a murderer going after Beth, right at this very minute. I've been trying to help the police catch him, and somehow, I think he found out. I'm afraid he's going to kill her. The police are already on their way, but I'm afraid they might not get there in time."

Sam never hesitated or questioned me. He said quietly, "Nobody will harm a hair on her head if I can help it. She'll be safe," and hung up.

CHAPTER 42

Kevin Harper felt comfortable in Atlanta. He saw a lot of similarities between the city and Chicago. Both were large centers of culture that sprawled for miles, forming concrete oases in verdant wastelands, at least in terms of sophisticated society. Both cities bragged about their international airports, which competed for the title of world's busiest, though Kevin considered it a dubious honor.

Of course, he could never live in suburbia like his brother. His work would have kept him near Emory, but unlike many of the doctors and professors there, Kevin would have bought a midtown condominium in a high rise. No lawn to maintain up high in the sky, looking down upon his fellow man scurrying around from point A to point B.

He parked his rental car on the street and hurried up to the house. He hadn't warned his brother of his pending arrival, not wanting to give Dan any excuse to say no.

# # #

Initially, Sam had only said he would check on Beth to humor Dan, who was, quite frankly, talking crazy talk. *His pregnant wife is in danger at this very second, right here in our neighborhood, in broad daylight?*

Sam brushed aside the window sheers and eyed Dan's house across the street, searching for any indications that his neighbor could be anything besides paranoid. He blinked at the unfamiliar car parked out front of the Harper residence.

I should go. I told him I would.

He still felt funny about getting his gun, particularly something as threatening as a shotgun, but that was his only option for a serious weapon. Sam feared scaring one of the neighborhood kids with the gun. Plenty of young ones had been running around the subdivision, playing in the middle of the afternoon on Easter Sunday. Nor did he want to get arrested for brandishing a loaded gun outside. His shotgun was right there in the coat closet at the top of the stairs, if he decided he needed it.

Sam started to relax when the second vehicle, a van, pulled up to the house. It looked familiar. He believed it had been there only yesterday.

Must be someone else Dan called to check on his wife. There is safety in numbers.

# # #

He felt the net tightening around him. Clayton sensed it was about time to disappear, get a new name, and find a new place to live. He'd made sure not to leave any DNA evidence through carelessness. The cops might consider him a person of interest, but he convinced himself smugly that there wasn't any physical evidence that could lead to a conviction.

He remembered how everything had gone to hell in a hand basket. Candy got away from him. The cops had been crawling all over Hidden Hills ever since they found the bodies on the golf course. Then, at the next place he planned to hit, a stranger showed up and damned near exposed him.

Who the hell is this guy Harper? Clayton asked himself. *First, he spoils my Lake Allatoona adventure. Then I get the shock of delivering an order right to his house. I'm sure this is where I followed the asshole yesterday morning. He seems as much responsible for my recent streak of bad luck as anybody. If the police already know who I am, why not make myself famous? I'm going to enjoy watching this guy die.*

Clayton briefly considered the smarter course of action. It might be best to torch the place in Hidden Hills if the cops weren't already crawling all over it. He could shed his skin and resurface in a new part of town with the insurance money, maybe even head out west to L.A. After living in that house for years, it would be impossible to erase every shred of evidence linking him to his adventures, if forensics ever recognized the place for what it was. Freezing, storing, and chopping up the chick he strangled probably had left some residual DNA. He knew the cops had her body parts and were trying to identify her. If they found his place, they had him. Clayton had made up his mind that he would never go to jail.

He donned his work jacket, selected a couple of props to carry up to the door, and rang the doorbell. A familiar looking man answered, but his face showed no recognition of Clayton. Apparently, his mysterious nemesis didn't know his true identity or the secret of how Clayton got inside the homes of his victims. The fool only noticed his white lab coat and the equipment, and the door opened wide.

"Come in," the man said, and stepped aside for Clayton, who readied his knife. He pounced on the man right there on the doorway, burying the blade into his chest. The shocked man clutched at the hilt of the blade, trying to gain control of the weapon lest his assailant pull the knife out himself in order to stab him again. He fell back and slid down the wall. His strength ebbed and his hands soon fell helplessly to his side. Clayton knew the wound should eventually kill him. The man was no longer a threat to him.

He was already moving toward the stairs, thinking about the woman. *She will scream before the bastard dies. I want her screams to be the last thing he hears. I want him to know how he failed her.*

The faster his world escalated out of control, the more Clayton began to feel like he had nothing left to lose.

# # #

A man in a white lab coat carried a box toward the door. Sam remembered the same man had brought IV equipment to the Harper house when Beth came home from the hospital. He almost stopped watching, but when the man in white attacked the man who answered the door at Dan's house, Sam realized he should not have doubted his neighbor's sanity. He took the stairs two at a time and grabbed his shotgun on the run.

351

As he bolted for the front door, he yelled up the stairs, "Barbara, stay put! Call the police."

Make noise. Call attention to yourself, instinct told him.

Completely inexperienced at stopping a fight, Sam waved his shotgun as he sprinted toward the surprised man in white. He ran to unknown danger with no hesitation, screaming at the top of his lungs.

# # #

He never shut the front door. From across the street, Clayton heard a voice calling. He turned and looked to see the man coming right at him on the dead run, wielding a shotgun.

Clayton quickly decided that he didn't want to die without a fair fight. His knife was no match for that shotgun. So he made a run for it, retreating deeper into the house toward the kitchen, and the door leading to the back yard.

As much as he ached to feel the release of breaking her skull, he forced himself to keep running. He didn't have time to go after the woman.

# # #

Sam saw that the attacker heard his shout and had fled through the back door of the Harper house, making his escape. The man in the lab coat circled around the house to his van, jumped inside, and burned rubber. Sam checked through the open door to make sure the van was gone and then called out to Beth, in the upstairs bedroom.

"Wh-what was that? Who is there?" Beth's frantic voice cried down in reply.

"Beth, this is Sam—I'm your neighbor from across the street. Please call 9-1-1 right now, and have them send an ambulance! A man was stabbed in your foyer. I'm keeping pressure on the wound, trying to keep him from bleeding to death."

Beth appeared at the top of the stairs, a dangling tube hanging out of her arm. She locked on the man slumped in the foyer.

"Kevin! Kevin!" she screamed.

Sam looked up from the bleeding wound and saw something familiar in the man's face. He looked like Dan, but older.

"Call for help now, Beth! Kevin can't answer you."

Before she could move, sirens filled the air. She tore her eyes away from the blood covering Kevin's chest to see what looked like half the Roswell police force come pouring into her front yard.

CHAPTER 43

A different team of doctors from the ones who had helped Beth now worked on Kevin, desperately trying to stabilize his condition so they could save his life by emergency surgery. The doctor in charge shouted, "We've got to deal with this pneumothorax, ASAP. Let's get a chest tube in him through the mid axillary line to reinflate this lung and help his breathing. I'll deal with the internal injuries from this stab wound. How much fluid has he had?"

"Two liters of normal saline," one of his nurses answered.

"What are his vital signs?"

"Blood pressure is eighty over fifty, pulse one-twenty."

"Let's give him a unit of blood and reassess his vitals at that point, see if he's ready to be prepped for surgery."

# # #

My heart would not leave my throat, as I dialed Mom's number. My prayers went unheeded, because she answered her phone.

"Mom, I'm so sorry. I've got some really bad news," I began.

"Oh, my God. Is it Beth? The baby?"

"No, Mom. It's Kevin. He came down here to see about me, because he thought something was really wrong. I'm so sorry. He went to my house. I wasn't home. The man who has been killing people must have mistaken him for me. He stabbed him, Mom. And it's pretty bad." My voice started cracking, but I reminded myself that he'd come to Atlanta because he didn't believe me and thought I was crazy. I hadn't been crazy. The danger was still out there somewhere. I took a deep breath and got control of myself. "Kevin's lung collapsed, and he lost a lot of blood. The doctors said his condition has stabilized and he's out of surgery, but he's still got a tube in his chest and he hasn't woken up yet."

Mom wailed into the phone. "Is he going to die?"

"They don't think so. I will feel better when I see him awake, but the doctors don't seem worried because they have monitors showing he still has brain activity."

"Why wouldn't he have brain activity? God, what are you telling me?"

"From what I understand, Kevin was resuscitated at the hospital. His heart stopped beating in the ambulance, on the way there. It was a close call."

"But now he's going to get better, you told me the doctors said," Mom reminded.

"Yeah, Mom, that's what they said." I let her cling to that. She was in shock and there was no point in me making it worse by reminding her that doctors weren't God, either. They guessed just like the rest of us. Their guesses were more educated, but that was about it.

Mom forgot her misery long enough to chide me, "I hope you listened carefully to Kevin's doctors. I am sure they know what they're doing."

I should have let it go, but I bristled, "Yeah, right. You act like a doctor is the only person on earth with a lick of sense, because he's got a piece of paper that says he can practice medicine and I don't. I'm not stupid, and I'd appreciate it if you wouldn't act like it."

Mom was silent for a moment, then apologized, "I'm just worried about your brother. That's all."

"I know, Mom. I'm worried about Kevin, too. I'm sorry that I snapped at you. I'm sorry that Kevin came here to help me, and he got hurt instead of me. This man wanted to kill me, but he stabbed Kevin instead. It's my fault...just like Dad."

"What do you mean, Daniel?"

"Dad's heart attack—it was my fault. I got arrested and into trouble at school. Dad's heart attack was less than six months later. It seems safe to assume that the chance I might spend time in prison caused Dad the stress that led to his heart attack. I'm like the angel of death for the people you love the most."

"Daniel, son, don't you ever talk to me like that again. That's simply not true. You don't know what else was going on in your father's life when he died. It's not your burden to bear."

"I'm not so sure about that. I'm not sure about much of anything anymore. But I love you, Mom."

"I love you too, son. I'll be catching the next flight to Atlanta. While I've tolerated a good bit of your nonsense over the years, I won't forgive you if you don't pick me up from the airport. I'll call you again to let you know what time my flight arrives."

The thought that Clayton had not yet been apprehended nagged at me, but I didn't worry too much about it. Every cop in Atlanta was on the lookout for him. It was only a matter of time before time ran out for him.

CHAPTER 44

Agent Craig Gradick of the GBI officially took charge of the manhunt for Clayton Farmer. Atlanta was too big and too open to shut down all the airports, trains, buses, and interstates leading to Florida, Alabama, Tennessee, the Carolinas, and points beyond. He had to coordinate interviews with the media as well as law enforcement departments throughout the state. Sooner or later, Farmer would surface, and they needed to be ready for him. He directed that BOLO alerts be distributed to MARTA cops, the various police departments in the metropolitan Atlanta area, and federal marshals.

He wanted Clayton Farmer, and bad.

Instead of a massive dragnet, Gradick employed a small team of specialists who worked with a profiler to glean as much about the suspect as they could from multiple investigations and compile it into a profile. If they could get a good idea of what made Farmer tick, then they might be able to think like him, anticipate his next move. If it was possible to nail him before anybody else got hurt, they had to protect the public. And they knew they were after someone who enjoyed causing horrific pain.

The team thought he would try to run, and his profile showed that he liked to gamble. The police found receipts from a recent trip to the casinos in Mississippi. They figured he'd try to get to Biloxi if he could, because of familiarity with the place. He might go to Vegas, if he thought they were looking for him in Biloxi. The GBI put out an alert that had every cop in the greater Atlanta area looking for Farmer. Gradick worked with the FBI to add him to their Most Wanted list.

The profilers couldn't see him heading for the casinos up in Delaware, where he'd be more likely to stick out like a sore thumb. Maybe he would head for an Indian reservation with a large gambling operation. They were all sold on the idea that Clayton Farmer had turned rabbit and he was running for the safest hole in which to hide.

Everyone except Wassner. He knew the crazy bastard was so unpredictable that he was capable of just about anything. Clayton was most likely to do whatever the profilers were least likely to predict.

# # #

The surgeon came by to check on Kevin. He looked over his chart, scribbled a few new notes, and looked over at me. "Your brother, isn't he? The surgery went well. He will still need oxygen and the chest tube for another day or so, but barring complications, he should be up and around in a few days. The knife penetrated the lung and nicked his spleen, but we were able to get everything repaired."

The door opened, and an orderly carried in a large e-cylinder oxygen tank. "I got paged to bring an e-cylinder to this room. Since when do we go back to the old days, using tanks?"

The doctor answered, "We had to reinflate his lung, and I don't want it to collapse on me again. The patient is still on supplemental oxygen, and the valve controlling the flow coming out of the wall is frozen. Until maintenance finds time to get it repaired, we're going to have to rely on the tank."

The orderly went about his business of attaching the tank he had brought to Kevin's breathing apparatus. He stopped and turned to the doctor in confusion. "What are you talking about?" the orderly asked. "The valve just opened for me with no problem. Doctor, I've got him hooked up to the wall. We didn't need this tank. The O2 is flowing, just fine."

Before the doctor could respond, the intercom paged "Doctor Heart." It was the all-hands-on-deck code scramble for a heart attack.

"Mr. Harper, I have to answer this page. Someone will be back to check the status of your brother's oxygen feed as soon as possible," the doctor assured me. He motioned for the orderly to follow him and rushed out of Kevin's room.

Beth sat in the chair beside mine. She had already been in hospital emergency room, waiting for any word about Kevin when I arrived. Sam had driven her there, following the ambulance from our house. I had driven like a bat out of hell from Hidden Hills straight to our house, unaware my wife and brother were at the hospital. The uniformed cops securing my house with the familiar yellow crime scene tape had tackled me as I ran up the front steps. Somehow, one of them managed to calm me down enough to explain they were both still alive.

"Honey, I should eat something, I think. I'm going to walk around and look for a vending machine. Can I bring you anything?" she asked.

"No, why don't you stay here with Kevin? I'm antsy anyway. I'll run down to the lobby to see what I can find." It was getting to me, staring at Kevin's chest to make sure it moved.

Kevin remained unconscious, still recovering from his surgery. They managed to rouse him in recovery just long enough that they were sure he would be okay. He complained of so much pain they sedated him once more, quite heavily, and moved him into the private room.

The uniformed officer stationed outside Kevin's door looked bored. I offered to get him a magazine or something from the gift shop, but he politely declined, busy working the crossword puzzle in the paper.

I paced outside the elevators. An "out of order" sign on one of the three elevator cars meant waiting twice as long for one of the operable chutes to arrive.

The bell chimed to announce the elevator's arrival. An orderly or doctor in a scrub suit held the door for me while I stepped into the car. I nodded my thanks, scarcely paying him any attention. As I stepped past, I noticed a pattern on his extended forearm, a tattoo. I pushed the button for the lobby and leaned against the back wall of the elevator.

As the doors began to close, the significance of the tattooed image finally registered like an electric shock in my weary and addled brain.

It was a hooded cobra poised and ready to strike, coiled around and through the eye sockets of a skull. Various colors of ink depicted a snake wrapped around a skull. I had almost forgotten the old woman.

A snake skull tattoo!

Too far from the buttons to press "Door Open" in time, I lunged for shrinking gap between the closing elevator doors. The man I realized must be Clayton Farmer watched me patiently through the closing doors, amused by my futile efforts. His cruel, empty eyes locked on mine. The elevator doors closed like a curtain on a stage, the final scene. His malevolent smile told me everything that I needed to know.

Clayton had recognized me. And I knew where he was headed. He would kill the crossword-working policeman, my comatose brother, and my pregnant wife before I could get back to the hospital room. My only hope was that the cop would somehow recognize and stop him. But I had walked right by this sadistic killer without even a hint of recognition, not even a twinge in my gut, and I'd been in pursuit of him for days. What chance would the cop have?

Frantically, I punched the button for the next floor. I ran my fingers down all the buttons, desperate to get off at the first opportunity. An eternity passed before the doors finally opened three floors below. I jumped out and pressed the call button for the up elevator, with no intention of waiting for the next available car. If the one of the doors didn't open immediately, I would take my chances on the stairs.

Time was precious. I got my bearings, saw the stairwell, and dashed up the stairs as fast as I could, knowing I'd be stuck on the wrong side of the fire door when I got there. Undeterred, I planned to beat on the door as loud and long as it took to get someone to open the door. I couldn't stand there and wait for the elevators. I had seen how slow they were moving.

I fought panic and an impotent rage beyond words. My brother, wife, and unborn child were about to be murdered, and I had let their killer walk right past me.

# # #

Clayton knew what he wanted to find and where to look. The crash cart was kept next to the nurse's station because of all the drugs. He needed to move quickly since the pain in the ass had seen him. He needed a diversion to get rid of the nurses. Fewer would be working on Easter Sunday. He also expected there would be less staff working at night than during the day.

He stepped into a room just beyond their sight and turned off the heart monitor. With satisfaction, he heard an alert sound at the nurse's station. Then he ducked into an empty room about halfway between the nurse's station and his false alarm, and there he waited until he heard scurrying footsteps pass his hiding place.

His distraction successful and the nurse's station empty, Clayton stole the crash cart. He paused long enough to break the plastic lock off the door and inventory his potential weapons inside. There were hemostats, scalpels, scissors, and long needles that Clayton could use to stab somebody if necessary. He began pushing the cart toward the room and the stupid cop sitting outside in the hallway. He might as well have stapled a bull's-eye on his chest. Clayton would not have been able to come up with a plan and mount an attack as easily had the officer remained safely inside the room. The cop had foolishly made himself a vulnerable target.

The asshole responsible for all of his current grief had seen him and would be back up soon, probably on the next elevator. Clayton knew that he had to move fast. He knew the right room number, and headed in that direction, following the signs on the wall.

He wanted Harper's wife and the other man he had stabbed to be dead before his adversary made it back, so he could enjoy the pain on his enemy's face. He guessed the man he stabbed was Harper's brother, given the facial resemblance. That was just another chance to hand his real target some more hurt.

As he neared the room, the cop glanced up, registered Clayton's medical attire, and lost interest. His eyes started to lower to his newspaper, but the squeaking of the cart wheels accelerated as Clayton rushed him. The cop's head shot back up in alarm, but it was too late.

Using the crash cart as a battering ram, Clayton slammed into him, crushing man and chair into the wall with brutal force. The pinned man grunted in obvious pain, struggling to extract himself. Clayton heard stirring inside the room and kept moving quickly, sensing that time was running out.

He snatched up the defibrillator from the crash cart, spun a dial to jack up its power, and shocked the cop with the paddles. He flopped around uncontrollably on the floor, like a fish out of water. Clayton knew the strong jolt would cause arrhythmia or atrial fibrillation, either of which could easily kill the man, but he could not have cared less.

# # #

On exiting the elevator, Wassner immediately sensed that something was wrong. He looked down the corridor but didn't see any nurses at the corner station. He walked quickly down toward it, noting something was missing. *The crash cart.* It could explain why all the nurses were away from their station, but then again, maybe not.

As he broke into a trot toward Kevin Harper's room, he wondered if he was being a little too paranoid. He would rather apologize for being a little too nervous than end up dead for being a little too careless.

The cop lying on the floor told him everything he needed to know. Wassner drew his weapon. He checked for a pulse, but found none. Wassner hesitated at the door for a second, listening for any telltale sounds or voices, then kicked open the door, entering the room weapon first.

# # #

Clayton held Beth Harper with his arm around her throat, using her as a shield.

Wassner noticed right away that the scalpel in his hand was in an awkward position, a little too far from her throat for a quick kill. He would have to step away from her slightly to slit her throat, with her neck buried in the crook of his arm as it was. Clayton ought to have the scalpel in his free hand.

If he could only get a better angle on Clayton, Wassner could take him, even with Beth in the killer's grasp. He knew that it would be suicide to surrender his weapon to the sadistic murderer. That wasn't an option, though the nut cases always demanded it as part of hostage negotiations.

Wassner did not intend to negotiate with this lunatic.

He would have to take a head shot to get him cleanly. Just another step or two to the right, and he ought to be able to put Clayton down. He tried talking his way into position, while he maneuvered those final few steps...

"Don't cut her, Clayton. Let her go. You'll only make things worse for yourself. Right now, she's the only thing keeping you alive. You're out of options. Drop the scalpel, surrender peacefully, and you can get the best lawyer in town to defend you. You kill a pregnant woman and nobody will want to take your case. Not a jury in the world would acquit you. Lock you up, and throw away the key. Put down the scalpel, and we can get you medical help. You can talk to your lawyer, maybe plead insanity. Who knows?"

Beth tried to say something but Clayton cinched his elbow tighter and snarled, "Shut up!"

To Wassner he commanded, "Stay where you are, unless you want me to give her back to you in pieces!"

Wassner said, "It seems we are at an impasse." And took a half step to his right.

He was almost there. Beth rasped a warning, "No, you're too close!"

It was too late. From behind Beth, Clayton's other hand came out. He pointed the Taser taken from the downed officer in the hall at Wassner and fired. The slender wires followed the twin electrodes, quickly crossing the short distance between the two men. The sharp points embedded into Wassner's chest and the next thing the detective knew, his body was thrashing uncontrollably on the floor, muscles screaming in agony from the electric shock.

# # #

I raced up three flights of stairs and pounded my fist on the door to the stairwell, slightly out of breath but able to beat on the door.

Nothing.

I pounded harder and yelled at the top of my lungs.

Shit! It's a holiday...short staffed. There's nobody to hear me. Damn it! I should have waited for the elevator.

I pounded until both my fists throbbed.

When the door opened, I was still gasping for air, like a fish out of water. "What's the problem? How did you get stuck in the stairwell?"

Pushing past the orderly abruptly, I shouted, "Sorry, it's an emergency," and broke into a sprint, headed for Kevin's room. "Call the police! Now!"

CHAPTER 45

I raced toward the room and saw the cop lying on the floor, either unconscious or dead. I ran harder, not even thinking to grab something to use as a weapon. My only thought was saving Beth and the baby. I burst into the room to confront the animal there to murder me, my wife, and brother.

I was shocked to see Wassner lying on the floor and Clayton bending over to pick up the detective's gun, holding a scalpel in his other hand. I knew I couldn't let him get the gun. With a primal yell that came from depths of my soul, I tackled him. We fell together at my wife's feet, clutched in a struggle for her life.

The gun slid under the bed, out of reach as we grappled for control of the scalpel. Clayton sunk his teeth into my right hand and ripped the flesh open. Searing pain ran down my arm and the warm blood made my hand slick and sticky. I began to lose my grip on his arm.

He balled his empty hand into a fist and threw a punch aimed at the side of my head. Instead, it made contact with the corner of my eye. In desperation, I snapped my neck forward, my forehead smashing into Clayton's nose. He howled in pain, but his hand with the scalpel slipped free. He slashed at me as I rolled just out of reach.

Beth's scream reminded me that I couldn't run. I had to stand my ground and fight, even without a weapon. I scrambled to my feet and faced Clayton, just as he staggered up himself. He was out of his mind with rage, a dangerous wild animal coming in for the kill. I had to get between him and Beth.

From the floor, Wassner grabbed at Clayton's legs and tried to pull him down, distracting the maniac from me and Beth. Clayton viciously kicked him in the ribs, most likely cracking a couple of them in the process. Wassner expulsed a groan, but grabbed at Clayton's legs again in spite of the pain.

Beth shouted my name with authority, "Daniel." Nothing more.

I looked away from Clayton and Wassner struggling, and recognized the expression on her face. It was the look of supernatural contact.

She extended her hand toward the oxygen tank that the hospital staff still had not come to retrieve. I realized what she meant to do, which only gave me a split second to make a decision and act.

The whole world shifted into slow motion.

The tank teetered and wobbled. Her hand pushed the tank a little harder, and it began to fall. I saw it topple and watched the subtle change in its trajectory.

I knew what would happen if the pressurized tank landed wrong and ruptured. Wassner had risked his life to save my wife and brother, and he was in the path of the blast that I knew was coming. It was the right thing — the only thing — to do.

I dived toward Wassner, on the floor in front of us. The falling oxygen tank was pointed away from Beth, so I trusted that the intuition she had tapped into knew how to keep her safe.

My body moved through thick syrup, suspended in midair above the detective's helpless form as the tank headed toward the floor. From the corner of my eye, it seemed the metal base of Kevin's IV stand turned to catch the impact of the oxygen tank's valve. It aimed right at Clayton. I recognized the explosion was inevitable.

I made a split-second choice. Wassner had risked his life to save my wife and brother. I felt like I owed him mine in return. When my body landed, covering the vulnerable Wassner, I felt my forearm snap at contact with the floor, all my weight following behind it.

I cried out "Beth!" and all hell broke loose.

I was prepared for an explosion, but not the fury that was unleashed when the tank valve crashed into the sharp metal corner. The force fragmented the top of the tank, turning it into a dozen or so deadly projectiles. Shock waves rolled over my back. Shards of steel passed so close I felt the air stir and anticipated the pain of metal embedding in my flesh.

For a split-second after the blast, I waited in disbelief before opening my eyes. I felt unscathed, but that was impossible. The concussion of the blast left me stunned and disoriented, the echo of the explosion still ringing in my ears.

A misty vapor thicker than smoke filled the room. The foggy aftermath of the oxygen tank explosion made the hospital room a surreal parody of angels floating on clouds. I might have suspected that the blast had killed me, if my arm didn't still hurt. The pain reminded me that I was still alive.

I carefully rolled off Wassner. When the mist cleared enough that I could see again, it appeared that I didn't seem to have as much as a scratch on me from the blast.

I spun around to find Beth, remembering the lunatic had been intent on murdering her just before the tank exploded. She was safe, frozen in place beside the spot where the oxygen tank had stood only seconds before. My eyes widened in shock when I saw the other half of the tank embedded in the wall. The end of the tank had knocked a hole through the brick exterior wall and hung a good foot outside the building.

I looked at Beth, and she at me. Our eyes spoke a lifetime of love in that one look. Relief tinged with horror shook me as the devastation of the explosion sank in, as the thought of what *could* have happened took hold.

The slow motion sensation faded and reality returned.

A low moan escaped Clayton's lips. I turned to see the killer intent on butchering my family dying on the floor, only a few feet away from me. A serrated piece of shrapnel the size of my outstretched palm had torn off his leg, just above the kneecap.

Beth screamed, "Oh, my God! Behind you! The wall!"

I shifted, protecting my broken arm, to follow her gaze. The wall behind me was peppered with shrapnel. A dozen pieces or more, the size of a quarter or larger, had shredded the wall. It looked as if an invisible shield had cloaked me as my body had protected Wassner.

I struggled to my feet. Pulling himself to his elbows, Wassner followed our gaze and let out a low whistle.

Beth stammered, "I...I heard a voice, inside my head. It told me to push the tank, and everything would be okay. Dan, I almost killed you!"

Tears welled in her eyes, but I shook my head. "No, you did the right thing. It was the only way, really."

Clayton wallowed pathetically in a spreading pool of his own blood, as he tried in vain to figure out how to reattach his leg. His femoral artery had been severed, and the chance of survival was practically zero, unless he immediately stopped the bleeding. With my useless arm, I doubted that I would be able to secure a tourniquet in time to stop the bleeding, nor did I have any inclination to try.

As if reading my mind, Wassner said, "Don't bother. He's not gonna make it."

Clayton looked past me with glazed, confused eyes that seemed to register the presence of a great evil only he could see, waiting for him to take his last breath. His eyes widened in terror, and he struggled to drag himself toward the door, trying to extend his miserable life.

I felt a small measure of pity for him as I watched him struggle in vain against death. He saw something, and it scared the shit out of him. I shuddered to think what he saw.

Clayton wrapped his bloody arms around his head and screamed as the darkness took him.

Kevin still slept peacefully, an angelic expression on his face.

PART SIX
BRIGHT MONDAY

CHAPTER 46

Beth smiled at me apologetically. "I'm sorry that I ever had any doubts about you."

"Beth, would you please excuse us for a moment? I'd like Dan to help me get out of bed to answer the call of nature," Kevin said to her.

"I need to stretch my legs, anyway. The baby enjoys it too, because it relaxes me." Beth patted her distended stomach. She leaned over my chair, her lips brushing my forehead.

I was so relieved to see her up, eating normally, and wanting to get out and about. She looked healthy without a needle embedded in her arm. Now a normal healthy glow brightened her complexion.

A fierce wave of protectiveness filled my chest again. But now it was followed by the satisfaction of knowing I had fought off a madman last night. I had been willing to give my own life for her, for Kevin, and even for Wassner.

I glanced at Kevin, a little surprised at his request. "Sure, I can give you a hand," I said. "But I'm not sure the nurses want you to get out of bed just yet. Shouldn't I call them to make sure it's okay before you pull out a bunch of tubes by accident? Don't you still have a tube in your chest? There's no reason to rush things. I can have them bring you a bed pan."

Kevin gave me a withering look. "I think I know what I can and cannot do. Beth wanted to go for a walk anyway."

After the door closed behind her, I waited a couple of seconds before I asked, "The get-out-of-bed business was bullshit, right? What do you want to talk about?"

"Relax," Kevin said. "I wanted to speak with you privately for a minute. I don't want anybody else to hear what I'm about to say." He stared at me for a long moment, his eyes boring into mine, and then added, "Wipe that frown off your face. I'd better get right to the point before your imagination runs wild. I need to ask you a question. You called Mom and told her about me being in the hospital, right? It was only natural that you blamed yourself and told her that it was your fault, even though it wasn't, but why did you say that it was also your fault that Dad died?"

My jaw dropped. I stammered, "How could you possibly know what I told Mom? No one was in the room when I called except me. Mom couldn't have told you. What are you saying?"

Kevin looked tired. His eyes closed, as if he were drifting back to sleep. Suddenly, they popped back open; he appeared more alert than I expected.

"Sorry. I was thinking about how to start telling you what I have to say. I guess the best way is just to lay it all out there for you, and let you ask questions, if you have any. Um...how can I phrase this? My body died, briefly. Twice. The first time was in the ambulance. My heart stopped beating, and I had an out-of-body experience. I watched the paramedics working on me, and then I found myself in the room with you while you called Mom. I heard your half of the conversation. That's how I knew what you said to her. Dan, I don't know how else to say this except to come right out and say it."

"I went to heaven, or at least went partway to heaven. Dan, I saw Dad there. He's more than happy to be where he is. You don't need to feel guilty about anything. It wasn't your fault anyway. Too many years of eating Southern fried cooking clogged his arteries. It wasn't your legal trouble that killed him. It was simply his time."

The expression on my face must have been priceless. Kevin could not resist smiling.

"You are confirming that everything I just said is true," he said. "My view of the world has been altered drastically. I believed that near death experiences were nothing more than hallucinations brought on by naturally occurring psychotropic drugs. You know, Ketamine. It occurs naturally in the body, even if the attending physicians don't administer it. I believed the pharmacological explanation of a natural, explicable phenomenon was simply more plausible than the old invisible man in the sky nonsense."

Kevin seemed to be rambling.

"Did you need help going to the bathroom?" I asked.

"Dan, this is important. Listen to me," Kevin said. "I was the one who told you that Santa Claus didn't exist. I also said the Bible was a collection of myths, and that you just rot after you die, and that's it. For most of my life, I've taken a small measure of pleasure from destroying your beliefs in what I derisively considered fantasy. I still can't believe what happened to me after I died. It was too incredible. I won't be able to adequately describe everything that I saw. Let me just tell you this. The next world...heaven...is simply beautiful beyond description. You can't even begin to imagine the *colors*. There isn't just green; there is emerald, jade, jasper, teal, and a host of colors I couldn't begin to name."

I'd never before seen such an expression of ethereal bliss on my brother's face, not even on his wedding day. On the one hand, too many things had happened to me over the past several days to casually dismiss what he said. But Kevin was the strictest materialist I knew. While he didn't aggressively evangelize his atheism, Kevin would quietly mock and ridicule those who didn't share his doubts about God. In a congenial tone, of course.

"Kevin, what are you saying? Are you trying to tell me that you met God?"

His face fell. He looked mildly disappointed. "No. I told you, I saw Dad. He was very happy. He looked younger, like in the pictures from when he and Mom got married. I saw this incredible light in the distance. I asked Dad if the light was God. He said no; the light is created as God breathes. So I'm just standing there, talking with Dad like we don't have a care in the world, which I guess we didn't since we were both dead. Then Dad told me I had to come back."

I stared at my brother in open astonishment. He was beginning to sound a bit like a televangelist. My fragile psyche had been under assault, virtually non-stop, for five days. Any residual doubts about the permanence of my transformation during that time I had cast aside. Whatever started last Wednesday in the thrift store when I touched that fateful tie had changed my world forever. Only days ago, when we talked by phone, I could tell Kevin thought I was losing my mind, about to suffer a nervous breakdown. Now he sounded as crazy as I ever did.

But I believed him.

"It occurred to me that my own arguments questioning the validity of the near death experience and even the veracity of those who claim to have had one could be used against my own experience. I know Jung said that you could only say that you haven't had the same experience as me but you can't prove my experience wasn't real. Before, I always thought that was a fallacious philosophical argument. After all, you could claim to have had a religious experience with the flying spaghetti monster and I wouldn't be able to *prove* you hadn't, so it seemed an exercise in futility. Plus, there was the evidence of Ketamine causing hallucinations and Libet's experiments stimulating the somatosensory cortex of the brain that made me think it was all limited to the confines of the brain, and one's imagination stimulated by dying," he prattled on as I lost interest and hoped he would get to the point.

"However, there is no logical explanation of why I could know what you said to Mom, or why you blamed yourself for Dad's death. Mom never even told me that you almost got charged with a felony when you were in college. Don't you understand what this means? My mind created new memories while my physical body was elsewhere. In fact, my body was *dead*. This means the mind and the brain are truly separable."

A strange disappointment came over me. My heart sank. For once, my brother sounded like a real human being, at least for a couple of minutes. Now he was beginning to sound like the old Kevin, as if he were thinking, *now how do I devise an experiment to prove this new theory?* It had always been about the science with him, never about the human being he used the science to study.

His experience had changed Kevin, though. An epiphany came to him next.

"A colleague of mine mentioned not long ago that one of the larger hospice organizations in Chicago was looking for a new executive director. I think I might leave the university and take the job, assuming it is still open. I'm tired of teaching and consulting. Of course, it will probably mean I'll need to take a pay cut, but I'm sure we can make do with less."

"Before you make any rash decisions, I think you'd better discuss any major life changes with your wife, don't you? Don't you think Stephanie will get a little bit upset if you take a job earning considerably less than what you currently make without even discussing it with her?"

"Stephanie has been unhappy in our marriage for years. She won't divorce me. Nor would she allow herself to have an affair. But, in her words, my emotional detachment left her very unhappy. She felt unfulfilled, inadequate as a wife because my work has always been more important to me than her. I denied her the blessings of motherhood. But it's never too late. I may not be able to undo the past, but I'm willing to try. If the doctors can't reverse my vasectomy, we can always adopt."

Someone had stolen my brother and replaced him with an exact duplicate. The funny thing was I liked the duplicate a lot better than the original. "Jesus, Mary, and Joseph," I laughed. "Somebody better warn Stephanie before she gets here to see you. She may insist you start having blood transfusions once a week, if this is the result."

Kevin didn't smile back. In fact, his face darkened and he looked a little crestfallen as he said, "I would have liked to meet Jesus. Dad implied that I hadn't earned the privilege. In fact, I think I was going to end up in hell."

I started laughing a little harder. "Don't tell me you're going to get all religious on me now, are you? Put the fear of God in you? Are you going to become a Jesus freak, or what?"

Kevin stared at me. "You don't get it, do you? I came to Atlanta because I thought you'd gone crazy and started believing in psychics and ghosts. And you had, hadn't you? It had become perfectly normal to you, or at least you were no longer able to deny what you saw and experienced. You confirmed the things you saw in your dreams or visions, whatever they were, had actually happened. Yet you are now going to ridicule me for saying that when I died, I went to heaven and saw our long-dead father? Have you forgotten that only a few seconds ago, you confirmed that an exchange you had with our mother that I could not possibly have heard actually happened as I described? How do you think I did that, by magic? The only way I could have known was if I *listened* to you as you spoke."

I stared back at him, speechless. What else could I say? As usual, he was right. Unless he was pulling my leg, Kevin believed what he was telling me. He had never been that good a liar and certainly wasn't cut out to be an actor.

I didn't know quite what to say, so I changed the subject. "Have you spoken with Stephanie? Do you know when her flight is due from Chicago? The last time I talked with her, she hadn't had time to make plans."

"I was kind of thinking I'd save her the trip and just go home," Kevin said. He grinned mischievously and said, "I'm going to be okay. You know, I always thought Chicago was a tough town. You know — Al Capone, the most corrupt city in America, including Philly and the Big Apple, yadda, yadda, yadda. I live in the toughest city in America. But then I almost get killed in Atlanta, inside my brother's house, in the *suburbs*."

I shook my head in amazement. This was indeed a new version of Kevin. I hoped Stephanie liked him better, too. I sure did. He appeared much more relaxed and acted kind of goofy, but that was a lot better than being a prick all the time.

Something is out there...more than what we can see, feel, or touch. Different journeys had brought us here, but Kevin and I now both believed and accepted the idea. And we were both okay with it.

CHAPTER 47

On our way home, I realized where we were and stole a glance at Beth. She felt my eyes and met them, asking, "What?"

"If you don't mind, I'd like to make a quick detour," I said.

Something had changed between us. Beth didn't challenge me. If either of us ever had any doubts about our relationship, they were gone for good. Now we trusted each other, openly and completely. Together for the long haul.

"Sure," she shrugged.

I pulled off Alpharetta Highway and parked in the lot. Sister Anita waited in her doorway, obviously expecting us. She greeted Beth like a long-lost friend, with a great big hug. Suddenly her eyes widened, and she pulled back in surprise.

Sister Anita looked over at me. "I knew that you had the gift. But now I see you have much more than that...you have a *blessing*. This child will be special—

no, he will be extraordinary. The two of you will face challenges, keeping this one safe in this changing world. Dark forces will be intent to stop him, in fear of his gift and what it could mean to the world. Your son will surpass the truth of his father, which will be recognized and sought by many. Your path will be difficult, even dangerous. But I am confident you will be equal to the challenge."

Beth looked more beautiful than ever, serene even at hearing her somewhat troubling prediction. She smiled at Sister Anita and said, "Thank you. I will protect him like a mother tiger would defend her cub."

Sister Anita laughed, "And I pity the fool who comes between you." She turned to me, "Daniel? I have a message for you."

"Yes?"

"An older gentleman, a man named Peter came to see me and asked that I give you a message. He said thank you, and goodbye. The time has come for him to go into the light. You were magnificent, and he wanted you to know how sorry he was that he caused you to lose so much sleep. He's also sorry you broke your arm. He promised not to bother you again."

I thanked her, but shook my head.

"What's the matter?" she asked.

"Peter may be gone, but we both know that others will find me now. I get new impressions from things I touch. This *gift*, as you call it, isn't going away."

Sister Anita smiled, "I never said it would, sugar."

To Beth she said, "It's been nice meeting you."

"It was nice to meet you, too," Beth answered. Then she looked at me and I knew she understood our lives would never be normal again. But whatever that meant, she'd share it with me.

"Daniel," she whispered, "let's go home."

ABOUT THE AUTHOR

John L. Leonard wrote this novel under the pen name of Rocky Leonard in honor of his father. In real life, Rocky Leonard was one of the most colorful characters you could ever want to meet. John credits his dad for the sarcastic wit and cynicism of the Robert Mercer character.

The author routinely writes articles for online publications and was interviewed on the Dennis Miller radio show. *Coastal Empire* is his first novel. He has also written short stories for an anthology about animals and is editing his second detective novel, *Secondhand Sight*.

John holds a BBA from the University of Georgia and worked as a computer programmer for more than twenty years before becoming a writer. His writing has also been influenced by shorter stints working as a bartender, real estate investor and landlord.

He has been married to wife Lisa for twenty-two years. John is the proud father of two and grandfather of three, as well as pack leader for several wonderful dogs and one crazy cat.

Born in Savannah, John has spent most of his adult life in the northern suburbs of Atlanta. The local color in his writing is equally authentic whether the setting is a Georgia beach, downtown Atlanta, or the Appalachian foothills in north Georgia.

Connect with John online at
www.southernprose.com.

DON'T MISS

The inaugural Robert Mercer Mystery

COASTAL EMPIRE

by

Rocky Leonard

Available now from www.eachvoicepub.com

"You underestimate my desire, Mercer. I can always make you suffer in agony for a while before you die. Once you are out of the way, we can torch your house in case you hid them there. We'll spread around a little money. Lance probably knows a cop he can buy if we need to. Enough money and advance warning gives us time to do damage control," Yarborough shouted.

A second voice said, "Hey! I think I see something moving out there!"

Well, I guess that settles it, Mercer thought. Let the games begin.

"Let's see you control this damage," Mercer said as he stepped into the open.

# # #

Wealthy and beautiful Sarah Reid hires private detective Robert Mercer to investigate her husband Barry, a real estate mogul whom she believes may be unfaithful. Mercer embarks on a case of possible identity theft and probable murder. He uncovers a vicious web of real estate fraud and jewelry theft that leads him to Kelly, an alluring woman with a few secrets of her own.

As Mercer pieces the puzzle together, the dead bodies begin to pile up and events threaten to spin out of control. With his canine partner Ox, a large black German Shepherd Dog, and John Sutlive, an old Marine buddy, Mercer and his motley crew do battle with a small army of villains in a fight to the death for his client.

This novel, set in sultry and mysterious Savannah, Georgia, is the inaugural book in the Robert Mercer detective series of great mysteries with irresistible supernatural twists.

COASTAL EMPIRE
PREVIEW

CHAPTER 2

Sarah Reid was sure she had the wrong address. Her friend had directed her to River Drive in Thunderbolt, but the street had houses on one side of the road, a marina and river bluff overlooking the Intercoastal Waterway on the other. She drove slowly past the Thunderbolt City Hall and the Public Library, more houses, a vacant lot, and there—a discreet sign marked a driveway leading to a small brick ranch.

A picturesque old oak tree shaded the drive. Wisps of Spanish moss waved in the stiff cool breeze blowing off the river. The familiar smell of marsh and salt water rode the wind inland where it swirled around Sarah, pelting her car with a few acorns from the oak.

For January, the day was unseasonably warm, cool but not really cold. The high temperature might reach the low sixties, But in the early morning, the chill took on an edge with the damp of the salty air, and it nipped at her. Sarah buttoned her coat. She hesitated at the front door.

Do you knock first when entering a house that contains a business inside?

The interior of the building looked like any other old house. It *was* just an old house, with wood floors and white walls, a sort of minimalist look to it and not much in the way of furniture. It was definitely Spartan.

A small sign outside discreetly advertised the business as Mercer and Associates. The weathered brick and the architectural style suggested the house had been built in the fifties or sixties. The structure appeared dated but it had new windows and recently painted white trim. The overall effect made it look quiet and inviting, a well-kept older home on a relatively quiet, shady street.

She glanced around as she stepped through the door. She had never dealt with a detective agency before and had no frame of reference.

After she decided to hire a detective, she had no idea what to expect except for the stereotypical images she'd seen in the movies. Less than twenty four hours ago, the thought of this had never crossed her mind.

Things change, particularly when you can no longer trust your husband.

The front door opened into a living room where a man sat at a large wooden desk facing the door. A section of newspaper lay open on his desk in front of him. The sparsely decorated room had a couple of movie posters hung in oak frames adorning various walls. A certificate or license of some sort hung on the wall next to his desk. Next to a leather couch, a small black filing cabinet sat like an unmatched bookend.

She decided she expected more people. There should be maybe a gun or two in a wall cabinet. Sarah no longer felt so sure about being here. She didn't know what a private detective agency was supposed to look like, but something made her think this wasn't it.

The man worked the crossword puzzle in the paper using an ink pen. He looked up as she entered, folded the paper, and put it aside. Like any Southern gentleman, he stood to greet her. A couple of empty chairs faced his desk.

Sarah glanced around the room once more, thinking she may be making a mistake. On the other hand, she didn't know anyone else she could ask for help. A good friend had recommended these people. If that wasn't going to be good enough, she was going to have to figure this one out alone. Her confidence in her own ability to do so had been shaken to the point she had come this far.

The man smiled to greet her, ambling around his desk to shake her hand without her having to take a seat. "Hi, can I help you?"

She looked hesitant. "Are you Mr. Mercer?"

He nodded. "Yes ma'am, I'm Robert Mercer. What can I do for you?"

"You're a detective?" She thinly disguised her doubts.

"I am indeed," he said. "Do you need one?"

"I think so." She shook his hand. "I'm sorry, but I don't have an appointment or anything…"

Mercer smiled broadly and said, "Don't worry about it, ma'am. This morning has been kinda slow. You caught me working the crossword puzzle." He paused a few seconds, watching her relax a little. "Please, have a seat and tell me what I can do for you. Would you like something to drink? Some coffee? Water?"

"No thank you."

She tried to stifle a laugh, and then said, "It's funny. My first impression was that you don't look like a detective, but then it occurred to me that I have no idea what a detective is supposed to look like. As I drove here, I suppose I started building a mental image of what I should expect. You have a very nice location for your office. It almost seems out of place compared to the rest of the neighborhood. I guess I expected your office to be next to a police station or a bail bondsman, but now I have to admit that I don't know why." She laughed nervously.

Mercer poured himself a cup of coffee and sat back down. Usually female clients were worried about their husbands being unfaithful. But Sarah Reid was one of the prettiest women he'd ever met in person. She had platinum blonde hair, crystal blue eyes, and a cover girl smile. She wore more makeup than he liked, especially when he noticed she used it to cover the sprinkling of freckles across her nose, which he found very appealing.

Connect the dots…

If she had not been wearing a rock the size of Gibraltar on her ring finger, he suspected he would be hitting on her by now.

Is her husband an idiot, or what?

The woman glanced around the room, surreptitiously taking in her surroundings. When she wasn't looking at him, Mercer could stare at her for a few seconds. She had been crying earlier; her eyes were still red and puffy. He decided to give her time, let her tell her story when she was ready.

But if he had to bet, he would guess she cried because she found something incriminating about her husband and now doubted his fidelity. Mercer sat back, waiting patiently.

Her eyes flicked back and forth between the few framed movie posters on his office wall. "I recognize Humphrey Bogart. He was in *Casablanca* with Ingrid Bergman. You must be a movie buff."

"I must be," he smiled. "But I haven't seen many movies lately."

"What made you choose these movies?" she asked. "They're not exactly pop culture, are they?"

"Well, I got the poster for *The Maltese Falcon* because that was the first detective movie I ever watched. I saw it when I was a kid with my dad, not long before he passed away. He liked it and let me stay up late to watch it with him on a school night. He never did that kind of stuff, but that one time he did."

He sipped his coffee while he looked at her thoughtfully. "Humphrey Bogart was Sam Spade, the first private detective I ever saw in action on the silver screen. Seeing the movie made me want to grow up and become a private detective."

Mercer turned his head and looked at the other poster. "As for *Memento*, it's about a guy searching for his wife's killer. He's a regular guy playing private detective, and he's pretty good at it because he used to be an insurance investigator. *Memento* had maybe the most brilliant plot of any movie I've ever seen. I've watched it a half dozen times, and I'm still not sure I could tell you what really happened."

"That doesn't sound very good," Sarah said.

"You've got to see it for yourself to understand," Mercer said. "I don't want to spoil it for you, but the reason it's hard to explain what the movie's about is because it's told from the perspective of the main character, the husband playing private detective. He has no short term memory, so he tattoos clues about his wife's murder on his own body."

Mercer smiled and added, "I got the obligatory Marine Corps tattoo on the first weekend when we all got drunk after boot camp, but these days for case notes I use pen and paper, not body parts."

"Don't worry that you've spoiled anything," Sarah said. "It doesn't sound like a movie I'd be interested in watching."

"Your loss," Mercer shrugged.

"Don't you have any employees?" She was stalling, trying to avoid dealing with her pain.

"You'd like to meet my associates? Unconvinced I can get the job done?. I have all the help I need whenever I need it—and a secret weapon. I have the mighty Ox."

At the sound of his name, a large jet black German Shepherd Dog leapt off the leather couch and bounded over to Mercer.

The woman startled. "Jesus Christ!"

"No, it's Ox," Mercer grinned.

"He's huge! Will he bite?"

"Absolutely not….unless someone tries to hurt me. My partner Ox here is a natural stalker and hunter. He uses that black filing cabinet next to the sofa to help him blend in with the scenery. It camouflages him pretty good as he lounges on the couch, watching everything that moves."

He sipped more coffee and rubbed the dog's head.

"The thing is, he's smart enough that he knows it. Sometimes even I have trouble seeing if he's there, and I know where to look. I thought about moving the filing cabinet so it would be easier to see him, but that would deprive my boy of one of his great joys in life….startling people occasionally while he keeps a low profile. He's a bright boy. He did that on purpose, just to see your reaction."

She muttered sarcastically, "I almost jumped out of my skin."

The dog looked as if he were smiling.

"He must be very well trained," the woman observed after a pause. "He didn't bark or come sniff me when I came inside. I thought every dog on the planet barked at strangers. Oh, my God—you didn't have his vocal cords surgically removed, did you? I think that's cruel. You wouldn't do that to your dog, would you? Why hasn't he barked? I don't remember the dog making a sound since I got here. I don't have a dog, but I assume they could remove vocal cords so the dog can't bark. Did you do that, Mr. Mercer? I'm not sure I could do business with a man who could be so cruel."

Mercer almost laughed. If she weren't such a wreck, he probably would have said something sarcastic.

Man, she is all over the place.

Questions were flying at him in staccato bursts. She was a bundle of nervous energy. Her emotions ran amok as she tried to avoid telling him the real reason she was in his office.

He chose to smile gently. "No ma'am, I haven't done anything mean to my dog. I do appreciate your concern about animal cruelty. It's a pretty low excuse for a human being that hurts a defenseless animal. But to set your mind at ease, Ox barks just fine whenever he wants. If he didn't like you or thought you were dangerous, he would have barked his head off. Well actually, if he really thought you were a threat he'd probably skip that step and express his displeasure more directly."

He looked at Ox. "Ox, speak!" he ordered.

The dog barked sharply once in quick response. Mercer looked at Sarah. "Okay?"

Sarah was impressed.

A broad smile crossed Mercer's face and his voice softened as if he were speaking platitudes to a child. "Just for the record, Ox doesn't think you're gonna try to hurt me. I believe he thinks you are a nice lady with a problem. Isn't that right, boy?"

Ox licked at his face. Mercer turned his head and scratched at the dog's chest.

Mercer broke eye contact. Sarah continued to stare at him, boring holes in the top of his head with her eyes as if to read his thoughts. "How would he know?" she demanded.

"Mostly because that's what I think. Dogs don't recognize speech as much as body language. He reads human emotion quicker than I can read the newspaper. Ox thinks you're okay because I think you're okay. Ox thinks you're upset because I think you're upset. Of course, he could tell without my help. Even if I could be wrong about you, you'd tell him….he'd pick up on your aura, and then Ox would tell me."

Ox nuzzled his arm, so Mercer leaned over and scratched his ears. As the dog came closer, Sarah tentatively extended her hand. He sniffed and then licked her palm. When Ox raised his head, Sarah noticed a sprinkling of grey under his chin. The dog had a few years on him, but his muscular build and intelligent eyes exuded confidence. Satisfied she had passed inspection, Ox wandered back to his spot on the couch.

The woman looked at Mercer for a long moment. "My name is Sarah Reid," she finally said. After waiting a moment for recognition that did not come, she added, "My husband is Barry Reid."

The name was familiar. He asked "The real estate guy, with the billboards?"

Mercer visualized a billboard he passed frequently, with a larger-than-life image of a boyishly handsome young man with Hollywood-caliber good looks. Put an emblem on his blazer and his picture would fit right into the Savannah Christian senior yearbook. He looked about seventeen.

A very *wealthy* seventeen.

She nodded her head in confirmation. Mercer digested that morsel of information for a moment. One of several thoughts that flitted through his mind was that she could afford to pay his fee.

Reid had his own real estate agency and sold more than twice as many houses in Savannah as his nearest competitor. Blond, blue-eyed, and very handsome, Reid apparently discovered the Fountain of Youth, with his improbable baby face very appealing to the recent divorcees in town. He probably sold at least half the community property in Savannah. Mercer could not help but wonder if one of the more voluptuous soon-to-be-single property owners had seduced Reid.

Reid was rather effeminate looking, almost a pretty man. Mercer also thought Reid's wife was gorgeous. With the steady stream of vengeful divorcees wanting to sell their homes, Mercer could imagine Reid faced some serious temptation to cheat from time to time.

Some guys could have the best of everything, and still feel like it wasn't enough. Maybe Reid fit into that category. Anyway, they both knew why she was in his office, but they still needed to go through the ritual of her explaining the reason for her visit and his display of an appropriate level of shock and surprise when she did.

Mercer guessed Sarah stood about 5'5" or so when they faced each other in those initial moments. It was tough to tell for sure because of her high heels. He decided she was in her late twenties to early thirties, maybe ten years younger than he was, but was she older than her husband?

Her ring was probably worth more than he made in a year. Diamonds might be a girl's best friend, but that camaraderie must have cost Barry a fortune.

Mercer could not imagine a larger diamond fitting in a ring she could wear on her finger. It was a big, sparkling chunk of ice. And that was how it looked under room lights; Mercer could only imagine what the ring did in natural sunlight. It would probably freaking blind somebody, the reflections coming off this stone.

Sarah's face now bore a look of resolve. She had convinced herself it was finally time to confront her worst fears.

Mercer kept a tape recorder in his desk drawer, which he pulled out, turned on, and left on top of his desk. Mercer took notes, but he didn't like to ask his clients to repeat themselves. The recorder alone would have sufficed, but he liked having something to do with his hands when he interviewed someone.

The act of writing notes of the essential facts tended to cement them in his mind. More often than not, he would write down a phone number and then be able to recall it on demand. He sipped his coffee, wrote her name on his note pad, and underlined it.

"Now, how can I help you?" he asked gently. He had a strong suspicion he knew already, but Sarah needed to confirm it.

"Are you related?…"

"To Johnny Mercer?" he anticipated. "No ma'am, but I get asked that question a lot. I'd never even heard of Johnny Mercer before I came to Savannah….I grew up in Oklahoma."

"I was going to say Bobby Murcer….but the name is spelled differently, isn't it?"

Mercer grinned. "I'm impressed. You know your baseball."

"I have a big brother." Sarah shifted in her seat, finally ready to quit stalling for time. "I'm sorry. I'll get to the point. This is difficult to talk about with a complete stranger."

Her brow furrowed. She paused before adding, "Actually, I don't really think this would be easier to discuss with someone I know. I believe I want to hire you...need to hire you."

She cleared her throat and said, "Recently I've come to suspect my husband is having an affair." Tears began to stream down her face as she said the words.

Mercer was a little surprised she hadn't taken even longer to get to the point. The really pretty ones typically had more trouble accepting the fact their husbands could still cheat. Sarah's nose turned red; he sensed her embarrassment had become acute. He concentrated on his notepad, though he had nothing really to write.

Crying unsettled him, especially with babies or women he barely knew. He got uncomfortable because he didn't know what to say or how to act that would comfort them.

Now if he'd deliberately made her cry, he'd have expected it when the dam burst, been better prepared. Other than offering her a tissue, what could he do, pat her on the back?

He made sure to keep a big box of Kleenex strategically positioned on top of his desk where a client could reach one or a handful if needed. She was not his first client to burst into tears. Hell, half the men who hired him because of a cheating wife started crying, too. That *really* bothered Mercer, watching another man cry.

He hated adultery cases but they paid the bills. And if there was a cheating spouse, Mercer caught them in the act. He hated infidelity, which is one major reason he never married. If he didn't trust himself, how could a wife trust him?

Mercer was old school when it came to marriage. He'd been raised to believe marriage was an "until death do you part" kind of deal. He felt once you made the commitment you ought to stick to it.

If you asked him to describe the perfect woman, he would not have described Sarah Reid. His taste ran to brunettes or redheads. Even so, looking at her Mercer had to wonder if the man who had her and cheated was insane. She was a truly beautiful woman, classy and appeared to be sharp as a tack.

Sarah regained her composure. She never really burst into tears, just sniffled a bit before recovering. Instead, she began to look angry. She said, "My husband recently talked me into trying to get pregnant. I haven't been taking the pill for the last couple of months. I felt like I'd been played for a fool, couldn't believe it when I read this card."

She reached into her purse, extracting a card that had *THANK YOU* embossed on front in elegant script lettering. He read the note inside. When finished, he folded the note closed, took a deep breath, and looked directly into Sarah's eyes.

"How long have you two been married?" Mercer asked.

"Three years".

"Happy?"

"Yes. Well, I thought so."

"Do you two fight much?"

"Not really. Normal disagreements like anybody else. My husband and I have gotten along well in the course of our marriage."

"Has he ever cheated before?"

"*NO.*" She bristled at the implication that she had tolerated a previous incident.

"You?"

"Of course not!" she snapped.

"Sorry, but I have to ask questions or I'm gonna be wasting your money. No offense meant."

"How can you say, "No offense" when you're asking such an offensive question?" Sarah glared at Mercer, expecting an answer. He ignored the question, but was secretly amused to see that she had a feisty streak in her, too.

Mercer looked down at the card Sarah had given him. Elegant block lettering adorned a handwritten note thanking her husband rather effusively for his purchase. A man named Walter Danielson appeared to have signed it. Mercer frowned at Sarah. "This handwriting is kind of effeminate for a guy named Walter, isn't it? I'm guessing you didn't get jewelry for Christmas. But I've just assumed your religion. You aren't Jewish, are you? Please forgive me..."

"No. We're Lutheran. We celebrate Christmas." She was momentarily distracted from her anger.

Mercer said, "What did you get for your present, if you don't mind my asking?"

"My Christmas present was the BMW outside," Sarah answered. "I thought I'd need the bigger car for transporting the baby....if we were going to get pregnant. I refused to drive a cliché. Minivans are ubiquitous!"

A smile struggled to emerge but he crushed the urge to allow it. "I drive a minivan," Mercer said in a matter-of-fact voice.

His remark flustered her. She blinked twice before muttering somewhat sarcastically, "I'm sure it's a wonderful vehicle."

Now Mercer smiled. "I'm sorry. I should mention it is my vehicle of choice because of Ox. The remote door openers are fantastic. You mentioned having a baby?" Mercer said.

"We've been trying to get pregnant," Sarah repeated. "That's why I don't understand why Barry would be cheating on me. He...says he loves me, Mr. Mercer. I thought he was sincere, but now, I don't know what to think." She sniffed as if tears were imminent.

Mercer looked back down and resumed staring at the notepad. Crying women always made him uncomfortable. He never heard of a jewelry store that sent a thank you note for buying something in the store. But Mercer wasn't too surprised because he had not spent more than a thousand bucks on jewelry in any one purchase in his entire life. He didn't know what it was like to be considered a high roller.

"I'm wondering how much money you have to spend before you rate a personal thank you note," he said aloud without soliciting Sarah's opinion. After a few seconds, he focused his attention back on Sarah. "Have you called the store and asked them about this?" he asked.

"Of course," she said impatiently. "It was the first thing I did. Mr. Danielson was evasive, citing their customer privacy policy. He made it clear that I was not his customer and intimated he'd written no such note. I asked what my husband bought; he remained polite and apologetic, but insisted he had to honor the confidential relationship with his customer,assuming the note was not just some sort of mistake."

Finally, Mercer had something else to write— *Walter Danielson.*

Mercer liked Sarah. She had spunk. She carried herself well. He liked smart women. Apparently, her husband was not very bright...assuming he really was cheating on her, of course.

"Has your husband been going out unexpectedly, staying out late at night? Strange phone calls to his cell phone at odd hours? Any unusual behavior you've noticed before the note came?"

She shook her head, emphasizing her answer. "No, no, no! Mr. Mercer, that's why I feel so stupid. This was completely out of the blue."

"If all you have is the note, why do you think he's cheating? Have you checked his credit report?"

"So far, all I've done is to decide I need to hire a professional to investigate this for me."

Mercer pressed his lips together and breathed out through his nose, trying not to snort in the process. Guys like Barry Reid really pissed him off. They had it all, and it still wasn't good enough. He stared at the return address on the envelope that came with the card. "This store isn't local."

He thought he should mention his fee. Sympathy didn't pay the bills.

"A trip to Atlanta is probably going to run you at least a thousand dollars plus expenses. Realistically, you're probably looking at two grand on the low end for me to go up there and figure out what he bought and for whom. I will get results, though. If you want your husband kept under surveillance while I'm in Atlanta, you're looking at more like five to seven grand over a couple of weeks."

The money didn't appear to faze her. "What do you recommend?"

"If it were me and the note my only evidence, I'd wait to find out what comes from my trip to Atlanta.

The note doesn't look good, but it's circumstantial. Really, it doesn't make sense — it doesn't jibe with everything else you're telling me."

"What do you mean?"

"Look at it this way….if he is having an affair, who is the other woman? Who comes to mind first?"

"I don't know — Charlize Theron."

"That's not what I meant. Not including every available option on the planet, of the women you know, who does *he* know that might seduce him?"

He had chosen his words carefully, not wanting to rub salt in an open wound. The thought of an unfaithful spouse was painful enough without believing it had been his idea to cheat.

"I can't think of anybody."

"Ok. I'd never argue the point."

After a second she realized she'd been complimented, and blushed slightly.

"Have you said anything to your husband?"

"About this? Of course not! I wouldn't know what to say. I've avoided speaking with Barry since receiving the card."

Sarah opened her purse and fished out a bank envelope that she handed to Mercer. "Here's two thousand dollars cash for a retainer. I hope you will help me, Mr. Mercer. This is like a bad dream. I want my happy marriage back...either help restore my faith in my husband or give me the proof I need for a clean break divorce. If I can't trust him, our marriage is over."

She drew a deep breath and stared at Mercer for several moments. Her next words were calm and measured. "I still love my husband, Mr. Mercer. I would like to believe I'm wrong. I'm hoping you will prove I'm wrong. Long ago, I made it very clear to Barry that the one thing I will not tolerate is cheating. If there's something he wants me to do, he only has to ask."

Mercer was pretty sure she was intentionally teasing him with that last remark.

"I won't tolerate Barry sleeping around with other women. I refuse to share my husband. If he wants someone else he can have her, but not me too."

Mercer saw no need to respond to that. Instead, he said, "Your husband is a successful businessman. I assume if he is cheating, you'll want hard evidence to produce in court.

Otherwise he'll get a good lawyer to contest the divorce and fight for a minimal settlement."

"I don't care about Barry's money, Mr. Mercer."

Mercer thought about that statement for a long moment. "Then what *do* you want?"

She explained, "I have my own inheritance and a trust fund. My daddy was an executive for Dixie Crystals Sugar Refinery. He bought stock in Coca-Cola. This is about trust, not Barry's money."

Mercer decided she didn't need him to apologize for not knowing she had her own money. "I'll start tomorrow morning. I'm going to need some information. How would you like me to communicate with you when I have something to report?"

"I've been thinking about that. I don't want my husband to know I've hired you. If he isn't cheating, I'd rather he never found out I doubted him. Therefore, discretion is going to be very important to me. Can you send me an email and arrange another meeting that way? If that's inconvenient I'll give you my cell phone number. However, I am not a very good actress. If you call and Barry overhears, he might ask me some difficult questions I couldn't answer. I'm not used to the idea of lying to him about anything important."

Mercer said, "I'm going to need some personal and financial information from you about Barry—banking information, Social Security and credit card numbers and their expiration dates, driver's license information if you can get it."

He rather expected her to balk at handing over her financial information, but she didn't protest at all.

"I'm glad you reminded me." Sarah surprised him by reaching into her purse and taking out a folded piece of notebook paper. She said, "I didn't think about getting his driver's license number and I don't know it off the top of my head, but it had occurred to me you would need to figure out how Barry paid for whatever he bought."

The page was divided into two columns, one filled with bank and credit card company names and the other with account numbers. Mercer was impressed;

this woman was well organized. She even thought to bring him a picture of her husband. He doubted there were any billboards for his business in Atlanta. While his face was well known in Savannah, no one in Atlanta would have any idea who he was.

"You can keep the picture" she said. "It's a copy I had made this morning."

Geez, I wish I was this organized, he thought.

Mercer stared into her eyes. She held his gaze until he said to her quietly, "I can't promise you anything but the truth. What I can tell you right now is I've seen too many cases where the most obvious answers don't match up with the questions. Everything is not always as it seems. This does look bad on the surface, but that's all you've scratched so far. I've seen a lot worse."

For the first time since she came into his office, Mercer saw a small glimmer of hope in her eyes. "It's so weird...this came completely out of the blue. I had no suspicions or doubts about Barry whatsoever before this note came in the mail. Barry has an office downtown and one at home, where he works half the time. He almost always gets home for dinner. I usually travel with him if he goes out of town. He plays golf at the club once or twice a month without me. It's not like he's got a lot of opportunities to cheat on me."

She looked lost and confused. "I don't see how Barry has time for a mistress. But I also don't understand the thank you note..."

Mercer thought about it. Her description of Barry didn't match up with a guy cheating on his wife and buying expensive jewelry for his mistress.

Sarah Reid rose to leave. "Thank you, Mr. Mercer. I look forward to your email."

Walking her to the door, he tried to think of any other questions to ask. As she stepped outside he said, "I've got a funny feeling about this. It might not be what it looks like. I'll let you know what I found out as soon as I can. You can trust me."

She shook his hand again. "I do, Mr. Mercer. I have faith in you."

That sounded good. He hoped she felt a little better leaving than she had when she arrived.

He wished he really felt the confidence he offered, suggesting he believed that her husband could be innocent. All too often, the worst suspicions are the ones that turn out to be true.

CPSIA information can be obtained at www.ICGtesting.com
Printed in the USA
BVOW04s1919150614

356346BV00011BA/205/P